Deception's Princess

ALSO BY ESTHER FRIESNER

Nobody's Princess
Nobody's Prize
Sphinx's Princess
Sphinx's Queen
Spirit's Princess
Spirit's Chosen

DECEPTION'S PRINCESS

ESTHER FRIESNER

Random House 🏠 New York

Text copyright © 2014 by Esther Friesner
Jacket art copyright © 2014 by Larry Rostant

All rights reserved. Published in the United States by Random House Children's Books, a division of Random House LLC, a Penguin Random House Company, New York.

Random House and the colophon are registered trademarks of Random House LLC.

Visit us on the Web! randomhouse.com/teens

Educators and librarians, for a variety of teaching tools,
visit us at RHTeachersLibrarians.com

Library of Congress Cataloging-in-Publication Data
Friesner, Esther M.
Deception's princess / Esther Friesner. — First edition.
p. cm.
Summary: In Iron Age Ireland, Maeve, the fierce, willful youngest daughter of King Eochu of Connacht, is caught in a web of lies after rebelling to avoid an arranged marriage.
ISBN 978-0-449-81863-3 (trade) — ISBN 978-0-449-81864-0 (lib. bdg.) —
ISBN 978-0-449-81865-7 (ebook)
1. Medb (Legendary character)—Juvenile fiction. [1. Medb (Legendary character)—Fiction. 2. Princesses—Fiction. 3. Kings, queens, rulers, etc.—Fiction. 4. Family life—Ireland—Fiction. 5. Conduct of life—Fiction. 6. Ireland—History—To 1172—Fiction.] I. Title.
PZ7.F91662Dec 2014 [Fic]—dc23 2013002948

Printed in the United States of America
10 9 8 7 6 5 4 3 2 1
First Edition

For Lee Martindale

Bard, Warrior, and Friend
Extraordinaire

Contents

Èriu

IRELAND IN
THE IRON AGE

DÙN BEITHE

Ulster

ÉMAIN MACHA

FIR
DOMNANN

CRUACHAN

Connacht

TAILTEANN

TARA

ISLE OF
Avallach

Leinster

Munster

N

TECH DUINN

THIS WAY TO
Tír Na nÓg

miles
0 10 20 30 40 50 60

CHAPTER ONE

The King of Connacht's Daughter

I AM TOO young to be a part of so many lies. I'd blame the bards for it, if I could. It would be easy to say that they never let the truth get in the way of a marvelous story, but my life's tale is more complicated than that. Whose is not?

Though the bards I've known tell no lies, sometimes they will craft their songs without knowing all the facts. I am two summers shy of eighteen, yet they are already singing about me as if I were a grown woman and queen in my own right. (Well, I *would* like that, but I can't say the same for all of their songs about me.) It almost makes me wish I were a bard myself instead of the royal princess of Connacht. Maybe then the *whole* truth would have a fair chance of being heard.

Above all, I hate the way they waste so much time praising how *beautiful* they think I am. Whether or not that's so, it annoys me. The flash of sunlight on a sword blade is also beautiful, but it distracts you from seeing the worth of the steel. As if I were nothing but the sum of eyes and lips, height and grace, slenderness and strength, fair skin and fiery hair! I am much more than that: I am Maeve.

If I had my sister Derbriu's gift for music, I'd make sure my true story reached every ear in the length and breadth of Èriu, from the High King's seat at Tara to the humblest farmer's hut. I know exactly how I'd begin it too. I'd start with what happened on that spring morning some dozen years ago, when I danced with the black bull.

I didn't think it was a matter of any importance when I did it, but what did I know? I was five years old. I've been called Maeve the Spoiled, Maeve the Proud, Maeve the Sneak, and, worst of all, Maeve Two-Tongues, Maeve the Liar. Nobody ever called me Maeve the Wise, then or now. One small adventure, done on a whim, and it changed my world forever.

The black bull was my father's pride, a prize taken in one of the countless cattle raids he led against our neighbors. A king must show his strength as a warrior by capturing the cattle of lesser men. To me, that meant my father was obliged to steal every herd in the land. As far as I was concerned, all men were inferior to Eochu, royal lord of the realm of Connacht, which he ruled from within the ringfort of Cruachan.

In those days, I didn't think of Cruachan as a fortress. It was simply my home. One could enter its walls of beaten earth only through a single narrow gateway. The king's great house and many other buildings stood safe within. I knew nothing of the importance of making a stronghold hard to attack, easy to defend. As far as I was concerned, Cruachan's battlements were placed atop a high mound strictly for my pleasure, so that I could enjoy a fine view of the surrounding countryside. And the armed men on watch? Obviously their sole purpose was to make sure I didn't slip off the wall.

On the morning I crossed paths with the black bull, Father had set out on yet another raid, or so I thought. All the house rose early, a few of our warriors groaning pitiably from the effects of the previous night's leave-taking feast. Too soon for me, Father finished breakfast and strode off, bawling for his chariot driver, Fechin, to attend him. The warriors of Connacht grabbed a few last mouthfuls of meat and bread before following their leader. They were as eager to race into battle as their high-spirited horses. I overheard some of them boasting about how they would shine in battle and come home to claim the hero's portion, the best cut of roasted meat served at the victory banquet.

My mother, Cloithfinn, matched Father pace for pace all the way to his waiting chariot, her hip-length waves of golden hair swinging like a heavy silken cloak. My five sisters were already there, lingering beside the king's horses. There were kisses for us all. I wanted to cry, but the air was already loud with the wailing of many young women, clinging to their sweethearts. Mother wouldn't embarrass Father like that. She carried herself tall and proud, with a cheerful face, and held us to her example. We knew this might be the last time we would see our father alive, but we were a king's daughters and we had to be brave.

As Father's chariot passed through the gateway and down the steep side of Cruachan's mound, Mother led us to the top of the wall. We stood with the other women, shouting encouragement to our departing heroes. The weather cut short our

farewells; a barrier of fog settled over the land, so that Father and his followers vanished from sight quickly, as if the Fair Folk had risen from the Otherworld and swathed them in capes of silk, cold and gray.

My favorite sister, Derbriu, squeezed my hand as we all began our descent from the battlements. "Are you all right, Maeve, dearest?" She often spoke to me in that motherly way. If there's one truth I know in the world, it's this: five sisters are four too many if they tease you all the time for being the baby of the family. Derbriu never did. Until my birth, three years after hers, she'd been the youngest, so she knew how much those taunts of "Baby!" stung.

I smiled, just for her. "I'm fine."

She knew I was lying. "You mustn't fret while Father's gone. Think of how happy we'll be when we see him home safe again."

"I'll be happy for that," I said solemnly. "And because of the cows."

Derbriu laughed so hard it drew our eldest sister's attention. "What's so funny?" Clothru asked.

"Maeve's eager to get the cows Father promised us."

"Well, so am I," said Eithne and Èile in chorus. Our twin sisters often spoke with one voice. It always made me giggle.

"And I!" our middle sister, Mugain, exclaimed. "Five cows apiece for doing next to nothing? It's a windfall." She grinned with delight.

Mother overheard. "Don't count your cows too soon, my girls—not with the easy way you all fall to bickering. Your father's so fed up with it, he's willing to *buy* peace. Five cows for each of you if he finds you little she-wolves lying down in friendship when he comes home." The severe look she gave us added: *See that it happens.*

"Do *we* get to choose?" I piped up.

"Choose?" Mugain echoed, raising her eyebrows.

I folded my arms. "They'll be *my* cows. I want to pick them."

She snickered. "You can hardly wipe your own nose, Maeve. When did you become a judge of cattle?"

"Tame your tongue, Mugain," Mother snapped. "This is how quarrels start. Maeve has a good point: you girls should have a hand in matters that affect your future. I'm not raising you to be helpless or lazy or to expect you'll lead perfect lives simply because you're princesses. My daughters will *not* be empty bowls, waiting idly for someone else to decide if you'll hold the hero's portion or scraps for dogs. It's not enough to be *given* things. You must also—"

"So you *want* us to pick our own cows, Mother?" I interrupted, grabbing her arm and bouncing up and down. "Can we? Will you promise?"

"She can't do that, Maeve," Clothru said in her most annoying I-know-everything voice. "She has to ask Father."

Mother's eyes flashed at my eldest sister. "Beg *his* permission to give *my* word? Your father will honor my pledge because he honors *me*. And if you girls wish to be respected by your husbands when you're grown up, gone, and managing your own households, you will take care to—"

I didn't linger to hear the rest of Mother's lecture. Whenever she started talking of husbands, I knew she couldn't mean me. I didn't want one, not if being married meant leaving home, not as long as my life held so many more interesting things to do.

I might never want a husband, but I did want a knife, and now. I stole away so nimbly that not even Derbriu noticed my departure. I sneaked into the great hall and spirited off a small, keen-edged blade from the place where the women prepared our meals. My plan was simple: find five cows that I'd be proud to own and cut off half the tuft of coarse hair at the end of their tails to mark them as mine.

The need for haste blinded me to all else. If I waited, one of my sisters might get a cow *I* wanted. I didn't spare a moment to take off the fine clothes I'd worn for Father's leave-taking or waste a thought over how dangerous cattle could be.

As I said, no one ever called me Maeve the Wise.

I plunged into the fog that had swallowed up Father's raiding party, happy to have it conceal my departure from Cruachan, but once I reached the grazing fields, my elation faded. The mist wasn't burning off fast enough to suit me. How was I supposed to choose cows I couldn't see? I wanted to stamp in frustration, but cold droplets soaked the hem of my tunic and dense grass hampered my feet. I scowled into the haze and struggled on. The thick, unmistakable smell of cattle was all I had to guide me along.

And then, between one step and the next, I met the bull. He loomed through the slowly thinning fog like one of the Fair Folk's stone monuments leading to the Otherworld. A feeble glimmer of sunlight made his black-tipped horns glow with an unearthly light. He was less than seven paces away and seemed unconcerned by my presence. I could have flung a pebble and hit his flank easily, but I would have died before committing such sacrilege. His glorious strength and lordly presence stole my breath. I knew that I had to have him.

The bull was grazing as I crept closer. From time to time he lifted his heavy head and turned it slowly from side to side as if sifting the different scents on the morning air. When he did this, I froze in place, willing him to mistake me for a part of the landscape. I wasn't a *complete* fool: I understood that what I wanted to do was perilous. Now that I saw the full measure of the beast before me, I recognized him. This was not just any of my father's cattle. This was Dubh, the fire-hearted black bull whose horns had laid open a man's leg from hip to knee when Father first brought the creature home. This was the one whose blood ran so hot that our cowherds had to keep him far from the other cattle outside of breeding time.

This was the bull I was born to own.

I slipped off my tunic and tied the sleeves loosely around my neck. If I suddenly had to turn and run, I couldn't have that dew-drenched garment holding me back. But it wasn't just any tunic of wool or linen, to be dropped in the field and retrieved later—if the bull's hooves spared it. I'd chosen to wear my best one for Father's leave-taking, a family treasure made from silk the deep blue of twilight.

The tunic's soaking hem fell against the backs of my thighs and clung there. That didn't matter; my legs were free. I was ready. My palms grew damp, my mouth dry. I licked my lips; it didn't help. The bull continued grazing. I edged closer, coming up behind him. A misstep plunged my right foot into one of his droppings. I think the familiar stink of his own waste masked my true scent just long enough for me to lift his tail and slash a chunk free with my blade.

Oh, how I ran after that! I raced through the grass, one foot a reeking mess, one hand clutching the precious spoils of my adventure. My heart pounded in my ears, but not half as loud as the rumble of the bull's hooves. I'd struck swiftly, but not swiftly enough to escape undetected. Great Dubh knew he'd been challenged, and he bawled his outrage to the skies. I didn't look back, but I could hear him closing the gap between us. Now the morning mist was lifting and I could see Cruachan's high earthen walls in the distance. A stand of trees sprang up to my right, but too far off for me to reach them before the black bull reached me. From the left I heard the lowing of many cows as the king's herds were driven to milking. Those were the beasts I'd been seeking when I found the bull. If I could reach them and lose myself in the herd, I might survive Dubh's charge. Could my small legs cover so much distance in time?

I clenched my teeth and drew in deep, desperate breaths through my nostrils. As hard as I ran, as dire as the fate at my heels, I never let go of the tuft of bull's hair in my left hand. *I won't give it up!* I thought angrily. *It's proof he's mine! And if he overtakes me, I'll . . . I'll . . .* My right hand closed more tightly on the little knife. In my heart I knew that even if I managed to stab the maddened bull with that pitiful blade, it would be no more to him than a fly's bite. Still I clung to false notions that I was not entirely helpless. I stoked my fury like a blacksmith's fire until it blazed away the panic in my bones.

The sound of many voices raised in fear came from across the fields: my father's cowherds. The sun had erased the last of the mist, giving them a clear view of my wild, hopeless dash. They were horrified but too far off to help me. Even if they could have conjured wings and covered the space between us, would they have been able to stop the beast? They'd have had better luck using a reed to hold back a thunderstorm!

My chest tightened and burned. I stepped on a tuft of grass and staggered sideways, stumbling halfway to my knees but recovering quickly. Something tugged at my left foot as I rose. I kicked backward violently, thrusting clear of whatever had snared me, and ran on.

It wasn't until I'd covered forty strides that I became aware of the change all around me. The cowherds' cries of alarm had turned to cheers. The bull's ever-closer presence was fading. The sun and wind poured over my back, which was now bare as an egg, and my neck was no longer encircled by the silk tunic's sleeves. What was happening? I couldn't resist the temptation to pause in my flight and turn around. Dubh the Mighty, Dubh the Fierce, Dubh the Bull of Bulls, my father's most valued beast, no longer chased me. Instead of plunging on, eager to avenge his clipped tail with my blood, the huge animal was trampling and goring and tearing the life out of . . . my tunic. Most of it lay in a damp wad under his hooves, the rich blue silk a muddy brown. A scrap of fabric trailed from one of his horns, forever just out of reach, tormenting him. He bawled and shook his head, but it was there to stay.

"I'm glad your father's not here to see that, Princess." A man's voice sounded at my side. One of the cowherds had arrived. "He'd offer some outlandish prize to the man bold enough to steal old Dubh's ribbon and I'd lose at least four of my stupidest lads to that contest." A fresh bellow from the bull made him chuckle. "*Now* hear him. Pitiful, like he is begging me to free him from that rag: 'Oh, please, won't you save me, dear friend? I promise by all I hold dearest, cows and cud, that I won't hurt you. I'll stand as tame as an old dog, and once you've plucked this accursed thing off my horn, I'll let you leave in peace.' Ha! Find a different fool to believe *that*, Dubh," he called out through cupped hands; then he lifted me onto his shoulder just like Father would and carried me home.

What a return that was! From the moment the cowherd brought me back to my mother I was scrubbed and kissed, praised and scolded, spanked and stuffed with the best tidbits at dinner. She ordered me to tell her what had happened, but I was so proud of my successful adventure that she didn't need to *demand* an explanation. I recounted the whole tale to her, to her attending ladies, to my sisters, and soon to all those who hadn't accompanied Father on his raid. Everyone who heard it repeated it, and sometimes added to it, until the ripples of the story ran out from Cruachan to meet Father halfway on his road home.

His driver, Fechin, raced the horses up the slope at such a furious pace that our watchmen scarcely had time to announce their lord's approach before Father was leaping down from his chariot, shouting my name. When Mother and all of us girls rushed out to welcome him, he scooped me up and threw me so high that I gasped with delight.

"What have you done now, Maeve?" he shouted. It was the only time anyone would say those words to me in praise. "What have you done to that poor, helpless bull? Bested by a girl! Will he ever recover from the shame?"

He placed me on my feet before him so that I could catch my breath and reply, "I only wanted to make sure my sisters couldn't take him when we choose the cows you promised us for not quarreling. And we didn't, not even once."

"Who said *you* could choose a gift of *my* giving, little spark?" Father tried to sound serious and failed utterly.

"It was my idea," I told him. "But Mother agreed it was a good one and said you'd do it."

"Is that so? Just like that?" Thick, spear-calloused fingers smoothed his mustache, which was as red as my hair. He smiled at Mother. "What sort of bold behavior are you teaching your daughters, my clever one?"

She tossed her chin high. "The same that I'm teaching *your* daughters, old boar." Everyone laughed, Father loudest of all.

Circling Mother's waist with one arm, he said, "Ah, Cloith-finn, are you sure you haven't been misleading me all these years?"

"What are you bleating about, calling me deceitful?" Mother tried to push free of his embrace. Her scowl looked deadly.

He kissed her heartily and earned a slap for it. Chuckling, he replied, "Haven't you been hiding the fact that our Maeve's no girl-child after all?"

"Do you even hear the nonsense you speak, boy?" Mother snapped at him. She must have known he was teasing, but she was in no mood to play along. If she hoped hard words would make him seal his lips, she failed.

"Be reasonable, love. What girl goes romping off to capture a full-grown bull? Our Maeve's got a spirit fierce enough for her to make a fine son, one that any king would be proud to call his heir. When Maeve was born, your good friend Lady Íde came to tell me she'd seen the baby come into the daylight with its fists clenched, ready for a fight. The midwife saw this as such a powerful omen that it took her a while before she noticed she'd delivered yet another princess."

" 'Yet *another* princess'?" Mother repeated, a dangerous note in her voice.

Father stepped away from her and raised both hands as if to shield himself from a blow. His ready smile wavered.

I was too young to tell if this was more of their usual sparring or if they were quarreling in earnest. I threw myself between them and begged, "Don't fight! I promise I won't take my bull or the cows if you make up. It's Father's homecoming. We should all be happy."

My plea eased the tension. Father sighed and smiled fondly at Mother. "She has your wisdom, Cloithfinn. We should heed it." He offered me his hand, huge and rough, and Mother gave me hers, small yet strong. Soon I was shrieking with glee as we entered our stronghold, my parents swinging me high into the air at every third stride.

As we approached our great house, I saw a group of Father's men crowding the stone-framed entry. Flanking it were the severed heads of warriors who had fallen most valiantly in battle with Lord Eochu, each carefully embalmed with cedar oil and displayed in a niche. I had grown up seeing these grisly trophies, a tribute to my father's skill with the sword. The worthiest of the king's fallen adversaries was shown the greatest respect by having his head set on the lintel above the doorway, but this place of honor had remained vacant for over a year.

No longer. The warriors who had just mounted the fresh trophy there turned to greet Father with loud cheers. He scooped me off my feet and held me against his battle-scarred chest so that I could have a better look at his newly taken prize.

"See there, Maeve?" he said gravely. "That's the fate of a man who thought he could betray me and escape the consequences just because he was High King of Èriu." He gave the sightless eyes a mocking look. "I taught you otherwise, eh, Fachtna Fáthach?"

I stared at the severed head in wonderment, remembering the times when Father had spoken about attending the High King at Tara or sending him gifts. A man so high-ranked that other kings paid him tribute, yet now he was . . . gone.

"What did he do to you, Father?" I asked.

"You don't need to burden yourself with such things, my spark. It's men's business. All that touches you is this: I'm High King of Èriu now, and you're my bold, bull-hunting daughter." With that, he jounced me in his arms and carried me into the house.

If I had any further questions for him, they were swept out of my mind by the storm of preparations for his victory feast. It began that night, went on for thirty more, and the din of it rocked Cruachan to its roots.

We were not the only ones sharing the celebration. The road to our ringfort soon teemed with noblemen arriving from all parts of Èriu. Every one of them bowed and brought gifts. My ruined silk tunic was soon replaced by a more splendid one. My sisters received equally magnificent garb.

Gold ringed every neck under our roof. No sooner was a heavy torque finished, polished, and placed in Father's hands than he awarded it. It was very funny to see some of his younger, thinner fighters struggling to stand tall under the weight of such a precious yoke. I couldn't begin to count how many animals were slaughtered to feed the shifting crowd. We breathed the scent of roasting pork and stewing beef for so long that I forgot what fresh air smelled like.

My sisters and I soon grew tired of so much revelry. Even though we were always welcome at the nightly carousing, we often stayed in our room after eating.

"It's so *boring*," I complained to Derbriu. "Every night Devnet the bard sings nothing but songs about how Father cut off the High King's head."

"That's the truth." Derbriu cleared her throat and burst into a hilarious imitation of our house bard performing the tale of how Eochu Feidlech, son of Finn, rode out to avenge an act of treachery by Lord Fachtna Fáthach, and won. All of my sisters giggled, but very softly. It was dangerous to make fun of a bard. If he learned about it, you could find yourself the target of a satire cruel enough to kill, or so Mother said.

Silence followed the laughter. Clothru said, "It's all going to be different for us now." She didn't sound happy.

"Why?" I asked.

"Because now we're the *High King's* daughters. We're more important than before."

"Too important," Èile said glumly. "It means there'll be no more putting off sending us into fosterage."

Fosterage . . .

I was well aware of the custom that called for highborn children to be raised in other households. Some went as young as a year old. Boys were sent to learn the skills of a warrior, girls to prepare themselves for marriage. Fosterage forged lasting bonds between families. Mother said it was also good for the children, making them more self-reliant, helping them to grow up strong, far away from softhearted parents who might be too ready to offer sympathy for every hurt or to make excuses for every failure.

No one asked the children if they wanted to go.

"It won't touch you, Maeve," Clothru said. "Father will flatter his strongest allies by awarding the rest of us to them, but he'll want to hold on to you as his pet bargaining token."

"It's not fair," Èile sulked. "Just because she's the youngest—"

I opened my mouth to protest, but before I could speak, Mother entered our room. "Your father wants you all to join the feast."

"Do we *have* to?" Mugain whined. "I'm tired."

"All right, girl," Mother said crisply. "If you're so weary, I'll tell your father he can take the cattle he was going to present to you and give them to your sisters instead."

Cattle! We'd all forgotten about Father's promise to reward our good behavior with five cows apiece. We scrambled after Mother like a tumble of puppies.

A fire blazed high in the stone-ringed central hearth of the king's great house. Men sat crowded on the benches that lined the walls or stood packed hip to hip, feasting and drinking. I expected we'd have to struggle through their midst to reach Father's seat, but they moved aside for us like grass bending in the wind.

"Ah, there they are!" Father exclaimed when he saw us. "My prized, beautiful daughters. Come here, girls."

We arranged ourselves in a row before him while he told the assembled men of Èriu of his promise to us. "You can't make peace with women using sword or spear, so you must buy it," he declared, red-faced and grinning. "Five cows each was a fair price, but I've changed my mind. My daughters have come up in the world. They'll each have *ten* cattle"—we six danced for joy while the warriors loudly approved their new High King's generosity—"except for Maeve."

I was stricken. "Father, why—"

"Patience, my spark." He beckoned our bard to step forward. "Sing for us, Devnet, a new song. Give us something different, the tale of how the Fair Folk put a prince's heart in a girl-child's body." He pointed at me.

"Yes, my lord." With a mischievous look, Devnet began to sing about my adventure with Dubh. I was so enchanted to hear a bard transform me into a heroine that I forgot my distress over losing those promised cows. He took some liberties with the tale, toying with it so merrily, so blatantly, that his listeners had to know it was all a joke. When he reached the point where I grabbed Dubh's tail, he claimed I used it to swing myself onto the bull's back and ride him to Tara and home again. His song served up the truth as well. Though he praised my courage, Devnet reminded everyone that I owed my life to luck, and he didn't forget to include a comical account of how I stepped in a pile of the bull's manure. I would have blushed if I hadn't been giggling. There was no real malice in his words. He had everyone else in the hall laughing and cheering for me until the end, when he described my "noble warrior's stink, her fair skin adorned with the brown smear of triumph."

Father rewarded our bard with a gleaming armband, then had me sit in his lap. "You see, my friends? All of my daughters shine, but my youngest shows a champion's heart. Mark me, someday she'll be a prize worthy of none but the greatest lord in Èriu." He smiled at me. "It's a shame I can't reward your exploits with the hero's portion, my spark. I'll have to give you twenty cows instead."

"Nineteen," I corrected him solemnly. "Nineteen and Dubh."

He laughed, praised my courage, and said, "How could any man deny you whatever you desire, Maeve?" But days later, when I first went out to see my newly given herd, there were twenty cows and no sign of the bull.

CHAPTER TWO

A Promise and a Path

MY SISTERS HAD said things would change for us now that
Father was High King. They were right, but they never guessed
how soon those changes would come. Clothru was sent out to
fosterage by midsummer. Eithne and Èile, as next oldest, soon
followed. Mugain went just before the first hard frost. In spite
of how often they'd teased me for being the baby, I cried like
an infant when each of them left home.

Derbriu was the last to go. On that sad morning, six years
after our other sisters had been put to fosterage, I became the
lone princess in the High King's house. Father drove away
with Derbriu by his side. Mother's women chattered ceaselessly
about what a fine place the king had found for his sweet-voiced
daughter. She was going to be raised by a noble family of the
Ulaidh whose realm included Emain Macha, a site of sacred
power.

All I knew was that my favorite sister was being taken far
from me and that I might never see her again. I stood watching

her fly away into the dawn and wondered why I couldn't weep. Instead of drowning in my own tears, I felt hollow, dry, and as brittle as an overbaked clay jar.

That aching emptiness wasn't my only burden. Now that I spent more time in my own company, I began to notice something odd: No matter where I went, if any of Father's warriors were nearby, I was watched. Every way I turned my head, every time I glanced up from a task, I saw men's eyes on me. Nearly all of them did it, from our older fosterling boys to men three times my age. If our gazes met, they'd smile and wish me well, but it was no casual greeting. There was something disturbing behind it, though I was unable to give it a name. It was worse when they tried to draw me into conversation. The boys' attempts were painfully awkward, but when the men did it, I felt my skin creep. Why were they suddenly so fascinated by anything an eleven-year-old girl could say?

I wished Father would hurry home from taking Derbriu to the lands of the Ulaidh. He would set things right when he came back; I was convinced of that. Meanwhile, I did what I could for myself. I became skilled at avoiding the men's eyes, dodging their greetings, escaping from any chance of conversation, but it was still hard while I remained within Cruachan's walls.

That was why I took to ranging the countryside. The early morning sun never found me at home. I became a rover, a wanderer, a cloud's shadow blown across the grass and gone. Bog land and forest, streams and ponds, deer paths and grazing fields for cattle, all of these became my realm. I was a frequent visitor to the homes of farmers and the huts of cowherds. Most of them didn't know who I was, and the sudden appearance of

a solitary girl was startling. There were moments when I was mistaken for one of the Fair Folk, and sometimes I couldn't resist the urge to play along. If instead of simple curiosity I saw an awestruck look in the eyes of a plowman or his family, I would burst into a weird, wavering song and dance away, beckoning them to follow. No one ever did.

An uncanny transformation overtook me. I'd begun my wanderings to avoid facing unpleasantness at home, but the longer I followed this new path, the more I came to love it for its own sake. Away from the eyes that haunted me, the encounters that put me on edge, and the lessons that aimed to stitch me into a life I'd never chosen, I started to savor something new: freedom. Freedom, honey-sweet and heady. I gulped it down the way Father and his warriors drank mead.

Mother had no idea of my feelings. She disapproved of what she called my waywardness and chided me for it every night at dinner. "Do you hate learning your future duties so much?" she demanded. "Or do you simply have no respect for me?"

I wanted to tell her what was wrong. I wanted to say, "Men are looking at me all the time. Men are talking to me, and I don't like it." But I couldn't. When I put my feelings into words while alone, they sounded stupid. I was sure Mother would think I'd lost my wits.

I hunched over my meal and mumbled, "Sorry." It was all I'd do until Father came home again. Then I'd tell *him* and everything would be set right.

He was gone a long time. Besides accompanying Derbriu to her new home, he had much to do as High King of Èriu. Samhain came while he was away. Samhain, the time of shadows, the turning of the year from light to dark. The border between our world and the realm of the spirits grew as thin as frost on a blade of grass. Few dared to venture outside on that night for fear of meeting the Fair Folk or the dead.

Mother worked with our most trusted stewards to oversee the last stage of harvesting and food storage. She also approved which cattle would be slaughtered so that there'd be enough food to see the rest of the herd through the coming winter. When the purification bonfires were lit across our land, she astonished everyone by leaping over the blaze as gracefully as a doe, with not so much as a spark touching her tunic. I followed, with less success, and it took a man with a pot of water to douse my burning hem.

"Where did you get the idea you were old enough to try *that* madness?" Mother yelled, shaking me. I laughed and pretended I was going to attempt it again. I expected her to hold me back, but to my surprise, she didn't. Arms folded, she watched me prepare to make a second jump across the fire, her lips pressed into a small, hard line. I took a few steps back, dashed forward, and stopped short, suddenly afraid. My cheeks were hot, but not from the nearness of the bonfire.

"I was only joking," I mumbled as I made my retreat.

"Good." Mother's voice was filled with satisfaction. "So you're no fool, in spite of how irresponsibly you've been acting." She tapped the side of my head with her forefinger. "Maybe there's a mind inside this nutshell, not just a tangle of impulses."

I wished I were as impulsive as she thought. Maybe then I would have blurted out everything troubling me, heart and spirit. Instead I fell back into a silence that resolved nothing at all.

An unspoken truth is often cousin to a lie.

Some dozen days before Father's homecoming, I woke up shivering. I pulled on my tunic and shoes, swung my blanket over my shoulders, and flitted to the house doorway. The great hall and hearth were deserted. It was very early, and the intense chill seemed to be encouraging the rest of the household to stay snug under their covers.

I looked outside. Whiteness was everywhere. I couldn't recall the last time snow had fallen on Cruachan, or even if I'd been alive to see it. Winter usually brought rain and fog, not this bright, shining view. When I gasped with delight, my breath hung on the air in a tiny cloud. I ducked back into the hall just long enough to grab a chunk of bread from a basket near the hearth, and soon I was no more than a streak of red hair fading into the distance and a scattering of footprints in the snow.

I had no destination in mind when I set out that morning, caught up as I was in the beauty I saw everywhere. This snow-fall was a gift from the Fair Folk, from the gods, a magical spell that transformed familiar places with glittering enchantment. I took deep breaths and released them in great gusts of laughter. I scooped up double handfuls of snow and flung them into the sky, thrilling to feel countless tiny points of icy moisture shower over my upturned face. I walked farther and farther from home, forbidding myself to surrender to the cold. My feet began to tingle and my hands felt raw, but I went on.

I don't know when the wolf caught my scent or how long it followed me before I realized it was there. The only sounds that weren't hushed by that day's wintry stillness were the harsh cries of a flock of crows flying across the pale sky. All I can remember is a strange prickling at the back of my neck and the abrupt awareness of something intently watching me.

Don't be such a baby, I told myself scornfully. *You're imagining—*

Then I saw the beast. It was big-boned but scraggly, one ear badly torn and hanging limp. When it realized I'd spotted it, the wolf snarled, lips lifted to show red gums and a flash of sharp teeth, a fearsome look in its eyes. As it held me with that wild golden gaze, the hackles of its patchy gray pelt rose and it flattened its unwounded ear. I watched the creature pull back into a crouch and wondered if I had any chance at all of escape. The white silence between us stretched to eternity.

A war-shout tore through the air, riding the shaft of a warrior's spear. The wolf yelped, pierced through the ribs with such force that its body made a long swath across the snow. A pitiful whimper, a few twitches of those huge paws, and it was over.

"Lady Maeve, are you all right?" A tall, rangy young man came loping toward me, black braids slapping against his bare back. Even in this weather, he only wore breeches, something Father's less seasoned warriors commonly did to toughen themselves. There were no scars marking his body, a sure sign that he hadn't yet seen battle.

"I— Yes, I am." I glanced at the wolf's corpse. Blood matted the gray fur and seeped into the snow. "Thank you." I spoke no louder than a mouse's squeak.

"Not a bad throw," my rescuer said, bracing one foot against the dead animal's hind leg and yanking his spear free. "I'm glad I woke in time and saw you leave Cruachan. If I hadn't decided to follow you . . ." He nodded at the wolf.

"Why did you?" I must have spoken more harshly than I intended. He jerked his head back as though I'd slapped him.

"I meant no harm, Princess. I was intending to make an early start this morning anyhow, to try my luck at hunting."

Now that I'd had a moment to really look at him, I saw that my rescuer wasn't one of the men who'd been hounding me. I lowered my eyes, embarrassed. "I'm sorry. I thought you were . . . were someone else."

He shrugged. "I'm no one but Kelan, Lady Maeve, and all I want is to see you safely home."

I was too shaken by my close escape to object. I waited while he skinned the dead wolf, and secretly admired the swift, neat way he did it. He grinned as he slung the pelt over his shoulder. "I can't wait to tell everyone how I took this trophy."

I grabbed his arm. "But you can't tell! Please, you mustn't do it. If my mother hears what happened, she'll never let me leave the hall again. She'll tie me to a post, like a dog. She'll treat me like an infant!"

"Which is it going to be, my lady, dog or infant?" He chuckled. "Never mind, I'll keep your secret, I promise."

Could I believe him? Our warriors loved to boast about their achievements. He didn't look older than sixteen, yet he'd just killed a wolf with a single spear-cast *and* saved a princess. Would he be able to resist the temptation to brag?

"I hope you'll do that for me," I said. "But don't make a promise you can't keep."

He laid one hand on the thin bronze torque around his neck. "I, Kelan, give you my oath, sworn on your own father's gift to me. Will that do?"

I smiled. "I hope the day comes when you can swear an oath on a torque made of gold."

As Kelan and I walked back together, under the shadow of snow-laden boughs, he asked, "Why was it that you left the house this morning, in weather like this?"

I made a dismissive gesture. "I go out every day, in all weather."

"So you do. People talk about it constantly. Some of the men are even laying wagers about it."

"What sort of wagers?" I was on guard.

He shrugged. "Wagers over why no one sees you inside the ringfort from dawn to dusk. Most of them bet that you're meeting a lad. Some say he's a peasant, some that he's one of our own, and a few claim you've enchanted a prince of the Fair Folk, no less. The highest stakes are riding on the lucky fellow's name, though if you ask me, it's just so they can hunt him down and give him the beating of his life."

"Then I'm glad there's no such person. Why would they want to do such a mean, stupid thing?"

"Ah, simple enough—because they're all in love with you, Princess."

My cheeks flamed. "That's ridiculous!"

"No, it's real enough. You're the High King's daughter, the one he's favored over all the rest since the day you showed that you were brave as any boy—braver!"

"The black bull . . . ," I muttered.

Kelan nodded. "I was there among the other fosterling boys when Lord Eochu honored you for it, twenty cows to your sisters' ten. Our warriors and highborn guests talked about it for days afterward, and the news spread across all Èriu when the visiting nobles went home. That gift marked you forever as someone special, and now your father's added to the tales surrounding you by keeping you home as his treasure. Everyone says the man who gets you gets Connacht. It's easy to fall in love with a girl who brings her husband a kingdom." He laughed.

I wasn't amused. The wolf pelt draped over Kelan's shoulder mocked me. Was that what I'd become? A trophy to be taken, a prize, a reward more precious than any golden torque? "So that's why they stare at me all the time," I said, half to myself.

"They want you to notice them. Our fellows believe they're so irresistible that if you take a liking to one of them, your doting father will honor your preference before the highborn of other kingdoms begin making their offers. The first sign of interest you show to any man, he'll leap on it like a starving dog on a meaty bone." His lips twisted. "And the others will likely leap on *him*. You've spared them all plenty of bruises and broken heads by the way you always flee anything in breeches."

I wanted to protest, to say I wasn't running away like a coward. *But that's exactly what I've been doing,* I thought, though I hated to admit a truth that made me despise myself.

"If that's how it is, you'd better not walk me back all the way, Kelan," I said softly. "The other men will see us together. They'll think I'm favoring you, and then—"

"I'm safe, Lady Maeve. My comrades know I'd never have a horse in this race. My sweetheart, Bláithín, would kill me. For one of your mother's serving girls, she's got pride worthy of a queen." His mirth rang out through the icy air.

I wished my heart were as light as his. *Why am I caught in this snare?* I thought, my jaw set. *Why am I letting our men—* anyone—*make me feel so uncomfortable in my own home that I have to run away? When Father comes back, I'll tell him everything and he'll put a stop to—*

Will he? The afterthought took me by surprise. I remembered something my sister Clothru had said on the day that a gift of twenty cows set me apart from my sisters forever: "Father will flatter his strongest allies by *awarding* the rest of us to them, but he'll want to hold on to you as his pet bargaining token."

That is *how Father sees me, isn't it?* I realized as I tramped through the snow, head bent, eyes on the ground. *I'm a gift to be given, like those cows. What I want doesn't matter, no more than when I wanted Dubh. Father spoke as though he were going to give me the black bull, but he never did, and I had to swallow that. His choices are the only ones that count, the way he decides which warrior will have the hero's portion when we feast.* I clenched my fists at my sides. *That's what I am to him: the hero's portion. And what can I do about that?*

Kelan and I emerged from the trees into the open fields. I lifted my gaze and saw Cruachan, dominating the land, massive in the sunlight. Now that I knew how things truly stood for me inside those walls, my home looked like a holding pen where cattle were confined while their fates were decided for them. My spirit felt as heavy as my sodden shoes.

Suddenly, a shrill cry slashed across the brilliance of the winter sky. The fierce, commanding call tore my eyes from the ringfort to where a solitary bird hovered effortlessly in the heavens, its elegantly shaped wings sharply outlined against the blue. It was too far away for me to see its color or markings, especially

with the sun in my eyes, but when it suddenly plunged earth-
ward, I knew it was a bird of prey. Somewhere among the fields,
a mouse or some other unlucky small creature had just lost its
life to that bird's talons. I waited patiently and after a while saw
the bird rise up again, soaring free.

How beautiful, I thought, my admiration mixed with pierc-
ing splinters of envy. Devnet sang of an ancient princess of
Connacht, Caer Ibormeith, who lived every other year of her
life as a swan until the god Aengus chose her. Instead of turning her into a human, he changed himself into a swan and they
flew off together. His action had always puzzled me, but on
that winter day, in that moment of seeing the raptor's flight, all
at once I knew that Aengus had chosen wisely.

"A kestrel," Kelan said, shading his eyes. "They're fierce
little things—good hunters, especially that one, finding prey
when the cold weather drives small creatures deep into their
nests. Clever bird. Clever and stubborn."

I scarcely heard him. My eyes were too filled with the kestrel's grace, its strength, its freedom. The sight of it broke the
spell of gloom and resignation that had settled over my heart.
In that moment I knew that what I desired—what I was *born*
to do—was to claim those wings for my own. I spread my arms
and imagined that it was already so. I was no longer Father's
bargaining token, destined to await the day he *told* me what my
life would have to be. Only cattle are driven; kestrels fly free.

I embraced my dream. I didn't know exactly how I'd manage to fulfill it—to choose, hold, and defend my fate, to tell my
father, High King of all Èriu, no. But I would; I *would.* I would
learn. I would find a way. The wild kestrel was gone from sight,

but its image had become a part of me, a sign as sure as any bard's vision.

I touched the gold torque circling my neck and silently made a binding promise: someday I would have my wings.

That wolf's pelt became Kelan's badge of honor. He flaunted it before all the men, both the green boys and the seasoned fighters. He told the tale so many times over dinner that his companions complained he was trying to turn himself into a bard. If Devnet had been there to hear him instead of with Father, he might have had a sarcastic thing or two to say about that.

No matter how often Kelan added details to his recital, my part in the story stayed hidden. He never mentioned my name, though sometimes he'd wink at me when no one else was looking. He kept his word and my secret.

One morning I awoke to find a blue cloak covering my feet. It was trimmed with a thick collar of gray wolf fur. My cry of surprise and delight fetched Mother so quickly that I suspected she'd been lurking just outside my doorway.

"Do you like it? Be sure to thank Kelan. He asked me if one of my ladies could make that for you. It's not every lad who'd sacrifice his precious trophy to make a little lass happy. If I didn't know how bound he is to my girl Bláithín, I'd say he was in love with you," she teased.

"He's not."

I wrapped my new cloak around me and buried my nose in the fur. Was it an illusion or did the wolf's pelt still hold the clean, cold smell of that snowy day? The scent conjured visions of my kestrel, wings wide, eyes fixed on its desire.

"Well, I suppose he's just another of those men who think they'll get your father's favor by being nice to you. You'd better be aware of that, Maeve, and not be misled by false kindness."

"Yes, Mother," I said dutifully. I didn't feel I needed to tell her that I already knew the difference between a false kindness and a true friend like Kelan.

My run-in with the wolf didn't stop my rambling ways; it just made me stay more alert to my surroundings. I wore the furred cloak as a talisman, a charm to keep me safe wherever I went. I'd made one great change in what sent me wandering: Now I left the ringfort solely because it was my choice, for my pleasure. I was no longer running away. I refused to let anyone, fosterling or warrior, drive me from my home. Whenever I felt men's eyes on me, I met their stares with the full force of my gaze. It was impossible to mistake it for flirtation. When I did it, I stepped into the feathered skin of the kestrel, small but bold, and looked at them as if they were my lawful prey, free to live or doomed to die by *my* decision.

Yes, do stare at me, you mouse! Do it if you dare. You won't like the consequences.

The effect was all I could have wanted: Even the most seasoned warriors recoiled when my fearless eyes struck them—they weren't expecting a challenge from a girl just out of childhood. While the shock of it still lingered, I softened my expression and greeted them politely, but with the same distant courtesy Mother used when telling her servants what she wanted them to do.

Poor men, I confused them badly. It was wonderful. I'd broken their spears, spoiled their hunt, and freed myself from fearing their attention. Mother was happier too. Ever since I'd reclaimed the right to live without harassment, I no longer had to dodge my lessons in order to dodge my "admirers." Best of all, I'd fixed things without having to wait for Father to come home and do it for me.

That was good, but it was only a start. If I was ever going to be truly free, I needed a way to persuade Father that the daughter he loved was more than just a prize to be awarded. I thought of how he treated Mother. There was more than love between them. He joked with her, teased her, but he also went to her for counsel. He called her beautiful, but he called her clever too. Anyone with eyes and ears could stand witness to how much he respected her for her wisdom. He gave her full authority over his holdings while he was gone.

I wanted him to give me the respect he gave to her. I didn't need it to make choices for a kingdom, or even for a household, just for me. The sooner Father came back, the sooner I could set myself to gaining it. I could hardly wait for his return.

I never suspected what that homecoming would bring.

On the cold, foggy day when Father's chariot returned to Cruachan, I'd finished my sewing lesson early, to Mother's satisfaction, and rewarded myself with a solitary ramble. I was well away from the ringfort and saw his horses long before any of our watchmen.

"Father!" I darted from the roadside, waving my arms. "Father, it's me, Maeve!" I was careful to identify myself loudly. I knew how fast a warrior could fling a spear, especially if some mysterious shape suddenly came at him out of the mist. "Welcome home!"

My greeting fell away into a great silence. The fog played tricks on my eyes and ears, making it look like there was only one man in the king's chariot. *Why is Father driving himself home?* I wondered, peering at the oddly shrunken shape holding the reins. *Did something happen to Fechin? How awful! Father says there's no better man for his horses.* I prayed it wasn't true.

The gods seemed to listen. I heard Fechin's familiar voice rise tentatively over the horses' slow footfalls. "My lady? Where are you?"

I came closer until we could see each other. I saw the sadness in his eyes a moment before he saw the terror in mine: Fechin was driving the High King's chariot but his master was not there. My chest filled with pain and a great wail of grief rose to my lips.

"Lady Maeve, no!" Fechin clutched the reins in one hand, his other making rapid hushing motions. "Lord Eochu's with us. He's alive. He's coming home and"—he bit his lip—"he sent me ahead, that's all. You have nothing to fear."

"Where is he, Fechin?" The strange, harsh quality of my voice startled me. It echoed between us as if we were standing inside the curved iron walls of a giant's cauldron.

"Coming, he's coming, I swear! He's riding in a wagon, along with the tribute his subject kings gave him when we were all at Tara for the Samhain rites."

"Father would *never* ride in a wagon. No warrior would. What happened to him? Tell me!" I was afraid, uncertain, and it made me sharp-tongued.

Fechin blinked, then frowned at my demanding tone. I was too caught up with worrying about Father to explain, apologize, or even hear what I sounded like. "You'll be told when you need to know—when and *if*! Now step up or step aside and let me pass. I've been sent ahead with a message for Lady Cloithfinn."

I chose to go with him. It wasn't because I craved the thrill of a chariot ride. I wanted answers *now,* and was sure I'd get them when Fechin spoke with Mother.

Once we were within the ringfort, Fechlin threw the chariot reins to the first able-bodied man he saw and raced into the great house. By the time I ran after him, he was deep in conference with Mother. They spoke in whispers, and when I tried to creep close enough to hear what they were saying, a line of her attendants blocked me.

"Let me pass!" I cried, trying to shove my way between them. They ignored my protests. Three of the women laid hold of me and began leading me firmly away. I struggled in their grip and even kicked one of them by accident as I shouted, "Mother! Mother!"

"Maeve, stop acting like a wild thing and *go.*" Mother's voice was tense and strained. "This doesn't concern you."

"It's about Father. It *does.*"

Mother didn't bother to debate with me. She ordered her attendants to take me to my chamber and keep me there. By the time I was allowed to emerge again, Father and the rest of his party were home. He greeted me with all of his old warmth, but when I begged him to toss me high, he smiled wistfully and said, "You're too old for that now, Maeve."

The grand homecoming feast was delayed. He spent the rest of that day and the next in his sleeping chamber, with his highest-ranking men going in and out. Every face was grave.

My home became a place of whispers, where each conversation was an exchange of secrets. I learned none of them.

When Father finally left the confines of his room, he looked tired and preoccupied. I caught Mother looking his way many times with an expression of worry carving notches beside her mouth and between her brows. When I asked her what was wrong, she dismissed me angrily. Something had made her mad at the world.

I don't know what's done this to you, Mother, but I'll find out, I thought.

Determination turned me from Maeve the Wanderer to Maeve Stay-at-Home, Maeve Bide-by-the-Fire, Maeve Mouse-in-the-Shadows. Mother was pleased to find me suddenly devoted to learning the ways of loom and spindle, needle and thread.

She didn't notice that I always found a way to do my work within eavesdropping distance of our household's most notorious gossips, male and female. I thought I was being very wily, but no one spoke about what I wanted to know.

I had no better luck when I tried approaching the men and boys who'd hounded me in Father's absence. No matter how I tried to draw them out, they put up walls and took their earliest chance to flee me the way I'd once fled them.

My drive to uncover what was hidden soon became a force that was driving *me,* taking me down a bad road. I even tried taking advantage of Kelan's good nature. He turned away from my incessant questions with an apology and such an unhappy expression that I immediately regretted what I'd done.

I was lingering in a doorway, trying to catch a conversation between two of Father's attendants, when a voice behind me said, "Hear anything that interests you, my lady?" Our bard's soft, lilting murmur made me jump and utter a little shriek as if he'd bellowed in my ear. Devnet laughed as the two men stared at me before taking their talk elsewhere.

"What an odd occupation you've adopted," he went on. "Can't a princess find better entertainment than eavesdropping?"

"It's not entertainment. There's something I need to know and I can't discover it any other way. I've tried."

"Have you tried asking me?" His smile was almost as kindly as the warmth in his deep blue eyes. "No need for that. I can guess what's driving you to play the spy. You're fretful over your father."

"How did you know?"

"Knowing you." He passed one hand through his unkempt silver hair. "Knowing how much you and he love each other. Lord Eochu has six daughters, but only one is his spark."

"He came home in a *wagon*." I blurted the unthinkable, the unnatural. It was like accusing the sky of sending a rain of fishes or the earth of giving birth to a harvest of swords.

"So he did." The bard's face grew serious. "Because of how direly he was wounded at Tara, and of how close he came to death."

My jaw dropped. If Devnet hadn't flashed a warning look at me, I would have filled the house with my cry of dismay. He jerked his chin, silently bidding me to go with him outside. There, far from any witnesses, he told me everything.

After Father placed Derbriu in her new home, he rode to the sacred hill of Tara for the Samhain rites. A close kinsman of Lord Fachtna, the High King my father had slain, confronted him, declaring he had no right to rule. The poison-tongued creature swore that Father's claims of treachery against Lord Fachtna were false, a weak excuse to kill him and satisfy his own ambition.

"Such words could not stand," Devnet said gravely. "The two men fought with all the lesser kings to witness it. Lord Eochu sent his challenger to feed the crows, though not before the man nearly did the same to him. It was only thanks to the druids of Tara that he survived. It was a long recovery, and neither peaceful nor complete. Your father's loyal warriors and allied kings had to cut down more than one hand raised against him while he lay helpless. His healers were outraged when he insisted on going home before he was fully mended, but he wanted everyone here to see he was alive before some false rumor of his death could spread to the ears of power-hungry men or reach Cruachan and wound those he loves. If the price of that was to come back in a wagon like an ailing woman, he paid it willingly."

I began to tremble. "Father . . . Father almost died?" I had a gruesome vision of unknown hands removing Lord Fachtna's embalmed head from our great house's lintel and replacing it with Father's. Floods of tears streamed down my cheeks before I realized I was weeping.

Devnet regarded me with compassion. "This is why Lord Eochu commanded us to preserve your ignorance, child. He was certain the news would undo you and he loves you too much to burden you with men's business." A rueful smile twitched one corner of his mouth. "Did I ever tell you of the dream I had before you were born? I woke from it convinced you'd be the valiant son your father longed to have—a son to make him secure in his kingship, a son to free him from worrying about the unknown fate you, your mother, and sisters would face if he died in battle. It's worse now that he's High King. The eagle atop the tallest tree makes the easiest target. Your father is my friend as well as my lord, Lady Maeve. He's told me many times how much he loves his daughters, but he *needs* a son. Sons provide for their families in the hunt, protect them in war, and bring them honor by their bravery. They say that when Lord Eochu killed Lord Fachtna and took his head, his son Conchobar saw it all without shedding a single tear."

He sighed. "My dream was wrong, Princess, but it remains with me. Though you weren't born a boy, that deceitful dream of mine still made me seek a boy's courage in you. When you were five years old and dared to challenge that bull, I felt justified, but now . . ." His shoulders rose and fell. "I should have heeded your father and shielded you. I'm sorry my mistake hurt you so deeply."

"I'm not hurt." Indignant, I dashed away the tears with the back of my hand. "And I don't need to be shielded. I'm *not* weak."

"Perhaps you're not, for a girl. But a girl is what you are, to your very heart." His old, ingratiating smile returned. "A pitying heart, I hope? One that cares enough to keep this talk of ours from your father's ears and spare me his laughter for clinging to a meaningless dream?"

What king would dare to laugh at a bard? I thought. "I promise to do as you ask."

"You're a good girl, Maeve. Thank you."

I watched him return to the great hall and thought, *What's the use of being a good girl when my father needs a son?*

Chapter Three

Quest and Consequence

I WAS GOING to become a boy. It was as simple as that.

Well, not *that* simple. I'd need help, and there was only one person I could rely on for it: Kelan.

I managed to catch him alone and begged him to meet me outside the ringfort. He agreed once I assured him I wouldn't keep pecking for answers about Father.

"Someone told you, didn't they," he stated. I nodded sheepishly. "That's what I thought." He sounded resigned. "Just don't slip and tell Lord Eochu the name of the luckless boy who blabbed. If you scooped him clean of secrets, at least you can spare his hide."

"How did you know it was a boy?"

His look as good as said, *Don't make me waste time answering a silly question.* But I swear by all I love, at that age I asked it honestly.

I decided it would be best if Kelan and I weren't seen

leaving the ringfort together. I gave him directions to meet me in a safe place I'd discovered, a sweet refuge under the protective springtime canopy of a willow tree. It grew on the bank of a stream that ran close enough to Cruachan to be handy but far away enough from home to remain my secret.

The moment that Kelan pushed aside the curtain of sword-shaped leaves, I poured out my plan.

"You want to become *what*?" He stared at me as if an owl had popped out of my head.

"A boy," I said, then realized that in my eagerness, I'd misspoken. "Not to *become* a boy. It would take the Fair Folk's magic to do that. I want—I need—to learn how to *act* like one."

"You mean wear breeches?"

"I need a boy's *skills,* not his clothes. If you put a horse's harness on a frog, it can't pull a chariot. Kelan, listen—I'm doing this for Father's sake. I don't want him to go on thinking he's our family's sole protector."

"But he's not. The warriors of Connacht would shield y—"

"Not if Father fell. They'd follow the new king then, true?"

"I . . . I guess so." Kelan rubbed the back of his head. "I never thought about it."

"The new king would take *everything*—cattle, gold, silver, whatever he liked. Who'd stop him?" I went on. "My mother, my sisters, we'd all be left with nothing. That's Father's worst fear, and it never leaves him. If he can't put it from his mind, someday it might distract him in a fight and then—" I shook my head. "He won't be free of it until he knows someone will keep us safe even when he can't do it anymore."

"Someone like you?" Kelan had the kindness not to laugh at me straightaway.

"I hope so. I can't be the son he needs, but I *can* learn all the things a prince of Connacht would know. I'll be strong, skilled with weapons. I'll be so swift to challenge any man who speaks against him that they'll have to face my sword, not his. I won't let him have the chance to fight them. When he rides to war, my chariot will race beside his. I'll do all that"—I spread my hands wide—"because you'll train me."

I waited for Kelan's reply. He remained silent, a young man who had turned to stone. The only sounds were the rushing of the stream, the music of songbirds, and the distant cawing of a flock of crows. At last he took a deep breath. "Well, you're not asking *too* much, are you?" He tried to sound playful, but it rang false. "Or is there more to your wish? Do you hunger to rule all Èriu? Do you see yourself as our next High King?"

"This is no jest," I said firmly. "I only want to ease Father's mind, to have him know my spear and sword will protect us as well as his."

Kelan sucked in his lower lip in thought. "Your spear and sword . . . Do you know the first thing about how to use them? Can you even *lift* them?"

"I will, once you teach me."

He looked as if he pitied me. "Lady Maeve, you should pick a better guide for this road. I've trained with weapons since I was seven years old and I'm still no match for most of Lord Eochu's men."

"You're the only one who *can* teach me, Kelan, the only one

I trust to keep such a secret. You're good enough to kill a wolf with one spear-cast. You saved my life and I'll never forget that, but"—I brushed his knuckles with my fingertips—"now I have to learn to save myself."

"You sound like your father." Kelan leaned back, resting his shoulders against the willow and watching the dance of light and shadow among the branches. "If he doesn't find a doorway, he batters down the wall."

"I'm not asking you to do this as a favor, Kelan," I said. "I'll repay you. The man who tends my cattle says the herd is thriving. Take twenty—no, *thirty.* Father wouldn't give me Dubh, but he let him be my herd's sire for five years, so almost any cows you'll choose come from the best bull in Connacht."

"Lord Eochu will give me a different kind of payment if I do this," Kelan said, but he didn't sound fearful; he sounded as if he were giving my offer serious consideration.

"Forty," I pressed. "Forty cattle and a gold torque."

"And when your father sees it around my neck, how do I explain where I got it?"

"He'll know, because *he'll* give it to you. Once I'm trained, I'll show him what you taught me and he'll be so impressed, he'll let you name your own reward."

"Hmmm, forty cows, a golden torque, and arms-master to the prince-princess of Connacht? Not bad." Kelan was joking again. It was a hopeful sign. "Wouldn't that be grand news to send to my father and sister. You remind me of her, Lady Maeve. She's about your age. I haven't seen her for a long while, but I do remember how stubborn she can be."

That's how you described the kestrel too, I thought. Stubborn but clever . . . clever and stubborn enough to get what it needs to survive.

Like me.

"I . . . *hate* . . . this!" A rapid series of blows battered at my shield, making my arm sting when I blocked them and bruising my body when I failed. The only times I was able to avoid being hit was when my teacher and I circled one another in the moments before combat. The oak-fenced clearing that was our practice ground lay far enough from Cruachan to let me shout out my frustration with no danger of being discovered. "I . . . really . . . really . . . *really* hate this!"

"Maybe you wouldn't hate it so much if you stopped talking and started fighting," Kelan replied lightly. Unlike me, he could speak without panting for breath. He wasn't even sweating. It wasn't fair!

Enraged, I lunged for him, raising the heavy stick he'd given me to use as a sword. He sidestepped without a second thought and let me rush past until I tripped over a tree root and sprawled on the ground. "At least you kept your mouth shut that time," he mused as I sat up and wiped dirt from my face. "That's progress."

I left my stick and shield where they'd fallen and hugged my knees. If looks were lightning, I would have turned Kelan into a pile of ashes.

"Don't give me that face," he said. "It's scarcely thirty days since we began. Did you imagine you'd master weapons so quickly?" When I scowled in reply, he added, "You're acting as if these lessons were my idea, Princess." Kelan sent his own weighty "sword" twirling high into the air and coolly caught it before it could touch the earth. "How do you expect to protect your kin if you hate learning how? You have no love for the sword. I can tell."

"The peasant doesn't *love* his plow," I shot back scornfully. "Mother doesn't *love* her spindle. I don't have to *love* my weapons. I just have to use them." I stood up slowly, hampered by pain, and winced as I picked up the sword-stick. "Come on," I said, facing him in the first fighter's stance he'd taught me.

He waved aside my challenge. "That's enough for today."

I glanced at the sky. "Why? It's early! We haven't done spear practice yet." I didn't hate the spear quite so much as the sword. Although I despised how foolish I looked when my best efforts fell far short of the target, I considered any weapons lesson that spared me further black-and-blue marks to be a good one.

"Another time," Kelan said mildly.

"Well, then, can you start teaching me how to track game?"

"Not today either. I want to see you do better with the spear first."

"That means never."

"You do sound like my little sister." Kelan smiled. "She was impatient too. I will teach you how to hunt, Lady Maeve, and in time we'll seek a way for you to learn how to drive a chariot. We can't have the prince-princess of Cruachan waging her battles on foot."

I looked at him hopefully. "Do you mean that, Kelan?"

He touched his torque and nodded. "Lord Eochu's going to banish me from Connacht if he finds out about all this, so I might as well make the offense worth the punishment."

I cast aside my sword-stick and raced to hug him. "I'll *never* let Father banish you. He'll have to send me away too. You're the best, bravest, kindest man in all Cruachan!"

"Well, it's good to know you'll keep me safe, Princess." He returned my hug with a brother's fondness. "I'd hate to tell Bláithín that I've been daring your father's wrath for nothing. She's already had plenty of hard words for me about these lessons."

"She knows?"

"I tried to keep it secret. Blame her for having keen eyes and a sharp mind." Sheepishly, he added, "Blame me for not being more careful about where I was hiding those."

He nodded at the pair of breeches I wore for my weapons training. They were Kelan's, outgrown and somehow not handed down to another boy. I couldn't wield sword or spear with a dress tangling around my legs and I couldn't risk having Mother or a servant find those breeches if I kept them in my room, so it fell to Kelan to safeguard them between lessons.

"She found them and wanted to know why I was holding on to clothing I couldn't use. If only I had my father's gift for words, I might've come up with a believable excuse!" He shrugged and set about wrapping up our practice weapons before hiding them in the boughs of an oak. "No harm done. Bláithín won't betray us. It would just make trouble for me, maybe even get me sent away. She doesn't want that, I hope, especially now that I'm about to become the father of her baby."

"A baby? Oh, Kelan!" He laughed to hear my whoop of joy and to see how happily I danced in spite of all my bruises.

My friend was going to be a father. I hugged the happy news to my heart as I stood with my parents at the Beltane celebration marking the start of summer and my twelfth year. It was a time of revelry, of light coming out of darkness. Every flame in the land was extinguished, to be rekindled from the twin bonfires now blazing at the foot of Cruachan's ringfort mound. Father had already dispatched the runners who'd carry the blessed torches, passing warmth and light from hand to hand until all the land blazed with renewed life and joy.

I smiled with pride as herdsmen drove our cattle between the fires to purify them and keep them safe from harm in the coming year. I was convinced I could tell which ones were *my* cows, sure that they were the best of the lot. Many of the beasts wore garlands of yellow flowers, the same blooms that decorated our house. Their loud lowing nearly drowned out the sound of human voices raised in song.

"Those are fine cattle, Lady Maeve." A voice at my elbow made me turn. It came from Lord Guaire of the Gangani, one of the many visitors who'd traveled from other kingdoms for our Beltane festivities. "I keep searching for the black bull among them."

"There's more than one black bull in our herds," I replied.

He stooped just enough so that his lips brushed my ear as he murmured, "But only one that was captured by the most beautiful girl in Èriu."

This again? Lord Guaire was far from the first of our guests to sidle up to me with honeyed words. From the moment the men of other kingdoms began arriving at Cruachan, the highest ranked among them made it a point to seek me out and heap flattery at my feet. Did they think I was vain or hollow-headed enough to believe they were wooing *me*? I knew better: I was just the go-between, the one who'd let them wed their *true* love, the kingdom of Connacht.

I wanted to laugh at Lord Guaire, but that would be discourteous. He was our guest, and older than Father. "You must mean Dubh, my lord," I said. "He died last year in a fight with another bull."

"That must have been a sad loss for you, my lady, but that's the way it is with bulls." His teeth gleamed in the firelight like a hungry dog's. "The strongest and most experienced always takes the prize."

"Or the youngest and smartest," I replied. "The cowherd who witnessed the battle said that Dubh's rival wasn't brawny but knew enough to force him onto treacherous ground, where he took a misstep, fell, and broke his leg. Our beast keepers had to kill him. The other bull didn't need to bloody his horns. I admire brains more than brute strength." I gave Lord Guaire an innocent look. "Don't you?"

It took every bit of self-control I had to keep a straight face as he muttered his excuses and left me. Too soon he was replaced by Áed, a prince of the Menapi whose father's realm lay east of Connacht. He was attended by a matched pair of enormous wolfhounds. The male was so tall that the top of his head came almost up to my shoulder, and he seemed to be forever growling. The female was silent, but she had a wicked look, unlike our more sweet-natured hounds. I didn't trust either one of them or their master.

"Well, Lady Maeve, have you made your choice?" Áed asked casually. The question took me by surprise. Then I remembered he was talking about the dogs. As soon as we'd been introduced, he'd offered me one of them. Now he said, "I'd give you both, but I'm afraid they might be too much for an inexperienced girl of your age to handle safely." He made a silly show of pretending to think before exclaiming, "But if you'd like me to stay with you here and help you manage them—"

"I wouldn't put you to the trouble," I said blandly. "If I do accept your generous gift, someone from our household can teach me to control a pair of dogs."

"With respect, Lady Maeve, these aren't ordinary dogs," he persisted.

I raised my brows. "Are you telling me that Lord Eochu, the High King himself, has *no one* in his service good enough to master your wolfhounds? Or are you saying that all of my father's dogs are ordinary?"

Lord Áed became flustered and promptly found a reason to be elsewhere. His hounds went with him, but he was the only one retreating with his tail between his legs.

Though I'd freed myself of Áed's and Guaire's unwanted attention, they weren't the last pests to swarm me that night. The area around the Beltane fires teemed with highborn men and celebrated warriors. Before the night ended, I felt like I was a honey cake and every one of them was trying to steal a bite. I was flattered and wooed and bothered every time I stepped away from my parents. If my suitors were young, they implored me to watch as they jumped over the bonfires, trying to impress me with their daring and agility. I thought they looked like a bunch of grasshoppers. If they were old, or already married, they insisted on filling my ears with the virtues of their unwed kinsmen. That was just boring.

Some of them didn't bother talking to me at all. They went straight to Father, tongues wagging, eager to let him know how sincerely they admired his *perfect* daughter. I heard them praising my skin, my hair, my eyes, taking me to pieces like ravens pecking at a dead thing. If any of them mentioned my wit, I missed it. At long last, they began to drop away one by one, overcome by all the mead and Gaulish wine they'd been drinking.

Our Beltane guests hung around Cruachan like the smell of rotting fish. Most of them returned to their own lands after the festival, but enough of them lingered to annoy me. Not only did they continue to waste my time pouring globs of sticky-sweet compliments in my lap, but their continued presence made it impossible for Kelan to give me my weaponry lessons. I lived in terror of having them announce they'd be staying with us until spring.

I took my irritation to Father. Good fortune let me shake off my admirers long enough to catch him by himself in one of the more distant outbuildings. It was a storeplace for all manner of discarded gear awaiting either repair or doom as kindling. Splintered spear shafts, broken baskets, even pieces of smashed chariots took up most of the space. The rest had been claimed by a bright-eyed hunting hound who had never been told that winter was not the right time to have pups.

"Would you look at that?" Father said, gesturing to where the new mother lay nursing her young ones. "*Twelve!* Twelve, and not a runt in the lot." He'd brought a basket of meat scraps with him, and now he tossed one to the hound. She caught it neatly, without disturbing her litter. "Tsk. They'll eat her alive. I'd be doing her a favor if I drowned half of them."

"I'll help," I grumbled.

"What?" Father blinked.

"Not the puppies—our guests." It wasn't the most gracious thing to say, but I was fed up. "Why won't they *leave*?"

He put one arm around me. "Blame me, my precious spark. It's my doing. Didn't you wonder why I stayed at Cruachan to celebrate Beltane? Why I summoned so many of our nobility to attend me here instead of holding the rites at Tara?"

I think I know, Father, I told myself. *You stayed because you're still recovering from your wound, and the druids of Tara who healed you allowed it for the sake of peace.* But what I said was, "I'm just happy you're here with us. I don't care why."

"My sweet girl." He pressed his cheek to mine so that stray strands of his long mustache tickled my nose. "I'm never going to find the man worthy of having you for his wife."

"You had plenty to choose from at the bonfires," I retorted. "Every man there was *supremely* worthy. You only had to ask them, *if* they gave you a chance to do that before they told you."

"And just like that, your sweetness is gone." Father snapped his fingers, startling the nursing hound, who snarled. "Or like that," he added with a rascal's smile and a nod in her direction. "How hard did *you* snap at our noble visitors when they vexed you?"

"I know better," I replied with the same dignity Mother assumed whenever Father began to tease her. (She only swatted him when he persisted.) "They're our guests—princes, kings, and warriors—and they're important. All I did was remind them that you're *more* important. If that helps them remember that I'm important too, then good."

"Is that how you handled them?" Father was plainly impressed. "Did they take offense?"

"One or two of them might've been embarrassed," I confessed. "But they'll never admit it. They're grown men, and I'm only a girl." I purposely gave Father my most guileless look.

He roared with laughter so loudly that the hound leaped to her feet, shaking off puppies left and right, and made a false lunge for him. He pacified her with a fistful of tidbits. "Those poor men. I'm sorry for them. Who taught you to play kings' games like that? Your mother has some skill at guiding people the way she wants them to go, then letting them think it was their own idea. Of course she doesn't try such tricks with me."

I snorted and turned it into a cough. "Maybe she could guide our dawdling visitors onto the road home," I suggested.

"Patience, my spark. It's good for me if they stay, easier to keep an eye on them, overhear any rumors that they're not so loyal as I'd like." He took a bit of meat from the dog's basket and began to chew it absentmindedly. "I've been generous and honored every man as he deserves, but honor counts for nothing with the greedy ones. They'd turn against me the instant anyone convinced them they'd grow richer if a different High King ruled Èriu."

"Is that how it is with all the lesser kings? Can't we trust any of them?" Angry for Father's sake, I closed my fingers on the hilt of a sword that existed only in my imagination.

He misinterpreted my words. "Don't be afraid of them while I'm here to shield you, daughter. My girls should fill their minds with happier things. Clothru and the twins are going to be wed by summer's end, and I'll see to it that Mugain and Derbriu are both betrothed at the Lughnasadh festival." He spread the fingers of one hand. "*Five* strong sons-in-law before next Beltane. Powerful kin make the best allies."

He talked about marrying off my sisters the way Mother spoke of household chores to be accomplished: *Card the wool to spin the thread to weave the cloth to make the gown to dress the daughter to send away forever as some man's bride. Done. Who's next?*

"What about a sixth?" I asked the question as calmly as I could. "What are you going to do with me?" If Father intended to serve me up along with my sisters this year, I didn't want it to come as a surprise. It's better to fight a battle you can anticipate than a raid that descends out of nowhere.

He threw the last of the meat to the dog. "I'm not ready to give you up quite yet, dearest. When I matched your sisters to their future husbands, I had my hands full putting out all the wildfires of envy that broke out among the men I *didn't* choose. I'd like to catch my breath before I go through that again."

I felt relieved enough to joke, "Why don't I just run away with a cowherd's son tomorrow and save you the trouble?"

"Why don't *I* just give you to that little snot-nose Conchobar today and solve all my problems?" he replied in kind.

"Conchobar?" I echoed. "Lord Fachtna's son?" I remembered Devnet speaking of how bravely that young prince witnessed my father take his father's head.

"Why not?" Father strode to the doorway, leaving me to run after him with the empty scrap basket. "Wedding you to him would please the two-tongued schemers who've been striving to overthrow me from the moment I became High King. They've turned that accursed boy into their tool. Down I come, up he goes, into the High King's seat, and then he fills their hands with gold. But if I make him my son-in-law and heir, his hidden masters *might* let me live out my days in peace, free to let down my guard, to give up testing myself against my opponents the way our best smith tests a sword." His mustache lifted in a grin. "Where's the meat in a life like that?"

"Who are they?" I asked. "The men plotting against you, what are their names? Why don't you call them out, challenge them, and be rid of them?"

"Why not ask me to kill the boy and be done with it?" he said sarcastically. "My sword against a lad who's what, eleven? Twelve? *That* would make the bards call me a hero!"

"You're not taking me seriously."

"You're taking yourself seriously enough for the both of us," he countered. "You're trying to meddle with something that a girl can't understand and that's not your business."

"How is this not my business?" I cried. "If you're in danger, aren't we all, our whole family?"

He clicked his tongue. "Maeve, I told you not to trouble your mind with this. It's *my* place to handle it."

"And what's mine?" I would not shout at him. I would not give him the chance to claim I had no more control over my temper than a cranky child. "To sit and sew?"

"That," he said lightly, "and to go on as you've been with our visitors, my spark. Keep their interest, keep yourself just beyond their reach, and keep the peace for me. Oh, and one more thing." Arrow-swift his hand shot under the basket

I carried and knocked it out of my hands, over my head. "Keep your eyes open." He swaggered back to the great house, laughing.

"I'm *not* picking that up again!" I called after him. But I did.

There's something inexplicably adorable about new puppies. I found myself returning to that distant storage building almost daily, just to watch them squirm against their mother's belly, pink noses speckled with milk. Their tiny whimpers and soft barks wove a love spell worthy of the Fair Folk.

I wasn't the only one entranced by those little lives. Though I never crossed paths with the puppies' other admirers, I saw proof of their visits in the many beef bones cluttering the floor. The mother dog received so many gifts, you'd think she gave birth to twelve princes. I followed Father's lead and always brought her scraps, not bones, which left no mess behind and which she gobbled up gratefully.

One day I arrived at the dog's "great house" to find a familiar face. There was the serving girl Bláithín, ankle-deep in pups, trying to tidy the floor. Her swelling belly made stooping to gather up the old bones difficult, but the mother dog's determination to hold on to every one of them, no matter how bare, marrowless, or splintered, made it impossible.

"Let me help you, Bláithín," I said by way of greeting. "If you keep her distracted, I can pick up the bones."

"Thank you, Lady Maeve, but you shouldn't do my work for me," Kelan's sweetheart replied. She sounded tired and looked drawn.

"It won't be work. It'll be a game," I assured her. "How

many bones can I whisk away before the dog knows what I'm doing? Here, use this." I thrust the basket of scraps into her hands and grabbed the empty one she'd been unsuccessfully trying to fill with the hound's leftovers.

It all worked so well, I could hardly believe it. I whisked out of the storage building with a heaping basket before Bláithín managed to feed the dog half the meat I'd brought. "I'll be right back as soon as I dump these on the midden!" I called over one shoulder.

As I passed through the ringfort, I had the good luck to meet one of our other servants with his own pile of refuse. He offered to let me dump the contents of my basket into his and I was glad to be spared the long walk to the midden. It meant I could rush back to Bláithín and finish our task sooner. I did so with light feet and a happy heart, eager to help my good friend's sweetheart.

Then I heard the screams.

I was the only one who could hear them. The place the mother dog had chosen to birth her pups was set well apart from the rest of the ringfort's structures. Its sturdy walls muffled the sound of Bláithín's terror, and the furious barking of dogs, and all the other sounds of a desperate struggle inside.

I raced through the doorway to see Lord Áed's huge male wolfhound menacing the serving girl. The beast must have gotten away from his master and caught wind of the meat scraps I'd brought. Our hound faced the interloper bravely, defending her puppies, but she was only half his size. Two small bodies already lay lifeless on the floor between them. A confrontation that had begun over food had turned murderous, and bad luck put Bláithín in the middle of it, her path to the doorway blocked by a snarling, bloody-mouthed wolfhound that looked ready to close his jaws on anything that came near.

My eyes darted left and right, seeking some way to save her. A heavy piece of wood stuck up from the ruins of a broken chariot. I grabbed it with both hands and pulled, grunting with the effort, until it came free. It was longer and heavier than the false sword Kelan gave me for fighting practice, but it would have to do.

"Bláithín, I have him—run!" I shouted, slamming it down on the wolfhound's hindquarters as hard as I could.

The monstrous dog yelped and wheeled to face me, eyes alight with fury. I moved quickly, becoming a wall between him and Kelan's beloved, opening a clear escape route for her. I didn't dare take my eyes off the wolfhound, but I heard her shift behind me, her fear-choked throat uttering a weak, "Lady Maeve, I can't let you—"

"I said *run*!" I raised my makeshift weapon in the way Kelan had taught me. "Get help, go!"

She gave a small sob of terror and obeyed. The wolfhound lunged after her, fangs snapping, but I was her shield, deflecting the attack with a blow to his snout. He staggered sideways but did not fall. I cursed myself for not being bigger, stronger, a more seasoned fighter with the power to put an end to this. The beast shook off his daze too soon and gathered himself for another leap. I was his target now.

Every word, every lesson Kelan ever gave me whirled through my mind as I wielded that splintered staff like a warrior's blade. As I fought, a chilling certainty fell over me: *This is to the death.* I shouted a challenge in the wolfhound's face, forcing myself to cast away the thought that I might be the one to die. I was Maeve of Connacht, clever Cloithfinn's child, daughter of bold Eochú the High King, princess of Èriu! I would not let doubt weaken me. I would not accept defeat until the moment I reached Tech Duinn, the isle where the god Donn reigned over the dead.

I did not fight alone. The mother dog stood with me, protecting what was hers. She darted at her giant enemy, keen teeth drawing blood before she jumped aside, dodging his answering bite. We played him between us like the *sliotar* ball in a game of hurling. Bad luck: he was as smart as he was vicious. The next time our hound made a feint at him, he didn't counter it. Instead he spun on those massive paws, as light-footed as a lad leaping the Beltane fire, and charged headlong into me.

His weight did what his teeth could not. I fell backward, feet snaring in my dress. I held fast to my weapon, still using it as though it were a blade capable of saving me. The wolfhound's muzzle was so close I could smell the rankness of his breath. I imagined he was gloating, sure of his kill now that I was down.

A shout cracked the air, and another. Blood spattered my face as a sword descended, opening the wolfhound's throat. The enormous dog toppled among the remaining bones.

"Lady Maeve, are you all right?" One of Father's warriors stood over me, offering a hand to help me back onto my feet. His other fist held the blade that had saved me. Two more men stood in the doorway, with Bláithín peeping anxiously between them.

"I'm not hurt," I replied. "But two of the puppies—"

For no good reason, I began to cry.

❧ ⊕ ❧

The three men who'd come to my aid were on sentry duty when Bláithín's shouts for help fetched them. Now all five of us stood before Father in the great house, with me still in my bloodstained dress, as he tried to bellow his way to the truth. His harsh questions were solely for the men. Bláithín and I were not asked to speak.

As the three warriors took turns explaining why a royal visitor's valued dog was dead and how the High King's daughter nearly came to die in its jaws, the buzz of titillated whispers from the onlookers turned our hearth into a hive of rumors. Lord Áed bided at the High King's side, the dead wolfhound's pelt in a heap at his feet. He speared our warriors one after the other with his eyes.

"Well, which is it?" Father thundered at the sentry who'd killed the beast. "Did you save my daughter or didn't you?"

The young man met Father's eyes without wavering. "Lord Eochu, it would be easy to say so and take my reward, but the gold would turn black with a liar's curse. I saw what I saw, and these men saw it with me. We reached the storeplace only a few breaths before the dog bowled the princess off her feet, but in those moments we saw her fighting off the beast as ably as any of your fosterling boys being trained to the sword."

"I don't believe it. My daughter—my *child*—with a sword in her hands against a full-grown wolfhound?"

"It wasn't a sword," I said quietly. "It was a piece of wood."

"A piece of wood *you* used to torment my dog!" Lord Áed exploded. He wasn't talking to me.

Bláithín cringed. "My lord, I never—"

Áed wouldn't let her speak. "You must have done it. There's no other explanation for him turning savage enough to attack the princess. What evil impulse made you goad him like that? Were you bored? Idle? Or are you too stupid to live?" He toed the dog's pelt. "*Your* skin should be lying here. Nothing less would redeem you for causing my dog's death and endangering my beloved Lady Maeve."

The blameless serving girl crumpled, sobbing wildly. I caught sight of Kelan in the crowd, his face twisted with distress. Anyone could see how much he wanted to come forward, take Bláithín in his arms, defy every lie Lord Áed spewed at her. But doing so would insult the High King's noble guest. The consequences were unthinkable.

I dropped to one knee, hugged Bláithín warmly, and looked Áed in the eye. "No one used that stick against your dog but me."

"You're a sweet, softhearted girl, Lady Maeve," Áed replied smoothly. "You shouldn't waste your time trying to protect the wench this way."

I stood up slowly. Frost was in my voice, making me sound older than my years. "Which way is that? By lying for her?"

Áed suddenly saw the edge of the cliff to which his wagging tongue had brought him. As much as Father might want to keep peace between Connacht and the Menapi, he could not let any man call his daughter a liar and let it go unavenged.

"Forgive me, Princess, I spoke poorly. I know you'd never dishonor the truth. I believe you with all my heart." The words tumbled from his lips in a single breath.

"I do tell the truth," I said, letting my eyes travel around the encircling crowd before they came to rest on Father. "Everything these men said is true as well. I fought the dog, but not before it killed two of our own. It would have done the same to

Bláithín, and that would have been two more lives lost. Would *you* allow such a thing to happen and do nothing, Father?"

"I'm a trained warrior. You're not," he said sternly. "You're my precious child. Your safety comes first."

"I won't be truly safe if I can't take care of myself," I replied. "I'm not stupid or clumsy or cowardly. I can learn how to use a *real* sword, if you give me the chance." I closed my ears to the faint threads of laughter coming from the crowd.

"According to these three men, you already know the basics of that." Father leaned forward, one fist on his knee. "Who taught you?"

I sucked in a sharp, short breath.

"Well, Maeve?" he persisted. "No one learns weaponry without being taught. You heard my question. Answer."

I couldn't speak. My blood was pounding in my ears, deafening me. I fought to keep myself from trembling, to keep my gaze from straying to Bláithín, still crouched on the floor, or to Kelan where he stood as close to her as possible among the crowd.

"Nothing, girl?" Father made a disgusted sound. "Burying the truth is birthing a lie. You shame me. Go."

His words were knives. "Father, please, you must understand. I *can't* answer you. I—"

"I can, Lord Eochu." Kelan took two strides forward. His face was still a boy's, but his bearing was a man's. "I'll tell you everything."

Kelan's revelation was the talk of Cruachan and it grew with every retelling. If you stood by the round central hearth and asked each person who passed by, "What happened after that young warrior confessed?" you'd hear everything from *"When Lord Eochu learned Kelan taught the princess how to use a sword, he had the blacksmith grind the lad's own blade into powder and made him eat it"* to *"Lord Eochu was so pleased by Kelan's courage and honesty that he gave him half of Connacht and the princess."*

I found the truth with Kelan himself, down by the stables where he sat alone, cleaning a towering pile of gear for the chariot horses. He smiled sadly when he saw me. "Bringing my golden torque, are you, Princess? The one you said your father would give me when you surprised him with your sword skills?"

I dropped down beside him. "I'm sorry I made you give me those lessons, Kelan. I was foolish to dream Father would let me use them, no matter how good I got. I wouldn't be able to draw a sword against his enemies unless I fought him first."

"That's a pity, Princess. You would've grown to be a capable fighter. You were good enough with that piece of wood to save my Bláithín's life, and our baby's," Kelan said, polishing the metal fittings on the bridle in his hands. "That's worth any punishment Lord Eochu could throw at me."

"How—" I hesitated to ask the question. "How *is* he going to punish you?"

He brandished the glinting bridle. "What do you think *this* is?" His old grin was back. "Twenty days as a stable boy by day and a house servant by night. My comrades are going to laugh their throats raw before this is over. Eh, it could have been worse. At least he didn't banish me."

"But he could have, and I'd be to blame. You didn't deserve this. Why is he being so unfair? Oh, Kelan, there are times when he makes me so angry, I wonder if I still love him!"

"Don't talk like that, Princess. You know you do." My friend rubbed the bridle fittings harder. "It's not your fault that you're so young your father still wants to protect you but you're so brave you hate it when he does."

I knew that Father had recovered from his wound completely when he led our men on a cattle raid once more. It was a great success: It proved that Father was as formidable as ever, it brought Cruachan a wealth of cows, and it sent the last of our loitering guests home. Father's raid subtly reminded them that even if they had no plans for swooping down on other men's cattle that season, they should at least look after the safety of their own herds.

Kelan was not allowed to join the first cattle raid. He was still being punished for his part in setting my feet on the "wrong" path. When Father decreed a second raid and in the same breath announced that Kelan was forgiven, my friend looked so grateful I feared he would cry. He rode away proudly and returned triumphant.

I congratulated him that evening, before the victory feast. He radiated satisfaction as he replied, "Thank the gods it went so well for me, Princess. I'll have a fair share of the cattle we took and no regrets over losing the forty you offered me."

"Oh." I understood: Our lessons were over. I owed him nothing.

He read the disappointment in my face. "I'm sorry, Lady Maeve, but you know it's impossible now. If I hadn't taught you to use a sword, even a fake one, you'd never have dared take on that wolfhound. And if you'd died—" He shivered. "I'm lucky the High King was merciful and I won't tempt his mercy a second time. I've got to think about Bláithín and the baby, our future. Please understand."

"I do," I said. "I'll accept losing my teacher, Kelan, as long as I can keep my friend."

"Always, Princess." We parted with smiles as I went to take my place beside Mother for the feast.

It was one of the wildest celebrations I could remember. Father was so well pleased with all the fine cows now added to our herds that he ordered the servants to pour more and more mead for his followers. Soon the atmosphere in the great hall became so loud and unruly that Mother rose from her place and discreetly retired to her sleeping chamber. Her tactful withdrawal took all of the women with her, including me. Only the serving girls had to remain.

I didn't mind our enforced retreat. I was stuffed with good food and wanted to go to bed. The jolly uproar just beyond my door faded as I fell into a slumber so deep that a hundred warriors' gatherings couldn't wake me.

The sound that did rouse me the next morning was so soft that I thought I was dreaming it. Rubbing my eyes, I sat up and listened. Yes, there it was: someone was crying.

The great hall was a shambles. Benches were overturned, men and dogs lay sprawled on the ground, and rivulets of spilled mead trickled from dozens of fallen drinking vessels. The smell of smoke mingled with other, stronger reeks that made me cup a hand over my nose as I picked my way through the wreckage, trying to find the lonely weeper.

She was huddled behind my father's bench, one fist pressed hard against her mouth to stifle her sobs. When she became aware of my presence and lifted her face, I recognized Bláithín.

Before I could ask her what was wrong, she blurted out, "It was Caílte's doing. Caílte, fifteen years older than my sweet man and five times as skilled with the sword. Caílte, may his lying bones turn into worms of fire!" It was a soul-deep curse meant to be shouted loud enough to crack the sky, but her voice never rose above a fierce whisper. My belly twisted at the eeriness of it. "Your father gave him the hero's portion of the boar last night. Why didn't he choke on it? He claimed he overheard my darling mutter that someone else deserved that damned piece of meat. False! False! He refused to hear my beloved's oath that he'd said no such thing, challenged him to fight it out, and killed him at the second blow. Let him die old, maimed, sick, and shunned for taking the light of my heart away from me!" She buried her face in her knees.

That was how I learned that my friend Kelan was dead.

Chapter Four

A Shift of Seasons

KELAN WAS BURIED with his bronze torque, the silver brooch I pinned to his cloak, his spears, and what was left of his sword. The blade had broken during his duel with Caílte just before the older, more experienced fighter landed the death blow. Bláithín showed me the tiny iron shard she'd saved.

"I know you liked him, my lady, and he always smiled when your name was on his lips. He told me how much you reminded him of his sister. May the great mother Danú comfort all his kin. I want to share this remembrance of him with you. That is"—she hesitated, probably remembering that she was not a young woman talking with a girl but a servant speaking to her princess—"if you'll permit it."

She placed the shard in my hand. The iron splinter was the length of my smallest finger and almost thin enough to be mistaken for a needle. I returned it to her with respect. "Thank you, Bláithín. You've honored me."

"Someday I'm going to give it to our son," she told me, eyes shadowed by sorrow.

"When he's born, I'll make him a gift of forty cows, I promise."

"My lady, it's too generous, too much—"

"Not enough, Bláithín," I said. How could it ever be enough to make up for the loss we two were bound to share?

The moon changed faces and the seasons danced, but when the time came, neither Bláithín nor her infant survived the birth. While the women of our house prepared the two of them for burial, I helped by gathering up the dead serving girl's few belongings. She was already in the earth by the time I found the sword fragment tucked into the folds of her winter cloak so it couldn't go into the ground with her. Rather than let it rust away on top of Bláithín's grave, I decided to keep it in memory of Kelan and stored it safely in a small leather pouch. At Samhain, when the dead bring their grievances to the living, no angry spirit came to haunt me. That was how I knew I'd done the right thing.

Samhain and Beltane and all the other festivals turned the seasons around me until I was almost fifteen years old. All of my sisters were married women, queens in their own right, and I was the last tasty apple left hanging on the royal tree.

The older I got, the more frequently our household opened its gates to highborn visitors, always men. It had been four years since my last lesson on how to wield a sword, but I still found myself blocking and parrying all sorts of advances. I was always careful to discourage them without insulting them. I didn't want to give these men an excuse to pick a fight with Father. If I couldn't fight beside him with a son's weapons, at least I could fight for him with a daughter's wits.

It was wearying work, keeping each suitor close enough to retain his support for the High King but distant enough so that he wouldn't conclude he was assured of getting *this* hero's portion. I knew I'd have to wed one of them at last, some unlucky day, but these ongoing games of yes-no-maybe made me think of marriage as surrender and defeat. The idea turned my stomach sour.

Sometimes, when I'd managed to sidestep a particularly relentless princeling, I wondered if the poor thing believed that winning my affection meant winning the High King's consent. I wanted to take each one of my suitors, shake them awake, and tell them, *"Save your pretty words, your pleading looks, your silly gifts. My father loves me, but that doesn't mean he listens to me. If you want to give me something I can use, make it a way to gain enough of his respect so that my life becomes my choice alone."*

The days between Beltane and Lughnasadh were my favorite time of year. They brought a respite from visitors. Few of the highborn could afford to leave their lands during that busy, fruitful season. On one such sweet summer day, I sat with Mother and her closest friend, Lady Íde, all of us spinning wool into thread for the loom.

"You're getting better at that, Maeve," Lady Íde said, casting a critical eye over my work. "The thread's much smoother and more even." She was tall and rawboned, with a handsome face, blue eyes, and golden hair that swung from the crown of her head in dozens upon dozens of tiny braids.

"Let me see." Mother leaned closer and rolled the strand

lightly between her fingertips. "So it is! This will make a lovely blanket for the baby."

"What wonderful news. I'm so happy for you, Lady Íde," I said.

Mother and her friend laughed. They both sat up tall and pulled their tunics tight across their bellies. Lady Íde's was flat.

I dropped my spindle. My eyes grew big as the moon.

Lady Íde nudged Mother with her elbow. "This was fun, but I still want to be there when you tell Eochu."

Mother was going to have a child. The news flew across the land of Èriu. We were all swept away in a river of congratulations and Father was half buried by a landslide of earthy jokes from his men. There was no counting the number of offerings my parents made to the goddess Brigid in her role as blesser and helper of childbirth.

Once I got over the surprise, I was overjoyed to learn that I'd be a big sister when winter came. I could hardly wait. So far, nothing else in my life had seemed to have the magic needed to change me from being the "baby." It didn't even matter that I'd become able to have babies of my own *two full years* earlier than this.

I longed to share my elation with Derbriu and the others, but they all had lives of their own too distant from Connacht to undertake a visit until after the baby was born. They wouldn't come any earlier than the birth festivities without good cause. The best I could do was climb the ringfort wall and pretend my thoughts could reach them.

My feet took me to those heights more and more often, especially in fine weather. On one such day I reached the top and gasped at the beauty that met all of my senses. A sweet breeze blew from the east, fragrant with summer, and I spread my arms to embrace it. Thin white clouds made a lazy progress across a radiant sky. I turned my face to the sun and let its gentle fire burn away everything but my joy. I felt light enough for the wind to lift me up and send me flying. There was magic in that place, in that moment, an enchantment as powerful as any that the Fair Folk ever cast. My sensible side insisted such things could not happen, and yet I stood ready to believe that if I closed my eyes and wished with all my heart, I'd open them to see the tops of the tallest trees far below me. All I had to do was want it enough, and I did. Oh, how I did!

"Watch out there, milady. You're near the edge."

I opened my eyes, but not to anything I wanted to see. As always, a sentry patrolled the circular outer ramparts of Cruachan. This one was an older man, his hair streaked with gray, his right cheek lashed with a long white scar. I knew that face too well: Caílte, the one who'd killed my friend. The sight of him turned my mouth to a hard, small line and struck a black spark in my heart. I didn't react to his warning with thanks, argument, or any word at all. Showing him my back, I began to descend the ringfort's steep wall.

"This again?" Caílte flung his resentment at me like a spear. "How long will you carry a child's grudge against me? It was a fair fight. I did what I had to do. There was no choice!"

I stopped and looked back at him coldly. I had not spoken to the man since the day I'd learned he was to blame for Kelan's death. At first he wasn't aware of how much I hated him. He was a warrior, and not one of those who kept trailing after me; when would the two of us need to speak with one another?

But as time passed and I continued to treat him with silent, icy loathing during our few encounters, he finally grasped how things stood between us. From there, it was a small step for him to realize why.

"No choice?" I echoed, lifting one eyebrow. My skeptical smile was the next best thing to telling Caílte outright that I thought he was a liar.

He got the message. I saw his fingers tighten on the shaft of his spear and knew he wanted to throw it at me but didn't dare. I relished his frustration.

"You weren't there," he gritted. "You don't know everything."

"What don't I know? You claimed you heard Kelan whisper that you didn't deserve the hero's portion of the roast boar. Did you ever imagine you might have *mis*heard? You could have asked him to repeat the insult, if there even was one."

He looked away from me, color rising to his cheeks, making the livid scar stand out like lightning against a midnight sky. "I had to avenge my honor."

"Honor?" The word tasted sour on my tongue. "Compared to you, he was an infant with a blade. There's no honor in mowing down green grass!"

Caílte kept his face averted. "You are the High King's beloved daughter," he said dully. "Say whatever you like to me. His power protects you. If that weren't so—"

"What, then?" I demanded. "Say what you wish. Do what you will. I won't go running to my father. I swear it on my life."

He remained unmoving and silent.

"Nothing?" My lip curled. "My father gave the hero's portion to the wrong man after all." I spun around to go, so blinded by anger that I failed to mind my steps.

My foot touched empty air. I flailed my arms, uselessly fighting to regain my balance, and half slid, half rolled down the flank of the ringfort's outer wall. My head-over-heels tumble ended in the defensive ditch that encircled Cruachan. Before I could pull myself out, Caílte was there to offer me his hands. Like all of our best fighters, he was nimble as well as strong.

"Are you all right? Nothing broken? Can you stand?" His battle-hardened face was contorted with anxiety. This blooded warrior who'd taken countless enemy heads was fretting over me like a dog with her first litter of pups. It was so absurd I had to laugh, but it was very bitter laughter. I rejected his kindness—it only humiliated me—spurned his help getting out of the ditch, and marched back into the great hall with my rage and heartbreak like a heavy cloak wrapped tight around me.

I was walking past the hearth at the center of the hall when Mother saw me and let out a yelp of alarm.

"Maeve, you wild thing, *what* have you been up to this time?" She pointed an accusing finger at my dress. That poor garment had suffered worse than I from my fall into the ditch. It was so torn and filthy that even if the servants did get it clean again, I'd be a long time mending it.

I reached up to tuck my hair behind my ears and encountered a handful of debris from the ditch. Dead leaves, twigs, and a smelly, unidentifiable wad of *something* pattered to the floor. I put on an innocent smile. "I've been outside, Mother."

"As if even you could get this filthy inside *my* house! Tell me what you were doing, girl."

"Thinking." I kept that guileless look on my face. It wasn't fooling her, but if I let it slip, I'd burst into either mindless giggles or furious sobs.

"Thinking! Not crawling into holes to wrestle with badgers?"

"Tsk, I'm caught," I said with mock dejection. "And the worst part of it is, the badgers won."

The next morning was the more beautiful sister to the one that had come before. I asked the name of that day's watchman before leaving the house. When I heard it was not Caílte, I scrambled eagerly back to my perch atop the outer wall and recaptured the bliss of sun and wind and sky.

My happiness was not interrupted by any idle conversation. The sentry on the ramparts was no more than sixteen and painfully shy. He blushed when he saw me climb up to join him, mumbled a greeting, and spent the rest of our time together staying as far away from me as he could without actually leaving his post. That suited me perfectly.

I shaded my eyes and surveyed the world around me. The loveliness of fields and trees, roads and rivers soothed me. Looking up, I gave a small cry of joy: a kestrel was flying high in the glorious blue. Every time I saw one, I yearned to share its freedom. I opened my arms, closed my eyes, and for a few heartbeats I once again pretended I'd found enough magic in my life to give me wings. The bird's cry snapped me out of my reverie. I shaded my gaze and peered hungrily after it as it made a lazy circle over the open land and then flew toward the woodland south of Cruachan.

Before the creature was hidden by trees, a fresh sight caught my eye, banishing my daydreams of following it in flight. Four people emerged from the forest, heading toward us. I shouted to our sentry, but his eyes were as good as mine. He'd already seen them and was running to alert everyone within the ringfort.

The approaching figures didn't look threatening. They came on foot, and if they were armed, they would only have four swords and daggers against the full might of Father's men. Even at that distance I could see that they carried no spears. Two of them carried nothing at all, though their leader bore a blackthorn staff. As they came toward Cruachan, I saw that he also wore a magnificent cloak of six colors. It was thrown back over one shoulder on account of the heat, revealing a long, pale tunic, as speckled as a trout's flank. A druid. Only kings and queens had the right to flaunt more colors in their clothing.

A smaller person walked a few steps behind the druid—a tall, black-haired boy.

What is *that one wearing?* I wondered. *His cloak's wrapped around him as if we were in the coldest days of winter. It's even got a red fur collar that he's pulled up tight under his chin! Is he crazy?*

Crazy or sane, he was obviously a person of importance. He walked along unhindered by any burden, his hands empty. All of their traveling gear was carried for them by the pair of heavily laden men bringing up the rear of their short procession. These two wore long shirts of one color, yellow, marking them as slaves.

"Lady Maeve!" The sentry's head popped up over the lip of the wall, interrupting my observations. "The queen says you're to come inside at once. You must be ready to greet the visitors when they arrive."

This time my descent from the ringfort's heights was much

more dignified than when I'd ended up in the outer ditch. I found the great hall in turmoil, though it was a *controlled* confusion. Mother was at her best when she had little time and much to accomplish. Other women might throw their hands up and surrender to defeat and disaster, but she sent commands flying through the air like spears. Each of her ladies and servants had a specific task flung in her face, and the gods save them if they didn't get it done.

My part in this whirl of desperate action was disappointingly minor: "Maeve, wash your face, comb your hair, and change into your best clothing. Wear the shoes with the gilded bronze clasps and your silver brooch. And for the love of all things, *wash your face!*"

"You already told me to do that once, Mother."

"Well, it's grubby enough to benefit from being scrubbed twice. Don't stand there arguing with me. *Move!*"

I ducked into my sleeping chamber and found one of our oldest fosterling girls waiting for me. "What are you doing here, Guennola?"

I didn't know what to make of her presence. There was never any common ground for real friendship between the fosterlings and me. All that seemed to interest them was gossiping about one another or tittering about boys. From time to time a few did seem willing to share my company, until I found out their sole reason was to claim a bond with the High King's daughter. That ended that.

Guennola sniffed. "Lady Cloithfinn says I'm supposed to help you make ready to welcome the visitors," she said stiffly. It was clear she saw this assignment as glorified baby-tending.

I'd have liked to send that prim girl on her way, but her

orders came from Mother. Only heroes fight battles they can never win. I took off everything but my undershift, released my hair from its plait, and said, "You'd better start by bringing me a bowl of water and a towel. *Someone* thinks I need to wash my face. Twice."

Washing, dressing, and loading me with sufficient jewelry were easy. Combing the wildness out of my hair was hard. Guennola groaned and complained while working out the snarls, as if she were the one feeling massive fistfuls of hair being yanked out of her scalp. "I don't understand it," she whined. "Your hair was in a neat braid when you came in. I saw it! Where did this nest of briars come from?"

"It's . . . a wicked spell . . . cast over me . . . by the Fair Folk," I replied, wincing between words. "One of their—ow!— one of their ladies was—ow!—envious of my hair and— Oh, *please* just give me the comb!"

"But this is my job, Lady Maeve. Your mother said I was supposed to—"

"I won't tell. Will you? I'll comb, you braid."

"Lady Cloithfinn said you're to wear it loose. It looks prettier that way. I'm supposed to put flowers in it and tie silver beads to the strands near your cheeks."

"What a ridiculous fuss!" I exclaimed, gently guiding the comb through my much-abused tresses. "Who *are* these guests of ours?"

I had my answer soon enough, but not from Guennola. She ignored my question and began decorating my hair before I finished untangling it all, tying the last silver bead in place a heartbeat before Mother burst into my room.

"Aren't you done ye— Ah, you are. Good. Well done,

Guennola. Maeve, attend me." She spun about and sailed back into the great hall before either of us could catch a breath.

Our visitors were with Father, seated comfortably on benches at the far side of the central hearth. Servants were already filling their drinking horns with a choice of mead or fresh milk. Others were hurrying to offer food. Mother snatched a bowl of bread from one of them and thrust it into my hands. Her intention was clear: these guests were worthy of being served by a princess.

As I stepped forward with the bread, Father beamed. "This is my youngest daughter, Maeve. Maeve, this is a splendid day for us. Our home is privileged to welcome Master Íobar and his son, Odran." There was no need for him to mention Master Íobar's calling. The druid's ceremonial bronze sickle was in plain sight, hanging from his belt. "They've come from Munster in the south, bound for the holy island of Avallach, but they've consented to stay with us until it's time to set out for the Samhain rites at Tara."

"This is an honor," I said pleasantly, offering my bowl to the older man. His dark hair was heavily streaked with gray and he had the blackest eyes I'd ever seen. They drew me in and held me rapt. I was only dimly aware when he took a piece of bread and thanked me. I found myself unable to tear my gaze away from his until Father saved me.

"Maeve, I think Odran would like something to eat too."

Flustered, I shifted my attention to the druid's son. Even now, inside the great hall, he kept his cloak around him. The only parts of his body not concealed by wool and fur were his feet and his face. Blue-black hair lay long and thick down his back and fell in a smooth sweep across his high forehead. I was thankful to see that he didn't have his father's unfathomable eyes. His were the clear, honest blue of that morning's summer sky.

Perhaps he stays so wrapped up because he's been ill, I thought, taking in the pallor of his skin. There wasn't the faintest stain of healthy red on his cheeks, nor any sign that the sun had tanned him in all the days he'd been traveling.

"Please help yourself," I said, urging the bread on him.

He made no move to accept my invitation. His hands remained tucked away under his cloak. "Thank you, my lady," he said with a gentle smile. "I'm not hungry right now."

"But you've been traveling. You need to eat. If you don't want bread, there's cheese coming too, and lots of meat. I hope you're not worried about being a burden to this household. We have plenty to share and our guests make us happiest when they eat their fill. Here, have this." I took a large chunk of bread from the bowl and held it out to him.

He didn't move to take it. Something else did. The red fur collar ringing his neck shuddered, twisted, and raised a daintily pointed black snout from beneath the curtain of Odran's hair. The little fox's yellow eyes blinked sleepily at me before it roused itself completely and snatched the bread from my hand in one snap of its jaws.

I gasped with surprise as the swift creature jumped down from Odran's shoulder to hide itself and its prize under the boy's bench. "Your collar—" I began breathlessly.

The front of Odran's cloak squirmed. A small brown, round-eared head popped into view, eyes bright with curiosity. It was the first time I'd seen a stoat at such close quarters while the feisty creature was still alive. In one jump, it landed in my bowl and began tearing savagely at the bread. I yelped and reacted without thinking, throwing the bowl straight up over my head.

Odran moved almost as fast as his strange pets, shedding his cloak as he leaped forward, arms outstretched, eyes fixed on the flying bowl. He didn't see me in his way. Even if he had, I doubt it would have made a difference. His shoulder struck me aside as he grabbed the bread bowl in midair. My rump and his feet hit the ground at the same time.

"Odran!" Master Íobar's shout shook dust from the roof of the great hall. "You worthless toad dropping, what have you done to the princess?"

His father's rage had no visible effect on Odran. Now that he had the young stoat cradled safely in his arms, he stood there gazing at the rest of us in mild bewilderment. He reminded me of a puppy, caught making a mess indoors. His eyes seemed to ask: *What's wrong with you? Why are you yelling at me? I don't understand.*

I clambered back to my feet and tentatively laid one hand on Odran's arm. I didn't like being so close to the feeding stoat but felt that if I kept my distance now, his father would see it as proof I'd been insulted. "If you didn't want bread, you should have just told me so," I said genially.

His smile returned. "I believe I did, my lady."

"Then it's my fault for not listening, and I beg your pardon." I eyed the stoat uneasily as I spoke. The vicious little thing was gnawing avidly at a piece of bread, but who could say when it might grow bored with that bland food and want a taste of something with blood in it? My hand, for instance?

He misinterpreted why I was staring at the beast. "Would

you like to pet her?" he asked, making as if to pass the stoat to me.

"No!" I recoiled violently, as if he'd offered to dump a basket of fish guts onto my bed.

Father found my reaction to be the funniest thing he'd seen in a long while. "Tsk, Maeve, you're giving our furry guests a rough welcome," he said, chuckling. "Maybe you should ask Odran's creatures to excuse your bad manners."

I rolled my eyes at him. "I'll do that on the day after I hear *you* apologize to every cow you slaughter at Samhain and every tick you pluck off your favorite hound and crush between your fingers."

"That sounds like something your mother would say. What's happened here to make my little spark catch fire?" Deliberately and distinctly he slewed his glance in Odran's direction and laughed again, harder.

My cheeks flamed. I was in no mood for his teasing. Making myself as tall and dignified as I could, I turned to our guests and said, "Master Íobar, Odran, be welcome to Connacht." Then I marched to my sleeping chamber, ignoring my father's great guffaws, my mother's irate orders that I come back at once, and the high-pitched yipping of an overly excited small red fox.

CHAPTER FIVE

Runts and Strays

"YOU LIKE HIM, don't you?" Mother asked playfully as the two of us worked on embroidering a new tunic for Father to wear to the Samhain rites. It was another flawless morning, some nine days after our guests had arrived, and we'd had the servants move a bench outdoors so that we could take advantage of the sunlight.

"Who?" I asked, distracted. All my focus was on my needlework. It was an art I wanted to master but found slow going. My stitches were too long or too short and I kept getting knots in the thread.

"Odran. Who else could I mean?" Mother finished a spiral design banding one of the tunic's wrists. She was already done with the other wrist and the neckline of the garment, while I was still struggling with ornamenting the lower hem.

I looked at her as if she'd grown antlers. "Odran?" I repeated. "I do like him—"

"Aha!"

"—except not the way you're thinking."

"Oh." She seemed disappointed but shrugged it off in short order. "That's just as well, I'm sure. I don't want any of my girls to have broken hearts."

"I don't think Odran could break anyone's heart," I said. "He speaks politely to everyone, no matter their rank. I've never heard him give our servants commands, just requests. He's kindness itself to those animals he keeps, and he makes sure that no one but he has to deal with their meals and their messes. I've never heard him brag or bully or complain about anything." I shrugged. "He's so . . . nice."

Mother tied off a thread. "You say that as if it were a fault. Do you want one of those lads who's always scowling or picking fights or who's perpetually bored and so very *loud* about letting everyone know it?"

I made a face. "I don't want *anybody.*" Then I grew thoughtful and added, "Not just yet."

"So, if you *did* want someone—which you don't, of course—could that someone be a *nice* boy?"

"Do we *have* to dwell on this?" I slapped the cloth draped over my knees. "We used to talk about so many different things when we had work to do together. Now you talk like one of our girls, forever twisting the conversation back to boys and boys and *boys.*"

"And you keep twisting it away. You'll be married someday. You should know what you want in a husband."

"Don't you mean what Father wants?" I countered.

Mother examined her finished embroidery with a meticulous eye for any defects. "Not if you're my daughter. When the time comes, you'll find a way to make your desires known."

"I can do that now. It doesn't mean Father heeds me. For all I know, he'll come back from Tara and say, 'Look at the wonderful gift I've brought home for my little girl—a husband! Take him and like him.'"

"And you sound like a *very* little girl when you say such things," Mother replied. "Really, Maeve, there are more ways to fight for what you want than striking out with sword, spear, or even a stick. Griping isn't one of them. I hope your new sister won't whine like that." She set her stitchery by and rested one hand on her belly.

She wore a tranquil smile, as if she were the guardian spirit of the Fair Folk's treasure. I smarted from her remarks. *Do I really whine so much?* I thought. But seeing her so perfectly content gave me a warm feeling that overcame every resentment.

"The baby might be a boy," I said, placing my hand atop hers.

"You think so?" The baby kicked; we both gasped with delight. "I don't think I have the knack for birthing boys. I wonder if I'd even know how to raise one."

"You won't have to worry," I said, drawing my hand away and leaning back. "Father and his men will take charge of his upbringing from the moment he's born."

"Darling Maeve, can you even *picture* your father and his mighty warriors trying to keep a newborn's stomach full and its bottom clean?"

I clapped my fingers over my mouth and snickered. She pressed her lips together. We might have held on to our self-control, but we made the mistake of looking at one another. "Father . . . cleaning . . . *baby*," I sputtered, and we were both hysterical.

Mother brushed tears of mirth from her cheeks. "It's good for a child to be surrounded by joy, even before it's born." Her gaze shifted from her belly to me. "I want that for all of my children."

We returned to our stitchery. I bent my head over my needle and concentrated on embroidering a pattern of triquetras along the hem of Father's tunic. A triquetra was a simple figure that looked like three overlapping ash tree leaves, although without their jagged edges. My needlework left much to be desired, but Mother seemed content with it.

"You're improving, Maeve. Will you be finished with that hem soon?"

"I'd like to be done today," I said. "But I'm afraid it will take longer. I'm making so many bad stitches!"

She patted my forearm. "They aren't perfect, but they're not bad. Your father won't notice. He'll treasure this garment, knowing part of it comes from your hands." She went back to her own embroidery. The warm, pleasant silence of summer hovered over us like a dragonfly.

I was the one who swatted it out of the air.

"Oh no!" I held out my needle. I'd managed to snap it in two.

Mother clicked her tongue. "Let me give you a new one." She searched her basket diligently. "Hmph. None here."

"Do you want me to ask the other women?"

She shook her head. "We've done enough. Let's take your broken needle as a sign to lay aside our work and enjoy the day. I'm going to ask Lady Íde to join me for a stroll through the apple orchard. What about you?"

"I'll find something to do, don't worry." I gave her a kiss and dashed off.

Happily on my own, I set my footsteps on the path toward the stream, seeking my favorite retreat under the willow tree. It was a special place for me. Those tender, drooping branches were like the protective hand of a green goddess, preserving memories of the day when Kelan listened to my dream of seeking a prince's skills.

What would Mother say if I told her that Kelan was almost as good a friend to me as Derbriu? My mouth twisted in a wry smile. *She'd probably ask me if I "liked" him. The way she sees the world, boys and girls can't be friends unless they're sweethearts.*

I touched the pouch at my belt that held the splinter of Kelan's sword. Though I had once rejected the idea of leaving it on Bláithín's grave, now I considered burying it at the foot of the willow and covering the spot with a miniature cairn, a pile of stones to mark a special place, a secret monument to a lost friendship.

But if I do that, I won't have it anymore. I couldn't deny how many times the mere act of touching that tiny sliver of metal had brought me comforting memories.

I pushed aside the notion of parting with my talisman.

The last time I sat by this stream, I saw some fat brown trout by the bankside rocks. I should try to catch one. I liked the idea, even if it was all what and no how, as many summer notions are. I pictured myself coming home with my catch—a dozen fish, no less—and presenting them to Father in triumph. He'd pile praises on my head while the warriors of Connacht cheered my talent as an angler and Devnet sang of how every trout I caught contained a belly full of jewels. By the time I reached the willow and parted the cascade of slender branches, I was so caught up in my own daydreams that I didn't notice someone else had found my sanctuary.

"Hello, Lady Maeve," Odran said in his mild, amiable voice. He was sitting in the dappled shade with the fox cuddled against his hip and the stoat perched on his shoulder.

"What are *you* doing here?" I demanded. He didn't deserve such a hostile reaction, but his unexpected presence had spoiled my plans to enjoy solitude. I wasn't thinking about fairness, only: *This is my place, my special hideaway,* mine*! He has no right to come here uninvited, with or without those nasty beasts.*

"I'm sorry. I was wandering with Guennola and Muirín when we saw this tree and I was tired, so—"

I interrupted him. "You *named* these animals?"

The question took him by surprise, as if I'd asked whether water was wet. "Why shouldn't I? The king of Munster has names for all of his hunting hounds, his chariot horses, and the best bulls in his herds."

"The king's horses, hounds, and bulls are valuable and useful," I said peevishly.

"Guennola and Muirín are valuable to *me*," he replied, his voice taut with restrained anger.

I didn't care. "I can see how *you're* valuable to *them*," I jibed. "You give them food and attention, and you've obviously carried them all the way here from Munster. I don't know how many days the journey takes, but I'll wager it's a long one. Is that why your skin's so white? You wore that fox too tightly around your neck and it choked the blood out of your cheeks."

His high brow furrowed behind its swath of raven hair. "You sound like my father. He's ignorant too."

"No druid is ignorant. If he were, he wouldn't *be* a druid!"

"Ignorance isn't the same as lack of learning." Odran stood and snapped his fingers. The fox sprang to its feet and gave him an eager, inquiring look. The stoat clung to his shoulder, then reared up on its haunches, swaying slightly. "And telling a guest he's welcome isn't the same thing as making him welcome. Farewell, Lady Maeve."

I grabbed his arm as he turned his face away from me. My outburst of temper had exhausted itself. I realized I'd had no reasonable cause for lashing out at this gentle boy and I was ashamed. "Wait, Odran, please. I shouldn't have been so rude. It's inexcusable to break the bond of hospitality."

"Oh, don't worry. I won't tell Lord Eochu that his daughter forgot her manners. The 'bond of hospitality'—what a hollow eggshell *that* is!"

"You don't mean that. It's sacred!" I cried, repeating what I'd been taught since I was old enough to understand.

My protest struck the back of Odran's head. He would not look at me, and when I tried to step in front of him, he pivoted so that I was staring at his back once more. "If it were truly a sacred thing, it would *mean* something," he replied. "It would come from the heart, not from habit. My father and I have stayed with many kings on our travels. All of them honored the 'sacred' bond, but for most of them *welcome* was only a word. For some, it was an inconvenience. For many, it was a burden." He glanced at me over one shoulder. "Father loves himself too much to believe he's not a cherished guest everywhere he goes, but I've been unwanted often enough to recognize when 'Must you go so soon?' means 'Why didn't you leave sooner?'"

"Oh." I laid one hand on his shoulder in spite of the chance that the stoat might see it there. "That isn't my way. I do believe in the guest-bond, but that's not the only reason I'm asking your forgiveness. I spoke hot words in a bad temper. If I've hurt you, that's worse to me than breaking the pact of travelers' welcome. I'm very sorry."

The hardness in his eyes and in the deep creases framing his mouth began to soften. "I'm sorry too. I should never have insulted you like that."

"By calling me ignorant?"

"By saying you sound like my father." He lowered thick-lashed eyelids. "He'd never apologize for hurting me. He says, 'Hard speech is a blacksmith's hammer and anvil. It shatters useless metal, pounds out weakness and imperfection, and shapes the finest sword, the spearhead that flies truest to the target.'" Odran looked up at me again. "Those are his exact words. Kind, aren't they?"

"His *exact* words?" I was skeptical. I could accept that Master Íobar would speak so loftily, for druids and bards were often touched by Lugh, the god of poets. I could not believe Odran would remember them perfectly.

"Believe it," Odran said. "Father's spent years training me to remember things precisely as I hear them. When I was little, I thought it was a game and I enjoyed it. It was the only time he'd share my company outside of meals, good morning, and good night. The better I became at memory tricks, the longer we stayed together." A rueful memory stole the light from his eyes. "Then I found out there was no affection behind it. It was all part of his plan for me. Why ask me what I might want to do with my life? It was decided for me on the day I was born: I'd grow up to be a druid like my father."

"You sound as if you don't want that," I said.

He scratched the stoat's white belly. "There are parts of his calling that I do like. I could see myself as a healer. I just hate being told what I *must* do, be, and become. It was bad enough at home, hearing him lecture me every day. If I did poorly at my lessons, he'd either skin me alive with sarcasm or threaten to take Muirín and Guennola away from me. I'd hoped to have a break from that when we started on this journey, but he's made me recite lore and rites and history every step of the way."

"Is that why you came here?" I asked, indicating the willow's sheltering leaves. "To get away from him?"

"From him and from the lads your father's fostering." Odran clicked his tongue and the stoat slithered inside his tunic. It peeped out at me from the embroidered neckline. "They despise my friends as much as you do."

I was suddenly ashamed. "Odran, I don't despise them. It's—" I paused to seek the right way of putting things, but all I could muster was a lame, "It's complicated."

How could I tell him that his creatures filled me with misgivings? They weren't like the tame beasts I knew, dogs and horses, nor like the animals of the world beyond our ringfort's walls. An icy shiver of memory conjured up the wolf that would have had me if not for Kelan's spear. And if a trained dog like Lord Áed's wolfhound could turn vicious, how could anyone trust these sharp-toothed wild things? There was something fetching about them, but that made me uneasy too. If a mouse looks up to marvel at a kestrel's flight, she forgets about its talons.

I couldn't tell Odran my feelings. He wouldn't understand. He'd think I was a coward. He'd see me as just another of those girls who squealed when they saw a spider.

"Complicated . . . I see." Odran didn't press me for a more satisfactory explanation. I was grateful for that. "It's the other way around for your fosterling boys. Whenever they see Guennola and Muirín, they try to knock their brains out with slingstones. You can't get less complicated than that."

"They *dared*?" I was furious. "Come back to the ringfort and show me the ones who tried to kill your animals. Father will skin those brats alive!"

"No, Lady Maeve," Odran said patiently. "The High King will tell me to fight my own battles. This has happened before in other courts. I've learned that the best I can do for my friends is keep them out of harm's way."

"But I could—" I began. He shook his head. He'd made his choice and I had to honor it or truly become like his father, forcing my wishes over his. "All right. But if you change your mind, tell me. And if you want a good refuge, come here whenever you please. I'll let you have this place to yourself for as long as you stay at Cruachan."

"I wouldn't like that," Odran responded. "Muirín and Guennola are good creatures, but they're bad at conversation."

I settled myself onto one of the willow's roots. "Which is which?"

He sat down near enough to create an air of companionship but far enough to respect my uncertain feelings about his animals. "This is Muirín"—he patted the fox—"and this is Guennola." He tickled the stoat's chin. It bit him. I giggled until I snorted. "*Not* funny," Odran mumbled, sucking his finger.

"Wait until the *other* Guennola finds out the name of your little horror," I gloated. "A bite will be the least of your worries."

"It wouldn't be the first time my girl's name matched another lady's." He studied his finger. The tip was red but there was no blood. That bite had been no more than a friendly warning. "Your Guennola would have to be very stupid to believe I named the creature after her as an insult."

"Ah, but what if you named it after her as a compliment?" I asked impishly. "What if you did it as a tribute to her extraordinary beauty? What if you're out of your mind in love with her? What if—"

"What if I drop *my* Guennola down the back of your dress?"

"What if I push you into the stream?"

"Wouldn't that break the guest-bond, my lady?"

"I'm more worried that it'd scare off the trout."

"Trout?" He perked up with interest. "I like trout."

We were soon deep in a fish-catching conspiracy. I offered a plan: "If we broke off a willow sprig and one of us dangled it in the water, maybe that would hold a fish's interest long enough for the other to grab it."

"Worth a try."

My scheme went better than I'd hoped, probably because Odran was the one seizing the distracted trout. His long, thin hands were strong and fast, stabbing into the stream like a heron's bill. After we caught three fish, Odran's belt pouch produced a knife and a fire striker. He kindled a flame and soon the fish were roasting to a golden brown on sharpened sticks. Muirín and Guennola tussled over the entrails.

When the light began to wane, we agreed to go back to Cruachan separately. "My mother thinks I like you," I told

him. "I don't want to give her any more thread to keep on weaving *that* cloth."

"I thought you did like me." Odran looked hurt.

"I do," I reassured him. "The trouble is, Mother's idea of 'liking' isn't the same as mine. I'm afraid it ends in marriage."

Odran shuddered. I didn't know why seeing that gesture of repugnance irked me so much. "You're right, Lady Maeve. We do *not* want our parents getting the wrong idea about us. My father would call a thousand curses down on the High King's household if he imagined we were more than friends."

"The High King's daughter isn't good enough to be the wife of a druid's son?"

"It's not that. It's the timing. Right now there's room for only one thing in my life, according to my father, and that's getting me to Avallach so that I can finish my training and become exactly what he wants me to become. There can't be any distractions or diversions."

"Not even bringing them with you?" I pointed at Guennola and Muirín.

"Trust me, it took all my wits to persuade him to allow me their company. I've never asked Father for much and I've always tried to bend to his will, whether or not I like it. The only thing I've ever fought for in my life has been getting permission for this."

"I'd think that if Master Íobar's used to your constant obedience he'd be *less* likely to make an exception. My father's chariot driver, Fechin, always says that if you loosen the reins a little, the horse will yank them completely out of your hands."

"Then I'm glad Father knows nothing about horses." Odran grinned.

"I'm surprised he was willing to let you harbor wild things even before the two of you began this journey."

The druid's son grew serious. "I was born sickly. Not even Father's healing lore could bring a healthy color to my face or give me the endurance to run and scuffle with the other children. Then my mother died, and I mourned so deeply that I couldn't eat or sleep. Everyone said I was destined to follow her to Tech Duinn.

"And it would have been so, if not for my mother's dearest friend. That good woman brought a robin's nest to my bedside with a broken-legged birdling inside. 'I can't persuade the little one to eat,' she said. 'Won't you help me?' She showed me how to feed it by hand, how to keep it clean, how to check the binding on its leg and how to retie it. By the time the little robin could hop to the door and fly away, she'd saved two lives. After that, whenever I found an animal that was hurt or ailing and brought it home to heal, Father scowled but didn't interfere. Mother's friend was there to remind him that he owed my life to Flidais, the goddess who cares for wild things. If Father wanted to keep me, I must be allowed to keep my creatures."

"How many do you have?" I asked, picturing the ringfort of Munster with all the king's warriors ankle-deep in limping badgers and runny-nosed hedgehogs.

"Oh, I didn't mean that I *keep* every creature I heal. If I have the skill and good fortune to make them well again, I send them back to their true homes. It's only rarely I take one in who's meant to stay with me. Guennola and Muirín came into my care as orphaned babies. I couldn't teach them how to live wild. They'd die."

"I wonder how your teachers at Avallach will react to them."

"I'm hoping Father will bring them around." Odran dropped his voice to a conspiratorial whisper. "I've convinced him that these two rascals help me concentrate on my studies."

"I'd love to know what magic spell you used for that. You must be a born druid," I said drily.

"There was no magic at all to how I did it. One day I asked Mother's friend to keep Muirín and Guennola for me and went to my lessons without them. Father had been after me to rid myself of the creatures ever since I found Muirín abandoned in an empty den. He tolerated Guennola because my stoat could keep out of his sight inside my tunic, but a poor scrawny runt of a fox cub was too much for him."

"He never tried taking them away from you by force?"

"And have us waste precious learning time quarreling about it?" A dimple showed itself.

"He must have been pleased when you parted with them," I said.

"*Pleased* is a weak word for his reaction. Not even a bard could describe how overjoyed he was."

"A short-lived joy, I'm sure."

"You've hit it. All that day my hands kept straying to the place where Guennola usually nestled, my eyes drifted to Muirín's spot at my feet, and my mind"—he feigned a melancholy look—"my mind wandered so far away that my recitations of lore and ritual and history sounded like the babbling of an infant just learning how to talk."

"Was that all it took?" I asked. "A single day of stupidity?"

"Certainly not. It took at least seven days and as many beatings before Father began asking himself if my creatures weren't also my touchstones, living tokens to guard and build my power of memory. That was why he let me have them at lessons again."

"Either that or his arm grew tired from trying to whip sense into a block of wood. He had better things to do. You say his goal is to see you become a druid. He swallowed his annoyance and let you have your pets so that you'd stop playing games and get on with your education."

"Do you really think so?" Odran looked disillusioned. He plucked the stoat from the ground and said, "What a shame, Guennola. All this time we thought we'd been so cunning, outwitting Father that way, and here comes Lady Maeve to tell us he was twenty steps ahead of us."

"It's time for *you* to be twenty steps ahead of *me*," I remarked. "I'll see you at dinner."

"Whatever you say, Lady Maeve." He placed the stoat on his shoulder and whistled for Muirín to attend him.

"Wait, Odran. Before you go, there's unfinished business between us."

"You've already argued with me, fed me, mocked me, listened to my troubles, and as good as told me I'm a simpleton next to my father," he said in a friendly way. "What's left?"

"That you never again call me *Lady* Maeve."

"Is that all?" He placed his hand over his heart. "I swear it, now and forevermore."

And he sealed the new bond between us by waiting until my back was turned and tangling a sticky strand of trout bones in my hair.

Chapter Six

Fox and Hounds

Master Íobar's son must have had a large inborn share of his father's mystic power: he disappeared the day after our meeting under the willow.

To be truthful, he was invisible only by day. He ate with the rest of us every evening, suffered a tongue-lashing from his father, and went to bed. The reason for these nightly rebukes was Odran's daily absences. Master Íobar could not give lessons to a ghost or ask a phantom to repeat things from memory. The bitterly funny thing was that those scenes between father and son were so repetitive and unchanging, I found myself mouthing their words while the druid ranted about all the ways Odran was a disappointment and a failure, and Odran responded with the same passive apologies.

Never once did he promise to change his ways.

I tried to talk with him at meals, but he timed his arrival for after I was already seated. It would have drawn the wrong kind of notice if I'd risen from my place to sit beside him.

Once, I tried lying in wait, lingering at the doorway into the great hall until he arrived. He greeted me in a friendly way, walked in with me, shared my bench, then announced he had to answer the call of nature. When he returned from doing his business outside—his *alleged* business—he sat elsewhere.

What had I done to earn such treatment? I'd enjoyed his company and his conversation. I hadn't taken the slightest vengeance for the trout-bone incident. We had parted as friends. The more I thought about it, the angrier I got.

What in the name of all the gods is wrong *with him?* The question boiled in my brain. I wished I could scream it out loud. *And a hundred curses on him for acting like there's something wrong with* me!

Even though I knew there was no decent reason for Odran to be treating me that way, his behavior still hurt. Like a hound with a thorn in its paw, I retreated to nurse my wounded pride in private. When my brooding resentment left me, it was only because it had smoldered so long that it caught fire and became a burning desire to make *him* hurt for a change. I reached a cold conclusion: I was done with him. If he didn't want to be with me, I didn't want to be with him.

I'll ignore him from now on, I thought, then reconsidered. *No. Ignoring him's a good start, but not enough. I'll make sure he knows he's being ignored. Let Odran make himself vanish as long as he likes. I'll make him vanish the rest of the time! Who's the spell-caster now?*

I put my scheme into action that very night. He didn't notice. I wouldn't have minded if only he hadn't looked so content. For a moment no longer than a butterfly's wing beat I wished I could walk up to him, punch him in the shoulder, and shout in his face, *"Pay attention to me when I'm not paying attention to you!"*

I fought down that highly inhospitable impulse and soothed myself with the knowledge that even if my icy treatment hadn't worked that night, there were plenty of other nights to come.

Your eyes will open, Odran! I thought. *It will take time, but before the summer's over, you'll realize that I'm shutting you out the same as you're doing to me and you'll be sorry.*

My confidence was strong but turned out to be useless. While I was preoccupied with my plan of retaliation, other members of my family were also taking an interest in Odran's chronic absences. Mother brought up the matter when she and some of her ladies were supervising a thread-spinning lesson among the fosterlings.

"Look at how big I'm getting," she mused, studying the bulge of her unborn child. "And so soon! It feels like I'm carrying a warrior *and* his weapons. If it is a boy, I hope he'll give us less trouble than Master Íobar's son gives his poor father. Gone from sunup to sundown every day. What could he be doing?"

"Lady Maeve might know," Guennola said casually.

"Why would I?" I held myself aloof and cold. "I don't bother with him."

"You did." Her head bent over her spindle, a sly quirk tugging the corners of her thin lips. "When he and his father first came here, I saw the two of you coming back from— Well, I don't know *where* you'd been or what you'd been doing, but I did see you return home together."

"Together but not together," another girl put in. "We both saw them, Guennola, remember? You and I were sent to gather some herbs, and *there* was Master Íobar's boy, sauntering up the path from the stream, that filthy fox of his trotting beside him, and *there* came Lady Maeve along the same road, not more than thirty paces behind him. If that isn't proof that they'd been keeping company but wanted to keep it secret, I don't know what it *does* prove."

"It proves you two would rather gossip than work," I said calmly. "And that's like proving a fish can swim." Guennola and her comrade blushed and squirmed under a downpour of giggles from the rest of the women.

I hoped that would put an end to all talk of Odran, but Mother had other ideas.

"Wouldn't it be a delicious change for us all if there could be peace between Odran and his father? I'd rejoice to have one dinner without the same accursed clash between those two."

"You'll have some relief soon, my lady," one of Mother's attendants remarked. "When the king and his best horsemen go to Tailteann for the Lughnasadh races, Master Íobar will travel with him but not the boy—not after the way he's been provoking his father."

I doubted Odran would mind being deprived of a trip to watch horses run and men compete in countless athletic games to honor the god Lugh, but I saw no reason to mention this.

"Lughnasadh!" Guennola cried. "Is it so soon?"

"Soon enough," her friend said, sighing. "Another Lughnasadh and not one of us will be handfasted."

I rolled my eyes. It was this way every year among the older fosterlings. Many couples began wedded life at Lughnasadh by having their wrists bound together with ribbons in front of witnesses. It wasn't the only way to be married, but Father claimed it was the best because the man could walk away from it at the end of a year and a day. Mother agreed it was a good thing, adding that the women would like it better if it were changed to a month and a day instead.

"Stop your moaning, girls," Mother said placidly. "Finding a man is easy. The hard part is finding one you can please. The blessed part is finding one who'll please you." She added more fleece to her spindle, teasing out the fluffy fibers into a strong thread. "As for me, I have a good-enough husband"—everyone laughed—"and I don't mind making him happy. So to that end, I want you all to make those gossip-hungry ears and eyes of yours useful. Find out where Master Íobar's son goes each day and what takes up his time. If you succeed . . ." She touched the gold bracelet on her wrist meaningfully.

I didn't like what I was hearing. "Mother, are you serious? How is having Odran spied on going to make Father happy?"

"Once I learn his secret, he and I will make a bargain. If he's not sneaking off to do anything vile, he can continue, but not all day nor every day. He must swear to give at least half his time to lessons. If not, I'll tell Master Íobar everything. Odran's smart enough to know what *that* would mean. He'll accept my terms and assuage his father. That will put an end to all their arguments and *that,* dear Maeve, will make your father happy." She set her spindle aside and took off her bracelet. "Now, who would like to try this on?"

The fosterlings swarmed around her, vying for a turn to wear queenly gold. Even Mother's attendants crowded up. No one seemed to care when I stepped away from the mob, letting my spindle be trampled under their feet.

Why must she meddle in this? Whatever Odran's been doing, it's his *business,* I thought. Mother enjoyed bringing order out of chaos. The constant strife between father and son was upsetting her small world, but that didn't give her the right to sacrifice Odran's independence for her peace. *I'd like to see how she'd like it if I offered my gold torque to anyone who'd stifle her little spats with Father!*

I no longer cared that Odran had been avoiding and ignoring me. I threw away my resolution to act as if he didn't exist. I was determined to warn him about the snare being set.

If only I knew how to do it, I thought. *By tomorrow all of those beady eyes will be on him. The one thing working in his favor is that Mother's pack of she-hounds isn't trained to hunt. They can't shadow him; they'd make too much noise. What else might they do? Flirt with him so he'll confess? Try to coax his secret out of him?*

I imagined Guennola simpering at Odran, bringing her lips close to his ear, whispering endearments—

—and having her namesake stoat sink its teeth into her chin. I pictured her with the stubborn little beast clinging there like a long, skinny beard and laughed so hard my ribs ached.

I recovered to face a disturbing possibility. *Our fosterling girls aren't hunters, and flirting with Odran won't work, but what if they flirt with someone who is a hunter? A good one?* There were any number of young men under our roof who fit that description and who would willingly trade their tracking skills for kisses and the promise of more.

I have to tell Odran. I have to tell him now. Tonight, at dinner, before his father stirs up the usual brawl and he's sent to their sleeping chamber. He must be alerted to what's going on behind his back.

I decided to repeat the trick of waylaying him in the

doorway. As soon as our paths crossed, I'd take his arm and whisper everything he needed to know in order to safeguard his privacy.

It almost worked. Once again he greeted me as though he'd missed my company and couldn't wait for the chance to enjoy a conversation. His false warmth didn't fool me. I knew he was already plotting a way to escape me.

Fine, let him put the breadth of the whole house between us! I thought. *But not yet. Until I have my say with him, he'll stay to hear it—I'll make sure of that.* I reached out to clutch his arm.

Guennola the stoat stuck its head out of the neck of his tunic and hissed at me. I jumped back, nearly treading on his fox's paw. Odran chuckled. "I think she's jealous of you," he said.

"She can have you," I grumbled. "I don't want to sit next to you tonight, so you won't need to bother summoning up an excuse to get away from me. I just want to tell you one thing, very important, that you need—"

"Aha, there's a happy sight!" Father's voice rang out from his place on the king's bench. His good fortune had given him eyes as far-seeing as any falcon's. My bad luck made him turn them in our direction before I could tell Odran what he needed to know. "They make a handsome couple, don't they, Master Íobar?"

Odran's father made a sour face. "You flatter my boy too much, Lord Eochu. He would never dare to set his sights on your child. She's destined for a king's bed."

"So you say, but can your arts let you foresee which king will be worthy of my Maeve?" Father drank deep from his cup of beer. "She's already rich in her own right, and I won't let my dearest girl go to her husband without adding much more to what she holds. In fact, it might make more sense for her to stay here and wed a man who'd come to her."

What is Father doing? Every word he spoke to Master Íobar made me cringe. It was the old story: *I'm being dangled before that man like a bit of meat to tempt a hound. If Father would even* consider *having me marry anyone less than a prince or a famous warrior, why Odran? What is this game?*

Whatever it was, Master Íobar was as loath as I to play along.

"Odran's future is the only one I know," he said. "It's an enviable one. Any intelligent boy would desire it and work with all his heart toward achieving it. Perhaps we could exchange tasks, O King. I'll find the right royal mate for your youngest girl and you'll convince my stone-headed son to apply himself to his lessons."

Father stroked his chin, mulling over the druid's words. "That's not a bad idea. He could be fostered here and study with Master Niall and Master Owain. It would save you the journey to Avallach, but—"

"My lord, forgive me, I spoke too lightly." Master Íobar's grizzled brows made a shape like a down-thrusting spearhead between his eyes. "My son cannot consider marriage until after he has completed his studies and become my colleague. Learning must be his one love. It was that way for me and I know that Master Owain and Master Niall will attest to it being the same for them."

He looked at the two druids who served us at Cruachan. Both nodded in agreement with their brother. "There will be time enough for such things after he achieves his goal," Master

Owain intoned solemnly. "I lost nothing by being patient and putting learning ahead of wedding."

A handful of Father's favored warriors heard this and snickered among themselves. Everyone under our roof knew that white-haired Master Owain had been forced to take a local cowherd's young daughter for his wife because all his offers of marriage to wellborn women were rejected. It was an honor to be a druid's wife, but when that druid was as old as the lady's father, it became an honor easily refused. We'd all heard Master Owain's bride weeping herself to sleep every night from Lughnasadh to Beltane. In time, she seemed to accept her fate and showed the world a smiling face. In a little *more* time, she also showed the world a baby boy who looked very much like Fechin, Father's chariot driver.

A baleful stare from Mother silenced the young men's amusement. "Can finding mates for our children wait until after we've eaten?" she asked, putting bite into the question. There was a general rumble of agreement, especially from our chief cook and his helpers. As they began ladling portions out of the huge cauldron of stew on the fire, an air of happy, hungry anticipation settled over the hall.

"I have to take my place, Maeve," Odran murmured, moving away from me. "I'm sorry I can't sit with you, but Father would see it the wrong way if we remain together. You heard him."

"But, Odran, all I want is—" He was away before I could finish the sentence. I was left giving my warning to the air.

I had a bad dinner. It wasn't the food, but the frustration. Half my stomach burned with annoyance because I'd failed to caution Odran that when tomorrow came, he'd be the girls' quarry. The other half tied itself in knots because I couldn't help thinking it would serve him right if they caught him. All of it was made worse by knowing that I'd missed the opportunity to speak with him before dinner. Would I be given another chance to warn him in time?

Pride and pity are not good mealtime companions. They stole my appetite and left me glumly picking at my food.

Father noticed. "What's ailing you, my spark? Come sit beside me and share some of my portion."

I went to him gladly. There was something deeply comforting about leaning against him and knowing that every bit of that strong body and brave spirit was devoted to my protection.

Even when you don't want to be protected? The wayward thought flicked through my mind, there and gone. It stayed as briefly as the glint of sunlight on a honeybee's wing, but that was time enough for it to do its work.

Father loves me, but he sees no difference between holding me out of harm's way and holding me on a tether. Master Íobar is worse. He'd tie Odran to him hand and foot if he could. And now Mother's helping him.

My eyes narrowed. Whatever knots they tried to use to bind that gentle, kind, infuriating boy, I would be the knife that gave him back his liberty.

Master Íobar's voice rose over the level of common conversation in the hall. "There he goes again," Father muttered. "Why doesn't he try governing his son at some other time than dinner? It puts me off my food." He promptly gave this the lie by stuffing a chunk of meat into his mouth and chewing vigorously. He swallowed, smacked his lips, and added, "I gave them a sleeping chamber of their own. He could flay the boy's ears in private, *after* we've all had a pleasant meal, but that wouldn't suit our venerable guest. He likes an audience."

"Be quiet, Eochu. He'll hear you," Mother reprimanded him.

"Pfft!" Father blew a scornful breath through his lips. "Where have you been all this time, my love? You know that once that fellow's started his attack, he doesn't hear anything but the sound of his own voice telling the lad what a rotten son he is."

"Right, *that's* going to make the boy eager to change." Fechin spoke up from his place nearby. He kept his voice pitched discreetly low. "I know that when *I* want a new horse, I just pick out a pig and beat it until it grows a mane."

I giggled.

"Who wants to bet how long it will be before he sends the boy to their chamber tonight?" Another one of Father's men turned to Devnet. "Master Bard, I wager this bronze brooch of mine that if you begin the tale of how Aengus loved the swan-maiden Caer Ibormeith, young Odran will be sent off before you reach the point where the god first sees the lady."

"And I say it will happen before that, while you're still describing how handsome the god appeared," Fechin chimed in, stripping one of his gold bracelets from his arm as his stake. Other men sidled nearer, all wanting to take part in the game.

This talk of how soon Master Íobar's rage would boil over gave me an inspiration. I leaned heavily against Father's arm and whimpered.

"What is it, dear one?" he asked tenderly. "You can't be ill, can you? You were just now laughing at Fechin's wit."

"It's nothing, Father," I said in a piteous voice. "It's only that I'd like to leave." I didn't lie, though a finicky judge might argue that I used misdirection to dodge telling the full truth.

"Do as you please, darling," he said, patting me on the head. "Go to your chamber and rest. You'll feel better in the morning."

I kissed his cheek and left the circle of light cast by the central cook fire. I heard Mother urgently asking Father what was ailing me and likewise heard him assure her that it was no more than some minor touch of stomach trouble. Then their voices were engulfed by the overall ebb and flow of conversation, slashed through here and there by Master Íobar's customary berating of his son.

I know that *tone. It won't be much longer.* I was certain that if I'd stayed and joined in the betting about the moment of Odran's banishment, I'd win. *I must move quickly.* With one backward glance to make sure no eyes were following my retreat into the shadows, I slipped into the sleeping chamber I sought.

Odran's room was almost fully dark. The only light was what leaked in at the edges of the hide curtain shielding the doorway. I moved cautiously, unfamiliar with the placement of the bed and our guests' possessions. I didn't want to stumble or, worse yet, knock over anything that might make noise and bring someone to investigate. By laying my hand flat against the wall and shuffling my feet as I went along, I was able to locate the bed. The thick layer of dried grass under the cloth covering released a sweet scent when I sat down. A pungent, animal reek slowly overwhelmed it.

What is *that smell?* I wondered, covering my nose and mouth

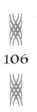

with one hand. *It's not the stench of waste—Mother would skin any beast who soiled her house and take its master's head for good measure. Ugh. Whatever it is, I hope I won't be trapped here with it for much longer.*

My wish for a short wait in the dark was granted. I heard a sudden roar from the hall—Master Íobar losing his temper, no doubt—and then the sound of footsteps coming closer. Their brisk approach was accompanied by the lighter, quicker pace of Muirín's trotting paws.

I bit my lip. What if the fox outdistanced its master, found me first, and attacked? That was what our household watch-dogs were trained to do when surprising interlopers. Who knew if Odran had taught his pet to do the same? I shuddered, already feeling the sting of those sharp little teeth, and began groping in the unfamiliar dark for anything I might use to fend off the animal harmlessly.

All that my blindly searching fingers could find was the bed-cover. I pulled it up around me, covering my head and swathing my face so that only my eyes were visible. *Bite me now, Muirín, and you'll get a mouthful of wool,* I thought smugly just as the hide door was pulled aside and a wedge of firelight fell over me.

"What— Who—" Odran's startled voice resounded loud as thunder to me.

"Hush, oh please, *hush!*" I whispered desperately, letting the bedcover drop away, revealing my face. Better a fox's bite than discovery. "It's me—it's Maeve. *Shhh!*"

He let the door fall closed behind him. I heard him make his way toward me with the confidence of knowing precisely where to walk without accident. The dried grass crunched as he landed heavily beside me.

"Maeve, what are you doing here?" He spoke so quietly that he was nearly inaudible. Every word sounded taut enough to snap at his next breath. "If my father finds you here—"

"He won't. Just listen to me and then I'm gone. When you leave Cruachan tomorrow, be on the alert. Mother has offered a reward to any of her girls who can find out where you go every day. If they fail to do it themselves, they might bribe some of the boys to dog you. Luck be with you." I rose to leave.

"Wait." His hand closed on my wrist. "Tomorrow, come to the willow by the stream, the place we met. I have something to tell you too."

I pulled my hand away roughly. I left him there in the darkness, without a yes or no.

My own room welcomed me. I fell onto the bed, grateful that my escapade had gone undetected by the adults still eating and drinking in the hall. I heard Devnet's clear, powerful voice raised in song and regretted that my false illness would keep me from being present to enjoy the bard's performance. It was a shame, but there would be other times and other songs to delight me. Tonight I'd been able to fulfill my self-imposed task and that would have to be satisfaction enough.

I've done what I can for you, Odran, I thought. *Whether or not you were worth the trouble, I warned you and now I can be finished with you.* With that, I fell into a sleep so deep that I should have remained abed until long after sunrise.

Instead, the dawn found my sleeping chamber empty and my racing feet carrying me through the mists to the shelter of the willow tree.

CHAPTER SEVEN

Eyes of Flame

"WHAT TOOK YOU so long, Odran?" I asked when he parted the willow branches and came to keep our meeting. I spoke casually, as if his arrival was as unimportant as a worm showing its head aboveground.

"That's a strange greeting." He sounded amused. "I was trying to follow some good advice a friend gave me last night. It takes more time to get where you're going when you have to look ahead, behind, and all around for every step you take."

"Were you followed?"

"Not unless the hunters on my trail have the magic to turn themselves invisible."

"Like you've been doing." I hadn't meant to speak of how he'd been avoiding me. I definitely didn't mean to be grouchy as a badger when I said it. So much for treating him coolly!

"Maeve, I'm sorry." He sat beside me and reached for my hand.

"Don't do that!" I snapped, hugging myself away from

him. "I don't want that stoat of yours to slither out of your sleeve and nip my finger until it's bloody."

"Guennola is fairly well behaved when she bites," Odran replied. "She's lost patience with me countless times, but those sharp teeth of hers have never yet broken my skin and made me bleed. I don't know where she learned to do that. *I* never tried to teach a stoat self-control. Anyway"—he linked his hands behind his head and leaned back against the tree trunk—"she isn't with me now."

Was he telling the truth? His stoat was a very thin, small creature. It couldn't have been longer, from nose to tail tip, than my forearm. The animal might be lurking inside his garments, disguised as a bulge of the fabric. I eyed Odran scrupulously, waiting for the telltale twitch and squirm beneath the cloth that would reveal Guennola's presence.

"I know what you're doing, Maeve," he said. "Do you want me to prove she's not here by shedding my tunic?"

I would *not* let him faze me. "Your fox doesn't seem to be with you either. What will you strip off to prove *that*?" I replied drily.

He opened his mouth and closed it again, at a loss. I tasted a sweet sip of a small victory.

"Enough about your beasts," I went on. "Last night you said you had something to tell me. You asked me to come here and here I am. I have better places to be, so speak. What do I need to hear from you?"

"An apology," he said, holding my gaze with his own. "That, and an explanation."

"What could you have to apologize for or explain to me?" I forced myself to break the hold of his eyes.

"You know that answer, Maeve. You said it yourself before we sat down to dinner last night."

"You'll have to remind me," I said, covering my wounded feelings with an artificial show of dignity. "I have a poor memory for unimportant things."

He let my barbed words pass. "You said that I've been making excuses to avoid your company. You're right, and I regret it. I want your forgiveness—"

"Is that all? Are we done here?"

"—but first I want to tell you why I behaved so rudely. It's your choice whether you hear me out or not. You can leave now and never say another word to me except farewell when Father and I travel on to Avallach. You're free."

I bent my head, prideful stiffness melting from me like a cloak of sun-touched frost. "I'll listen," I said.

"Of all the stupid things I've done—and Father would be happy to recite the full list—keeping you constantly at arm's length was the worst. The day I met you was the first time in my life I believed I'd made a friend. That was new to me. I had no such bonds back home. The boys who studied with Father never invited me to join them in play after our lessons and I was too shy to ask. The others—the young warriors in training—had no use for me except as the object of their 'jests,' or when they tried turning my creatures into targets for their weapons."

"That sounds familiar," I said, half joking. "I've had two friends in my life, and one was my sister Derbriu."

"I can't imagine you being too bashful to find companions," he said with a faint smile.

"There's a wide gap between *can't* and *won't,* Odran," I told him. "I don't see the good in heaping up friends like pebbles, just to have a pile of them. Mother doesn't understand that I'd rather be happy alone than miserable in a crowd."

My declaration bewildered him. "If that's how you feel, why are you so angry with me for staying away from you?"

"Because—" The tip of an invisible knife touched my throat. "Because you're the first person I've known since Kelan that I've wanted for a friend."

"Who's Kelan?"

"It doesn't matter," I said, the greatest lie of my life. "He's dead."

"May his soul know joy in the Land of Youth. I'm sorry you lost someone special to you."

"He wasn't my sweetheart," I said sharply.

"I never said he was. Can't he be special to you anyway?"

There was such innocent sincerity in Odran's question that I wanted to throw my arms around his neck. I had to settle for covering my face with my hands and exclaiming, "*Thank* you. If you only knew how sick I am of being teased about that sort of thing!"

"I have some idea," Odran replied. "We both got a taste of it last night. Your father has a powerful sense of humor. He almost had me believing he was serious about you and me becoming—"

I flung my head back and uttered a groan of pure aggravation. "If I were in love with anyone—if I even cared the slightest bit for a boy that way—why would I want to be taunted for it? I'd only have to lose him, unless he were a prince, a king, or a warrior famed enough to be given the High King's daughter as his hero's portion." I slumped against the tree.

"Poor Maeve." Odran's hand stole over mine so gently that I was scarcely aware of his touch at first. When I did notice, I made no move to escape it.

"Poor *you*," I countered. I turned my hand palm upward, let my fingers interweave with his, and leaned toward him without thinking. Away from his creatures, he smelled deliciously of fresh air, warm bread, and apples.

"Poor us?" he suggested lightly. We both laughed and let it numb us to the truth: Unless the Fair Folk granted us a heavy measure of their magic, our lives were not our own. Our fathers held them.

"Let's make a bargain, Odran," I said. "From one captive to another. Let's be true friends from now on. You'll leave us before Samhain and I'll never see you again unless one day my royal husband says, 'There's a new druid joining our household, Maeve. He's the strangest man you ever saw, with a fox for a torque and a stoat for a bracelet!'" I realized I was still holding his hand, squeezing it warmly. *What am I doing?* I released him, embarrassed, but reluctant too. I couldn't make sense of either feeling.

"At last, a future worth praying for," Odran said. "I'll take that bargain, Maeve, but first I still owe you the reason why I acted so badly toward you."

"You don't have to do that. It never happened. We're starting over, remember? Now let's find something fun to do. Do you want to go fishing again? Oh, I know! Come with me and I'll show you my cattle. There's a wonderful bullock in the herd, lastborn son of Dubh, the best bull Father ever owned."

"I've heard of Dubh," Odran said. "Isn't he the black bull

you tamed when you were three years old and rode all the way to Tara?"

"That's not exactly what happened." *Bards. Honestly. Devnet's song had traveled far and changed shape dreadfully in ten years.*

"Probably not." His wonderful blue eyes doubled the effect of his smile. "If a creature as small as Guennola scares you now, getting close to a bull when you were three would've been terrifying."

"I wasn't three—I was five—and I wasn't terrified until things got out of hand," I said. "Also, I am definitely not afraid of animals." I hesitated over that half-truth, then amended it. "I mean, I'm not afraid of *our* animals, the ones we keep, the horses and cattle and pigs and dogs."

"Just wild things, then?"

"Not all of them. I'd be an awful coward if I were scared of creatures like hares, deer, hedgehogs, and squirrels. It's the ones with an appetite for meat that I'd rather not encounter." And that was *another* near-truth to be corrected. "Except . . . except for the hunting birds. When I see them soaring or hovering or even when they make a kill, I wish I could hold them with my eyes forever."

I'd never spoken to anyone of how fiercely I loved the way a hawk's wings wrote *freedom* across the open sky. Why was it so easy to say such things to him? I fell silent, wondering if he'd laugh at me.

He wasn't laughing. He stood up and offered his hand. "Come with me, Maeve."

I clasped his hand again; it felt right. So did following him without question. We left the willow tree and the stream. We

raced like leaves on the wind. Our eyes scanned the landscape, but Mother's she-hounds must have had other business occupying them, for we were safe, alone and unobserved. Open country gave way to forest. Odran moved through the venerable oaks as if they were all his partners in a mystic dance. He never once let go of my hand, and I danced with them too.

The forest ended and we could no longer see any trace of Cruachan ringfort behind us. A few straggling trees seemed to mark our path to the edge of a bog. The sun warmed the green blanket of moss and added brilliance to the staggering flight of blue, orange, white, and golden yellow butterflies as they dipped and rose, seeking nectar from thickets of purple bell-shaped flowers.

"This way. Mind where you step." Those were the first words Odran spoke to me since we began this journey. He showed me a wooden walkway laid out on top of the bog. It looked very old and decrepit, and was so narrow that we had to go in single file, still holding hands.

"Is this where you've been going every day?" I asked. "No wonder we never see you. This is a world away!"

"It only seems that way because you don't know our destination," Odran replied over one shoulder. "Don't worry, we're almost there."

The walkway split into two. Odran led us onto the left-hand path, which soon brought us out of the bog and into another stand of trees. These were young pines, hardy and able to thrive near bog land. We stepped out of their fragrant shade to meet a fresh, moist breeze and to see a small lake rippling at our feet.

"We're here, Maeve. Look."

Odran pointed to a spot a little farther along the lakeshore where a double row of thick, sturdy pilings marched into the water. They supported a wooden walkway like the one that had taken us over the bog, and ended at a large, circular platform supported above the water by more of the anchored tree trunks. A round house rested there, its thatched roof showing so many holes that it resembled the hide of a mangy dog.

"This is where you've been coming?" I demanded in disbelief. "To that tumbledown crannog?"

"It's sturdy where it counts," Odran said staunchly. "The roof's the only part that's gone to ruin, and even so, we have plenty of places inside that are safe from the rain and can be made snug against the cold."

"We?" I echoed.

He took my hand again. "Let me show you."

I let him conduct me across the causeway to the crannog. The wind shifted as we approached, blowing landward and bringing a familiar scent. I wrinkled my nose: I knew where I'd smelled this before. As Odran plunged eagerly through the house's gaping doorway, I found myself dragging my feet and pulling back until my hand slipped out of his.

He turned a questioning look on me. "Are you frightened, Maeve? I swear, you're safe here."

"I'm not afraid. It's just . . . that smell is so—"

As I spoke, a familiar face showed itself around the doorpost. Odran's little red fox peered up at me with a smear of blood on her muzzle and such a smug expression that I immediately exclaimed, "Oh no! Muirín's eaten Guennola!"

"I'd like to see her try getting away with that. There'd be a lot more blood than this, and more than half of it would be hers." Odran lifted the fox into the crook of his arm and scratched her between the ears. She closed her eyes in bliss. "She's probably found some mice. They venture out here to steal food and end up becoming food themselves." He looked at me. "As for the smell, it's worse in there. I must be accustomed to it, but if you find it too much, you should stay outside. I'm sorry I brought you on such a tiring journey for nothing. It's just that after what you told me today, I thought you'd be pleased to see—"

"I may not be used to the stink, Odran, but I can endure it. I was able to put up with it while I was waiting for you in your room last night, wasn't I?" I pulled my shoulders back. "And for your information, it would take a far, far longer road than our little stroll today to tire me. Now stop treating me like I'm a buttercup petal and stand aside!" With a fine display of bravado I strode past Odran and into the house.

He was right: the stench *was* worse inside, in spite of the gaps in the roof that let in gust after gust of cleansing air. My stomach heaved. At first I was glad that I hadn't eaten anything that day except some wild blackberries picked on the road to the crannog, or had more to drink than a few handfuls of water when we encountered a brook. Then I grasped the dreadful fact that it's better to just throw up than to stand reeling while your stomach tries to empty itself of nothing.

"Here, Maeve, lean on me." Odran put his arm around my waist. I slumped against him and rested my head on his shoulder, even though he was still cradling the fox in his other elbow. I swear, I caught her smirking at my weakness!

Enough, I thought. I took a long, deep breath through my mouth, then blew it out forcefully.

"There, I'm better now. Let me stand on my own." I pushed him away gently. "Thank—"

I saw them then. Their eyes glittered at me from the make-shift beds Odran had constructed for them out of pine boughs and scraps of cloth and even a broken bowl. He had also built up miniature holding pens around those comfortable resting places so that none of them could escape too easily.

A small badger bared its teeth at me even while it shivered. I wondered what lay beneath the fabric strip binding its middle.

A pair of squirrels chattered to each other from nests attached to separate house beams.

A hedgehog stuck its nose out of a notch-shaped break in the upended clay pot sheltering it. The pot was positioned on a slab of wood and the wood was ringed by a thick, wide fence of brambles.

Odran saw me studying the arrangement and couldn't help bragging, "That is one of my best inventions. It keeps Muirín and Guennola from bothering him while he heals." He set down the fox, who eyed the hedgehog's ringfort sourly before sauntering off.

"Now I see why this place smells worse than a tanner's trough," I said. "So many animals! I didn't think Muirín and Guennola could produce that much stench on their own."

"I wish I could care for them better," Odran said. Pride in how he'd safeguarded the hedgehog faded from his voice as he admitted his failing. "I should scrub this place more thoroughly, but when? It takes so long to walk here every day, and then to be back to Cruachan in time for dinner! I have to use my time giving them fresh water, finding their food, and treating their wounds and ailments. If one of them has managed

to roll in his own filth, I have to deal with that immediately. I clear away their droppings as often as possible, but—"

"The smell gets *into* things," I finished for him. I surveyed the small enclosures. "Tomorrow I'll bring soap and some more rags. Try gathering some flowers to scatter on the floor. We won't be able to undo this stench in a single day, but we can make a start."

"You want to come back here with me?"

I shrugged. "If I can. Mother might have work for me. If that happens, I'll try to escape long enough to leave the cleaning supplies for you to take here on your own. I can hide them under the willow, though I do hope—"

"But you're afraid of wild creatures!" He sounded so vehement about it that I had to giggle.

"Don't you listen? I don't mind those." I indicated the squirrels and the hedgehog. "However, I'm not going to touch *that* one." The badger snapped at me when I pointed at it, then subsided into a permanent state of grumbling. "Nor your fox nor your stoat. By the way, where is Guennola?"

Odran went farther back into the house to a place where the roof was almost entirely intact and the shadows hid many things. I heard him shifting some heavy object, followed by a yelp of pain. He returned with the stoat on his shoulder and his forefinger in his mouth.

"The miserable ingrate bit me again," he muttered around it.

I coaxed his hand away from his mouth and examined his finger in the light. It was red, and I could see the prints of Guennola's teeth, but once again there was no blood drawn.

"Just as you said," I remarked. "She nips you, but she doesn't break the skin." I gave the stoat a look of admiration. She hissed at me. Again. I suppose even stoats have their traditions.

"I put her in the same sort of thorn-ringed enclosure as the hedgehog," Odran said. "It was the only way I could feel confident that she wouldn't do him any harm when I'm not around."

"Why is she here at all?" I asked. "And Muirín too. You have the stoat penned up safely, but your fox was free to greet us at the door. If you don't tether her, won't she run away?"

He whistled and Muirín came at his call. Odran picked her up again, just long enough to sink his thumb and forefinger into her neck fur and fish out a strand of braided leather that hung from a loop concealed by her pelt. The end was gnawed through. "Obviously the thought has crossed this vixen's mind. It was luck that brought us here before she could act on it. I can trust her untethered if I'm nearby, but I won't chance losing her or having her bother the ailing animals when we're apart."

"You ran a big risk. I know how much you love Muirín and Guennola, so why keep them here?"

"It's not the first time. Since I found this place, I've been leaving them here for a day or two at a time so they don't outstay their welcome at Cruachan."

"Really? I never noticed."

"No one did except Father." Odran's face fell. "How could he help that, sharing a sleeping chamber with us? Whenever he became aware that they were missing, it was as if the High King had heaped his hands with gold. You should have heard him: 'If those beasts are gone, it's the gods who've freed you

from them. Animals have no place with us unless they earn their keep. Now you can devote your attention where it rightfully belongs.' Oh, the *hope* in his voice when he told me that!" He shook his head. "And the look of doom he wore whenever I brought them back."

"Are you carrying them back and forth just to provoke your father?" I wouldn't have put it past him, and I wouldn't have blamed him for it either.

"I didn't intend it to be so. That would be like burning down a forest to find a stone. It doesn't take much to ignite Father's wrath. All I wanted was to prevent your parents from hating my pets as much as he does. Our stay with you will be the longest time we've remained with one host. Every other stop along our road has been for two or three days at most. Even after so short a stay, I've heard the royal mistress of the house complaining about the smell. I'd rather bring Muirín and Guennola out here and give your servants a fighting chance to defeat their scent markings."

I glanced after the fox, who had vanished into the recesses of the round house. "I guarantee they'll succeed, even if they have to tear down the great house and rebuild it overnight. My mother can be very *firm* about cleanliness. So can I. We should get started. Where do you keep the things you use to clean up the animals' waste?"

He nodded in the direction that Muirín had taken. "Back there, but—"

I ignored him, already on the hunt and eager to help. It didn't strike me as odd that Odran was shielding, nurturing, and trying to heal wild creatures. He wasn't the same as ordinary boys, so I couldn't hold him to the same measure of behavior. That would be like trying to force a bull into a badger's sett. I heard him call my name and hurry to catch up to me. His hand closed on my upper arm.

"Be careful, Maeve." His breath was warm on my ear. "If your eyes aren't used to the dark, you might stumble and fall. Please, stand still and let me bring you what we'll need."

"No need to bother," I said cheerfully. "There's more than enough light to see by once you're back here. It only looks dark from the front part of the house. I can see Guennola's nest, and there's Muirín, watching me from under that bench, and over there—"

My heart and my breath seemed to stop at the same time. My eyes filled with a sight that was both the most awesome and the most pitiable I'd ever beheld. Wings that should have been stretched out to catch the wind were folded around a small, dapple-feathered body. A strip of cloth held one of them immobile. Taloned feet grasped a wooden perch, and a hooked gray beak with a black tip parted to confront me with a sharp *kee-kee-kee!* The kestrel's eyes met mine. A bright yellow ring encircled each eye, matching the color of the small stripe bridging its beak. As I stood captive to that bold, unwavering stare, I saw the impossible: a flare of brilliance rose from the depths of those dark brown eyes, a moment of light in the darkness like the kindling of the need-fire on Beltane eve.

"You see it too?" Odran's voice broke my trance. "I thought I was the only one."

Her name was Ea: fire. Odran called her that when he first saw that unearthly flame that flashed and faded in her eyes. I agreed it was a good choice.

"What have you named the other creatures in your care?" I asked as we walked back home together.

"I don't give them names. I'm going to release them when they recover. If you name something, it's bound to you. Isn't that right, Muirín?"

He shifted the little vixen from one arm to the other. We were crossing the bog causeway and if he let her trot along with us, she might take it into her head to dash away and explore. Odran didn't want to chase her over deceptive ground, where a layer of greenery covering deep water might support her weight but not his. His care for her welfare meant he couldn't hold my hand on the way back. (Not that I needed him to guide my steps, but I couldn't help wishing for it anyway or feeling a little envious of Muirín.)

"Does that mean you're going to keep the kestrel?" Part of me was appalled at the possibility. *Is she so badly injured that she'll never fly again? How can she live, exiled from the sky! This will break her heart.* Another part of my spirit was thrilled to imagine how matters would play out if Odran couldn't set her free. *If he keeps her now, that means I'll be the one to have her eventually. He can't leave her on the crannog forever. Samhain will come. He'll have to travel on with his father, and Ea will be mine!*

Had I entertained such a selfish thought, even for a heartbeat? The memory of a raptor's unfettered flight shamed me so deeply that I almost didn't hear Odran answer:

"Ea isn't mine to own, and Flidais, goddess of wild creatures, would punish me if I tried to steal her. That bird doesn't need me the way Guennola and Muirín do. She's old enough to know how to fend for herself, to hunt, to nest, to find a mate

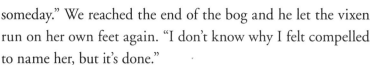

someday." We reached the end of the bog and he let the vixen run on her own feet again. "I don't know why I felt compelled to name her, but it's done."

We passed the rest of our return home talking about Odran's hideaway on the crannog and how we would arrange things so that he and the animals could remain unmolested in that far-off refuge.

"We can be thankful that Lughnasadh comes soon," I said. "Your father will accompany mine to Tailteann and you won't be shouted away from your dinner every night."

"I get enough to eat. Don't worry about me."

I would have believed his easygoing reply if his skinny body wasn't contradicting every word. I'd seen spiders with sturdier legs.

I dropped my voice and played the cunning schemer. "Yes, but if you stay through the entire meal, you can slip leftover pieces into a pouch and bring them to the creatures the next day. I'll do the same. That way we won't have to hunt for food for them, and that will give you more time for seeing to their other needs."

"That *would* be nice." Odran studied his hands; the nails were black with embedded soil in spite of repeated washings. He couldn't catch mice for Ea to eat, so he grubbed in the dirt to fetch her beetles and earthworms. His other meat eaters got the same fare.

"I have another idea. You'll teach me how to take care of the animals so that I can go to the crannog in your place. Think how happy your father will be to see you back at your lessons!"

"Maeve, are you moonstruck? I can't teach you all the healing skills you'd need to look after them on your own. And have

you forgotten that poor badger? He must be kept clean and comfortable, fed by hand when he won't feed himself. How do you expect to do that when you fear his teeth and claws?"

I stopped walking and clasped his hands. "I'd bury my fear and do what was needed. I saw how tenderly you treat those beasts, Odran. Why do you do it?"

"There you go, sounding like Father again."

"Odran, I'm serious." I dug my fingers into his hands as hard as I could, for emphasis. "It's like the way Fechin cares for his horses, but they're always going to be a part of his life. These are wild things you'll release and never see again."

He smiled sheepishly. "I don't know why I do it, Maeve. It's as much a mystery to me as why I gave Ea her name. Something in my spirit drives me to help them. Do you think it's a weakness? Am I so afraid of death that I have to fight it on all of these small battlefields?"

Cowardice? I thought. *Father's best warriors should learn courage from you!*

I squeezed his hands again, this time more gently. "I understand. It's confusing, but . . . but it's the same for me. After seeing the creatures in your care, I'm still afraid of some of them, and yet I know . . . I *know* that I'd risk any hurt they might give me if I can help them." *And you,* I thought.

So it was decided that Odran and I would become partners in ministering to the injured animals. Agreeing on the details nearly set us at each other's throats. We talked and debated and argued and fought about them all the way back to Cruachan.

It galled me that I couldn't go to the crannog on my own until Odran took me there at least twice more. He wanted to be reassured that I wouldn't get lost on the path and that I could fulfill each animal's needs. I accepted the second part readily, but I resented the first. The fields and forests, the bogs and lakes of Connacht were my home. I didn't need a newcomer to guide me through *my* land. So what if I'd never found my way to that abandoned crannog during any of my rambles? I wasn't being reasonable; I was being mad.

Odran had his own mouthful of gristle to swallow: I made him consent to resume lessons with his father. He began by doing so on alternate days, when I was with the creatures. Then I informed him it would be even better if I spent two days with them to his one.

"Just until our fathers depart for Tailteann," I cajoled. "We don't want people noticing that there's a pattern to our absences. If they do, they'll begin to ask questions."

"Why not break the pattern by having you go to the crannog once for every two of *my* trips?" he countered.

"*I'm* not the one who has to memorize so much," I said primly. "*I'm* not smart enough. I'm not going to become a great and mighty druid who can hurl down curses and read the future and sit in judgment. I'm merely a princess. All I have to do is look pretty and be charming and very, *very* sweeeeeeet." I fluttered my eyelashes and blew kisses at him.

"You have all the charm of Guennola and sharper teeth," Odran said. I punched him in the arm. "*That* wasn't sweet at all," he complained. But he gave in.

CHAPTER EIGHT

Bonds Made, Bonds Broken

ODRAN SOON LEARNED the wisdom of doing what I told him. One pebble rolling down a hill can nudge along larger and larger stones until it all becomes a roaring rockslide. Just so, my insistence that he go back to his studies soon brought us a host of benefits.

Master Íobar was pleased, of course. He saw Odran's compliance as an overdue win for his authority as father, teacher, and druid. Generous in victory, he didn't seem to mind it when Odran evaded him every few days, as long as he had his full attention and effort on the days they spent together.

Master Íobar's rage cooled even faster when Odran stopped bringing Muirín and Guennola to his lessons. The druid became positively jovial, no longer berating Odran or banishing him to their chamber every night. If he asked, "Where were you today? I missed you," and his son's only answer was a shrug and a smile, Master Íobar returned the smile and let the matter drop.

With peace between our guests, my parents were able to

enjoy food, drink, and companionship at dinner, free from the tension of wondering when the nightly storm would break. Our hall was loud with Devnet's songs instead of Master Íobar's ranting. I never saw Mother look more content.

As for me, I was as happy as the lucky mortals who found their way to Tír na nÓg, the isle of eternal youth and beauty in the western sea. Every day that was my turn to visit the crannog was another chance to be with Ea. When I was there, I became like a child who's been given a piece of honeycomb and deliberately holds off taking the first bite to prolong the treat. I saw to the needs of all the other creatures first, never rushing through my duties to them, until they were all fed, clean, and comfortable. Once that was done, I could give myself completely to Ea.

What went on behind those shining eyes of flame? How did she see me when I fed her, kept her perch clean, talked to her, even sang every one of Devnet's songs that spoke of birds, flight, freedom? Every time I tended her, I yearned to stroke those glossy feathers but reined myself in. I sensed she wouldn't like to be touched, though there were times I felt her refusal wasn't "No" but "Not yet." I respected her wishes. I loved her; I could wait.

Perhaps someday an enchantment would let us master the many languages of animals. Until we should have that gift, we could only hope for some sign that the creatures we loved understood just how much. I'd seen the spiderweb strands of devotion between Father's chariot horses and Fechin. Men called them the High King's steeds, but anyone with eyes knew how things really stood: they were Fechin's just as surely as he belonged to them. That was how it was between Ea and me.

Odran named her, but only I knew her. I couldn't hold her in my hands, but I didn't care as long as I held her to my heart.

On the day Father and Master Íobar went off to attend the Lughnasadh gathering, I reaped the final reward for herding Odran back to his studies. I wasn't expecting it and it came from an unforeseen source: the featherbrained babble of one of our fosterlings.

The arrangement Odran and I had made for us going to the crannog was disrupted by the royal departure. It would have looked much too suspicious if either of us failed to bid our fathers farewell.

My friend fidgeted dreadfully throughout the whole leave-taking. It was his turn to look after the little ones; he should have set out before dawn. I could almost read his thoughts: *I should be where I'm needed. Why don't these men* go?

I sidled up next to him and pressed my right foot down firmly on his left. I feared that if I didn't hold him in place somehow, he'd bolt before Father's party was out of sight. My ploy delayed him long enough to thwart any suspicion when he did vanish, and I was feeling rather proud of how discreetly I'd done it, until later that day.

I was at needlework with Mother and our fosterlings when a shrill, skin-scraping giggle tweaked my attention away from the garment I was sewing. It came from Sabha, a girl who never seemed able to speak without simpering.

"Lady Maeve, I hope *you* won't try to claim the queen's bracelet for finding out where Odran goes," she said. "You've got an unfair advantage over the rest of us—you could do it as quick as a kiss."

Before I could respond to the coy insinuation behind those

words, Mother spoke. "What are you talking about, Sabha?" she asked wearily. The baby was growing at an uncommonly fast rate, wearing out her patience as much as her body.

"Yes, Sabha, *what?*" I gave the too-chatty fosterling a hard stare.

Sabha made a *Who, me?* face and appealed to her companions for support. "Was I the only one who saw how things stand between Lady Maeve and Master Íobar's son? Because if you ask me, they stand very *close.*" She arched one brow.

Why was there never a rotten apple around when I wanted one? I would have settled for a clod of mud, but the weather had been dry. I had to make do with words: "Who'd ask *you* anything? You blabber just to hear your teeth knock together."

"Maeve—" Mother cautioned me.

Sabha was not discouraged. "There they were, side by side, so *adorable*! They couldn't hold hands, of course, but if you'd seen the way Lady Maeve was leaning against her sweetheart, you'd *know.*"

I leaped to my feet. "I *know* you're a troublemaker, Sabha. You stir things up because you're as bored with your own dull life as we are."

"I saw you and the druid's son too," Guennola barged in. "You were standing on his foot. You know, it's a mistake to *force* your sweetheart to stay close to you, Lady Maeve. It makes him want to escape."

"You know a lot about keeping sweethearts. Too bad you never had one," I sniped.

"That will be enough." Mother raised her hand. "Sabha, I'd know if my daughter had a sweetheart." One of Mother's ladies snickered, but a glare of queenly anger silenced her. "However,

since you think Maeve's guaranteed to win the prize . . ." She took the gold bracelet from her wrist and tossed it on top of the sewing in my lap. "And there's an end to it." A chorus of protests rose up around her, but Mother had spoken.

That evening, I waited for Odran just inside the ringfort gateway. I was so eager to give him the good news that I didn't care if I was acting exactly like a lovesick girl. When I saw him coming, it was all I could do to keep from running down the path to meet him.

"Odran, look!" I showed him the bracelet. "See what Mother gave me!"

"It's lovely, Maeve," he said, regarding my prize doubtfully. Guennola gave me the same inquisitive, uncertain look from her perch on his shoulder. "Is this some special day for you?"

"It's special for us both." I linked my arm through his, being careful to do it in a way that wouldn't alarm or irk the stoat. Guennola and I weren't friends, but my relationship with her precious Odran had forced her into a guarded truce with me. "This bracelet is your freedom." I told him how Mother had called off her she-hounds, though when it came to explaining why . . .

"Since you and your father stopped fighting every night, there's no more need to hunt you down, but someone had to get the prize she offered. If she'd given it to one of the other girls, the rest of them would have argued about it." And that was mostly true.

"Is it so?" Odran was visibly relieved. "I don't have to be wary of pursuers anymore?"

"Well, you might not want to relax your alertness *too* much, but the chief danger is past," I said jauntily.

"Maeve, do you know the best part?" His blue eyes shone with joy. "Your mother's put an end to the hunt and my father's away. We can stop playing hide-and-seek. We can go to the crannog together until he returns!"

Why couldn't I be as happy as Odran with our shared days in that half-ruined house over the lake? Something prevented me—the poignant knowledge that it couldn't last. Lughnasadh would end, our fathers would come back, and we'd have to renew our old ruse to deceive Master Íobar. That was bad, but it was nothing next to what else we'd have to face.

Too soon the light would fade, the days would shorten, the crops would be harvested, the cattle herds thinned, and Samhain would come. Odran would depart for Tara, and from there travel on to Avallach. He would take his healing lore with him. I'd picked up some of it from watching him and from the instructions he gave me for tending our creatures, but it wasn't enough. If I were left on my own, any small wild beasts who fell victim to injury or illness would have a sorry fate. I feared that I didn't have the knowledge necessary to help them.

That was what I told myself whenever the thought of his leave-taking stole my joy. I wasn't ready yet to admit why else I felt so miserable at the thought of a future without him. And how did he feel, knowing that in a brief time we would be parted? I yearned to know, but I didn't dare to ask.

My haunted thoughts distracted me. Not even Ea's bold, beautiful presence could lift my spirits. Once I became so caught up in them that I began stroking her feathers, until she clashed her beak at me. *Treat me like a puppy, will you? Pay me the attention I deserve or pay the price!* she told me with her fiery eyes. *And count yourself lucky that I chose to give you a warning, not a bite.*

I heeded Ea, but absentmindedness trickled into the way I cared for the other animals. I scrubbed the same spot on the floor until all the stoat's smell and half the wood were gone. I fed one squirrel her breakfast and promptly fed her the other squirrel's breakfast too, while he chattered angrily at me from his nest. I went down to the lake to fetch water and came back with a bucket full of minnows and weeds.

Odran noticed. A blind man would have noticed. The two of us were looking after the hedgehog—he examining its lame paw, I setting a fresh ring of brambles around its clay house— when he spoke up. "Maeve, that's the tenth time you've pricked your fingers and the third time you've knocked over that pot. If you break it, the little creature won't have any place to shelter tonight. I know you're not clumsy, so where's your mind wandering? This isn't how you took care of our animals when you were alone with them."

"What's wrong with the way I take care of—" I bit back my objection in mid-breath. I knew I'd fallen short. "I'm not happy, Odran."

"Yes, I can tell." He wasn't mocking me for saying something so obvious. "What's wrong? What have I done to make you feel that way?"

"Being you."

"I don't understand."

"You're going to be a druid. You're going to Avallach. You're going to leave me, and I can't—" I was on the point of saying too much when a twinge of pain made me gasp and wince. I turned over my palms and saw that they were bleeding from my mishandling of the brambles. Before I could cast my eyes around for water and a cloth, Odran was cleaning my hurts.

"I don't want to go, Maeve," he said softly as he smeared a beeswax salve over the scratches. His hands were warm and strong, but he had a tender touch. "I wish your father hadn't been joking when he suggested I stay here to study with Master Niall and Master Owain. I'd say yes to that in a heartbeat."

"And if you stayed, I . . . I could study too," I said. "You'd learn the druid's way from them, and I'd learn the healer's way from you. Then, if I found a wounded creature, I'd know what to do without needing you to tell me."

"I'd like it better if you always needed me, Maeve." His pale face turned bright red and he quickly bent his head over my injured hands. I was glad; it meant he couldn't see how those simple words had flustered me as well.

When he looked up again, he tried pretending he'd said nothing. "If you want to become a healer, I'll teach you what I can, but the best way to learn is by working on your own with the animals. If I'm here with you, you become my shadow. There's only one way to get around that."

He was going to say, *Let's come here separately again.* I knew it. I feared it.

No! I cried out inside. *I don't want to give up these precious days of being with you.* Before he could suggest that, I exclaimed, "I have it! Instead of us sharing the care of all the animals, let's each be sole caregivers for individual ones."

Odran considered this. "That's a good idea, better than mine. I'll take the ones that frighten you, and you—"

"That would leave you with no responsibilities at all."

"What? Are you saying that you're no longer shy of any of the creatures?"

"I've grown used to them."

He looked pleased but hesitant to believe me. "Even Guennola?"

To answer, I headed for the rear of the house, where the stoat's temporary enclosure stood near Ea's perch. Odran had put her there to keep her out of mischief while we saw to the hedgehog. I intended to pick her up with my own hands, to prove I was telling the truth.

"Maeve, no!" Odran seized my wrists and spun me around to face him before I could touch one hair of the stoat's pelt. "You've got fresh blood on your hands. Do you dip your fingers in stew before you pet your father's dogs?"

I yanked myself away. "I'd rather have you think I'm a fool than a coward," I declared. Then I realized what I'd said and blushed. "And if saying something like *that* doesn't prove how foolish I can be, nothing will."

"A fool couldn't have come up with plans as smart as yours," Odran said. "And having a few fears doesn't make you a coward."

We decided how to divide the creatures' care between us.

"There are two squirrels, so that's simple," I said. "Which do you want?"

"The male. He doesn't chatter so much."

"That suits me. The female doesn't find the need to pee everywhere." I met Odran's jest with one of my own.

"I should probably take charge of the badger."

"I told you, I'm not afraid of him anymore."

"It's not about fear. His wounds are the most serious, and I have more experience at healing than you do."

I had to give him that. *But not for long,* I thought. I was determined to learn everything Odran could teach me about helping wild things.

"If you have the badger, is the hedgehog mine?"

"Not if we want things to be even. We'll either have to share his care or cut him in half, and I don't think he'd like that."

"That's not funny, Odran, and it's not fair. It means I'm only in charge of the squirrel."

He gave me the strangest look, as if I'd said something unthinkably ridiculous. "Aren't you going to look after Ea?"

Did he just say that? "You want me to have the kestrel?" *If this is a joke—*

"You have her already." There was no hint of teasing in his voice. "And she has you. I've seen it. Whenever you have to do anything for her comfort, you always do more than enough. If I tell you to feed her, you catch the fattest beetles and earthworms and smile when that sharp, hooked beak of hers snaps them from your hand. When you clean up the droppings under her perch, you finish the job by scattering fragrant pine boughs over the floor."

"It's nothing," I murmured. "You do things for her that I can't. I've never loosened her bindings to examine her wing or retied them so she could continue to heal."

"That's my fault. I've never given you the chance. I know how much you want to. When I do those things, you stand so close that I feel your breath on the back of my neck."

"I wanted to be right there, in case you needed me to fetch something for her. I'm sorry if I crowded you."

"I wasn't complaining." His fingertips brushed my wrist. "Maeve, there's no special skill behind what I'm doing for Ea. When I found her, she was holding her right wing oddly, so I bound it to her body for support because I couldn't think what else to do. I don't even know if it's broken or merely sprained. You can already give her everything that I do—rest, food, sanctuary—and since you've watched me adjust her bandages, you can do that too. I know you can. But you can give her more. I've seen how you look at her, and how she looks at you. There's a bond between you. The fire in her eyes flashes more brightly when you're with her. Believe it."

I did, as sure as breathing.

Ea sensed that we were talking about her. Her *kee-kee-kee!* from the shadows as good as declared, *If I'm so important to you earthbound sticks, then look at me! Pay attention to me! Bah, what's the use? I'm doomed to suffer these ill-mannered servants.*

"We're sorry, pretty one," I said, drawing near. "You should be a part of this. Odran claims there's something special between us. Is he right? Will you give me your permission to take care of you until you're free to fly again? You know that means I'll have to touch you, but I promise to do it without hurting your pride. Let me try now, please? It won't be so bad." I raised my hand to stroke her.

"Maeve—"

This time, Odran's warning about putting blood-striped palms within reach of a meat eater came too late. I was already running my fingers over the sleek feathers of the kestrel's head. She twisted her neck and darted her head upward so quickly that I never saw her move. A flash of pain from my forefinger declared that Ea's beak had claimed its prey. I shrieked and jumped away, terrified that when I looked at my right hand, I'd count four fingers instead of five.

All of my fingers were still attached to my hand. I gaped at them, seeking some mark of the kestrel's attack. The only wounds I had were those I'd given myself, being absentminded with the brambles.

"Amazing." Odran was as slack-jawed as I. "Why did you scream if she didn't bite you?"

"She *did* bite," I said. "It was a warning." I looked back at the bird. *A second one,* I thought, recalling how she'd snapped her beak on empty air to make me mind her. *I don't deserve a third.* "Forgive me, Ea. From now on, you will be the one to say if I can touch you."

The kestrel's eyes glowed and faded. She cocked her head and gave me a pert look that said, *Ah, so you* can *be taught manners! Good.*

Lughnasadh came. Master Owain and Master Niall oversaw our celebration at Cruachan, though nearly every aspect of the gathering was underscored by the grumbles of those young men who had not been chosen to accompany Father to Tailteann. None of them had ever attended the games there, and yet they were all convinced that our own races and tests of strength and other contests were miserable in comparison.

The only aspect of the holiday that seemed to meet with their approval was when they went off with the girls for the traditional bilberry gathering. The lads were so avid to participate in that sacred custom that some of them stayed out all night.

If they came home without a single bilberry to show for it, perhaps it was because they and their ladies had to eat all they found or starve before dawn.

Mother was somewhat concerned when I didn't want to participate. "Don't you *like* bilberries, Maeve?" she asked coyly. "Odran's going."

"Odran is a druid's son. It would look bad if he didn't join in every bit of the celebration."

"It looks just as bad if you stay home. You're the High King's daughter. If your father were here, he'd insist you take part. The more young people who go, the more berries they'll find. Everyone knows that a plentiful bilberry gathering means a rich harvest."

"Why didn't you say that before? That's a *sensible* reason for me to spend the day with a mob of snickering boys and giggling girls. Why bring Odran into it? You were the one who told the fosterlings you'd know if I had a sweetheart. Don't you think *I'd* know it too?"

Mother shrugged. "You're young and pretty. You don't need to have a *real* sweetheart, but why can't you play with the notion? Flirt? Test your powers of persuasion? Try a few steps in a harmless dance while you can still hear the music?"

"Turn Odran into one of those scraps of cloth you used to give me when I was first learning how to sew?" I countered.

She folded her arms over the swell of her belly. Her brow furrowed. "Maeve—"

"Mother?"

"*Go.*"

I went. I loved my own skin too much to gamble it on back talk when she used *that* tone. I trudged off with the rest of the bilberry pickers, filled a basket with the small, round, purple-black fruits, came back to Cruachan before anyone else, including Odran, and went looking for Mother. She'd tucked herself away in a secluded, sunny spot, probably because she wanted a respite from all the to-do of Lughnasadh. She glanced up from the hank of wool she was carding just as I dropped my basket at her feet.

"Bilberries," I said, deadpan. "Yum."

"And Odran?" she asked hopefully.

"He can pick his own." I tried to keep a straight face when I said that to her, but our glances crossed and we both giggled worse than all the Lughnasadh berry pickers combined.

Lughnasadh was long over, yet the road from Tailteann stayed deserted and no messenger from the High King came to Cruachan. Mother began to fret over my father's delayed homecoming. Every night at dinner she turned the conversation to *When do you think they'll be back?* No one knew.

I didn't share her concern. I'd passed my fifteenth birthday that summer, yet still I clung to my childish belief that there was no challenge Father couldn't meet. When I recalled the time that I'd seen him come home from Tara gravely wounded, I didn't tremble over how close we'd come to losing him but exulted because he'd had the strength and will to survive.

I might have felt more of Mother's anxiety if not for my faith that all was well with Father and the fact that she and I now lived in different worlds. Her life centered on Cruachan, her husband, and the child she carried. Mine was fixed on the ruined crannog at the lake and the animals there.

Even the best of bards would be at a loss for how to describe

the depth and breadth of my happiness. It lifted my heart to watch my squirrel grow fat and cheeky, and on the day Odran declared that she was well enough to return to the wild, I grabbed his hands and danced for joy. My high jinks startled the squirrel so badly that she leaped out of her nest, hit the floor running, and dashed from the crannog without giving me the chance to say goodbye.

Odran's squirrel was fully healed two days later and had a more sedate send-off. His place was taken by an undersized young hare with a bad cut on her left flank. Odran brought her in but immediately handed her over to me.

"What do I do?" I asked, caught midway between excitement and dread.

"Use these," he said, bringing me a bowl of water, a little pot of salve, and cloth for bandages. "I'll tell you how, but you'll do it yourself."

He did so, then left me holding her while he went to prepare her nest. By the time he came back to see how I was getting along, I had the hare's wound cleaned, salved, and bandaged. Now I was working on cleaning all the scratches she'd given me in the process.

"You'll be glad to know there's nothing wrong with the beast's hind legs," I grumped, washing my generously scored forearms.

Just in case we'd missed the sound of shrill chattering, we acquired a new squirrel with a wound on his back that looked like the mark of talons.

"He must have fallen afoul of one of Ea's bigger cousins," Odran said.

"Bigger and clumsier," I remarked. "Luck was with him. If squirrels carry talismans, this one should cherish his and pass it along to his favorite pup."

I'd been given the hare, so Odran took the squirrel. That was for the best. Not only was it fair but it was also good for the harried beast. Every time I passed near his nest, he became desperately agitated. Odran guessed it was because I carried Ea's scent and even squirrels can retain unpleasant memories.

Hare, squirrel, and all the rest were soon joined by a she-otter. Odran found her limping on three sore paws at the far side of the lake when he went there to fish. He'd gone there to catch some tempting fish for the badger, who seemed to have no energy and whose appetite had turned scanty and worrisome. Instead, he came back with the largest animal we'd ever taken in, her thickly furred body measuring more than the length of my arm.

I tried not to envy Odran when he took full charge of her, but my longing to be close to the pretty creature must have showed on my face.

"I know you want her, Maeve," he said without prompting. "I'd let you have her, and take the hare, but I feel she should be mine."

I told him that I understood. The creature's name and his were the same. His mother must have been the one to call him Odran, because I couldn't imagine Master Íobar using the magical bond of names to link his son's life and fate to such a graceful, playful, and—for the druid—useless creature.

The otter turned both of us into dedicated anglers. She had

to have huge quantities of fish every day. At first we brought in enough to satisfy her, Ea, and the badger, but one morning we found that there was one less animal to feed: the badger was dead.

I thought I'd never be able to stop weeping. Odran held me while I sobbed, but he didn't cry. I didn't get the chance to ask him why he remained dry-eyed over the pitiable little body: he read the question from my heart.

"We did all we could for him, Maeve. I'll mourn him after I've seen to the living creatures here who need me." He carried the badger outside. I don't know if he buried the body or left it for Flidais to find.

Goddess of wild things, Lady Flidais, take back your own, I prayed. *Let the last gift of his body feed your other children. Let his spirit find peace.*

Odran came back and went directly to Ea's perch. He began unwrapping the cloth that immobilized her injured wing.

"What are you up to?" I wanted to know. "I just changed that bandage two days ago." I was going to add, *Did I do it wrong?* but put that aside. I *knew* I'd done it right, copying his work exactly.

"You'll see." He took off the binding strip and carefully touched the kestrel's wing. She darted her head at him, beak agape. He just managed to avoid a bite.

I stepped in without being asked and held her small body firmly, one hand at the back of her head so that she couldn't move it. She struggled and made sounds of distress that pained me.

"Hush, Ea," I whispered soothingly. "Hush, my beautiful

girl. This is just like what I did for you two days ago. We're not trying to hurt you. Be calm and we'll be done soon." She gave one final lurch against my grip and settled down into resentful stillness.

Odran examined the newly freed wing. "I think it might be ready," he said. "There's only one way to find out. Maeve, can you carry her outside?"

"Why? What for?"

"You are going to show your bird the sky again, and you're going to see if she's ready to fly."

I couldn't speak. I did as Odran said, cradling her against my body so that she couldn't slash my hands with her beak as I carried her out of the round house, but I wasn't able to ask a single question or say one word. My head was too crowded with thoughts, my heart with warring feelings. I rejoiced and cursed, prayed to see proof that she was healed and grieved that I was about to lose her. My mind cried, *It's too soon! Too soon! There are too many dangers. She's not ready!* and then, *I can't hold her back forever. Not if I love her. She must be free.*

We crossed the walkway to the shore and climbed to the top of a small hill. There was a warm, brisk breeze blowing toward us from the water. I tried coaxing Ea to sit on my shoulder the way Odran carried Guennola and would have succeeded if he hadn't spoken up: "That's a good way to lose an ear. Pull your sleeve down as far as it can go and let her perch on your arm. Wait, maybe I should do it. She's going to dig in her talons, and you might not—"

"We'll be all right," I said softly.

We were not. Ea's sharp grip pierced my sleeve as soon as

she set one foot there. I bit my lip. I would not risk startling her with a scream or even a whimper. More important to me, I wanted her to see that I was strong.

It wasn't easy. A small cry of pain escaped the corner of my mouth. Odran heard, saw what was happening, and winced in sympathy.

"Gods, I'm a fool. You're dressed for summer! That material's not enough to protect you from her talons. We should have covered your arm with something more substantial, a piece of leather, anything. Here, let me take her."

I shook my head emphatically, still grimacing. The kestrel wore a look of cool curiosity as she watched the faces I made while holding back the pain. Then she lifted her head into the gentle wind and stretched out her wings tentatively.

She's going to leave me now. That thought hurt more deeply than her talons in my arm. I prepared myself to accept it.

As it turned out, I was spared that day. Ea made no move to fly. Her injured wing had healed but was stiff from disuse.

"We need to keep her safe for a little while longer," Odran said as I set the kestrel back on her wooden perch. "The problem is, we want to leave her wings unbound but we don't want her able to pounce on the other animals when we leave."

I agreed. "The otter's too big to be her prey, and Ea wouldn't like trying to grasp a hedgehog's prickles, but if she recovers, nothing will protect the squirrel and the hare." We both sank into deep thought. I was the first to break the silence. "Odran, give me your knife; mine's too small."

"What are you going to do?" He handed it over, but he sounded doubtful.

I took the soft leather pouch from my belt. It held my most

precious talisman, the iron splinter that came from Kelan's shattered sword. I spilled that into the palm of my hand, set it aside reverently, and went to work. A few cuts were all it took.

"Hold her steady," I told Odran. He obeyed, though he was still looking at me askance. I moved quickly, slipping the altered belt pouch over the kestrel's head. "Now let go." She twisted her head this way and that and snapped her beak through the opening I'd made for it, but other than that, she kept very still. "It works!" I exclaimed, delighted. "She won't fly if she can't see!"

Odran gazed at my handiwork with admiration. "You ought to secure the hood somehow," he said.

"I'm going to take it home and fix it. I'll find a pin to fasten it at her neck," I said. "Meanwhile, would it hurt her to have that wing bound to her body again for just one more day?"

Odran liked my suggestion, though Ea made a loud, violent protest. She glared at us fiercely when we left her to return to Cruachan.

As we approached the ringfort hill, I noticed that the road we walked showed the recent marks of many horses' hooves and the fresh prints of chariot wheels. There would never be so much traffic unless—

"My father's home!" I exclaimed, pointing out the tracks to Odran.

"And mine," he said, resigned.

"Don't let him see *that* face. We have to keep you on his good side, remember."

"I know, I know." He sighed. "I just wish I could be as enthusiastic about seeing my father again as you are about seeing yours."

"I'm not just glad for me," I replied. "I'm happy for Mother.

Now she can stop worrying about him. Oh, I can't *wait* to see the greeting she gives him. She'll skin him alive for staying away so long and smother him with kisses for coming back."

"That sounds like a very, um, *vigorous* welcome," Odran said. "Do you take after your mother?"

I barely heard the question. In my eagerness to see my parents reunited I decided that I simply *had* to get home at once. Odran could catch up later. I broke into an all-out run. Odran shouted my name, but I had no time for explanations. I heard Muirín yipping frantically, the vixen's shrill barks fading fast at my heels. I shot up the slope, through the portal, and into the midst of a milling crowd. It wasn't unusual to find such a press of people massed so close to one another inside our walls. Father wasn't the only one coming home and Mother wasn't the only one wanting to welcome back all the men who'd gone to Tailteann. It was only when I burrowed into the thick of the mob that I became aware something was wrong.

Where were the smiles? Where were the cries of joy, the embraces, the kisses? Why did every face look filled with apprehension? Why were all eyes fixed on the portal of the great house?

And where was Father?

Panic struck. My absolute belief in his ability to survive anything fell to pieces as I saw the expressions of dread surrounding me. I no longer edged through the crowd but began fighting everyone who stood between me and the doorway, shoving men aside, grabbing women by the arms to drag them out of my way. As I struggled ahead, the severed heads of Father's most honored enemies seemed to mock me from their niches in the doorway. Lord Fachtna Fáthach leered down as I stumbled and fell at the threshold of my home.

"Maeve, are you all right?" Lady Íde stepped out of the house and helped me back onto my feet. Her face was distorted by anguish and so white that her tear-reddened eyes looked like pools of blood.

No! Oh no! "Lady Íde, what's happened? Is Father—"

"Oh, Maeve, precious child." She pulled me into her arms so violently that the force of our embrace sent us staggering. She would have fallen backward and dragged me down after her, but strong hands were at her shoulders to catch and support her.

I looked into the face of our rescuer, a face I had feared I'd nevermore see in the living world. I blinked and blinked, afraid that I had slipped into a cruel enchantment cast by the Fair Folk. I scarcely dared to speak, afraid that if I did, the spell would shatter and he'd vanish.

But if he was an illusion, I had to know.

"F-Father?"

He looked as though some giant's hand had wrung all the joy from his body and soul. One arm around Lady Íde, one around me, tears dripping from his cheeks, my father spoke: "Your mother . . . your mother and the child."

CHAPTER NINE

Those Who Leave Us

ODRAN CAME THROUGH the crowd to find me sobbing in Father's arms. My hair hung in tangles around my face in a swath of red, blinding me to everything but my grief and fear.

Father held me close and would not let me go. "Maeve, Maeve, my spark, my precious girl, you'll hurt yourself if you go on like this. Hush, breathe, hear me," he pleaded urgently. "She isn't dead. Yes, we nearly lost her—both of them—and the danger isn't past, but she's still alive. That's what matters. Come. We'll talk inside."

I allowed him to guide us into the house. He brought me to his bench by the hearth. My feet were weighed down with invisible stones and my vision was a blur. I was only half aware of holding Lady Íde's hand. Father's arms were over us like a great bird's wings. Odran hovered near, and Master Íobar soon joined him. Servants brought us food and drink, leaving them within reach before hastening away. Not one of us took a morsel or a sip, though my mouth was dry and sour and my stomach empty except for pain.

Finally, Lady Íde said, "The bleeding came over her this morning. Such things will sometimes happen before a child is ready to be born, but only a spot or two and no more. This was different. Cloithfinn called for help as soon as she realized how bad it was. Our druids rushed to attend her, as did all her women. While they were with her, Lord Eochu came home. Master Íobar joined his colleagues and their skills turned back the blood, but I insisted Lord Eochu send for a midwife."

"A midwife?" I tensed. As far as I knew, you only summoned the midwife when a woman was about to give birth, but it was too soon for Mother's child to be born and live.

"As a precaution," Lady Íde reassured me. "I doubt there's any immediate risk of . . . of what we fear, but we must make sure of it."

"Can I see her?"

"In a while. She's resting. When she wakes, we'll need to wash her and clean the room. Sleep is her best healer now. I'd better go back to keep watch." Lady Íde excused herself and ducked behind the bull-hide curtain to my parents' sleeping chamber.

Odran gazed at me from the shadows beyond the fire. He didn't speak, but his eyes met mine with a look of deep sorrow and compassion. I would have run to hold him and pour out my tears in the safety of his arms, but my place was with Father.

"I should have come home sooner," he said in a hoarse, broken voice. "As it is, pure luck brought us back from Tailteann today." He leaned forward on the bench, elbows on knees, hands hanging limp and useless. "I could have found a way to prevent this."

"Don't berate yourself, Lord Eochu," Master Íobar said. "There are some things you can't fight with spear and sword."

"I don't merit any words of consolation. I know how badly I've failed." Father shook his head. "I should have been here for her."

I clasped his hand between both of mine. "You're here now."

"For how long? I lingered too many days at Tailteann. So many of my subject kings came to me there with troubles to be settled, and I was too proud to say, 'This is work for the law-keepers.' I stayed until I'd given every judgment. I could have turned over such matters to Master Íobar and the other druids and come home. And now the days until Samhain are running through my fingers like dust." He looked at Master Íobar. "I once called the lesser kings here for Beltane. Could I do the same for—"

The druid's expression extinguished the faint hope in Father's eyes. "Samhain is too solemn an occasion. The barriers thin and vanish between the Otherworld and this one, between the realms of the living and the dead. My brethren will confirm what I say. The High King of Èriu must be at Tara for the rites."

Father wore a self-mocking smile. "A fine king, who can't protect his greatest treasures." His jaw set; sudden determination turned him from flesh to iron. "A hundred curses take it, I *will* stay here! If I can't stand between my people and the perils of the Otherworld on Connacht's soil, why would being at Tara give me that power?"

"Have you lost your senses, asking such a thing, Lord

Eochu?" The druid held himself with dignity, majestic and fearsome, a figure of unassailable authority. "Are you so weak that you'd sacrifice the safety of your people, the fate of all Èriu, and the gods' favor because you must cling fearfully to one woman's skirts? I tell you, you will bring a *thousand* curses on everything you love if you follow any path that keeps you from your appointed place at Tara this Samhain. I know it, for every one of those curses will come from my mouth and break over Cruachan like a thunderbolt mighty enough to shatter stone!"

I rose from my place, my arms protectively around Father's neck. "Master Íobar—" I began, but that was all I was allowed to say.

Before he knew whether I intended to defend him, to plead for mercy, to protest the druid's threats, or even to counter them with my own, Father pulled me down beside him again.

"Forgive me, Master Íobar," he said, shaken to the marrow of his bones by his belief in the druid's power. "What I said was madness. I beg you, don't punish anyone but me for that, especially not my Cloithfinn and the child. Guide me now. I'll follow."

Master Íobar's aspect softened. "That is wisdom. Walk with me. The first thing you must do is let your people know that Lady Cloithfinn lives."

"Thanks to you, Master Íobar," Father said. He spoke as if Master Niall, Master Owain, Lady Íde, and the other women had done nothing. It was pitiably clear that he was trying to curry favor with the druid, out of fear, but if Master Íobar knew he was being flattered, he didn't seem to mind.

"It is my honor to be useful to you, Lord Eochu," he said smoothly. "Odran, come!"

With a brief, apologetic look in my direction, the druid's son attended his father. My own went along without one backward glance, deep in conversation with Master Íobar. I remained on the bench where Father had left me, forgotten, dismissed, and made invisible by the power of two men talking. And so I learned that it doesn't require the spells of the Fair Folk to make a girl vanish.

The next morning I woke up to find Odran kneeling at my bedside. My eyes and mouth snapped wide open, but before I could make a sound, his hands clapped over my parted lips.

"Shhh. No one must discover me here," he whispered, moving his hand away.

"Did you need to tell *me* that?" I whispered back. "What's going on? Why are you in my room?"

"I wanted to let you know that I'm going to the crannog so that you wouldn't worry when you didn't see me today."

I sat up and held my blanket around me. "What about your father, your lessons? Now that he's back—"

"He's busy. The midwife arrived before dawn and was brought to Lady Cloithfinn before she even took off her cloak. Father heard the commotion and dashed out of our room to join her."

"That was good of him."

"Good to himself," Odran said with sarcasm a bard would envy. "He wants to be sure that she doesn't steal your father's gratitude from him. He'll also take credit for anything she accomplishes too, wait and see."

"Odran, I know things are bad between you and him, but how can you presume such things about your father?"

"He as good as said them himself. Last night, when we were in our room, he couldn't help reveling in how ready your father was to submit to him. He said, 'The High King rules Èriu, but only a druid has the power to rule the High King. Pay attention to how this plays out for us, boy, and you'll learn that a wise man can outsoar an eagle. Lord Eochu respects my skills, he fears my curses, and he loves his queen too dearly. That's a start.'" Odran's well-trained memory let him recite his father's speech precisely as he'd heard it, but he could not do it without distaste clinging to every word.

I was livid. "Did he actually— Of course he did. Why would you lie about it? I have to warn Father."

"Warn him about what? Something that hasn't happened and that you can't prove?"

"But if you could say—" I began, then bit it back. How could I ask Odran to betray his father, and for what gain? Master Íobar's aspirations were still vague, unknown. "Never mind. There's enough trouble under this roof right now. I can't burden Father with more, especially when it involves a master of the healing arts. My mother's recovery comes first."

"Just as well." Odran sighed. "No one wins a real challenge against my father."

"You did, when you got to keep Guennola and Muirín and—"

"I was lucky. He didn't think that was a battle worth fighting. I'd better go." He shifted his weight, preparing to rise. "The sun will be up soon and the creatures need me."

"Wait." I grabbed his wrist. "I have to stay, for Mother, but before you leave, take this." I groped along the floor beside my bed and handed him a scrap of leather. It was the hood I'd sewn for Ea.

Odran examined it as well as he could in the dimness of my chamber. "When did you do this?" he asked.

"Last night. I couldn't sleep at first, so I took a clay lamp and finished it. I didn't want Ea to spend another day with a bound wing. Use the pin to secure the hood around her neck. Tell her I'll be coming to see her soon."

"You've embroidered it." I wished Odran wouldn't speak of such a simple thing in such tones of awe.

"I told you, I couldn't sleep so I used the time to make it fancier than need be. My needlework's miserable, isn't it?"

He looked at me. "It's beautiful." He tried to clasp my hands, but all at once it became vital for me to hold my blanket tight around my body.

I turned my head away. "You should go."

He stood. "I'll be back this evening to tell you how Ea's getting on, and the others. I wish I could stay with you, help your mother somehow, but—"

"Every soul under this roof stands ready to look after her. Our animals have only you."

"They have *us,*" he corrected me. "I would let them fend for themselves for this one day and stay with you, but every moment counts. Autumn will soon be here and that's the season when the hedgehog has to make his den for the long sleep. I want him to be well and independent enough to do that before I have to leave for Tara. *All* of our creatures must be healed before I go."

Even you, my Ea, I thought. *But that's as it should be. There's no other way.*

"I wish you could stay at Cruachan, Odran," I said, trying and failing to keep the longing out of my voice. "I can look after the little ones on my own, and yet—" I silenced myself before I made things too awkward between us.

"They would be in good hands if they were in your sole care," he said quickly. "But I'd never want you to take on so much."

I was stung. "Don't you trust me?"

"With anything. It's not that. Maeve, it's a long road from here to the crannog. How can you travel it safely when the winter darkness comes? If you miss your path on the bog causeway—"

"If you stayed, we could travel there together," I muttered. "We can't hurry the healing of the otter, the squirrel, the hare. If we put them back into the wild before they're well, it's the same as letting them die. You *must* stay. I'll make it so. I'll speak with Father before he leaves for Tara and get his consent. But how can we persuade Master Íobar to delay your arrival at Avallach?"

"Maeve, I can't follow what you're saying," Odran protested.

"I'm thinking out loud, that's all, chasing ideas." I shrugged. "They might as well be butterflies, but I won't give up until I catch one."

Odran left, stealing from my room, the house, and the ringfort undetected. If our sentry spied his departure, there was no need to raise an alarm. Threats took the shape of men rushing *toward* Cruachan. A lone figure running *away* might rouse the watchman's curiosity at most, but the incident would be promptly forgotten.

I lay abed for some time after Odran's departure, thinking about what he'd told me. I couldn't warn Father about Master Íobar's ambition, but I could keep my own eyes open wide.

Resolved, I rose, dressed, and went straight to the doorway of my parents' sleeping chamber. The thick bull hide that curtained it didn't let any intelligible sounds escape, so I waited for Lady Íde to appear, or anyone else who could give me news. Some of Mother's ladies saw me lingering, and instead of lecturing me on the evils of eavesdropping, offered to bring me breakfast. They understood. I thanked them for their kindness, but said no.

My vigil broke when Father emerged from a different doorway. His anxiety for Mother and the baby had hardened into rage at the world. He looked ready to behead the first person who spoke to him. Our eyes met, but the only greeting he gave me was a terse, "Anything?" I shook my head. He muttered a curse, turned his back on me, and walked away.

I refused to be set aside and dogged him as he strode to the hearth. "Shall I go to her, Father? Is there something I can do? Is Lady Íde with her? Who else?"

He sat heavily on his bench and accepted the bread and butter and early apples our chief cook gave him. "If you don't stop battering my poor head, daughter, I'll cut the throat of one of your cows for every question you spit at me." He spoke with an awful calmness that convinced me this was no joke, but a true warning.

I sat next to him and folded my hands in my lap. "I want to know how she is this morning," I said evenly. "I want her to be well. I want to go to her, to see her, to help her. If there is anything I can do that will restore her—*anything*—I want to do it. Now you see, I haven't asked you one question, but if you insist on killing a thousand of my cows for each word I've just said, I'll hand you the knife myself."

A melancholy chuckle sounded deep in Father's chest. "Bold words for a girl who doesn't have a thousand cows. Anyway, you tell the truth. You asked no questions and so your herd is safe. How did I come by such a clever daughter? You get that trait from your mother. What did you get from me?"

"Impatience," I replied, trying to make him smile. "Father, you're the *king*. Why are you waiting for news to be brought to you? You should be in there, *taking* it."

"You and I are biding time out here for the same reason, my spark. We want to give the healers room to do their work, and we don't want to disturb your mother." He turned his gaze toward the hide-covered doorway of their sleeping chamber. "And maybe we're content to wait for word because we're both a bit afraid of what we might find on the other side of that curtain."

I leaned against him for comfort, but I think I gave more than I took. As I rested my head against his arm, I heard him murmur, "Oh my Cloithfinn, my beautiful girl, stay with us. I'll save you if I can. I'll go to Tara when Samhain comes and raise a barricade between the worlds with my body and my sword so that you and our child won't cross into the darkness."

I hugged him. "It will be all right, Father," I said softly.

He locked both arms around me. "It will."

There was no real news for us all day, aside from those few times when one of Mother's ladies tiptoed out of the sleeping chamber to reassure us that there'd been no changes for the worse. We had to be satisfied with that.

The midwife finally came forward with her report at dinnertime. Master Íobar escorted her from Mother's room to

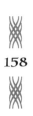

the hearth, where the household had gathered to take a somber meal. She was a fairly young woman, competent but not yet confident. From the way she kept darting timid glances at the druid, you could see that she was helplessly in awe of him. When she spoke, it sounded as if she were only voicing his words with his permission.

"All's well with the queen and the baby, Lord Eochu, but there's a chance this could happen again. I have good reason to believe she's carrying more than one child."

"Twins, my lord," Master Íobar said, neatly stealing the midwife's credit for bringing good news. "They're already acting like warriors, fighting for position. It's a great strain on Lady Cloithfinn, but with proper precautions—"

"She must rest completely, stay in bed until the birth," the midwife said, accidentally interrupting Master Íobar. He gave her a withering look.

"*As I was saying,* to safeguard the queen and the lives she carries, no one must disturb her, give her any cause for alarm, or trouble her in any way. Can you guarantee this, Lord Eochu?"

"With my life," Father said forcefully. "I'll see to it."

"So will I," I said, but no one heard me. The men were cheering for their king, and the women were heatedly reminding them to lower their voices and let the queen have her rest.

The young midwife left Cruachan the next morning, heaped with a fortune in gifts. She rode away in Father's best chariot. It was a great honor, but the poor woman looked as though she feared someone was going to ambush her and decree that she deserved none of it.

Once Mother's care became only a matter of keeping her

calm, clean, and well fed, Master Íobar and our druids left the maintenance work to the women. Lady Íde took charge of the rest. She had a pallet laid for her in Mother's room and ran the household from there, sharing some of her authority with the queen's most seasoned and trusted attendants. She never thought to call on me to help, and when I volunteered, she sent me off, saying, "There's nothing you need to do, Maeve. You have enough on your mind to occupy you."

Enough on my mind? Perhaps, but far from enough in my hands. Yes, I could have gone to the crannog, but in those first days of Mother's recovery, I couldn't bear to go so far from her bedside. Father and I visited her daily, though she was so weak and slept so much that we couldn't really keep her company.

One day, I found myself alone with her. Lady Íde had to give orders to our chief cook and none of her deputies was near enough to take over tending Mother. "I'll be back as soon as I can. She's sleeping, but if she wakes up, ask her if she wants to eat or drink. Here's water, and here's a platter of bread and meat. If you need me, stick your head out through the curtain and call. *Don't* leave the room."

"She speaks to me as if I'm three years old," I murmured, looking down at Mother's tranquil face. "But at least she's giving me something to do for you. I want to do more, but no one will let me." I tilted my head back and closed my eyes. "I'm so useless."

"Not to me." The words were little more than a whisper. My eyes snapped open and saw my mother's waking smile. Her too-white hand found mine. "You'll never be useless to me."

I took comfort from knowing Mother needed me, but if only Lady Íde shared her feelings! Mother's dearest friend had seen the birth of my sisters and me. Her love and devotion were absolute. She was an inextricable part of our lives.

All of which made her utterly certain that she knew what was best for us, and she was going to see to it that we agreed. For me, that meant being affectionately rebuffed every time I offered to do a woman's share of our household work while Mother recovered. How many times did I need to hear, "You're a good girl, Maeve, but no"?

I gave up. She won. But for once the loser in a challenge carried away the prize: the liberty to return daily to the crannog again was mine.

I did so with a clear conscience. Mother was getting better, and aside from our daily visits, what was there to keep me in the ringfort? The grown women of Cruachan were preoccupied, following Lady Íde's directives. As a result, teaching us girls about the loom and the needle, the spindle, the carding combs, and every aspect of feeding and managing a household fell by the wayside. The fosterlings soon learned that they could spend their days in gossip and flirtation as long as they disguised their lack of real employment with a hank of unspun wool or a piece of eternally unfinished embroidery.

I went where I could put my hands to better use. I scavenged for discarded scraps of leather and made them into a sleeve that would protect my arm from Ea's talons. My fingers grew astonishingly nimble at whisking off her hood, revealing those fiery eyes. I carried her out into the open, letting her see the shining blue realm awaiting her return.

"It's going to break my heart when you're set free," I told her. "I wish I could keep you forever, but"—I took a deep breath—"how can I do that and still claim I love you?"

Ea gazed at me steadily, and all at once I thought I saw something more than the familiar flash of flame in the depths of her eyes. Tentatively I raised my free hand and touched a fingertip to the feathers on her back. She made no move to warn me off. I stroked her head and she allowed it. The enchantment of that moment lingered over us until she declared *Enough!* by gaping her beak and stamping her feet on my leather sleeve.

I wanted to tell Odran all about the priceless gift I'd been given. He'd touched the little kestrel many times, but with the experienced, dispassionate hands of a trained healer. What had passed between Ea and me was more than that. He would understand.

I understood, too, that I couldn't speak to him about it until he was again free to visit the crannog. How could I flaunt my liberty in his face when he had so little? Master Íobar's delayed homecoming filled the druid with an obsessive drive to make up for lost time with his son's lessons. His zeal prevented Odran from visiting the crannog for four days in a row and now my friend was trying to catch up on the changes that had taken place in his absence.

"Maeve, you're a marvel," he said as he surveyed my work. "Are you sure there aren't three of you? You've done so much. The hedgehog's gone?" he asked, seeing the empty enclosure.

"I set him outside two days ago. Look!" I showed him my palms. "I picked him up without a single prickle."

"You're sure he was healthy enough to go?"

"No doubt about it. He let me carry him to the woods and took off the moment I set him down. Oh, that plump little body waddling away was the most adorable thing I ever saw!"

"You did very well." Odran sounded pleased. "Are any of the other animals ready to be released?"

"I'm not sure." My pride over having successfully returned the hedgehog to his natural place in the world gave way to apprehension. *He's talking about Ea.*

I was right. He was already heading for the kestrel's perch. Ea turned toward us at the sound of our approach. Even with her hood on, her sense of hearing was excellent. Odran ran his hands over the small, sleekly feathered body. "I can't feel any difference between her injured wing and the other one. We should take her out today and see—" He paused, surprised. "What's this?" His fingers touched a tightly braided strand of hair tied to the kestrel's right leg. "Is this yours?"

"Whose else would it be? It isn't doing her any harm and she doesn't mind that it's there," I said hotly. "She sat absolutely still when I put it on her. She didn't even try to peck at me."

"But why—"

I could have told him, *I don't know.* I could have said it was an impulse, but that wasn't true. The second day he'd been kept away from the crannog by his lessons, I'd examined Ea's wings myself. She had spread them wide and beat the air energetically as if to tell me, *See what I can do! See how strong I am!* And then, more cruelly, *See the proof that I'm ready to leave you forever.*

Yes, you will, I thought, burning her image into my memory so that none could take it away from me. *You'll be ready, even if I'll never be prepared for losing you. I have to let you go, except . . . except . . .*

That was when I used my knife to cut a long tress of my bright red hair, wove it into the thinnest of braids, and secured it tenderly to Ea.

"It's not to claim her," I said to Odran. "That would be wrong, impossible. She's not my property, but somehow, some different way, she's mine. I hoped . . ." Would my words sound foolish? "I hoped that if she wore it, she'd remember me." I looked into his eyes and silently pleaded for him to understand.

He nodded. "Then there's no question. It should stay."

That day I carried Ea to the lakeshore, removed her hood, and let her taste the air. Her wings ruffled in the wind. There was a short, firm pressure as her talons closed on my arm, then a sudden release as she threw herself into the sky. I watched her climb the clouds and hover against the blue. I was so entranced that I didn't feel the need to weep and I never felt the instant when Odran put his arm around my shoulders and held me close.

How long did the two of us stand there together, watching the kestrel's flight? How long did the beauty of those unbound wings divert me from the heart-piercing thought that I was never going to see her again? Time can hover too, suspend itself, hold its breath in the presence of magic. Devnet sang songs about how the mortals who did find entrance to the Otherworld believed they'd spent a single Samhain eve among the Fair Folk, but when they came out of the mound they discovered that a hundred Samhains had come and gone.

I spent the following day at home while Odran went to the crannog. I could have gone with him, but the previous evening Father had given me a mournful look and said, "It will soon be time to thin the herds for winter, Maeve. I wonder . . . would you care to come with me and tell me which ones you think should be culled?"

His invitation took me by surprise. The great responsibility of choosing which cows should be fed through the winter and which slaughtered for food wasn't something you shared with your "little girl," the daughter you saw as nothing more than some nobleman's marriage prize. Did he truly trust my judgment or was this another of his jests? Would he accept my choices or would he laugh and say, "Now let me show you how to do it the *right* way"?

Hear yourself! I thought. *You're seeing deception where there might be none. You'll know soon enough if he's playing with you. Give him a chance.*

"Thank you, Father," I said sincerely. "I'll try my best."

"Don't be modest. You've got your mother's eye for judging cattle. Didn't you choose my best bull for yourself when you were no more than an infant?"

"I think I was a *bit* older than that," I replied with a smile. "And even though I chose him, you didn't give him to me."

His weak smile answered mine. "You can't get milk from a bull, so it was no fit gift for an infant."

"Did you ever try?" I asked, and banished the last of his melancholy with laughter.

So I went with him to the fields early the next morning. We made the rounds in two chariots because I'd grown too big for his to carry us both and Fechin. Father considered it a shame for a warrior to guide his own team of horses unless an enemy's spear, sword, or slingstone had killed his driver.

At first it looked like he was going to go back on his offer. I stood in his shadow while he spoke with the cowherds, told them which animals to separate from the others, congratulated those whose careful husbandry showed in the health of their cattle, and berated those whose laziness had done harm. The sun was directly overhead when he looked at me and said, "Now it's your turn, Maeve." The rest of the day's decisions became mine. I'm sure that he wouldn't have hesitated to overrule me if I were about to make a gross error in judgment, but he never stepped in. My choices pleased him, and the trust he'd shown in my judgment pleased me.

As our chariots approached Cruachan on the homeward road, Father's came to an unexpected halt. He dismounted and strode back to mine.

"Let's walk together the rest of the way," he said.

He lifted me out of the chariot even though I could have done that for myself. We watched Fechin and my driver ride ahead and pass the ringfort gateway in the distance.

"What will people say when they see those two return without us?" I asked lightly.

"Hmm." Father pretended to ponder the matter seriously, then spoke in a womanish voice: "'Fechin, you scatterbrained lout, only you could misplace the High King of Èriu!'"

"*And* his beautiful daughter," I prompted.

"Does he think you're beautiful?"

"Who?"

"The druid's son. Your sweetheart."

I stopped walking. All the joy of sharing Father's work was gone. He was no longer treating me like a person whose opinions he respected. His teasing words turned me back into a girl like every other: all that I *must* want was marriage, all that I *must* care about until then was boys.

"Odran is *not* my sweetheart." I uttered the same denial that always came to my lips whenever my parents tried pushing me down the only path they saw for my future. The more they prodded, the deeper I dug in my heels.

This time, an errant thought came unbidden: *He's not? But wouldn't you like him to be?* I thrust it away, declaring, "He and I are friends, nothing more."

"What, girl! Would you prefer to be married to your enemy?" Father chuckled.

I decided to deflect his joke by pretending he'd spoken in earnest. "If I married Odran, I wouldn't need to look far for an enemy. His father would curse me from the top of my skull to the soles of my feet for keeping his son away from his studies."

"Master Íobar?" Father's mouth quirked. "Hardly that. What a prize it would be for him to become a High King's kinsman through his boy! The man isn't flesh and blood—he's ambition and pride."

"Why do you say that?" I asked. I knew I hadn't shared any of what Odran had told me.

"You might not understand this, not being a man, but when two warriors face one another, it's not just sword skill that decides the winner. The best fighters learn how to observe their enemies, know their moves before they make them." He made a wry face. "I wish they were all as easy to read as Master Íobar."

"I thought he wanted Odran to become a druid." I was confused but secretly delighted. Father was aware of Master Íobar's nature and no longer sounded like the chastened man who'd yielded to him so readily.

"He does, but he's the sort who eats from every dish. If he

could have a high-ranking druid for a son *and* royal blood ties *and* the generous dowry I'll give you, he'd still gnaw on his own sickle in an ugly temper because no one gave him wings!" He hugged me. "Never mind, my spark. I won't see you married to anyone but a king."

And all my elation was gone.

That evening, the chief cook gave us roast boar and Lady Íde served us good news. "Lady Cloithfinn wanted a second portion of meat, and after she devoured that, she did the same with a third!" She beamed. "The children she carries have fighting spirits that grow as fast as their bodies. Mark me, Lord Eochu, you'll have twin heroes on your hands!"

Father tried to reward Lady Íde with gold for her words but she refused, arguing that Mother's health was her reward. While the two of them were wrangling, Odran slid onto my bench.

"Maeve, will you come to the crannog tomorrow?" he asked in an undertone.

"I don't know if I will," I replied. "Father might want me to be with him."

"I understand, but"—his voice dropped even lower—"you *need* to come with me."

I asked him to give me a reason for it. He behaved as though I hadn't spoken, and I couldn't press him for an explanation without attracting unwanted attention from those near us at dinner. He remained stubbornly reticent when the two of us left Cruachan before dawn the next day. All the way through woodland and bog, he either chatted about trivial things or dropped into silence when I tried to make him give up his secret. Walled out by his silence, I imagined all sorts of dreadful, ghastly, tragic possibilities. By the time the crannog came into sight, rising from the mists of the lake, I couldn't stand to wait anymore.

I covered the last bit of distance at a run, with Odran at my heels, imploring me to stop. Curiosity sealed my ears. I struck thunder from the wooden walkway over the water and burst into the house.

Muirín yipped a greeting at the end of her tether. Guennola hissed and uttered sharp barks from inside her ring of thorns. The other animals made vague stirring noises or none at all. I looked all around but saw nothing out of the ordinary.

Odran caught up and took my hand. "You're worse than Muirín for running off," he said, breathless.

"And you should be ashamed of yourself, insisting that I come here but refusing to say why, making me worry, making me think you were holding on to some horrible mystery that—"

Kee-kee-kee! A kestrel's cry pierced the air. I gasped and let go of Odran's hand, pulled toward that sound as surely as if there were a rope around my waist.

She was there, on her old perch in the rear of the house. Her fiery eyes were hidden by the hood I'd made for her, but I knew her. Even if I hadn't seen the red braid tied to her leg, I would have known her, my Ea, my sweet bird, my precious one.

CHAPTER TEN

The King's Word

ODRAN TOLD ME all that he knew about Ea's return. "I went to draw water from the lake and when I came back, there she was, shifting from foot to foot on her old perch. It was as if she'd never left."

"There's nothing wrong with her, is there?" I asked, apprehensive.

"Nothing I can see or feel. She's fully recovered and she's been hunting successfully out there." He glanced at the squirrel's nest. "She came back fully fed. I found no evidence that she'd tried bothering that little fellow. I think he really does have a lucky talisman, though the gods alone know where he's keeping it." I giggled. "Of course I put the hood back on her right away. There's no sense in asking *too* much of a protective charm."

"She doesn't need food and she doesn't need care, and yet she still returned." I spoke in a voice made soft with awe, but my heart sang, *To me! She came back to* me! I wanted to dance. I wanted to weep for joy.

I controlled my impulses, refusing to look like a giddy child. "Maybe the braid I tied to her foot holds some of the Fair Folk's magic, a spell to bind her to this place," I said lightly.

"It was plaited from your hair, Maeve. Are you one of them in disguise? Let me see what you're hiding." For one amazing moment his hand cupped my chin. I lost the skill to breathe. "It could be true," he said, looking into my eyes as if searching for gateways to the Otherworld.

"Odran—"

His hand dropped abruptly. "Sorry," he said sheepishly. And before I could tell him that I wasn't sorry, he turned swiftly back to Ea. "If she's going to be free, then she's going to come flying in here whenever she likes. If she comes with an empty belly, that will put our smaller creatures in jeopardy. We can't bar her from this house, so what *can* we do?"

He'd gone from poetic to practical so fast that I saw no choice but to follow, reluctantly. "The otter's safe, and you can stop leaving Muirín and Guennola here alone. Isn't the hare too big to be Ea's prey?"

"The hare's size alone won't save her if any problem arises from her wound," Odran replied. "I've seen a nobleman's biggest, most formidable hunting dog stretched out helpless when a thorn in his paw caused a swelling."

A sick animal and a hungry raptor made a bad combination, and there was still the squirrel to worry about, to say nothing of any new creatures we might encounter who needed care. If Ea was going to come and go as she wished, we needed a plan.

In the end, I lit upon the answer: the squirrel and hare might panic if we put them under clay bowls like the hedgehog, but a large, sturdy basket, properly secured, would thwart Ea well enough.

"I'll bring a pair of them tomorrow, while you're at your lessons," I promised. "Meanwhile, we'll leave Ea here, properly hooded." I caressed her back. "You'll forgive me, won't you, my heart?" She snapped her beak at me petulantly.

Oh, what do you *have to be upset about, Ea?* I thought with an irrational flare of temper. *You can come and go at will, travel as far away as you please or stay here as long as you like. Odran will have to leave before winter, be hauled off to a place he doesn't want to go, and I . . . I don't want him to go either. But what can I do?*

In the moment before I pulled the hood over her head, I read the answer in my Ea's eyes: *When I want to fly, I don't wait for someone else to spread my wings.*

"Where were you today, my spark?" Father greeted me at dinner with a woeful look. "I thought you'd ride out with me again, but I couldn't find you."

I made some feeble excuse or other, all the while thinking, *This is the first time he's ever taken such a close interest in my whereabouts.*

Lady Íde was present, piling meat on a platter to bring to Mother. "Let the girl be, Lord Eochu." She spoke to Father with the easy familiarity born of her years-long standing as Mother's dearest friend. "Did you never find reasons to go roving when you were young?"

"Yes, but why can't my daughter do that with me?" he responded. "She was a great help when we were together

yesterday, and I hoped that was how she and I would pass the time before I leave for Tara."

"If that's what you want, Father, you've only got to ask," I said from my place. "It was my pleasure to help you with the cattle. What task do you have for me tomorrow?"

"Cattle?" one of our men called out cheerfully. "What did our princess do? Ride another bull?" Everyone guffawed.

Was I never going to live down that tale?

"I'm too old for childish escapades like that," I said demurely. "The king trusted me to choose the beasts we'll slaughter for winter. If he thinks I did that job well enough, I hope he'll give me new responsibilities."

The last time I saw a grown man give me such an incredulous look, it was just after I told Kelan I was going to become a boy. That same expression was now on the face of every one of the High King's warriors. Everyone knew how much our common comfort depended on thinning the herds wisely. If I'd had a hand in it this year, it changed the way they'd see me from now on.

And that was what I wanted.

"What are you mindless minnows gaping at?" Father bawled. "My daughter did a fine job! She's got a mind like her mother's, sharp enough to outthink ten ordinary girls!"

Our women and fosterlings grumbled until Devnet casually added, "Or twenty ordinary men." The only one who didn't laugh at that was Lady Íde, who scolded everyone for making too much noise and strode off to deliver Mother's meal.

Father stood up and called for attention. "Master Owain, Master Niall, attend me." As they came forward, I chanced to look at Master Íobar. He'd begun to rise as soon as he heard the

High King call the other druids' names, presuming his would follow. Now that he saw he was not included, he settled back as though he'd only moved in order to settle his bones more comfortably. The look he shot at Father was short but venomous.

"What may we do for you, Lord Eochu?" Master Niall asked.

"I want you to witness my words," Father replied. "I intend to have your princess accompany me as I continue seeing to our winter preparations. She'll share in everything I do, from surveying the harvest to inspecting the stores of food to hearing the complaints our people may bring to me before I leave for Tara."

Master Owain, the elder and more formal of the two, looked perturbed. "My lord, she's so young, and these responsibilities are so—"

"She won't be handling them alone," Father replied firmly. "She'll be by my side, learning. If she does well, she'll be worthy to take my place at Cruachan's Samhain rites while I fulfill my duties at Tara. I call on both of you to heed my wishes in this matter."

"Lord Eochu, you say *if* she does well . . . ," Master Owain said with an uncertain, sidelong glance at me. "Who will judge that?"

"I will, of course." Father's expression darkened, daring the druid to object.

I laid my hand on his arm. "Father, you have enough to do without measuring my work. Why not leave that to Master Owain or Master Niall? They can see the results and decide if I merit representing you." *And everyone else can see that I* earn *my honors,* I thought. *They're not just given to me because I'm your daughter.* "If they don't feel I'm trustworthy enough to stand with them, I'd rather stand aside. Too much is at stake for all Connacht, all Èriu, at Samhain."

"Is that what you want, my spark?" Father looked proud of me. I nodded.

"She does have Lady Cloithfinn's wisdom," Master Owain said, now regarding me with respect.

"And her beauty!" one of the men shouted. A chorus of agreement answered him. Father beamed, taking the compliment for his own.

"I wager she'll win this challenge," someone else called out. "Lady Maeve will prove herself and take Lord Eochu's part at Samhain. Who wants to bet against me?"

"Why bother, friend? You're such a luckless wretch you've got nothing left worth winning," a third man joked.

"Is that so?" Father was grinning. "I won't stand that. If any of you wish to wager, I'll give you the stakes for it here and now, in thanks for your courage and loyalty."

He proved his words on the spot by stripping every gold ornament from his body and clothing, except for the thick torque around his neck, a prize that was worthy of no one but a High King. He distributed these to his followers and called the trusted servant who guarded the royal treasures to bring more. No one was overlooked, whether or not they had said anything. Master Íobar's mouth stretched into a thready smile as he added a ring to the glittering adornments he already wore. A cloak pin rested in the palm of Odran's hand. He sat gazing at the king's gift, making no move to close his fingers over it, until his father snatched it from him with an impatient snort.

Devnet came forward and filled the hall with songs praising

Father's open-handed bounty. One of a king's highest virtues was his generosity to his followers, and it was a bard's task to make sure that everyone knew it. When he finished singing, he received Father's own drinking cup, the rim decorated with bands of silver and gold, in recompense.

The bard inclined his head. "Why do I bother singing about your liberality, Lord Eochu, when you give me something like this for my reward?"

"What's wrong with it, Devnet?" Father asked, struggling to keep himself from sounding too nervous. If a bard felt he'd been insulted or undervalued, he'd use his talents to satirize the man who'd offended him. A sword or a spear could take a king's life, but a bard's wicked way with words could make him look so ridiculous that no self-respecting warrior would serve him. "Is it not enough for you?"

"My lord, the trouble is that this gift is so rich it makes my praise of your generosity look poor by comparison." Devnet's eyes crinkled with good humor.

"Is that so?" Father laughed, relieved. "I'm afraid I can do nothing to amend that."

"Perhaps you can," the bard replied. "You know that I was born wandering. I love to travel, to wake up under new skies, to meet with my fellow bards and exchange songs, stories"—he winked—"and gossip. With your leave, I'd like to go journeying after I've attended you at Tara. Will you grant me that?"

My father turned to me. "What shall I say to this fellow, Maeve? Shall I let him leave us?"

"You should *make* him go, and do it now," I decreed. "Don't wait for Samhain. Such a cruel man shouldn't be allowed to linger at Cruachan."

"How am I cruel, my lady?" Devnet looked wounded, but it was as much a sham as the little game we now played.

"If you go on your way after Samhain, you leave this household without any songs to cheer us through the dark days until spring." The men of Cruachan applauded my pert answer. After their roar of approval diminished, I added, "What's more, you're doubly cruel, acting as though you need the king's permission to desert us. You're a free man, a free bard, and you have the freest tongue for empty courtesy that I ever heard." This time the cheers were so loud they made my ears throb. Even if everyone there knew that Devnet and I were merely joking, it wasn't every day that someone served a bard the same dish he set before others.

Devnet laid one hand over his heart. "I may be a free man, Princess, but from this day I am *your* man. Command me."

I stood up and climbed onto my bench so that no one in the hall could miss seeing me strike a haughty pose. "This is what I want from you, my bard: go with my blessing, return to my welcome, and bring me—bring all of us!—enough new songs to last us for all the winters to come!"

The bard made a graceful gesture of submission. "I swear it, my lady. Your wishes will be fulfilled."

"See that they are," I said crisply, with a dramatic toss of my head. The effect would have been magnificent except I followed it by catching the toe of my shoe on the hem of my dress and tumbling headfirst off the bench and into Devnet's arms. The assembled warriors howled and barked and bellowed in such a riot of hilarity that Father had to tell the servants *twice* to bring out more mead, enough for a victory feast.

As the silver-haired bard set me back on my feet, I gritted my teeth and whispered, "If you make a song about that misstep of mine, I will learn to drive a chariot just so I can run you down."

"My song will be silence, Princess," he assured me. "Out of respect for you and pity for your horses."

I enjoyed working at Father's side, even though it meant I wasn't entirely free to visit the crannog anymore. It was wonderfully satisfying to see the approval in his eyes whenever I assumed his duties and to hear him speak to me as one adult to another. And yet, on those days when he had tasks I couldn't share, I raced back to the crannog so fast that lightning would have lost the race to me.

Odran understood my situation. He always understood. We found ways to redivide our creatures' care so that one of us would always be there for them. When luck set us both at liberty, we went to the crannog together. Nothing let my spirit touch the sun as much as those few, precious days, not even when our druids told Father they'd be content to have me in his place at Samhain.

On such days, my favorite thing to do in Odran's company was unhood my Ea, send her off, and watch her flight.

"Look at her, Odran!" I cried, pointing across the lake to where Ea was an ever-shrinking shape against the clouds. "See how far she's going, and how high!"

"At least as high and far as she flew yesterday," he said. "Yet she always comes back."

"I hope she won't have a change of heart when winter comes," I said plaintively.

"She won't." Odran's arm slipped around my waist. "She always comes back to you."

His lips still held the taste of the bread I'd brought for us to share and hid a faint savor of sweetness. I was so startled by his kiss that though I kissed him back, I stood like a stone in his arms.

To my disappointment, he pulled away. "Are you mad at me, Maeve?" he asked.

I shook my head. "I liked it."

He looked relieved. "So did I, but . . . but you froze. I thought I'd scared you, or that I was doing it wrong, or that I should have asked your permission before—"

"I would've given it," I said, smiling. "But you'd better not try surprising any other girls like that," I joked, trying to gain a little time to catch my breath and let my racing heart slow a bit.

"No others," he said, so serious in that instant that he seemed much older. "You're the only one." He was about to gather me into his arms again, but I was quicker. Now I knew what I wanted, and I was the one who led the way. Oh, such a soaring feeling! So sweet, so free, and so wrapped in its own enchantment that we hovered in a moment outside of time.

When our lips parted, he sighed. "I wish that Avallach would sink into the sea. I wish that I could learn the Fair Folk's magic and find a way to change my father's mind. I wish"—he kissed me—"I wish this were my home. I wish— *Ow!* Muirín, you pest!"

I had to laugh. The jealous little fox had grown tired of being ignored and so she'd nipped his ankle. He dropped to one knee on the lakeshore to scratch her ears. She was always at his heels these days, refusing to be separated from him. I could understand the feeling. When he visited the crannog and tied her to a post so he could do his chores, she set up a wretched howl and would not stop unless he went back and took her with him.

"What were you about to wish for?" I asked as he scooped up the intrusive creature.

"That your father were mine. Lord Eochu loves you so dearly, I doubt he could deny you anything."

"Except the black bull."

"That was long ago. He treats you almost as an equal. Was it always that way between you?"

I thought hard about what Odran asked. I couldn't recall a time without my father's love, even if his protectiveness sometimes made me wish he loved me less and trusted me more. As a child, I'd been in awe of him. To my eyes, he was like the Fair Folk, more than human, capable of riding thunderclouds.

Things were different now. They'd changed since Mother's enforced retreat created an emptiness in his life that brief visits to her bedside failed to fill. I never knew how much he depended on her always being there for him until the lack of it beat him down the way no enemy's sword had ever done. My presence couldn't replace hers, but it could comfort him. He needed that comfort desperately. In the midst of a stronghold teeming with warriors, women, fosterlings, servants, people of every sort and temperament, he was lonely. That was why he sought me out and set me at his side, asking my opinions as a person, not as a girl-child. It was also why he looked so lost on days when I stole off to the crannog.

"He's always loved me, Odran," I replied. "Now he's finally beginning to value me."

"I could have taught him how to do that much sooner," Odran said. "Look at all time he wasted! Do you think he'd let me stay on as his teacher so he doesn't make more mistakes like that?"

"I wish he would."

But wishes aren't wings.

"Father?" I crept up behind him as he stood conferring with Fechin near the horse enclosure.

"Maeve, my spark!" His joy at seeing me was obvious. Fechin smiled as well. "I missed you today. Sneaking off to tryst with your sweetheart?"

I pretended to be cross, the way I always got whenever my parents teased me about boys, but I didn't waste a breath saying no about what I could no longer honestly deny. "Father, may I speak with you?"

"Why not?"

"Alone."

He consented. I took his hand and led him to a deserted space in the lee of the ringfort walls. He looked bemused but never uttered a word until I released my grip and said, "Father, if there were something that I needed, really *needed,* for my happiness and you had the power to give it to me, would you?"

That took him aback. "*There's* a question. Have I denied your wishes so often?"

"Please, I want your answer," I said stubbornly. "And if it's yes, then I want your sworn word that you'll—"

"That I'll what?" He cut me off. "Promise to grant you something without knowing what it is? My oath is the king's word. I don't give it lightly, not even to you, and I don't buy swords still in the sack."

"You make me sound sly as a Gaulish merchant." I was hurt but kept a proud face. "I only want you to swear to hear me out, to let me tell you what I want and *why*. Let me have my say—my full say, without interruption—as if I were someone whose words you trust."

Father ran his thumb over one side of his mustache, then the other. "I've asked your opinion about matters that are beyond an ordinary girl's understanding. I've told you how much I prize your insights. I've poured out gifts to celebrate the moment Master Owain took me aside to tell me that he and Master Niall are pleased to have you take my place here at Samhain. As High King, I must attend the rites at Tara. Any one of these things would be proof of how deeply I trust you. Why don't you trust *me* enough to say what you're after frankly, directly, without all this talk of oaths?"

I met his eyes and held them. "I want your word."

"Very well, you have it. What's so vital to your happiness that needs my oath to guarantee it a fair hearing?"

I breathed deeply and calmed myself. I didn't want to sound like a beggar or a spoiled, demanding child. "Let Odran stay."

Father's mouth fell open, but he remembered his promise and said nothing.

"Let Odran remain at Cruachan," I went on. "Not forever, just for a while. You're the High King. Master Íobar must consent if you tell him it will only delay Odran's trip to Avallach for a season. I swear to you by my head and my hand and my spirit, nothing in this world would bring me greater happiness.

You have the power to make it so." I fell silent, awaiting his reaction.

Father's expression was unreadable. "I always forget how old you are," he said. "I look at you and my memories show me a little girl, not a young woman in love."

"When did I say I loved him?" I exclaimed, hoping that if my cheeks turned pink, Father would think it was from the flush of temper. "Before everything else, he's my friend. We understand each other. Do you know how special something like that is to me?"

"Ah, your friend. I see. Your mother and I often spoke about how you never seemed to have any friends at all, except for Derbriu, so this is very good." Father smiled faintly. "And there's no need for me to share you with another just yet, so that's even better." He scratched the back of his head. "I'll see what I can do."

"Do you promise?" I had to be sure.

He kissed my brow. "You have the king's word."

He'd said, *I'll see what I can do.* My father was Lord Eochu, High King of Ériu. His enemies' heads framed our doorway. He led the greatest warriors in Connacht. His word commanded kings. What *couldn't* he do?

Master Íobar would give his consent at once. Odran would stay. I knew it must be so. I had the king's word.

I held on to that smug feeling for five days before it began to slip away. I didn't expect to be told that I'd gotten my wish immediately, but I did think I'd hear *something*. Five days, and not a hint about Odran's fate. Five days, and nothing to suggest that Father had succeeded, or that he was giving Master Íobar time to think it over, or even that he'd spoken to the druid at all.

To add to my uncertainty, Father no longer acted eager for my companionship. I didn't need to elude him in order to go to the crannog; he avoided me. Dinner was the one time of day we had to be in each other's company, but it was easy for him to keep me at arm's length then too. Once again Cruachan was besieged by highborn guests, the kings and warriors who were traveling to Tara. I couldn't object if he honored a different one every night by giving the guest my place beside him.

I only wish he hadn't also rewarded an additional pair of visitors with the two places flanking me. Odran's fate was on my mind, leaving me no patience for their tiresome flattery and flirtation. I forced myself to tolerate it anyway. If I gave our guests a curt answer or accidental insult, it would destroy the harmony of our home, buy trouble for the High King, and cause strife that would hurt Mother's condition.

I finally decided that if answers wouldn't come to me, I'd hunt them down. I sought Father out while he was overseeing the preservation of meat for the winter. He was so fanatical about deciding which of the newly slaughtered animals should be salted and which should be smoked that Mother used to poke fun at him for it, claiming he'd make a better cook than a king.

He didn't look happy to see me. "What brings you here, daughter?" he asked. "If you came to help, this is no task for you." He made a sweeping gesture, including the team of bare-chested men whose arms and torsos were spattered with blood from the carcasses they were shifting. "You might as well go back to the house."

Why is he trying so hard to send me away? "I will, as soon as I have your answer. You know what I mean."

His face closed and hardened. "We'll speak of it later. There's no time for that nonsense now."

Nonsense? "How much time does it take to say yes or no?"

He loosed a barking laugh. "Did you hear that, men?" he asked, turning to the workers. "Have any of you known a girl to be satisfied with yes or no? Even when they're told what they want to hear, they nag a man with 'What do you mean by yes?' and 'Are you sure you intended to say no? Tell me *why* and *how* you decided, and *who* swayed your mind, and if the moon weeps drops of cheese! Why don't you speak? I only want a *simple* answer.'" They all relished his shallow joke.

"Then why won't you give me one?" I said just loud enough for Father to hear. "I've already been given your promise."

Father's hand dropped onto my shoulder like a stone. Every hint of love had vanished from his eyes. "Go home, Maeve." He didn't raise his voice or tighten his fingers, but his entire being radiated threat. "Now."

I held myself steady, even when the pulse fluttering at the base of my throat was beating out a rapid *runrunrunrunRUN!* With a slight bob of my head, I walked off as slowly and serenely as I could. I would not let him know he'd made me so suddenly afraid.

The doorway to the great house was in sight when Father caught up to me. This time there was tenderness in the hand that clasped my arm and gently turned me around. "I'm sorry, child," he said. "I couldn't speak in front of those men about the business between us, and I do want to be frank with you."

"But you don't," I responded quietly. "Five days—no, now

it's *six* since you promised to speak with Master Íobar—and you've done everything you can to flee from me. Why, Father? Is it because he told you no?"

He nodded. "I didn't want to disappoint you, my spark."

He was hurting; I saw it in his face. I hugged him as hard as I could. "You can never do that, Father."

His arms closed around me. "Thank you for your faith, dear one. It warms me better than the sun."

"How can you disappoint me when this isn't over?" I said brightly. "Have you ever won a battle after only one spear-cast? Next time, tell Master Íobar you want him to stay as well, to hold a post of honor in the High King's household. He'd snap at *that* like a hungry salmon. Sweeten everything with gifts—gold, silver, cattle. I'll contribute half my herd if he'll—"

"Maeve, stop. There will be no second asking. Master Íobar has spoken. Odran will go to Avallach."

"Father, if you *tell* him—"

"I'm telling *you* now, let it drop! I can't stand against the will of a druid."

"But you're the king, king of Connacht, High King of Èriu!"

"And he is a man who can speak to the gods! He reads their desires and commands our sacrifices. If he turns his word against me, calls me accursed, it would give my enemies an excuse to rebel and attack. He could bring an end to everything I've built for us. Maeve, he has the power to curse us down to the marrow of our *children's* bones!"

He looked into my face and smiled sadly at what he saw there. "So. It seems that I can disappoint you after all."

I let Odran go alone to the crannog the next day. I'd looked forward to giving him good news, but now that I saw how matters stood between Father and Master Íobar, there was no chance of that. Failure felt raw and agonizing, like the mark of boiling water spilled over my skin.

I found three of Mother's ladies and two of the fosterlings weaving together and took a place among them. A servant fetched me a loom and one of the women guided my work as I sent the shuttle back and forth, creating a vivid checkered pattern on the cloth. When it was finished, she inspected it and was satisfied.

"You should apply yourself to such things more often, Lady Maeve. But I suppose that since you've been sharing Lord Eochu's tasks, you now think women's work is beneath you."

"With respect, I think that my idea of women's work isn't the same as yours." I took back my weaving and left.

I didn't dawdle in the great house. That was a good way to run into one of our visitors. I did *not* want to hear any more about how my hair shimmered, how my skin glowed, how my eyes shone, how my teeth sparkled. I'd be too tempted to ask my suitors if they wanted me for a wife or a torch.

I decided to pass what remained of the daylight revisiting one of my favorite places, under the streamside willow tree. It was beginning to lose its yellowing leaves, but there were still enough left to veil me from the outer world. I lay on my stomach, chin resting on my folded hands, and watched the play of light and shadow on the rushing water just beyond the curtain of trailing branches. The sound lulled me into peaceful slumber. In dreams, I stood with Odran on the shore of our lake, watching Ea soar and glide and hover, her tail dragging a rainbow out of the sun, her fiery eyes shining, growing larger and larger until they engulfed the stars.

I awoke and saw that the shadows had lengthened drastically. Rising to my feet, I shook dirt and dead leaves from my dress before heading homeward. As I passed through the ring-fort gateway and neared the great house, I heard a deep male voice behind me, calling my name. Master Íobar came striding toward me, a pair of dead waterfowl swinging by their necks from his hand.

"This is an unexpected pleasure, Princess," he said in a jolly tone that suited him like a cramped, ill-fitting shoe. "Odran and I have enjoyed the High King's hospitality all this time, but I've yet to have the chance to speak with his pretty daughter."

"That's my fault, Master Íobar," I responded carefully. Something about his uncommon friendliness set me on guard. "I didn't think you'd find my company worthwhile. What could I have to say to a man of your rank and wisdom?"

"Don't undervalue yourself, Lady Maeve. You and I should be able to find at least one subject that interests us both."

"Not hunting, I hope." I motioned at the ducks and made myself smile.

"Are you really so tenderhearted?" His grizzled eyebrows rose in mock surprise. "But I always see you eating your meat with a good appetite! Tsk. I was going to have the king's chief cook prepare one of these just for you, the other for your father, but if you won't enjoy it—"

"You misunderstand me," I said. "All I meant was that if you wanted to talk to me about hunting, I'd have nothing to say."

"Nor would I, or at least not much." He held the ducks

high, their orange feet dangling. "What is there to tell? I've been a good, quick shot with a sling since I was a boy. I saw these two down by the curve of the stream over there, where the big willow grows. I whipped a pair of stones at them, and here's your dinner."

"Thank you, Master Íobar." I shivered a little, knowing that he'd been so close to my hideaway. Either I was a deep sleeper or the druid had a born huntsman's undetectable footfall. "Shall we find the cook? I want to tell him to serve portions of the ducks to you and your son too. Father will insist on it. He'll say that the meat won't taste good unless the hunter has his reward."

"Your father is an eloquent man with a gift for saying what people want to hear." His teeth showed for an instant. "You can never go wrong praising a man's children. I was honored to hear he prizes my son's presence here so much, he hates to see him go. I can't remember the last time I was so pleased by a conversation."

Pleased . . . My eyes widened at the word. "If what Father told you—*asked* you—was so pleasant, why was your answer no? It was a simple request, even if it came from your king—let Odran stay here with us when you leave for Tara."

"Very simple. Except it didn't really come from the king, did it?" His clumsy attempt at coyness made me grit my teeth. He wanted to continue the game between us, but it was nothing like Devnet's easy banter. I tasted malice and I was done playing.

"If I had the authority to say who stays and goes inside Cruachan's walls, I would have spoken to you directly," I said reasonably. "But the High King's word rules all of us."

He looked disappointed that I hadn't reacted more sharply to his goading. "Tell me, Princess, did you ever stop to think how this 'simple' request of yours would destroy my son's future?"

"Master Íobar, Odran's future is as precious to me as my own. I don't want him to stay away from his studies forever, just for a season."

"I see. Would you care to tell me why?"

"I thought my father explained." I prayed that Master Íobar would admit that he already knew the reason for my request. I cringed at the prospect of revealing any part of my heart to this man.

"I want to hear it from you."

So there was no way around it. "Odran's my friend," I said. "I have no other. Think of what it will be like for me here after he leaves, when the days turn darker and the sun dies. Please, reconsider." I bent my head. "Please." It was his turn, make or break.

His chuckle was a slap across the face.

"Oh, Princess, aren't you ashamed to tell such lies?" Master Íobar's grin reminded me of the trophy heads of Father's enemies, displayed above our door. "Is it because you're afraid of angering me if you say what you really mean?"

"I've told you nothing but the truth!" I couldn't let him call me a liar and still stay calm. "If you're going to ridicule me for it, I wish I'd told you nothing at all."

My raised voice attracted the attention of the people coming and going by the great house. Some were honest enough to stare. Others instantly assumed looks of disinterest, which could only mean that they were paying very close attention to every word Master Íobar and I exchanged.

The druid didn't want an audience. "Lower your voice, girl," he growled. His false air of warmth was gone. This was the Master Íobar I knew.

I obeyed grudgingly. "Don't laugh at me, then. And don't accuse me of lying."

"It was my poor attempt at humor. I take no pleasure in seeing you sad."

"Is that why you rejected Father's request? To make me *happy*?" I muttered.

"Forgive me, Princess." His black, unfathomable eyes were momentarily hooded. "If I told the High King no, it was out of the selfish desire to see your face now when I tell you yes."

I should have gasped for joy. I should have heaped Master Íobar with thanks. I should have laughed and danced and seized his hands to try to make him dance with me. Instead, I could do nothing but stand where I was and stare, speechless.

My subdued reaction amused him. "Dumbstruck? That's natural. You'll rejoice well enough tonight when I announce my decision before all of the king's household." He glanced at the declining sun. "I'd better find the cook." He slung the dead ducks over his shoulder and added, "Don't worry, Princess. When you've had a few moments to yourself, you'll be able to believe your good fortune."

Maybe, I thought, watching him disappear into the great house. *But can I believe you?*

CHAPTER ELEVEN

The Druid's Power

I WENT TO my sleeping chamber to ponder Master Íobar's uncharacteristic generosity. He never struck me as the sort of person who'd give you your heart's desire without having his eye on getting something better in return. I remembered what Father had said about him: *"The man isn't flesh and blood—he's ambition and pride."*

But there must be more to him than that, I thought. *He raised a son who's gentle and kind, and did it alone. If he didn't love Odran, he wouldn't care so much about his future. Maybe he wouldn't be so harsh with his son if Odran's mother had lived to teach Master Íobar softer ways. She might have showed him to draw their child along the druid's path instead of shoving him along.*

I can't be too quick to judge him. I have to give Master Íobar a chance.

I arrived at the hearth as everyone was settling into their places. There was quite a crowd. The closer we came to the

Samhain leave-taking, the more of Èriu's highborn came to Cruachan to share at least one meal with their High King. I recognized some faces from previous visits, though others were new to me. Now if only one of them would come up with some new way to court me! I still wouldn't be interested, but at least it would be a nice change from hair-eyes-skin-teeth— Oh, how I love you and your dowry.

The air smelled of wood smoke and bore the delectable aroma of roasted venison in addition to the usual scent of the stewpot. I saw Odran seated by himself, with no sign of his father's presence. He waved for me to join him.

"How were they today?" I whispered as I sat beside him. He knew what I meant. "Tell me quickly, before Father sticks me between two of our guests."

"All of them are better than the last time I visited them. I think the otter might be ready for you to set her free tomorrow."

"Is she healthy enough to survive?"

"You'll examine her and decide. You don't know all my recipes for salves and medicines, but otherwise you're a capable healer." He grinned. "It's a shame I can't be there when you give the otter the good news."

My fingers brushed the back of his hand. "It must be a lucky time of year for otters," I said, playing with the meaning of his name. "You're going to have some good news yourself soon."

Master Íobar joined us before Odran could ask me the obvious question. The druid had decked himself out with so many pieces of gold and silver jewelry that the leaping firelight turned him into a pillar of glittering sparks. I glanced in Father's direction and saw him staring at Master Íobar warily.

Although we were hosting many nobles, we were merely having dinner, not a feast, not a celebration. This was not an occasion for displaying so much finery.

I stood up hastily to give Master Íobar my place beside his son.

"Stay where you are, Princess. You're so at ease, it would be a crime to disturb you," he said with the same unnaturally benevolent smile he'd worn when we'd spoken earlier.

Why does a little thing like that unnerve me? I chided myself.

"But I must go, Master Íobar," I replied. "Father will expect me to take my usual seat and entertain two of our guests."

"Not this night." The druid turned his eyes to Father and gestured at me, silently inquiring if the king approved. To my surprise, Father nodded, but he wasn't happy. His brooding look grew deeper when the nobles waiting for me to join them realized I would remain where I was. Their faces clouded and they began muttering to one another.

If Master Íobar noticed their discontent, he didn't seem to care. His cheerful gaze drifted over the hearth, the fretting cooks and bustling servants, and the platters that were being heaped with food. "My dear son, I don't see the special dish that I provided for Lady Maeve and her father. Find out what's become of it."

"Yes, sir." Odran went swiftly.

Master Íobar took his place at my side. "I hope the duck will be prepared to your liking. They're plump birds with plenty of meat on them. A fine roasted duck is one of my favorite dishes."

"Then you'll share mine," I said, encouraging myself to warm to him. *There's nothing wrong with his smile except disuse,* I thought. *He's not like Devnet, whose work is merriment. He's a high-ranking druid with many serious matters to concern him. No wonder that his face looks more natural in a frown!*

"How kind of you, Princess. However, I'll be seated with the king tonight and he is sure to offer me a portion of the duck I killed for him. Why don't you share yours with my son? I think he merits a treat for bringing me so much joy."

"He's done well with his lessons?"

The druid looked momentarily taken by surprise. "Mmmm, yes, that, of course. I've had your Master Owain and Master Niall examine him. My brethren tell me he has an intellect I can be proud of. They will continue his education after I leave him here."

"After I leave him here"! Hearing him repeat his new plans for Odran in front of an audience was even better than hearing them for the first time. With five words Master Íobar filled my heart with light and quashed all my misgivings about him.

Odran returned to say that the ducks were done to a crisp, delicious-looking brown and would be presented shortly. "The chief cook also bids me tell you that your instructions will be followed, Father," he added, looking somewhat puzzled.

"What instructions, Master Íobar?" I asked, itching with curiosity. It wasn't as if our chief cook needed to be told how to prepare a duck.

"Wait and see, Princess," he replied. I was starting to become accustomed to his strange smile. "We're all entitled to our secrets. I know you'll be happy when this one's revealed." He walked away to sit at Father's side. Every eye was on him. I heard two men near me speculate about why the druid was so gorgeously adorned.

"No one dresses up like that unless they want something," one muttered.

The second man grunted agreement. "Whenever I see my girl's wearing her best clothes and heaviest gold, I know I'm going to pay for it one way or the other. But that fellow's worse."

"True. When he's done up like that, I can't think of him as just a man. You can say no to a man."

"Thank the gods I've got nothing he could want."

"Not even that girl of yours?" They both guffawed.

The meal progressed. Plates were piled high with slices of venison. Bowls were filled with stew from the cauldrons. Chunks of honeycomb oozed liquid gold in the firelight. Mead and beer flowed. I heard Devnet pluck a few tentative notes from the strings of his harp, waiting for the right moment to begin his songs.

A servant brought me the duck Master Íobar had promised. The roasted skin gleamed with luscious fat, making my mouth water. I set my knife to carving it, offering the first piece to Odran.

He held up both hands. "No, no, you should taste it before I do. It's my father's gift to you. He'd slap the ears off my skull if he saw me accept that." He indicated the juicy, steaming leg I was trying to serve him.

"But I don't want to eat the whole thing by myself," I protested. "Master Íobar said he hoped we'd share this."

"Well . . ." Odran still looked dubious. "All right, but maybe I should wait until the king's been served."

"Wait? Doesn't he have—" I glanced to where Master Íobar was sitting with Father. The only foods before them were the usual fare. The second duck was nowhere to be seen.

"Oh no. Someone's made an awful mistake," I said for Odran's ears exclusively. "When there's a special dish, the king must have it before anyone else, and then it's his turn to offer some to his most honored guest. If Father sees that I've been given this"—I gestured at the duck with a sweep of its own roasted leg—"he'll punish the servant who brought it to me ahead of him, the one who failed to present the dish to him first, and the cook who neglected to give them the proper instructions!"

"Do you think the penalty will be severe?"

"Probably. Father's not a brute, but this is a matter of maintaining the king's dignity. If he lets one offense slip by without a strong rebuke, someone might take it as a sign that he's growing too weak to defend his rule as High King."

"This is why I'm glad I was never destined to become a warrior. They fight about the strangest things."

"I know." I thought of my friend Kelan and endured the painful memory of how he'd died in a quarrel over a piece of roasted boar. "I don't want anyone to suffer because of this stupid duck."

"How can we prevent it?"

I sought the answer frantically. Father and Master Íobar were deep in conversation. Neither one was looking in our direction. I'd have to act fast, before they did. For a moment, I wished I were gifted with the Fair Folk's magic so that I could cast a spell of concealment over the bird. Since that wasn't going to happen, I did the next best thing: I cast my skirt over it. Placing the platter on the floor, I lifted the hem of my dress and shoved the duck back between my feet, out of sight.

"Lady Maeve? Why did you do that?" The voice of one of

the men who'd been discussing Master Íobar's striking garb made me realize that my work had its witnesses, even if Father and the druid had seen nothing.

"It . . . I . . . You see . . ." I faltered over half a dozen explanations, none of which would have convinced a newborn hedgehog.

"The princess's action is a favor to my father," Odran said, giving the man a cool, challenging look worthy of Master Íobar himself. "Would you like me to tell him that you've taken an interest in his personal business?"

The man paled slightly. "No, no, never mind. I was just curious, but it doesn't concern me." He shifted his position so that his back was to us.

I leaned close to Odran. "Don't tell me you weren't born to be a warrior," I whispered. "You just faced down one of Father's best fighters, and you didn't even have to bare a blade."

"Who needs a blade? My father's a better weapon," Odran replied wryly. "He scares people."

"I've noticed." I was thinking about my own father and how Master Íobar terrified a man of so much strength and authority. Once again I saw his hangdog face and heard the shame in his voice as he told me, *"So. It seems that I can disappoint you after all."*

"It's because of his calling," Odran went on. "People revere the druids, but there's always a thread of fear running through their respect."

Master Íobar could scare people even if he were a cowherd, I thought. *Thank the gods our Master Owain and Master Niall are different.*

At that moment, I spied one of our head cook's assistants

approaching Father's bench carrying a large platter. I recognized the shape of a roasted bird and saw Master Íobar rise to meet the servant before she could set down her burden. It was obvious that the druid was going to turn a simple presentation of food into a striking event.

"Oh, good! The second duck's being served," I murmured. "Now we can eat ours." I bent over to drag it out from under my hem while Master Íobar motioned for silence in the great house.

"My lord Eochu, the goddess Áine's moon has changed faces many times since you first welcomed my son and me to Cruachan. May you be blessed for your hospitality. Truly your reputation for having an open hand is as well deserved as your fame in battle." He went on to enumerate all of the ways that Father had shown himself to be the perfect host as well as the perfect king. Íobar was eloquent, warm, and gracious.

His words were also as ever-flowing as a river. There seemed to be no end to them. While he spoke, no one moved. Who would dare risk insulting the druid by inattention? All other talk was suspended. Devnet set his harp aside. No cup was raised; no morsel of food was eaten. It was a good thing that the woman carrying the king's duck had muscular arms and stamina born of long days hauling cook pots and stirring cauldrons or she would have dropped it.

Odran slumped against me. "I'm starving," he whispered. Our duck lay in plain sight at my feet. He gazed at it with longing.

"Starving? Starving? How can you be starving, greedy guts?" I hissed back. "You ate enough of the venison to build a fawn in your stomach."

"But I haven't had any duck and I loooooove it," he said plaintively.

"Eat, then," I muttered. "Help yourself. Take that leg I cut for you."

"Yes, but if my father sees me eating while he's speaking—"

"Then he'll see me eating too, and serve him right for not telling us all to go on enjoying our food. We'd appreciate his speech much more if that were so." I stooped to pick up the duck leg, tore off a piece of the succulent flesh with my teeth, and chewed blissfully. Odran's eyes shone with envy, but he didn't stir to take a piece of duck for himself. It annoyed me beyond all reason.

Is he that frightened of Master Íobar? I thought peevishly. *And so is Father! Has either of them seen proof that he can cast a curse that* works? *They're men! They're supposed to be brave! Why do I have to show them how it's done?*

"Oh, here," I growled impatiently, and crammed a chunk of meat into Odran's mouth just as Master Íobar said:

". . . whose beautiful daughter, Lady Maeve, has shown me that the greater good for us all will not come from bringing my son to Avallach, but from leaving him to pursue his studies here. Lady Maeve, you have my thanks."

Everyone turned to look at me.

"Rrrrfff?" I responded, wide-eyed, my mouth full of roast duck, my greasy fingers caught between Odran's lips.

Feared as he was, Master Íobar was not feared enough to hold back the roar of laughter that now filled our hall. All he could do was wait for it to die away. Father tried to restore order but was hampered by the fact that he was hoarse from his

own loud mirth. The only three people who didn't join in the helpless glee were Master Íobar, Odran, and me.

"Did I hear right?" Odran asked. "Did he say I'm to stay?" I bobbed my head. "So that's what you meant about it being a lucky time for otters. You knew about this; you made it happen for me. Oh, Maeve!" He clutched my hand.

If I made it happen, I may have ruined it too, I thought. *What if Master Íobar believes these people are laughing at him, not me? If he changes his mind and takes Odran to Avallach to avenge the insult, I can't stop him, and Father . . . would Father even try?*

The last chuckles and titters in the great house faded, replaced by an uneasy silence. Unless I had no skill for reading faces, everyone I saw had realized that their outburst might have consequences if Master Íobar took it badly. Our mightiest warriors looked as nervous as boys caught stealing apples, our highborn guests shared their unease, and even Master Owain and Master Niall looked uncomfortable.

Only Devnet remained untroubled, smiling his drowsy smile.

Is Master Íobar so high-ranked or so formidable that even his fellow druids fear him? I wondered. *Which side would they take if it came down to Father's authority set against Master Íobar's? Would they stand with their king against his curses or hide in silence?* I didn't like the possibilities.

Father stood up, coughed a few times, and began to express his regret for what had happened, but Master Íobar would not let him apologize.

"It was my fault for interrupting Lady Maeve's dinner," he said, waving a hand so sparkling with rings it looked as though he were juggling live coals. "How happy I am to see her relishing my gift! Lord Eochu, you will pardon me for having seen to it that your lovely daughter was served ahead of you. It is my poor way of paying tribute to her countless merits. If I have offended you by doing this, name my penalty." The submissive words flowed from his tongue easily, but his eyes added, *If you dare.*

"Master Íobar, say no more about it. When you honor my daughter, you honor me," Father replied. He sounded relieved by the way matters had played out. "Now let's have some of this fine duck before it grows cold."

"As you say, Lord Eochu. I hope you will find it to your taste." Master Íobar motioned imperiously for the servant to set down the platter for Father. Was I the only one who disliked the way that the druid was giving orders to our people?

"The duck will taste better if you have the first portion, Master Íobar," Father said cordially. "It's good for friends and allies to eat from the same dish."

"It's better when husbands and wives do the same." The druid's smile stretched wide, and his glittering black eyes fastened onto Odran and me. Every gaze in the great house followed his. "Even if the marriage bond still lies in their future. See how prettily she feeds my son the best tidbits with her own hands. She makes no secret of her feelings for him. Be careful, Odran! You've been given a treasure. Every man here is jealous of you tonight."

Was there truth in the notion that the druids were masters of magic? Did they control the weather, the seasons, the fortunes of living things, and even time itself? I could believe it, for Master Íobar's words caused the flow of all actions around me to slow to a crawl. I watched Father's expression go through

painful changes from serenity to shock as the thing we'd once joked about became reality. I felt his astonishment spread out from him to encompass everyone there.

Our highborn guests, the men who'd seen me as their hero's portion, now sat glowering as Master Íobar whisked it from under their noses. Why didn't they speak out? Were they like Father, dreading his power too deeply? If so, that didn't keep them from muttering. My ears caught scraps of their outrage.

They loathed Master Íobar for his blatant ploy to advance himself through his son. With one breath they scorned Father for not destroying the presumptuous druid, yet with another they agreed that if Master Íobar intimidated the High King so badly, none of them would hazard challenging him. They called my father weak as self-righteously as if they didn't share his weakness.

They murmured, "If our king's that gutless, let the princess have the druid's boy and let that stripling have Connacht. Then let's see how long he holds on to what his father won for him. His head will fall to the first man who finds an excuse to challenge him. Maiden or widow, Lady Maeve will still be a sweet prize."

The rumble of their anger rose. I looked at Odran and saw him staring at his father, astounded by what that man had sprung upon us. His face was stiff and white with shock, only his lips trembling over what he didn't dare to say.

I dared.

I rose to my feet. "Odran is safe from any man's envy, Master Íobar. You have no worries. We are not betrothed."

My brashness caused a fresh stir. I had done what none of the grown men present had the nerve to do. Father looked ready to leap forward and rush me away, out of the hall, out of the house, out of the ringfort—to carry me as far as necessary to shield me from paying the cost of contradicting Master Íobar publicly.

The druid was unfazed. His benign look remained in place. "You're right, Princess," he said. "You and Odran are not formally pledged. Not yet, but we can seal the bond tomorrow and celebrate it properly the day after, before your father and I leave for Tara. Then he and I will have those happy memories to ease our journey."

"I'm sorry to deprive you of that pleasure." I held my ground, but inside I was shaking so badly I imagined I heard my bones clattering together. "There will be no bond and no betrothal. Odran and I will not marry."

What are you doing? a panicky voice shrieked through my mind. *Shut your stupid mouth before you lose everything. Let Master Íobar have this betrothal, if that's the price for keeping Odran here.*

That price is too high. I banished the idea of surrender. *Odran is dear to me*—the pulse at the base of my throat fluttered as I recalled how easy it was to lose myself when we kissed—*very dear, but that's why I can't let this happen. If we marry, if we're even betrothed, it will be an unforgettable insult to every warrior and king who ever saw himself as my husband. They'll kill Odran and rise up against Father, thinking he's too weak to be High King. Whether or not he wins against them, our people will suffer. I am Connacht's princess. I won't let that come to pass.*

So I held my ground, expecting an immediate attack from Master Íobar for what I'd said. It did not come. The druid's smile slipped just a bit, and that was all. His calm refusal to

speak gnawed at my nerves. Sweat trickled down my back and made my palms damp as I waited for him to end the heavy silence, the silence he used like a sword.

And then I heard a voice murmur from the crowd, "Our princess has a king's courage. I wouldn't be ashamed to follow such a one." I never did learn who spoke, but his admiration gave me strength to fight on.

"Master Íobar, please forgive the girl," Father broke in, distraught. "I've spoiled her. Turn your anger against me, if you must."

"Lord Eochu, my king, my friend, why are you so upset?" the druid replied mildly. "Did you think I was cursing this child?" His laughter was as believable as his smile. "I can't destroy your daughter with the same mouth that praises your generosity, or what sort of guest would I be?"

"I'm sorry." Father sounded as though he'd dragged himself away from a beating. "When you didn't say a word for so long, I feared—"

"I was gathering my thoughts, that's all. You must admit, Lady Maeve has a talent for knocking a man's legs out from under him, even when all she does is open her lips." He inclined his head to me slightly. "You will excuse me, Princess. I haven't much experience with the ways of young girls. I didn't expect to hear you reject my son so emphatically after the bold way you've been behaving with him."

My fists clenched. "What's so bold about sharing a special dish with an honored guest, Master Íobar?"

"I've heard others say that you two are sharing more than that. You and Odran have been noticed by many eyes, Princess, and many tongues find it amusing to chatter about you. They speak of those long, meaningful looks the two of you exchange when you think no one is watching. They snicker over how the pair of you vanished from this house from sunup to sundown every day that I was at Tailteann. What reason could you have for doing that if not to play lovers' games?"

"Dogs bark for the love of barking and rumormongers prattle to hear their tongues clack," I said. "You've been misled through no fault of your own."

"Have I? I don't hear you denying this gossip." He gave me a long, close stare, as if trying to drink all of my secrets through my eyes. "Come, child, admit how well you love—"

"I won't," I said firmly. "And I will not marry your son."

Master Íobar's calm expression cracked. He turned to Father, scowling. "So, the true ruler of Connacht has spoken," he said coldly.

"Pay her no mind," Father urged. "She's only being shy. She'll change her mind, I know it."

"Shy?" The druid's face went from anger to false pity. "My poor lord Eochu, now I see why you've failed to father a boy. The gods sent this girl to test you with her unnatural ways, her arrogant tongue, her impudence. Instead of ruling her, you've raised her too high, pretending her judgment is as good as a man's, and now she thinks she's entitled to assume a prince's role. If you can't govern a rebellious girl-child, you wouldn't know what to do with a son."

There was a disquieting murmur of speculation and agreement from certain visitors. I took special notice of them, especially one tall, wolf-snouted man who smirked at every barb Master Íobar shot at Father for having only daughters. *He'll bear watching,* I thought.

Father was desperate to placate the druid. "Master Íobar, I assure you, Maeve's betrothal is in *my* hands, now as always. If I say so, she will marry—"

"No. Not after the way she's humiliated my boy. Let some other man have her. No doubt she'll make the choice, and no doubt you'll give her what she demands of you."

This last remark went too far. Father's brow creased with indignation. He loomed up from his place and growled, "If I say my daughter will marry your son, then your son *will* marry my daughter. If I say the marriage will take place tomorrow, then you"—he jabbed a finger at the men around our hearth—"*all* of you will form a hunting party to supply the bridal feast. I rule this house. I rule Connacht. I rule Èriu!"

"You rule everything but your daughter," someone muttered.

Other voices joined the first. Some cried out against any man who spoke against the High King. Some snidely reminded anyone who'd listen about how Father had cringed before Master Íobar. Some called Lord Eochu a hero, others named him a weakling, but all the voices began to rise as warriors sprang to their feet. Insults were shouted, and the hearth fire in our midst burned cold compared to the flames of rage leaping around it.

In the middle of all this, I turned to Odran. He looked stricken, confused, and hurt. I wanted to speak with him, to share and heal his distress, but before I could say anything, I spied Lady Íde standing in the doorway to Mother's chamber. Her horrified expression yanked my mind away from Master Íobar, Father, and all the squabbling strife that wild ambition had provoked in our home.

Mother's hearing all of this! The realization hit me hard. *She'll want to know what's wrong. She'll try to find out. She'll leave her bed or fight the women keeping her there, and then—*

I didn't want to follow that thought to its end.

I pelted across the floor to where Devnet sat with his harp idle. Kneeling at his feet, I clutched his knees and implored, "Make them hear me, I beg of you! Silence them and summon their eyes!"

"At your command, Princess," he drawled, and took a deep breath.

The wild, skirling, eerie song that poured from the bard's lips was like none he'd ever sung before. It was not louder than the din stirred up in the great hall, but it was impossible to ignore. The melody was so enthralling that the words didn't matter. Every other voice dwindled and died before that insistent, wailing music.

Devnet's song ceased. The hall was utterly still and everyone was looking at us. The bard winked at me as if to say, *There. Just as you requested.*

I stepped into the silence with my arms flung wide. "Thank you, noble guests," I said. "Thank you for your kindness, for remembering that Lady Cloithfinn must have peace. My father often says how much he prizes all of you for your wisdom and goodwill, as well as your swords and spears."

I turned to address Father: "Lord Eochu, High King, how could anyone imagine I'd defy you? If it sounded that way, I apologize. And Master Íobar, I know how much reverence I owe you. When I said I wouldn't marry your son, I spoke as the princess of Connacht. I have a duty to my people that comes

ahead of my own desires. For their sake, the man I marry must be strong enough to protect this land. He must command champions."

A ripple of approval passed through the hall. The kings and warriors we hosted were pleased with what I'd said. I saw admiration in their eyes, even if some gave it grudgingly. I went on:

"Odran is destined for the druid's path. You said so yourself, Master Íobar, unless"—I gave him a hopeful look—"you've changed your mind?" I got no response to that except the glint of stony eyes. I'd expected as much and shrugged it aside. "With your permission, Odran could stay here to begin a warrior's training. Without those skills, how could he protect the herds and lands and treasures of Connacht, or even himself? The greatest druid's word is not enough to stop a spear or turn aside a sword, but I'm sure that someone as wise as you knows this."

I moved quickly and seized Master Íobar's hands so that he couldn't withdraw them without looking churlish. "You heard the rumors about your son and me and thought it would be a blessing if we could be together always. I'll never be able to thank you properly for your unselfish wish to please us, but by now you must see why it's impossible."

"I do see, Lady Maeve." Master Íobar pursed his lips. "I see clearly." He twisted his hands free slowly, so that no one would be able to accuse him of rudeness, and turned to Father. "My son isn't good enough for this princess of yours."

"I didn't say—" I tried to protest.

"I ask all of you to excuse me for disturbing the peace of

your house." He strode from the hearth to his sleeping chamber, ignoring Father's repeated appeals that he return.

"Odran, lad," Father said urgently. "Go to your father. See if you can fetch him."

"I'll go to him as you bid, Lord Eochu," Odran replied. "With your permission—" He glanced at me for the time it takes to blink before following his father into seclusion. Neither one came back.

The next morning there was an edginess to the atmosphere in the great house. People walked with a light, timid tread and it seemed like we were all holding our breath. No one passed the doorway to Master Íobar's room without giving it an anxious sideways look, the way you'd regard a cave mouth where a monster of the Otherworld might be lurking, ready to spring out and devour you.

The tension broke when the druid and his son emerged, Odran sullen, his father serene. One of our servants sprinted out of the house as soon as they sat down to have some breakfast. The purpose of his hasty exit became clear when he came back at the High King's heels. Father must have given orders to be notified as soon as Master Íobar showed himself.

The druid greeted Father cordially. His every word and tone were soothing and kind. Father accepted this renewed friendliness warily. I watched it all from out of sight, having tucked myself behind one of the massive pillars supporting our roof. Master Íobar would be accompanying the High King on the long journey to Tara, so it was to his advantage to pretend there were no hard feelings between them, but I was sure it would be a different story if the druid saw me. I didn't intend

to linger. I'd stay just long enough to determine that Father was safe from retaliation for what I'd said last night, then sneak away to tend the creatures on the crannog.

"Well, look who's there! Won't you share our company this morning, Lady Maeve?"

Apparently I wasn't as stealthy as I fancied myself, or else Master Íobar was genuinely gifted with a natural hunter's eye. I stepped out of my insufficient hiding place and joined them. Keeping my gaze downcast, I murmured the hope that everyone had slept well. Odran's voice was conspicuously absent from the polite replies. I was not the only one who noticed this.

"Odran, the princess asked you a question." Master Íobar spoke severely to his son. "Didn't I teach you courtesy?"

His reprimand forced a response. "I slept well," Odran said without emotion. "Thank you."

Master Íobar chuckled and looked at Father. "Children! These two are still nothing but sulky, stubborn children. What was I thinking, picturing them betrothed? Odran, I have to go with Lord Eochu to discuss a few things about our forthcoming journey. We'll have your lessons after that, so don't go wandering off for the day."

"You needn't worry," Odran replied.

"That's a good boy." Master Íobar and Father walked out of the great house together.

Odran ate a last bite of cheese, wiped his mouth, and only then looked up at me. "What are you waiting for?" he asked. "You have somewhere to go, don't you? The animals will want to be fed."

"Come with me," I said in a tight, strained voice. "I want to explain and I can't do it here, surrounded by all these tattlers."

"Don't bother." He got up. "I have to find meat for Muirín and Guennola. I want them to fatten up before we go. Their appetites always suffer on journeys."

He tried to get by me, but I took his hand and held fast. "Odran, if you won't come with me to hear what I've got to say, do it for the creatures. I need you to show me what to do for them after . . . after . . ." I couldn't say it. *After you're gone* sounded too final, as if his soul were sailing to Tech Duinn, the land of the dead.

His eyes fell to our clasped hands. "Are you forgetting so soon about what the gossips might say?" he asked, withdrawing his fingers. "You won't have to worry about the animals. They're all just about ready to be set free. You might even be able to release the squirrel today."

"I'm not certain he's fully healed. He seemed listless." I sounded miserable, but I couldn't help it. Odran's coldness was too much to bear. *Why won't you let me explain? How can you close your heart to me?*

"If you don't trust your own judgment, I'll go tomorrow— by myself—to check him and the others. I might even let them all go."

"Just like that? What if—"

"I'd never send them away if they weren't fully healed, if that's what you're thinking. Why would I? So you couldn't have them? To punish you for how you hurt me?" His words were bitter and his face became alarmingly like his father's when he said, "I wouldn't put something I love at risk over something as unimportant as you."

CHAPTER TWELVE

The Cost of Truth

I DIDN'T CRY—not while he stood there, throwing such cutting words in my face, not when he strode away from me, not afterward, when I was alone, never. I didn't shed a single tear. Odran's harshness was too vicious to be real, too vindictive to have come from the boy I knew, whose kisses were so tender. It left me too shocked to weep. Like one of the creatures in our care, he'd been injured and was snapping at any hand that came too near, especially the one that had wounded him.

I spent the day at the crannog, letting the placid spell of the isolated lake work its soothing magic on me. I tried and failed to burn away the ache inside by sinking myself in the fire of my Ea's eyes. I tried and failed to conjure a bit of healing laughter from the antics of the squirrel and the otter's comical face. My hands were busy, laboring over things like feeding the creatures and cleaning the messes they'd made. While I had that sort of work to do, my mind tumbled into a kind of slumber. It awoke only when it was time for me to examine the animals to see how they were healing.

Odran was right: the squirrel looked ready to resume his old life. I thought about letting him go, but a glance at Ea's empty perch made me reconsider. Now she was sailing the sky, out of sight but probably nearby, on the hunt.

"I'm sorry, little one," I told the squirrel. "I think you're well enough to go, but if you're still weak, you might turn into easy prey for Ea. I'd rest easier if Odran were the one to say you're fit." The squirrel fluffed his tail and chattered at me furiously, his tufted red ears twitching. At last I laughed. "Stop scolding me, you impatient thing! He'll be here tomorrow. One more day won't make a difference." I gave him a handful of the acorns I'd gathered on my way to the crannog and he was placated. "I'll miss you," I whispered.

That night after dinner I tried to tell Odran about how matters stood with the animals. He interrupted me with a terse, "I'll see for myself," and ducked into his room.

I went to my own room and got into bed, but I couldn't sleep. *Tomorrow is his last day here,* I thought, staring up into the darkness. *He'll leave hating me. Worse than that, he'll leave thinking I hate him.* I squeezed my eyes shut. *He's got to hear my reasons. If he still hates me after that, so be it. But I have to try.*

The sun rose through heavy fog the next day and never quite found the strength to burn through. Wrapped in my wolf-collared cloak, I moved through the mist along a well-known path, intent on my purpose. The earthy smells of autumn rose out of the damp earth and the fallen leaves, and a hint of wood smoke came from a distant hearth.

The fire in our own hearth was still banked when I left

the great house. I'd gotten up before any of the servants, wanting to reach the crannog ahead of Odran so I could be waiting for him with all I needed to say carefully arranged in my mind. I had paused outside his room, listening for the heavy breath of sleepers, but the bull's hide hanging in the doorway thwarted me.

Now I walked as briskly as the mist allowed, my eyes fixed on where I was going. Familiar or not, a path veiled by fog could disappear if you didn't take heed of every step, and when that path crossed a bog, losing your way meant losing your life. One blunder off the boards, one tumble into the muck, and you'd sink from sight forever.

I gave a huge gasp of relief after I left the bog behind, cut through the pine forest, and reached the lakeshore. The mist still hung over everything, thickly blanketing the water and sucking up the sound of my footsteps as I crossed the raised wooden walkway.

A small light was burning inside the round house, the simple clay lamp Odran used to help him examine our creatures. He'd come there ahead of me after all. I entered without announcing myself. He was kneeling beside the otter when I came in. Guennola was nowhere to be seen, but Muirín was hiding behind Odran and stealing peeks at the otter every few moments. When the little fox caught my scent, she perked her ears forward and yipped, her face one big grin.

Odran's reaction was not so welcoming. "What are you doing here?"

"I have to speak with you."

"Well, I don't have to listen." He stood up and brushed off his hands. "You can release the otter tomorrow. The hare may take another day or two—she's making a funny noise when she breathes—but the squirrel is ready today. I was going to set him free after I gave the place one last cleaning, but since you're here, you can handle that. Goodbye." He turned his back on me, heading for Guennola's enclosure.

I ran after him, grabbed his shoulder, and spun him around to face me. My fingers dug into his arms and I brought my face so close to his that our noses touched. "You *will* hear me. It won't take long. I won't cry. I won't beg. But I swear by my head that I *will not* let you leave this house until you let me say my piece."

"Do you think I'm *good enough* to hear a princess's words?" He flung his enlaced hands straight up within the circle of my arms and threw them wide apart, breaking my hold. When I tried to seize him again, he thrust one hand at my chest, sending me reeling backward until I lost my balance and fell on my rump. "Give orders to your servants."

I scrambled to my feet and dashed past him into the back of the house. Guennola was halfway out of her upside-down clay bowl when I pounced on it and cast it aside so recklessly that it shattered against a post. When I scooped her up, the stoat screeched a loud objection, biting the hand that held her close. I cried out in pain.

"What do you think you're doing?" Odran yelled. "Let her go!"

"Not until you listen to me." I'd sworn not to weep, but I couldn't control the tears that flowed as Guennola's teeth pierced my flesh.

"This is stupid! She'll tear your hand to tatters." He made a grab for her.

I wheeled sharply, blocking him with my shoulder. "If that's what it takes."

He rolled his eyes. "Fine. I surrender. Give her here and I'll listen to you, I promise."

That was good enough for me. I handed over the stoat and cradled my injured hand. There was a lot of blood; it made me queasy to look at it.

"The gods spare us, your face is white!" The anger was gone from Odran's voice. He set Guennola on his shoulder and put his arm around me, gently bringing us to where we kept the healing supplies. As he soaked and salved and bandaged my hand, I spoke:

"I had to say no, Odran, and not because you're 'unworthy' or anything else your father might have said. He was so blindly bound to the idea of our betrothal, he didn't see how many lives it would cost, including yours."

I told him everything I'd realized last night, helping him to see and hear it all through my eyes, my ears. I made him understand that when I'd said I had to wed a warrior, whether or not he was a king, it was a hard truth. He saw that my refusal was not a slap in the face, a declaration that he wasn't fit to win a princess. It was a decision that I'd had to make for the good of my family, my people—

"My love."

Odran kissed me. He moved so desperately fast that our teeth collided and my mouth was crushed. We both uttered a muffled "Ow!" but our lips didn't part. I thought I was going to die for lack of breath and I didn't care. This was the reality his father would never see through the smoke of his ambitious plans. This was all I longed for and knew I couldn't have without endangering a life as precious to me as my own. Even so, I yearned for him all the more and held him fast.

He ended it before I did, stepping back but still clasping my hands. His face was burning. "I don't want to leave you, Maeve."

"And I don't want you to go." I tightened my grip on his fingers. "We can't let that happen."

"It *is* happening. It's happening tomorrow."

"But not today. We have time. There must be a way to keep you here and safe and prevent my father's enemies from using your presence as an excuse to turn against him. We have to think. We have to try."

Why wasn't the crannog one of the mounds that sheltered a gateway to the Fair Folk's realm? Why couldn't we enter a world where each day lasted for a hundred years? We couldn't concentrate on crafting plans that might or might not work. We could only think *Tomorrow!* and cling to one another for consolation, warming the racing moments with our kisses.

We were still in each other's arms when Ea came flying into the crannog, alighting neatly on her perch.

"Hello, beauty," I said, happy to see her. "Be a good girl while I get your hood." Odran grumped when I left his embrace to look after the kestrel. "Shame on you," I told him, smiling. "You know I have to do this before she takes an interest in the other creatures." As I searched for Ea's hood, I said, "I have an idea: What if you told our fathers that you want to become a warrior? You could say you were going to keep your training secret, to fool any envious rivals who might harm you."

"Oh, *that* would work," Odran said with an ironic twist to his lips. "We'd just need to deal with a few details, like how I could learn weaponry in secret—"

"It's been done," I murmured.

"And how I'd live to take my first lesson before my father wrings my neck!"

"He won't do that," I replied confidently. "Not if he smells a second chance at getting what he's always wanted. It *will* work, Odran. Our fathers will consent to this—you'll see. And once Master Íobar leaves you behind, we'll be free to come here whenever we like. Do you think we'll find any new animals to tend when winter comes?"

"I hope not," Odran said sincerely.

"Me neither—I'd rather none were sick or injured—but isn't it a good thing to know we'll both still be here to help *if* we're needed?"

"Speak for yourself, Princess." Master Íobar stood framed in the misty doorway, a gnarled blackthorn staff in his hand. "My son will go with me."

"Master Íobar!" I exclaimed. All thought of finding Ea's hood vanished. "But there's no need for that. Odran and I . . . we . . . we've agreed to a betrothal after all." I was so rattled by his abrupt appearance that I spouted the first stupid thing that came to mind.

"Have you?" He entered the round house and approached us. He was wearing the same rough garb as when I'd met him coming home from the hunt. "Then that makes my morning walk through bog and forest well worthwhile. Imagine my joy at this news." I had to imagine it; there was no trace of pleasure

in his voice. "Shall we go back to give the High King his portion of happiness?"

"Yes, of course, we'll come with you as soon as—"

"Take your time. I can wait." The druid looked around
him, scrutinizing everything. "So, Odran, is this where you
come when you're nowhere else to be found? Is all that I see
here the lure that takes you from your lessons?" He cast a
hooded glance at Muirín, who was sitting near Odran's
feet. The vixen regarded him in her playful way, impudent
and bold.

The blackthorn stick lashed down. There was a sickening
sound of impact, an agonized yelp, and Muirín lay stretched
dead on the floor. I was still frozen by the horror of that small,
broken body when Master Íobar strode to where the hare
crouched, trembling, and destroyed her too. His cold eyes
swerved to the otter.

"Father, no!" Odran reached the beast before Master Íobar
could do so, shielding her with his own body. Hugging her
close, keeping his head down, he bolted for the doorway.

His father paused only for a moment, sweeping the house
for closer victims for his rage. He saw the squirrel's nest, but
not before I leaped to release the innocent little animal. As the
panic-stricken creature zigzagged wildly, dodging the druid's
blows, Ea set up a shrill cry, flapping her wings and launching
herself for the opening in the roof.

Cursing the squirrel's lifesaving nimbleness, Master Íobar
gave up trying to murder him and went after Odran. I chased
them both, yelling, "Stop! Stop! Don't do this!" I might as well
have tried to ward off a thunderbolt with a whisper.

Outside, the mist was lifting. Odran stood knee-deep in the water, watching the otter swim away. He turned a triumphant face to his father, but his moment of victory ended abruptly. Master Íobar grabbed a lakeshore stone, fitted it to his sling, and sent it whistling through the air. I heard a muffled thump as it struck its target and the lovely, graceful swimmer sank without a sound. Odran's wail of anguish would echo through my memory for days.

It wasn't over. Master Íobar caught sight of Ea and picked up another rock.

"Let her alone!" I shouted, holding my skirt high, running as fast as I could, launching myself at him and pounding on his back with my fists just as he whipped the sling forward and shot the stone over the water, through the sky, to where a frightened kestrel flew far, but not far enough.

I didn't hear the blow that struck her, but I saw her fall. I spun away from the druid, buried my face in my hands, and howled, refusing to witness her death. I shrieked and grieved until a hard slap across my face stunned me out of my unreasoning misery.

"Shut your mouth, you stupid girl," Master Íobar ordered, his hand raised to strike again. "It's only an animal."

"Wh-why?" I asked. "Why did you need to do that? They were harmless creatures!"

"He did it to punish us." Odran came to stand with me. His voice was as dead as the victims of Master Íobar's slaughter.

"For *what*?" I glared at Odran's father through my tears. "Didn't you hear what I told you? You were going to get what you wanted!"

"I heard many things." There wasn't a glimmer of remorse in Master Íobar's face. He was a man proud of a job well done.

"Eavesdropping," Odran said. "How long did you tarry outside the house before you showed yourself, Father? You should be ashamed!"

Master Íobar seized Odran's arm, yanked him away from me, and struck him so hard that he stumbled backward into the lake with a huge splash. "*Never* raise your voice to me," the druid gritted. "You're a young fool, drunk on your own desires. This girl has stolen your senses worse than the strongest mead. You've already forgotten how she rejected you yesterday and humiliated me before all of the High King's men. I tell you, she'll do the same to you again, on a whim. Today she fancies you, tomorrow she'll be done with you, and you're hollow-headed enough to eat that shame with a smile as long as it comes sweetened with her kisses. I thank the gods I'm here to save you from your own folly. Now get up. We're going."

Odran pushed himself out of the water. He was shivering, but I couldn't tell whether it was from a chill or from holding in his rage. His father seemed indifferent to the harm that might come to his son's health if he trudged back to Cruachan dripping wet in such weather. I flew to Odran and tossed my cloak over his shoulders. The autumn air was cold and the homeward road long, but I could endure it for his sake.

"Go with him," I whispered.

"What about you?"

"I'll come later. I know the path. I don't want to be near him."

"I'll stay too."

Odran's offer was bold but futile. His father lost patience

and grabbed him by the nape of his neck, like a puppy. Master Íobar was no longer young, but he had a fearsome strength. He dragged Odran away, pausing only to give me a backward glance and ask, "What are *you* waiting for?"

"For you to get out of my sight," I spat.

He smirked. "As you wish, Princess."

I waited until I could no longer see them or hear the sound of their retreating footsteps. Then I went back to the crannog to bury the dead.

It was hard labor. I had no practical tool for the job and had to dig a burial pit for Muirín and the hare using only a sharp stick. It was a mercy that the lakeshore soil was soft; I don't know how I would have made any progress with an injured hand. When I had their resting place ready, I considered seeking the otter's body but decided it would be a pointless gesture. She'd loved the water and now the water cradled her in the long sleep.

When I was done, I washed my hands and went back into the house. Ea's hood was there, the only token I'd ever have of her existence. I couldn't leave without it. As I searched the floor on hands and knees, I heard a faint sound and found myself staring at Guennola. Like the squirrel, Odran's pet stoat had escaped Master Íobar's rampage by agility coupled with luck.

"It pays to be small, doesn't it, Guennola?" I murmured. "He overlooked you." I held out my unbandaged hand to her. "And I overlooked him. He must have trailed me here. I should have been watching my back, but my mind was on Odran, and now I've lost him. It's my fault Muirín's dead, and my Ea, and the others."

The stoat didn't move or look away but kept her distance.

She didn't even hiss at me. It was like facing a creature carved of stone. The poor beast was probably fear-frozen, though in my state of mind I took her behavior as a silent accusation.

"I'm sorry," I said, my voice rasping. "We've both lost everything. I can't give you back to Odran. His father will kill you. Will you be mine instead? I promise I'll protect you. I'll take good care of—"

With a twist of her lithe body and a flick of her black-tipped tail, Guennola flashed past me and out of the round house. I was left alone in the haunted shadows.

I found Ea's hood and walked away from the crannog, hunching my shoulders against the deepening chill in the air. My flesh was cold, but inside I was burning with indignation and sorrow. Four small lives were gone, blotted out for no good reason. I would not let this crime go undiscovered and unpunished. I would demand justice.

Chapter Thirteen

The Bitter and the Sweet

"Nothing?" I cried, looking at Father in disbelief. "You'll do nothing about this? Not even reprimand him for what he did?"

We stood beside the king's chariot, which Fechin was inspecting before the next day's departure for Tara. The poor driver looked as if he were praying for the earth to swallow him whole. He'd tried to excuse himself when I first appeared and began pouring out the story of Master Íobar's atrocity, but Father ordered him to get on with his work. Now he was a captive of our confrontation.

"You heard me, Maeve," Father replied levelly. "I'll do nothing because there's no need for anything to be done, unless you want me to scold every hunter in our household. Master Íobar committed no crime. Those were all wild animals—foxes, otters, the rest—and he must have had a good reason for what he did. Even the smallest beasts can be dangerous.

Are you going to claim that hand of yours is bandaged because Master Íobar bit you?"

"Muirín wasn't wild," I protested. "She was Odran's pet, tame as any of your hounds or horses."

"All foxes are wild, and my hounds and horses earn their food. If the fox belonged to Odran, let him settle this with his father."

"Is that how you see it? Then I was wrong to come to you at all. If I want justice, I'll have to get it myself." I began to walk away.

"Come back here!" Father's roar at my back made me shrink inwardly, but I kept walking. "By the gods, you won't be satisfied until you've brought that man's curses down on us all. Is your mother's life worth less to you than a pack of vermin? You will *not* go after Master Íobar, not if I have to tie you to a pillar until we leave Cruachan!"

I walked on.

"You stubborn little— I said come *back*!" He overtook me, gripped my elbow, and spun me around. The violence of that turn tossed my hair back, away from my cheeks. The mark of Master Íobar's hand was revealed.

Father saw it. His brow creased, his rage against me cooling sharply. His calloused fingers grasped my chin with tenderness as he tilted my face to one side. "What's that bruise on your cheek? Did you fall?"

"I was slapped."

"Who did it? Who dared?" He was ready to take heads.

"No one *you* would dare touch." I pushed his hand aside and ran.

I didn't pursue Master Íobar after all. What was the use? I had no actual power to punish him for his cruelty. But *his* power was very real. Even if his curses were no more than words, enough people believed in them, and belief carries its own dark, self-fulfilling magic. Father was wrong: I did value Mother's life—and his—more than those the druid had stolen. Even Ea's. I abandoned seeking justice. Master Íobar had won.

I didn't leave my chamber for the rest of the day. The most I did was stick my head around the door frame and summon servants to bring me food and drink. I also dispatched one girl to discover what Odran was doing. As I suspected, he was isolated in his room like me, though not by his own choice.

"Find out if he's been fed," I told her. "If not, see to it."

She twiddled her fingers nervously. "Milady, what if it's because the druid's said he's not to have any food?"

"Are you afraid of him too?" She nodded and I narrowed my eyes. "He leaves tomorrow. I will still be here. You'd better start fearing me."

Dawn brought the High King's leave-taking, but I had no wish to bid Father farewell. I couldn't stand the thought of looking at him, standing tall in his chariot, seemingly so strong and bold, when I knew the humiliating truth: He was so afraid of Master Íobar that he wouldn't even try to prove if there was any real power to the druid's curses. Like a child told that a monster lurks beneath his bed, he'd never so much as peek there to see if it were so. The man I'd seen as a mountain had become a hollow hill of sand.

But as much as I scorned him for how he'd failed me, I didn't give in to the childish desire to hurt him by my absence from the leave-taking. One of us had to do what was right, no matter how bitter the taste it left in my mouth.

I rose from my bed and put on my best dress and ornaments. Shortly after that, I stood with the rest of the women on the ringfort ramparts, looking down at the men setting out on the road to Tara. Master Íobar had been given a place in one of the foremost chariots. Odran and their two slaves waited beside it. He kept his face turned away from Cruachan. It was just as well. I was afraid of how I might react if our eyes met. Our last goodbye would not be spoken.

Father saw me and waved. At first I kept my hands folded in front of me. It had taken all my willpower to come this far, given how badly I felt he'd let me down. I would attend his leave-taking, but that was all I'd do to mark our parting.

His arm dropped to his side. His self-confident grin faded into a look of such bewilderment and hurt that it sent a pang through my heart.

I can't let him ride away with this coldness between us, I thought. *I grew up so used to him as the bravest warrior of Èriu, my bold, beloved father, my hero, that I have trouble seeing him as human. I knew he feared the druid even before he refused to give me justice for the creatures' deaths. Why did I expect him to act otherwise? He can't help being who he is.*

I surrendered to kindness, raising one hand in a gesture of farewell. "Safe journey to you, Lord Eochu!" I shouted. "Safe homecoming, Father!"

In ordinary circumstances Father's absence would have put Mother in charge of overseeing the final Samhain preparations, but Lady Íde delegated that to me.

"If Lord Eochu trusted you with our cattle, you can certainly oversee the preparations for a feast. Of course you'll have Lady Kinnat and Lady Dealla to help," she said, naming two of Mother's ablest attendants.

I was thankful to have so much responsibility. It gave me the pleasure of feeling useful, testified that someone as formidable as Lady Íde considered me mature enough for the task, and most of all, took my mind off my aching heart. Sometimes, when I took a brief rest from supervising the preparations, I mused over the approaching festival, wondering if the veil between worlds would allow the souls of animals to pass through along with those of human beings. There was never any question in my mind that the creatures Odran and I had cared for had spirits that lived on.

I'll look at the moon and maybe I'll see my Ea's shadow hovering in the light, I thought. *Or perhaps I'll feel a furry body brush against my ankles and Muirín will be laughing up at me.* I smiled, thinking how I'd have to tell her to seek Odran at Tara and what a funny face the little fox would make—*What? Why didn't he tell me? Oh, that vexing human!*—before her spirit blew away like a thread of smoke from the blessed bonfires.

We had everything ready three days before Samhain eve. Mother was sleeping when I went to report this good news, so Lady Íde and I spoke outside the room. After I gave her all of the details concerning food, drink, and entertainment, I ended by saying, "I hope I've done well. I'd hate to disappoint you."

"You'd be wiser to *fear* doing that," Lady Íde jested. "If you'd failed to give this your best effort, you'd have to answer to me *and* Lady Clothru."

"Clothru?" My face broke into a smile of pure delight.

My childhood spats with my eldest sister were long gone. I felt nothing but joy to hear that I was going to see her again.

Then joy turned to misgiving. "Nothing . . . nothing's wrong, is it?" I asked anxiously. It wasn't normal for people to take to the road so near the shadows of Samhain just to visit their kin. "There's been no trouble with her husband, has there? He's still good to her?"

"Tsk. Of course he is. Rest easy, my dear. Lady Clothru will only stay with us until after Samhain's past and she's complied with the High King's wishes."

"His . . . wishes?"

"That she fulfill his role at the rites."

"But he promised that honor to me!"

Jolted, I cried out too loudly. Lady Íde shot me a warning look and rolled her eyes at the bull hide curtaining Mother's room. I lowered my voice, chastened, and repeated, "He promised it to me. I earned it. Master Niall and Master Owain approved. There must be some mistake."

Lady Íde cradled my face in her cool hands the way Mother sometimes did. "I'm sorry, dearest Maeve. Lord Eochu sent for your sister the day before he departed for Tara. He left word to keep her arrival as a surprise for you, but I was sure you already knew that he'd changed his mind about your part in the rites."

"Why would he bother to tell me? He gives and he takes away, with cause or on a whim. Nothing's changed since the day he let me think he'd give me Dubh but never did."

"Maeve, you mustn't be upset—"

"I'm not," I said, and was surprised to realize this was true. I was strangely calm after learning how Father had taken back the honor he'd given to me. I didn't try to work out his reasons.

There were many possibilities, everything from some unknown offense I'd committed to this being one final "gift" from Master Íobar. If the druid said *dance,* Father would caper, even if he trampled on a promise.

What could I do about it? No more than I'd done when I was five and all I'd risked to claim the black bull turned to nothing at one word from the High King.

Clothru arrived shortly after noon on the following day. She rode in a gorgeously decorated wagon, escorted by a numerous party of warriors. Master Niall and Master Owain directed me to take charge of her welcome. I think they felt sorry for me, so suddenly denied my place at the Samhain rites. I was supposed to stand in the ringfort gateway and say some ceremonial words of greeting before having our waiting servants serve cups of mead to the guests.

That was *their* plan. Mine was to throw aside all formality, barrel down the path, and jump into Clothru's wagon to embrace her. I don't know who was more surprised by that turn of events—the druids, my sister, or me.

We were inseparable for the few days left before Samhain. It felt strange to guide my sister through what once had been her home, and stranger still to hear her exclaim over how much had changed since she'd left us. She told me about her experiences as part of another household and about how hard it was to manage one of her own since she'd married Lord Cineád.

"Mother made it look easy," she said with a sigh.

I was a happy witness to Clothru's return to our mother's arms. It was only their mutual concern for the unborn twins that kept them from hugging each other hard enough to make their bones squeal in protest. Mother was so overwhelmed with happiness at having her oldest daughter with her once more that Lady Íde feared the excitement might be dangerous. She suggested limiting Clothru to a pair of brief visits daily.

Mother soon settled *that*. "Íde, I love you like a sister, but if you say one word to keep my Clothru away from me, I will get out of this bed and make you regret the day we met."

Lady Íde pursed her lips. "Too late." Clothru and I giggled.

My sister confided in me that she was apprehensive about the Samhain rites, but she carried out her part with dignity and grace. Everyone there remarked on how well she'd done and how proud the High King would have been of his eldest child. I fought down my envy and was glad for her sake.

Too soon Samhain was over and Clothru had to return to her home. Her departure was supposed to take place before dawn but we clung to one another so long that the sun was above the horizon before either of us could say a last goodbye.

"I'm sorry I was so terrible to you when we were children, Maeve," she whispered. "I wish I had more time to make up for it."

"Then come back soon." I hugged her fiercely. "The babies will be here before winter ends. Come back in the spring so that we can be with our dear oldest sister."

She toyed affectionately with a strand of my hair. "I'll be too big to travel by then."

"You—" I stared first at her face, then at her belly, as though I expected to see it already swollen with child. "Oh, Clothru!" Even with the tears of parting still wet on my face, I thought I would never be able to stop smiling.

With Samhain over and Clothru gone, I had too much

time left to spend with my thoughts. All of the major preparations for winter were done. There was only so much needlework and weaving I could do before my fingers cramped or the gabbling gossip of the other girls drove me away. Things would turn livelier when the men returned from Tara, but Devnet wouldn't be among them and I was so eager to lose myself in his songs!

And so it happened, but not in the way I'd hoped or ever could have imagined.

CHAPTER FOURTEEN

Tallying Trouble

I'D FINISHED MY work early and was loitering by our nearly empty horse pens on the day Father returned from Tara. He'd sent no messengers ahead to warn us of his arrival, so as far as anyone knew, this was just another day.

I was feeling especially glum. By some miracle all the real work in our household was either done or delegated—except the *vital* chore of gossiping—so I had nothing to distract me from sorrowful memories or the lingering resentment I felt over being shoved aside at Samhain. *Did Father truly think I was mature enough to be entrusted with sharing a king's work, or was that only his ploy to bind me close? He's been terribly lonely since Mother fell ill. Had he* ever *wanted my counsel, or only my company?*

One of Father's men took notice of me, standing there. His name was Bran and his chief duty was to look after our hunting hounds. Far older than anyone else at Cruachan, white-haired and wizened with age, he was still vigorous and able to keep the largest, rowdiest dogs in line. If he'd been within earshot the day Áed's accursed dog attacked Bláithín, how different my life might have been!

"Lady Maeve, is there anything you want here?" he asked.

"What? Oh. No, nothing," I replied without bothering to look at him, and sank back into thought.

"Well, if you haven't got anything better to do, would you come with me? It's time the dogs were fed and it might cheer you to watch them."

Bitter thoughts made dull company, and Bran always had some entertaining tale to tell about past hunts. Soon enough the two of us were standing outside the hounds' enclosure, tossing scraps to the pack and enjoying their antics.

"See there, Princess?" Bran said, pointing at a trio of the smallest, skinniest hounds, who were wrestling and growling over a wad of entrails. "Those are our youngest, all paws, bark, and energy. They'll make fine dogs if they don't get their throats torn out first."

I shuddered, remembering the murderous wolfhound. Bran saw and clicked his tongue. "Now, now, don't be upset. I'm exaggerating. When any of those three makes himself a nuisance to the older hounds, he gets a few nips to teach him better manners, nothing worse." As he spoke, one of the more seasoned dogs darted in under the young ones' noses and snatched the tidbit they'd been quarreling over. Bran and I laughed.

A gawky lad approached us, carrying a basket filled with meaty bones. He was so tall that I had to look closely at his beardless, pimply face before I realized he was probably younger than I. "Sorry I'm late," he said, ducking his head before Bran.

"You're not late, Colla," the older man said benevolently. "I brought Lady Maeve here to entertain her with feeding the hounds, but there's plenty left for you to do. Get along with it."

Colla nodded and set down his basket outside the enclosure but within reach of his long, skinny arms and climbed in among the dogs. Old Bran leaned toward me and in a voice that was pure mischief whispered, "Now you'll *really* laugh."

He was right. The dogs greeted Colla so enthusiastically, it was ridiculous. They leaped up, planted their huge paws on his shoulders, and licked his face until you couldn't see anything of the tall boy but dog tongues and drool. A less experienced person would have been knocked off his feet, but Colla held steady.

"Off, all of you!" The command would have sounded more masterful if Colla's voice hadn't cracked midway. When the dogs dropped back, he reached through the fence and grabbed a fistful of bones from the basket.

I blinked. Was there something else in his hand along with the meat-heavy ribs?

"Get it!" Colla showed the pack a bone, then made an overhand throw to the far side of the enclosure. The dogs bounded off to claim it. I heard a snap and the leader's yelp of confusion when his mouth closed on a dry stick instead of a beef rib. Colla laughed, called the hounds back, showed them the same bone, and tricked them with another stick all over again.

"Why are you letting him do this, Bran?" I was furious. I knew what it felt like to have something I dearly wanted dangled before me, then be snatched away. "It's a nasty game."

"Maybe, but it's not over. See that dog there?" He pointed to a tall, strong-limbed animal, with a square, sturdy muzzle,

a pure white pelt, and short, floppy red ears. She wasn't racing after Colla's decoy throws but remained aloof, dignified, and alert. "That's Treasa," the hound-keeper explained. "Watch her and wait."

I didn't have to wait long. Colla knew dogs well enough not to stretch their patience too far. He threw some of the real bones to quiet the pack leaders, then took fresh food and more sticks from the basket. As he stooped to do so, Treasa saw her chance. She ran into him like a young bull, knocked him sprawling in the dirt—and worse—of the hounds' pen, and grabbed the bones from his hand. A yelp of pain told me that the white hound had given Colla a lesson when she took her prize.

"That boy fooled her once when she was a pup, but never again," Bran said, gazing at Treasa with admiration. "The first time she taught him not to tease her, he tried paying her back with a beating, but he came out the loser, especially after I caught him at it. Now he daren't lift a hand against her."

"But he still taunts the others," I protested. "Why don't you put a stop to it?"

"Why don't *they*?" Bran countered, gesturing at the hounds still chasing meat and catching dry sticks. "Let them be Colla's fools until they turn clever enough to learn from Treasa, until the lad tires of this game, or until he grows up enough to know better, whichever comes first." He gave me a crooked smile. "My wager's on the dogs."

Father came home accompanied by the men who'd attended the High King's presence at Tara. Some were all too familiar, like Lord Áed. I was thankful to see that this time he hadn't brought more wolfhounds, though the unhappy little boy who walked beside his chariot clad in slave's yellow reminded me of a beaten dog.

Some new faces came in Father's train as well, or more accurately they were new to *me*. As the High King's guests entered Cruachan, Lady Íde ran out of the great house to embrace one of them enthusiastically. There were plenty of curious whispers from onlookers and raised brows at the placid way Lady Íde's husband watched his wife cover another man's face with kisses.

Then she cried, "Artegal! Oh, my dear, dear cousin, it's so good to see you again!" and that took the fun out of everything for some people.

Lady Íde's cousin was actually *Lord* Artegal, who ruled his realm from the ringfort of Dún Beithe, a ten days' march to the north. He was unique among our visitors because he'd come here from Tara to see his kinswoman, not to try winning me for himself or for any sons he might have. The others claimed they were breaking their homeward journeys at Cruachan to let Father know how devoted they were to their High King, but even the most naïve of our serving girls saw through that.

"Just look at them," I overheard one tell another with a harrumph. "All here sniffing after Lady Maeve."

"It's always easy for the pretty ones," the second girl said enviously.

Her friend snorted. "Pretty comes last with kings. What counts with those men is that she's been Lord Eochu's favorite since she was five. You know the tale of how she made the bull dance like a moon-mad hare before she broke off his horn with her bare hands and gave it to the king. That's why he promised she'd have Connacht for her dowry. *Now* do you understand what those hounds are hunting?"

If the serving girl didn't, I did. Once again I became the hub around which our visitors spun, vying for my attention. I'd grown adept at this game, though now I no longer cared if Father praised me for how well I played it. I loved him, but I no longer put my faith in him. The same breath that called me his "spark" blew icy cold with fear of Master Íobar. The same arms that I'd thought were stronger than any steel fell to his sides like willow branches when I begged him for justice. I couldn't look at him without recalling how he'd tossed me a bone that became a dry stick and crumbled into dust.

I was through depending on him for my happiness. Treasa had been fooled once and never again. She played no one's games. She didn't wait for someone else to tell her *Now you can have what you need, what you want, now, when* I *say so.* She used her wits to claim it for herself. So would I. To think that a dog had taught me more than any druid!

Father never knew how lucky he was that his wishes and my best interests overlapped. It was easy for me to keep all of my suitors equally near, equally far, since I was equally indifferent to them all. The hard part was remembering to resist the temptation to give some of them a richly deserved slap with my hand instead of my words.

The one who tried my patience most was Lord Áed. He'd brought a second slave with him besides the pinch-faced, scrawny little boy. She was a very pretty young woman, dark-haired, dark-eyed, and much better fed than her fellow captive. Though she wore the yellow garment custom demanded, she also wore a thin bronze torque around her neck, a valuable ornament for a slave, who'd usually have none. It was clear that Lord Áed treated her well, and more cruelly clear why. I never saw her smile except when he looked at her, and then I saw more fear than fondness in her expression.

I sympathized with her. I had to smile at Lord Áed, too, but at least my captivity ended after dinner.

They can't stay here forever, I consoled myself. *They'll have to go back to their own lands eventually. We are* not *going to feed these people through the winter. Oh gods, give me a spell to turn the guest-bond upside down and make them keen to* go away!

I didn't think the gods would answer, but they did.

Strange things began to happen at Cruachan. Baskets of wool were found soaked with water, delaying the task of carding the raw fleece into something fit to go on a spindle. Every spindle in the house vanished one day, only to turn up in the bottom of a cooking pot half filled with mud. An unseen hand filched tunics, cloaks, and trousers from our highborn visitors, returning the garments once they'd been "improved" with tiny rips and tears.

And one day we all awoke to . . . the stench. It seemed to be everywhere in the great house, vile and sickening. Father ordered our servants to search for the source, promising a reward for success. Our highborn guests gave their attendants the same task, though most of them promised punishment for failure.

Rumors began. I heard them from the servants first, talk of how Cruachan must be haunted or the target of one of the Fair Folk we'd displeased somehow. A few claimed it was evidence of a curse that had descended on us all, while others said it was merely a warning and we'd better find out the cause while there was time to ward off the malediction.

Our guests were not above joining in the gossip. I heard them doing so at dinner. They spoke low, but not low enough.

"So far no real harm's been done, though who knows how long that will last?" one of them said. "Today I woke up to find my shoes filled with squashed mushrooms and dead crickets."

"Is that all it takes to put your life in danger?" another jeered.

"Laugh, fool." The first man bristled. "The Fair Folk turn from mischief to malice in the blink of an eye. The same unearthly creature who put mushrooms in my shoes today could put toadstools in your stew tomorrow."

"Lord Eochu's druids ought to read the omens and see what he's done to offend the gods," a third man said.

I recognized him. He was Lord Morann of the Fir Domnann whose stronghold lay closest to our own. He was also the wolfish one who'd gloated most when Master Íobar gibed at Father for having no sons. "This has all the marks of a curse."

"Why do you think *he's* to blame, Morann?" the second man asked. "All of these pranks might be the petty work of some woman."

The first man snorted. "I doubt the gods would care about women's business."

"The Morrígan has her share of 'women's business,'" Lord Morann said sharply, invoking the name of the goddess of blood and battle, whose spells had the power to make and unmake kings. "Did you never think that all this mischief is a sign of her diminishing favor?"

Before either of the other men could respond, Lord Áed made himself an unwelcome part of the conversation. "How could you not? You weren't here before Samhain when the great Master Íobar said what many of us already think: If a man can't rule his own rebellious daughter, how can he rule Èriu?"

I couldn't let such talk continue. Pretending I'd heard nothing, I presented myself before Lord Morann and his companions with a jug of Gaulish wine in my hands. As I filled their drinking horns, I also filled their ears with gracious words and subtle flattery disguised as praise coming from Father, not me. Back in my own place again, I smiled to hear how my timely action changed the course of their talk.

"If that's rebellion, I'm a hedgehog," the first man said. "I've never heard it said that druids were the best judges of women's ways. It will be a lucky man who gets that girl for his wife."

"By which you mean your son, of course," the second joked.

Morann scowled. "Even if she has learned her place, it would be best for all of us if Eochu gave her to Conchobar."

"Conchobar? Fachtna Fáthach's boy?"

"That 'boy' is enough of a man to govern his late father's lands well and he's wise enough to heed the counsel of older, more experienced people," Morann declared.

Whose? I thought, simmering. *Yours?*

The first man turned serious. "She's a beautiful little thing, and she'll go to her husband with rich wedding gifts and Connacht thrown into the bargain. Still—" He hesitated.

"What more do you want? To have her dipped in gold?" Áed snickered.

His dubious comrade wasn't interested in hearing any jests. "Beautiful girls can bring their husbands more trouble than joy. The ones who *know* the power of their beauty are the worst. They can turn the strongest man into a spineless slave."

"Well, that explains why you married an ugly wife," Áed replied, then turned to the second man and added, "And why you have to ask *your* lovely bride for permission to sneeze." They were all just drunk enough to laugh instead of drawing steel. The conversation flowed into other channels and I could breathe easily again.

Well, as easily as any of us *could* breathe with the ever-growing stink haunting Cruachan. The problem worsened daily until there was no way to keep such a thing secret from Mother. Lady Íde was at her wits' end, trying to prevent her from getting out of bed to discover what was turning her pristine home into a reeking midden.

I joined the servants in the hunt, though I had to play my part secretly. It wouldn't look right for the High King's daughter to go sniffing through her father's great house like an eager puppy. But puppies have their uses. I was surprised that no one else thought of having Bran bring one of his hounds inside to seek the source of that awful smell. As soon as the dog came in, she began running in circles around the central hearth.

"Do you think something died up there?" Father asked his keeper of the hounds.

Bran shrugged. "I'm too old to climb and see."

"I can do it, Lord Eochu." Áed's little slave boy came forward. He shinnied up one of the wooden pillars and peered eagerly into the shadows, but when his feet were on the ground again he said he'd found nothing.

Father rewarded him with a bronze pin for his attempt. The child hadn't held it in his grubby hands for more than two breaths before his master, Lord Áed, snatched it away and gave him a resounding slap on the head for his failure. "Find the High King's chief cook and see if he can give you a task you won't botch," he growled at the boy. "Make yourself *worth* feeding, for a change."

The slave bobbed his head and darted away, but not before I'd noticed something strange: though there were tears on his cheeks from the hard blow he'd taken, he was smiling, and as he ran, he cast a smug backward glance up at the rafters.

I found him later behind the great house, wrestling with a cook pot twice his size, trying to scrub it clean. "Hello, Donal," I said, crouching beside him. My hand held out a generous portion of cheese and a whole loaf of bread.

The poor boy looked from my face to the food and back again with as much terror as if I were a monster offering him a feast of spiders. "P-Princess? How do . . . how do you know my name?"

"I asked your sister, Èile. She's got the same name as one of *my* sisters. Isn't that funny?"

Donal didn't think it was funny, not unless he came from a place where you turned white as a fish's belly and started shaking wildly just before you laughed. "You . . . what . . . why . . . Did I do something wrong?" The question finally burst from his thin lips, but his eyes answered it instantly: *I did, and I'm caught, and I'm doomed.*

"You're too skinny, and that's wrong, even if it's not your fault," I said, trying to calm him. "Here, eat. It's my thanks for what you did today." I pushed the food at him. When he only stared at it, I added, "You should never refuse a gift from a princess."

He didn't need another invitation. He gobbled the bread and cheese so fast I thought he'd choke. As the last crumbs vanished, I said, "I'm glad I found you out here. I wouldn't want you to have to eat indoors, what with that horrid reek everywhere. And that's just the latest nuisance that's come to Cruachan. Torn clothing, ruined wool, a fistful of worms in a king's bed. I think the rumors must be true—it's the work of the Fair Folk, playing countless small pranks because someone's angered and hurt them, someone too powerful for them to strike at face to face. They're probably disguised as birds so they can flit in and out of this house without being caught. Just today I could have sworn a handful of feathers came drifting down from the rafters. You were very brave to climb up there, not knowing what you'd find."

"I didn't find anything." He regarded me with deep unease.

"Maybe you didn't search carefully enough," I said, keeping my tone friendly. "I think you should make a second try. If you don't, the High King might decide it would be worthwhile to send one of our boys into the rafters. If that lad solves the stink riddle, he'll claim a reward that ought to be yours."

"You mean a reward that'll be Lord Áed's," the boy said bitterly.

"Perhaps. But if *our* boy discovers the source of the stench and reports it comes from something in plain sight, something you couldn't possibly have overlooked, Donal, then . . ." I spread my hands and left the rest to his imagination.

"Please don't let that happen, my lady!" he exclaimed. "I'll go up again now, at once. I don't care if Lord Áed and your chief cook *both* give me a beating!" He sprinted out of sight, leaving me with the half-scrubbed cook pot.

Everyone, including our chief cook, forgot about that cook pot when young Donal came down from the great house rafters holding the putrid body of a dead owl. I swear, he brandished that ghastly trophy as if he were a warrior bringing home his first severed head!

That night we were all entertained by a song about how a little slave boy climbed into the rafters of Cruachan's great house, ready to do battle with monsters. High over our heads, he was enveloped in a black cloud of demonic flies as big as bats. Their buzzing nearly deafened him as they tried to tear the flesh from his bones, but he fought them off, ripping their bodies in half with his bare hands. In the belly of the largest fly he found a knife, with which he boldly slew the malicious spirit of stench that had disguised itself as a man-sized owl, though by the time he climbed down from the rafters with the creature's corpse, it had shrunk to the size of an ordinary bird.

"Thus do all jealous enchanters seek to rob our heroes of their glory!" The last triumphant line of the tale fell from the lips of a harper in service to one of our royal visitors. Our own bard wasn't there. Devnet had set out on his wanderings right after the Samhain rites at Tara. I added my praise for the harper to that of everyone present, but I strongly believed Devnet would have done a better job. *His* demon flies would have been the size of *badgers*.

Áed was shamed into rewarding little Donal with gold. He did it grudgingly, taking a pair of rings from his fingers. Only a fool would believe he'd let the child keep them once they left Cruachan.

I was no fool. "My lord, your openhandedness shows that you're one of my father's noblest allies. But how far does it go?"

"I hope you're not questioning the limits of my generosity, my lady?" Áed said, on guard.

I gave him a disarming smile. "How could I? You once offered me two fine wolfhounds to show how much you admired me. I was too young to appreciate the gift or your attention then." I lowered my voice to draw him nearer. "It would be different now."

"You'd like a pair of wolfhounds?"

"I'm afraid they'd still be too much for me to handle. I'd like this boy instead." I indicated Donal.

Áed looked dubious, but only for a moment. I could almost read his thoughts: *What a good bargain, one skinny child in exchange for a princess's favor! And who knows where that might take me?* "I can't refuse you anything, my lady," he said smoothly. "He's yours, along with all the rewards I was about to bestow on him for his bravery." Everyone cheered his grand gesture.

I clasped his hands. "And the other?" I asked sweetly.

His brows met. "What other?"

"You did offer me *two* wolfhounds, Lord Áed. It's no less than anyone here would expect from such a gallant, generous man like you." I made a sweeping gesture, indicating the considerable audience of highborn guests, who raised a fresh cheer for poor, cornered Áed.

He gave me Donal's sister as well. I didn't give him a choice. The girl was summoned from Áed's room and was told about her new fate while she and her brother clung to one another, giddy with happiness.

Father softened Áed's consternation with gifts of his own. As he gave the outfoxed man a glittering brooch, I stole close and slipped a word into Father's ear.

"What's that, my spark?" I beckoned him closer and

whispered the same thing as before. "You want *me* to have them?" He glanced at Donal and Èile. "But they're Lord Áed's gift to you!"

"A gift I cherish," I replied, giving Áed a melting look. It might have been too much to be believed. His mouth shrank to the size of an acorn. He was no longer so willing to trust me nor so easy to be deceived. *So he's smart enough to learn,* I thought. *What a pity.*

"If you cherish it, daughter, why give it away?" Father asked.

"Didn't you hear the bard's song? Donal's bravery proves he's destined to become a valiant warrior who'll bring fame to you, his king"—I paused—"*with* the proper training. I wouldn't know where to begin, which is why I'm giving him to you. Of course, you'll have to accept Èile too. The bards would ridicule me forever if I only gave you half a gift."

Father laughed. "You mean you give me two new mouths to fill. Well, if I must have them, I'll have them free. Then maybe someday they can feed themselves." He pronounced the formal words for giving a slave liberty and declared Èile and Donal members of our household. Brother and sister struggled to embrace us both as they wept for joy.

Lord Morann was almost the last of our guests to go. I couldn't wait to see the back of him. I was going to scream if he didn't stop harping on the twin strings of "Conchobar would be the perfect mate for you" and "Even if he's not perfect, this alliance would strengthen Lord Eochu's rule. People are talking."

Talk you stir up whenever you can, I thought. But I honored the guest-bond and only let him see my smile.

I smiled in earnest on the night he announced, "Lord Eochu, beloved king, I'm sorry to part from you but I must go home tomorrow." Smile? I had to bite my lip to keep from cheering.

The next morning I went out to make sure that awful man was really leaving. Everywhere I looked, I saw the usual bustle that attends preparations for a journey. Lord Morann was nowhere to be seen, having left all of the arrangements in the charge of one of his men. The fellow could browbeat his own people as much as he wanted for all I cared, but I didn't like the way he was harrying *our* servants. As I watched, I saw him try to force Fechin to take orders from him. Father's charioteer just laughed and left him fuming.

"Hey, Fechin!" I waved for him to join me. "Who *is* that sack of wind?"

"A flea who thinks he's a falcon. The gall of him, treating a brother driver like I was no more than a fetch-and-carry!" He snorted. "The fool's so caught up with lording it over everyone that he's neglecting his own work. He had stable boys prepare his master's chariot for the road ahead. *Stable boys!* And he hasn't yet bothered to check their work. It'd serve him right if the horses came loose and dragged him bloody."

"Maybe you could take a look at it," I suggested.

"I'd better. No one else is going to do it. Want to come with me?"

I always liked Fechin's company. The chariot driver was a beloved, trusted member of the family, still boyish in spite of being close to Father's age. I accompanied him out of the gates and down the ringfort hill. A bored-looking boy stood holding the reins of two handsome brown stallions. He wasn't one of ours.

"Not keeping yourself *too* busy swallowing flies, are you?" Fechin greeted him sarcastically.

"I got told to mind the king's chariot and I'm doing it," the sullen boy replied.

"Good for you. With all that ambition, your master will have to take notice. Mark my words, today you're a lump of meat with eyes but tomorrow you'll rise all the way to being a log."

The boy grunted something ugly and made a rude gesture. Fechin threw one arm around his neck in what *might* have been a friendly manner if not for how tightly he closed his hold on the lad's throat.

"Was that the right way to act in front of our princess? Next time, think twice. Better yet, try thinking *once*," Fechin purred in his ear before letting him go. "Let's see if you're good for something. These manes are a disgrace. No chariot leaves Cruachan with horses that look so slovenly, not while I'm the High King's man. Bring me a comb and I'll groom them myself."

"Where am I supposed to get that?" The charmless oaf had a gift for whining.

"Find your master's charioteer and ask him. Or have a look around our horse pens for some help. We should have a few men working there. Don't come back without it."

The boy did as he was told: he didn't come back. Fechin conjured up a flock of curses on the incompetent lout while we waited. He and I ran out of things to talk about, which was no surprise. He loved me dearly, but I was still a child to him, and what would a battle-hardened chariot driver have in common with a child?

"What's taking that lump so long?" Fechin groused. "And who was the brainless creature who hitched these innocent animals to the chariot just to leave them standing idle? They're as bored as I am, and a bored horse is a dangerous horse, especially stallions." He jerked one thumb at the chariot. "Let's entertain them."

I held on to the front rail while Fechin kept the stallions to a leisurely gait. He even let me hold the reins for a little while. The horses immediately sensed that they'd been given into the care of an inexperienced hand and tossed their heads, trying to wrench control away from me.

"Hey! Don't try those tricks on Lady Maeve, you overgrown goats!" Fechin shouted. "And as for you, my lady, you've got to keep a tighter hold on those two than that." He showed me where I'd gone wrong, then took back the reins before I could correct my mistake.

"Another time, I promise. Right now we'd best see if all's ready for the leave-taking. It wouldn't do to keep a king waiting," he said, and drove the chariot back to where we'd found it.

There was still no sign of the boy. Fechin offered up a fresh round of curses as we got out of the chariot. "That does it! I'm going after him. If he hasn't found the comb, my foot'll find his backside. And if he *has* found it, I'll break it over his skull for making us wait like this!" He gave me the reins. "Hold firm and let them know you're their master, my lady. Don't worry, I won't be gone long."

Maybe I *should* have worried. Worry might have made me wise. Instead, I patted the stallions on their muzzles, told them how beautiful they were, and climbed into the chariot. All I wanted to do was have them take a few steps forward with my hand on the reins, just to prove to myself I could do it. It had been to play the part of a charioteer, to imagine what it must be like to drive into the heart of a battle, to maintain complete control over creatures who were half wind and half fire.

"Make way for Maeve, the war-maiden!" I declaimed, grinning. "Tremble before my mighty— *Waugh!!!*"

The stallions leaped forward without warning, taking off at a trot, then going into a canter, then an all-out gallop. I clutched the reins, wide-eyed with terror, and braced my feet, trying to pull them to a stop. But you can't fool a horse. They knew I was no more capable of mastering them than a chunk of cheese. They'd been put into harness, then kept waiting and waiting until they were weary of it. Now they had their chance to do what they'd been born and bred for: run!

I shrieked as the chariot jounced over the ground. Its careening course threw me from side to side so violently that my hips gathered countless bruises and my teeth clacked in my head. My hair flew out behind me, then whipped across my eyes when the horses decided it was time to make an abrupt turn. I didn't dare spare a hand to pull the tangled strands aside: hands were for holding a death grip on the reins and grabbing hold of the edge of the chariot.

The horses took another turn, scorning the road and pelting across open country. Blinking through my curtain of hair, I thought I saw water shimmering in the distance. *Oh no, not the stream!* I didn't know much about horses—I was proving the truth of *that* with every breath I took—but I was sure nothing good would come of a galloping team plunging into unknown water. I gritted my teeth, breathed in, spun my wrists up and over the reins several times to take up as much slack as

I could, and threw myself backward so that the full weight of my body was pulling against the horses.

It was my best attempt and not good enough. The chariot rolled on, but at least my effort made the horses swerve away from the stream. Now we were hurtling toward the ringfort. I saw a mob of people streaming down the slope, including several men on horseback. *Thank the gods!* I thought. *They'll overtake us, seize the bridles, and make these triple-cursed beasts stop.*

Apparently the same notion occurred to the stallions, who weren't through with their playtime. They wheeled about once more and redoubled their pace, the thunderous rumble of their hooves filling my ears. The water drew them on. In spite of my pleas and shouts and sobs, they flew off the bank and into the water with a colossal splash. I heard a loud crack and felt the chariot heel over to the left as the axle broke, and I slid into the stream.

The water wasn't deep, but it was icy. My legs began to go numb just as the first rider reached me. My wrists were hopelessly snarled in the reins, so he used a knife to slash them free. Other men arrived and started taking the stallions out of harness. My rescuer lifted me in his arms the way he'd treat an infant and carried me to the bank, where I was passed to another mounted man. Someone tossed him a dry cloak to wrap around me while a third rider sped ahead of us to deliver a report to Cruachan.

We entered the ringfort through a crowd of worried faces. Father and Lord Morann awaited us outside the great house. The most skilled bard would have struggled to describe the look of cold outrage on our guest's face.

He's got cause for anger, I thought. *I broke his chariot and might have harmed his stallions. Thank the gods they're all right! He'll have less to forgive me for.*

I jumped off the horse. Water trickled around my feet from under the borrowed cloak. "I'm truly sorry for what happened, Lord Morann. It was an accident."

He didn't respond to my apology except with a short, cynical quirk of his lips. "Another accident, eh, Lord Eochu?" he said. "Why do you think your stronghold's been beset by so many? I've heard whispers that such things were all the Fair Folk's doing, but perhaps they were no more than . . . accidents." He made it a point to stare at me.

Father's face clouded. "Someone bring Fechin," he called over the heads of the crowd. "Tell him that my brother king, Lord Morann, is to have my chariot, my two best horses, and half the cattle in Lady Maeve's herd to atone for this atrocious breach of hospitality. I want it done before the sun clears the ringfort wall."

What was I hearing? Did my father actually believe that I was the one to blame for Donal's work? Why was one word from Lord Morann enough to make him look at me as if I'd been caught putting a dead owl in the great hall rafters?

"Father, I tell you, it was an *accident*. I didn't—"

I pleaded my case, insisting that the wild chariot ride was nothing I'd planned, not mischief but mischance. I begged Fechin to defend me, to explain the circumstances. Father's chariot driver looked unhappy as he said, "I'm sorry, Lady Maeve, but I wasn't there when you . . . when the horses started running. I can't be your witness." Desperate to be absolved, I cried out, "What possible reason would I have to play pranks on the High King's guests?"

"Peace, Maeve," Father said coldly. "Accident or not, you and I are honor-bound to share the burden of compensating Lord Morann for his loss, but for nothing else. The spiteful tricks we all suffered were a coward's petty vengeance. As you say, why would *you* do such things unless you carried a grudge over some supposed injustice?"

His words seemed to defend me. The meaning behind them let me know I was guilty in his eyes. *He thinks I'm responsible for all that mischief because he refused to punish Master Íobar!* The revelation left me stunned, but I had to rouse myself enough to play out the last move of our game.

"Thank you for your confidence in me, Father," I said, bowing my head under the weight of our unspoken lies.

CHAPTER FIFTEEN

Seeds of Truth, Seeds of Change

LORD MORANN RODE off, taking my reputation with him, though I didn't know it right away. My friendless ways kept me at a distance from the whispers that followed me everywhere. Father had said that I was guiltless of that rash of household tricks, even if he thought otherwise, but scandal was a tastier dish than truth, as all the hungry gossips of Cruachan agreed.

Winter's chill, misty days brought them fresh meat to chew. A gray-haired, ruddy woman, plainly dressed, arrived at the ringfort walls in Father's best remaining chariot and was promptly brought into Mother's room. I was there visiting when Lady Íde ushered her in.

"Ah, Cera, good morning!" Mother greeted her like an old friend. "How are you? Is your family well?" Her eyes flickered over the older woman's dress. "You're not wearing the brooch I sent you?"

"My daughter has it in safekeeping. I treasure it."

"Good. I feared you took offense when a different woman was summoned to attend me after Lughnasadh."

"Milady, am I a jealous fool? I live much farther from Cruachan than the midwife who saved you and your babies, may Brigid bless her. Time matters in a crisis. I'm not wearing your gift now because I won't put it on until after our business is successfully accomplished. You know that's how I've always done things."

Mother laughed. "Of course. Pardon me for having forgotten, but it has been a while since the last time." She gestured at me. "You see how well you do your work, Cera? Maeve has grown up beautifully, even if you did mistake her for a boy when you first saw her."

She's the midwife who birthed me! I realized, and stared at her in wonder. It was no small thing to meet the person who'd welcomed me into the world. "I'm pleased to greet you," I said with reverence. "Tell me if I can help you in any way."

"Have you ever seen a birth, milady?" I admitted I had not. "Then maybe you'd better steer clear when the time comes."

I prickled. "Wasn't there a time when *you* first saw a child born?" I asked. "And yet you managed to get through that experience and many more."

Cera's chuckle was deep and hearty. "Oho, such feisty words! I remember you—the fighter. See, your fists are clenched now, just as they were when you let loose your first squall. I will call on you for help when it's your mother's time, but be warned: You know she's carrying twins again, and that can mean difficulties, especially for a woman of her age. The babes are so cramped inside their mother that it makes them impatient to be born, and they often come early. Poor, ignorant creatures, they don't know how unwise it is to rush into this world. That's why they're punier than other infants, sometimes too small to live."

I shivered to hear the midwife pronounce that dark hint of unthinkable possibilities. "Please don't say such things," I told her. "It sounds too much like ill-wishing." Cera glared at me for that.

Mother took my hands. "Dear Maeve, Cera told me all this years ago, when I carried Eithne and Èile. She didn't soothe me with falsehoods but gave me the hard truth, so I'd be prepared. Then she fought as bravely as a dozen of your father's warriors to help me and my babies survive."

"*Some* people value honesty," the midwife snapped.

"I'm sorry I offended you, Cera," I said. "I do appreciate the truth."

She cocked one eyebrow at me. "If you say so, Princess."

What does she mean by that? I wondered.

Mother went into labor early, as Cera had foreseen. The winter solstice was three days away when her pains came on. I was summoned from sleep to attend her. I awoke to see Sabha's bland, drowsy face looming over me, lit from below by the oil lamp in her hand.

"You'd better hurry if you want to see the birth, Lady Maeve. Cera says they're coming *really* fast." She turned to leave, taking the lamp with her.

"Hey! Wait! I can't dress in the dark," I exclaimed.

"Oh?" She blinked and yawned, rubbing her eyes. "Right . . . sorry."

I didn't waste time picking and choosing what to wear. I laid hands on the nearest piece of cloth big enough to cover my body, stuck a few strategic brooches through the material, and was ready to go. Sabha goggled at the weird picture I made.

"You're only wearing a cloak?"

"The twins won't care," I replied, and off we went.

We ran past Father, seated by the hearth with some of his men. He looked deeply worried, but he smiled wistfully and held out his arms when he saw me.

"Sit with me, my spark," he pleaded. "Keep me company while we wait to hear how your mother fares."

"I can't, Father," I called over one shoulder. "She wants me with her."

"But I *need* you with me!" he cried plaintively as I slipped past the door hide and into their chamber.

Lady Íde caught me as I darted in. The room was aglow with many lamps. The smell of burning fat blended sickeningly with the smells of sweat and blood. I tried to push past Mother's friend, but she held me tightly and refused to budge.

"Steady, child," she said. "There's not a lot of space in here."

"But I want to help."

"Then you should have come sooner. It's over."

I stared at Lady Íde, my whole body suddenly icy with dread. It took me an agonizing moment before I realized her face was serene.

"Oh my, I've frightened you. Forgive me." She released her hold and lovingly tucked back my sleep-tousled curls. "When I said it's over, I only meant that the babies have been born. Our women are getting them cleaned up and warmly wrapped while Cera looks after your mother. I don't think any of us expected them to be born *that* fast." She chuckled. "There's nothing here for you to do, unless you'd like to go tell Lord Eochu that Cloithfinn and the babies are all alive, all well."

"All boys." Mother's weary, happy voice came from behind Lady Íde. "Come here, my dearest. See your new brothers."

Cera was right about Mother giving birth early, but both she and Mother were wrong about how many babies would be born: there were three.

When I carried that news to Father, his roar of joy was so loud it felt as though he'd made the walls of the great house shake. His men joined in until our home held the din of a pitched battle, as deafening as if we were surrounded by horses galloping, chariots rumbling, men beating spears against the rims of their shields, and countless, thunderous war cries, enough to deafen the gods.

Lady Íde stormed into the midst of this tumult to scold them all for upsetting the babies. "They're newborn and small. They need sleep if they're going to grow healthy!"

"Small?" Father took her around the waist, tossed her at the rafters, caught her as she fell, and swung her around until both of them staggered, when he finally set her back on her feet. "There's nothing 'small' about my sons. They'll grow tall and mighty enough to cast shadows across all of Èriu, mark me!"

"Maybe so," Lady Íde replied, shaking her disheveled gown back into order. "But right now they'd rather have milk and sleep. We'll want three good, reliable wet nurses here before sunrise. Can your men see to that or are they useless old dogs like you, all howl and no hunt?"

In ordinary circumstances, she would have paid for giving Father so much cheek, regardless of whether she was Mother's

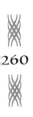

closest friend. On this night our world was left standing on its head and she could get away with anything. He was too drunk with happiness to care. He dispatched ten men to seek wet nurses, then strode into the chamber where his sons were waiting.

Father named the boys Bres, Nár, and Lothar, but people took to calling them the *findemna,* the fair-haired triplets, because they'd been born with golden hair like Mother's. They thrived, and by the spring equinox, Cera pronounced them so well bound to life that their delayed birth-feast could be celebrated.

It was a grand event, a festival graced by the presence of many highborn guests, a triumph. Three of our most trusted and competent fosterling girls were given the honor of carrying my brothers around the hall so that all of our guests could admire them. Harpers made the air resound with the exploits of gods and heroes so that the infants might develop a taste for glory to partner their taste for milk. The lavish gifts Father bestowed on everyone attending secured his reputation for generosity. From that day on, any bard who dared to describe Lord Eochu as a tight-fisted king would be hooted down and called seven kinds of liar.

Cera left us a few days after the feast. Father and Mother sent her home with a hundred cows and three gold bracelets. Before she left, she came looking for me.

"I couldn't go without making peace between us, my lady," she said.

Her words startled me. "I didn't know we'd quarreled, Cera."

"Not a quarrel, but an injustice. I haven't been fair to you.

I live far from Cruachan, and share a farmstead with my daughter and her husband. Our friends and kin know that I'm Lady Cloithfinn's chosen midwife, so whenever there's news of the High King's family, they see that it reaches me." She frowned. "They brought me lies about you, Lady Maeve. I don't know where they found such rubbish, but they stuffed my ears with it before I came here."

I could guess where the tales had come from. They'd sprouted from Lord Morann's insinuations and spread like creeping thistle. I could shrug off the lie "Lady Maeve put dead insects in my shoe," but what if it grew into something like "Lady Maeve put a rotted swan in the stewpot"?

And what if those false, ugly stories flew as far as Avallach? It had been months since Odran left me, but even if we never met again among the living, it was somehow extremely important that he never hear anything shameful about me.

"Never mind that anymore, Cera," I said with an assurance I didn't really feel. "The important thing now is that you know who I really am and you'll speak of it to others."

She brightened. "I will, my lady. And if I could root out all the falsehoods told about you, I would."

I took her hands. "They'll die out soon enough on their own."

Chapter Sixteen

Singers and Seekers

Spring made our land lovely. My brothers grew bigger and more demanding every day. I tried to do my part in helping Mother raise them, but Father was taking no chances about the boys' care. He recruited a small army of new servants to support the wet nurses and to aid the ladies already looking after our three princes.

And somehow, in the midst of so much joy, I vanished.

Mother didn't see me go. She no longer needed to remain abed, but since the boys' arrival she had become even more withdrawn from me than when she was awaiting their birth. Her waking world centered on them.

If I tried to become a part of it, I was pushed aside. Whenever I volunteered to join the group of women serving my brothers, they shooed me away.

"Thank you, Lady Maeve, but we have all the help we need."

"This job is for one person, milady."

"Don't waste your time with us, dear. Spend it with girls your own age."

"I'll send for you if you're wanted."

"Haven't you got something else to do than pester me?"

I tried speaking with Mother about it tactfully, on one of the few occasions that she and I were able to talk alone, but her response wasn't what I'd hoped for: "What a good sister you are. You'll have plenty of opportunities to look after the boys, but not now. Your brothers are the long-awaited princes of Connacht. Even if they can't inherit Eochu's rank, they can grow up to earn it, and your father will strive to see that they do. The women watching over Nár, Lothar, and Bres know that, so they work to earn royal favor from Eochu now and will eventually work to earn it from the boys themselves. That's not something most people want to share."

"They're jealous, then? Of *me*?"

"Of anyone who might take their reward. Let them be, Maeve. The king already favors you." She smiled.

How could I tell her that she was wrong? Ever since my brothers' birth, I had become a phantom to Father. The man who'd implored me to sit with him on the night the boys were born, crying, "But I *need* you with me!" now needed no one but them. He marked every event since their arrival by linking it to one of their *magnificent* accomplishments. When our bard Devnet returned at last from his wanderings, Father said, "Ah yes, he came back on the day Lothar learned how to turn himself onto his stomach. I remember it very well."

The final stone on the cairn that buried me from sight came when a pair of visitors arrived at Cruachan. I knew them—young men, minor kings from the south, two of my most ardent pursuers—and braced myself for renewed assaults of courtship.

These never happened. Our guests greeted me politely and then gave all their attention to food, drink, Father, and the boys. One of the young men did make a halfhearted attempt to steal a kiss, but when I refused he didn't bother making a second attempt. I didn't know whether to be annoyed or relieved.

Then I realized it wouldn't matter if I reacted either way. My father had sons to inherit the lordship of his lands, even if none of them ever rose to be High King. I was no longer the prize of prizes, great Lord Eochu's favorite child, the princess who would bring her husband Connacht for a wedding gift. It was a *kind* of freedom, becoming unimportant—the wrong kind.

And so I floated along the surface of life at Cruachan, unheeded and unneeded. Filling my days was harder than you'd think. There was only so much spinning, weaving, sewing, and embroidering I could do before the repetitive ordinariness of my tasks made me careless. I stabbed my fingers so many times that my blood spattered the cloth like yew tree berries. I lost skills I'd previously mastered. My spindle became a nest of knots; my loom looked like the web of a drunken spider.

Mother doesn't need me. Father doesn't see me. What am I doing here at all?

It became harder and harder to smile. The only times I found cause was when Devnet sang, especially one of his comical songs. My favorite was about how the foremost kings of the land challenged each other to fight for the honor of having me in their households but each met a ridiculous death on his way to the battlefield and I had to be fostered by a flock of swans. In the last verse, my foster parents taught me how to fly, and I became the queen of Èriu by burying my rivals with droppings from the sky. I wasn't the only one who liked it. Father called for it at every meal. Poor Devnet grew sick and tired of so many repetitions and declared, "I wish *I'd* died in a landslide of swan dung before I composed it!"

Our bard's songs were only occasional diversions; they couldn't fill my days. I found myself wandering the battlements more often, seeking forgetfulness in solitude. The trouble was, as long as my eyes could be drawn to the willow by the stream, to the path that eventually led through forest and over bog to the crannog, to a sky where Ea no longer flew, I was never really alone.

Where was the magic strong enough to let me banish memories? If I tried to empty my mind of them, striving to think about nothing at all, I failed. The oddest little things would twitch me out of my reverie: two guards talking about the best way to skin a hare, someone calling the name of our fosterling Guennola, the sight of a cloud curved like a kestrel's wing. Then the dull ache came, the persistent pain that blurred my eyes whenever I remembered Master Íobar's cold cruelty, Father's refusal to utter the smallest protest, and Odran—

I couldn't think about him. It hurt too much, and when I tried to push the pain away, it slipped through my fingers and buried itself in my heart.

I was seated on the top of the ringfort walls, chin on knees, when I heard a piping voice exclaim, "Here she is, Master Devnet! I found her!"

I turned my head to see Donal trotting toward me with our bard coming along behind him at a more sedate pace. I'd seen the boy nearly every day since I'd contrived to free him and his sister from Lord Áed, but it was still a happy surprise each time I saw him. The former slave boy no longer had a pinched, half-starved look and he wore the blue-gray tunic of a free person proudly. His sister was equally happy in her new life, and rumor claimed she'd soon be married to the same young man who was teaching her brother a warrior's skills.

Boy and bard settled themselves down on either side of me without a word of greeting. The sentry on duty gave us an inquiring look but went about his business. He wasn't the only one touched by curiosity.

"What brings you up here, Devnet?" I asked at last. "If you need me for anything, just say the word."

"I'm here for the boy's good," our bard replied. "He has a burden on his spirit. His sister noticed and came to me for help because she couldn't make him talk about it and we bards have a reputation for charming away silence. I succeeded in learning what ails him, but only you can heal it."

I turned to Donal. The boy looked glum and ashamed. "What's wrong?" I asked gently.

He began to cry. I put my arms around him instinctively but my eyes were on Devnet, silently imploring him to explain what all this was about. The bard only shrugged.

"Oh, Lady Maeve, I'm so sorry!" Donal finally managed to gasp. "Èile and I owe you everything, and I've repaid you badly."

"Hush, Donal, you owe me nothing," I murmured. "It makes me happy to see you free."

"But I'm *not* free," he countered. "Not while everyone thinks you're to blame for the mischief *I* caused when . . . when . . ." Sobs stole his voice.

"Pff! Hasn't that silly gossip died out yet?" I patted the child's head. "I don't worry about it, so neither should you."

"On the contrary, Princess," Devnet said, dead serious. "You should. The tales have run wild. I spoke with one of the bards attending our most recent visitors. I saw how doubtfully he kept eyeing you and asked him why. He told me how surprised he was to see that you were an ordinary girl—a very pretty one, but that was all."

"What did he expect to see?" I didn't like where this was leading.

"What the whispers and the stories and the songs that have spread across Èriu promise—Lady Maeve is famed for her beauty but notorious for her waywardness. She inflicts a hundred incidents of malice and destruction on everyone under her father's roof. Her strong spirit proves Lord Eochu's weakness. Not even kings are safe from her antics. When she's unable to cause havoc on her own, she sows discord and conflict among all the young men. To see her is to desire her and to desire her is to destroy yourself."

"Is that all?" I laughed and hugged the little boy in my arms. "Dry your eyes, Donal. You're not the one who wove all these lies about me."

He looked up at me and sniffled. "But I was the one who played the tricks that—"

"You were, you had your reasons, and you're sorry for them

now, aren't you?" He nodded vigorously. "Then it's over. It's not your fault if gossips jabber and bards turn mice into dragons. Go and be happy."

His face turned to pure light with a smile. A hug and a hasty kiss, and he was gone, leaving me in Devnet's company.

"Was that justice, Princess?" the bard asked. "Letting the boy dodge responsibility and escape punishment for mischief he committed?"

"He was a slave, Devnet, helpless. His life was a punishment. Those pranks were the only way he could prove to himself that he had power over *something.*"

"Mmm." Devnet tilted his head back and looked into the sky. "It's noble of you to take the blame for that poor boy's actions. I wish things hadn't gotten out of hand."

"I do sound fearsome, don't I?" I had to giggle. "I thought I had to be at least seventeen years old before I could destroy men with a single glance."

"It isn't funny, Princess."

"Or important," I replied. "I'm no longer the hero's portion, Devnet. Father has the *findemna* now, my brothers. Connacht will be theirs. Do you want to know something that *is* funny? I'm glad that Lord Morann was so good at muddying my reputation across all Èriu. If Father ever gets around to noticing I'm still here, he might not be able to find a king, a warrior, or any man willing to have me. I could live my own life here, as long as I liked. What's a little mud compared to that?"

"Even if Odran hears the tales?" Devnet asked softly. He saw me tense at the name. "I traveled with him and his father from Tara to the island of Avallach after Samhain. Master

Íobar kept to himself, but Odran welcomed my company. He couldn't stop talking about you, though secretly so his father wouldn't overhear. It wasn't out of fear, but because men tend to seal away their most cherished treasures. You have no idea how precious your memory is to him, Princess."

"As his is to me." I stood up and offered the bard my hand. "Will you help me, Devnet?"

He got to his feet as well. "Always, Princess. How may I serve you?"

I smiled. "How good are you at cleaning mud?"

Devnet rejoiced to hear I was going to fight to clear my name. "You must love that boy very much," he said.

"That doesn't matter. We'll never meet again. I do hate the thought of him believing lies about me, but do you know what, Devnet? I've realized those falsehoods have to be destroyed for *me*, for my own sake. If I close my eyes and ears to slander, I'm giving others the power to say who I am. No one gets to do that—not Lord Morann, not Lord Áed, not the bards, not the worst gossipmongers in Èriu—*no one*."

"As you say, Princess." I'd never seen Devnet wear such a proud, beaming smile.

The plan I made for saving my name was simply to fight words with words, old lies with new truths. Devnet would leave Cruachan and use his sweet songs to counter the nasty rumors against me and to influence his fellow bards to do the same.

"That will be easy, if I bring them songs worth singing," he said. "Songs that tell how wicked, tricksy Maeve, devourer of men's hearts, was actually an envious spirit of the Otherworld.

Only fools believe that the *real* Lady Maeve played that creature's pranks! For how could such a peerless princess, as wise and kind as she is beautiful, even think of—"

"Don't make me sound *too* perfect, Devnet," I teased. "Remember, you want to be believed."

My father roared like a wounded bull when Devnet stood up before the whole household and "asked" for his permission to go roaming again. "You just came home!"

"Lord Eochu, if you continue exaggerating like that, you'll be mistaken for a bard," Devnet replied. "You wouldn't want that. We have such a reputation for making up the worst satires against those who displease us." He spoke lightly, making everyone present laugh at his jest, but Father didn't take it that way.

"Fine, *go,*" he grunted. "The farther you wander, the less likely you are to aim that barbed tongue of yours at me."

"My lord, I assure you that the only reason for my going is to praise you and your family throughout Èriu," the bard said with an innocent smile. "I intend to give special attention to the virtues of your children. Who wouldn't wish to hear about how the courageous *findemna* slew a horde of fire-eyed wild boars without leaving their cradles?"

"Get out," said Father, now laughing louder than everyone.

Devnet left us the next day. "Where will you go first?" I asked.

"If you want to drink the purest water, go to the head of the stream," he replied, with an air of mystery.

"Why can't you tell me?"

"Oh, where's the fun in that, Princess? If what I have in

mind succeeds, I'll be home all the sooner, and if you guess right before I return, I'll reward your cleverness with both hands."

Devnet's riddle solved itself. The answer came to Cruachan from the mouth of a man from the land of the Fir Domnann, where Lord Morann ruled. He steadfastly refused to state his business publicly, to Father's irritation, but once the two of them retreated to a side chamber, we all soon learned it was nothing good. Father's bellow of bloody rage told us as much.

And that was all anyone did discover about the enigmatic messenger, until dinner. After his first furious eruption, Father remained quietly confined with the man for the rest of the day. He pulled the bull-hide curtain aside only once, to summon two warriors, but once he gave them their orders to keep all would-be eavesdroppers at a lengthy distance, he stayed hidden.

When it was time to eat, he led the stranger to a place of honor by his side. All ears in the great house were focused on the two of them, including Mother's. I liked seeing glimmers of her old self, before her difficult pregnancy took her out of the mainstream of our lives. It gave me hope that someday I'd have her back the way she'd been, high-spirited and even a little testy, nothing like the soft, baby-centered person she'd become since the triplets' birth.

At last Father called for attention. Everyone was so avid to find out the visiting stranger's identity and errand that even our rowdiest warriors fell silent in an instant.

"I have good news, my friends," Father announced in tones that were a better fit for *I have news that someone's died*. "After many years of seeking, I've finally found a household willing and worthy to accept my precious lastborn daughter, Maeve, into fosterage."

His announcement created quite the commotion. Mother gasped and laid one hand on her chest, as if trying to hold her heart back from leaping free. Scores of whispered questions raced around the hearth. Through it all, our mysterious guest kept his eyes on his food and continued to chew slowly and deliberately.

"Maeve, come here." Father motioned for me to stand before him. "We'll soon be favored by a visit from Lord Morann of the Fir Domnann. He's coming to escort you personally to your new home. It's a very great honor. Tomorrow we'll begin making preparations for your departure."

Lord Morann! *That* man? The one who'd falsely implicated me as the one to blame for Donal's pranks, whose greed took half my cattle in reparation for a "crime" that was an accident, who'd used his bards to smear my name?

And after he'd done so much to make me an unwelcome addition to any royal household, *now* he wanted me as a part of his own? This smelled worse than the rotting owl in the rafters.

I could have objected on the spot, but what would that have accomplished? I read Father's expression: he hated this situation as much as I did, but something had penned him into it. I stood tall and told him how much I appreciated having a father who always kept my happiness in mind, but inwardly I vowed to find out the truth.

Later that night, when I was about to blow out my oil lamp and attempt to sleep, I heard his voice outside my door. "May I come in, little spark?"

I pushed aside the door curtain. He dropped onto my bed

with a sigh of defeat. "You should be told what's happened," he said. "It's your life that bears the brunt of all this. You have a right to know."

By the flickering lamplight, he revealed everything. "Devnet's wanderings bought him trouble. He went to Lord Morann's stronghold, expecting to be treated as an honored guest. Instead he was taken hostage. You are the price I have to pay if our bard is going to be released alive."

I was staggered. Where to begin counting the layer upon layer of evil behind that one act? In a single breath, Morann had violated the sacred guest-bond, laid hands on a bard, threatened his life, and forced the High King, his overlord, to become his helpless servant.

And it was all my fault. Devnet left Cruachan at my bidding, to help clear my name. Now I knew the answer to his riddle: *If you want to drink the purest water, go to the head of the stream.* The smears against me began with Lord Morann. Devnet had gone to that man's stronghold seeking to persuade his fellow bard that it was time to sing a different song about me. Now this.

"I have no choice," Father went on. "Lord Morann's man let me know that if I refuse, our bard will meet his death in a way that casts all the blame on me, none on his master. I can't risk putting that to the test."

I patted Father's hand. "We must save Devnet," I said. "Give Morann what he wants. If he's so keen to have me as his fosterling, you know he'll treat me well." I offered a weak smile. "I should be flattered, having such a powerful lord willing to use such desperate means to claim me."

Father wasn't comforted. "He wants you as more than a

fosterling. He's one of several kings who want to take back my rule over Èriu but are too cowardly to do it in the right way, by coming against me in single combat. They support Fachtna Fáthach's son, Conchobar, as High King." He chuckled drily. "The boy wouldn't last two breaths if he fought me, so their plan is to advance his cause by having him marry you."

"That's madness," I protested. "No one becomes High King by marriage, and Connacht is my brothers' inheritance now. I'm a road that leads nowhere."

"You're still a road Lord Morann wants Conchobar to take. The messenger gave me no reasons, only orders. The arrogance of the man! I'm to have you ready to leave us and on the road to meet his master in three days' time. Lord Morann is so sure of my surrender that he's already set out for Cruachan, in the chariot *I* gave him, attended by at least a dozen warriors."

"And Devnet," I said quietly.

Father was surprised. "How did you know?"

"Our bard is Lord Morann's precious bargaining token and his shield. He wouldn't leave him behind, out of his control, and if you attack his party, he'll have him killed on the spot."

"And make it look like my doing, no doubt. You do have your mother's wisdom." Father was on the point of tears. "I wish I could throw that messenger's severed head at Lord Morann's feet the moment before I took *his* own. All I ever wanted was to protect you, my spark, and now I've failed."

I hugged him and reassured him that everything would be all right. I sent him back to Mother after making him promise he'd sleep without worrying about me. I told him that I wasn't afraid to go to Lord Morann and that I could take care of myself.

I am no liar.

I didn't wait for dawn, but dressed by touch in the dark and flitted from my room. My ears were alert for any sound coming from the chamber where my parents slept with the boys. The smallest whimper from one of the babies could quickly turn into the three of them wailing, rousing all sleepers.

I lingered under the rafters of the great house only long enough to pack a leather bag with food, drink, and the means to strike a fire. My knife was too small for protection, so I stole into the storehouse where I'd fought Áed's wolfhound and carried away a piece of broken wood very like the one I'd used to hold off the dog. It would have to be enough.

I wasn't going to sit and wait for my fate to find me. I was going to meet Lord Morann's approaching party before they reached Cruachan. I didn't know how I'd do it, but I pledged to secure our bard's safe release without sacrificing myself.

I talked Áed out of two slaves, I thought as I threw Kelan's wolf-collared cloak over my shoulders. *I talked Master Íobar's ambitions into dust, even if it all ended so badly. I talked countless kings and warriors into thinking they could claim me when I was always far beyond their grasp. I may not have the Fair Folk's magic, but I have spells of my own, and I'll use them to save my friend.*

With that purpose in my heart, I left my father's house and chose my road.

Devnet was a bard and so a man with a memory trained to hold on to the precise details of innumerable poems, songs, and stories. He was like a child of the Fair Folk, gifted with an enchanted net that could capture every aspect of a moment

in its meshes and preserve it forever. Whenever he came back from his wanderings, he spun tales of his days on the road that described every route he'd ever taken. If you paid attention and recalled his words, you could travel to any of the royal strongholds in Èriu and not miss your way.

I hoped my memory was good enough to take me on the right road now. I encouraged myself by thinking, *If Devnet's descriptions of his last trip to Fir Domnann lands are accurate, if nothing's altered the landmarks he described, I'll know soon enough if I'm on the road I need to intercept Morann. But if that isn't so, I can still do this. Nothing changes the fact that the Fir Domnann live west of us and that there aren't many roads fit for a king's chariot between here and there.*

I walked at a brisk pace, striving to put as much distance between myself and home as I could. I didn't know how closely Lord Morann was following his messenger, but the man told Father he had three days to prepare me to leave. That probably meant Morann was lagging *more* than three days' journey behind, and it was a trip that wouldn't bring him all the way to the gates of Cruachan. Morann might be arrogant, but he wasn't stupid. He wouldn't bring his hostage into the heart of a ringfort where his twelve warriors could be overwhelmed by all of Father's men.

Father's men . . . now *there* was a problem I shared with Morann.

How long did I have before my departure was discovered? How long before Father sent his hunters to pick up my trail and bring me home?

One day, I thought. *That's all I've got. They'll be too busy packing my things to care about where I am until it's time for dinner. If I'm lucky, it will be too dark by then for Father to send out search parties, but they'll be after me by dawn, and then—*

I walked faster.

A drenching rain overtook me that night. I found refuge under a massive oak tree, but the downpour was so strong and unrelenting that not even the forest canopy could shield me from it completely. My cloak provided some warmth, which was a good thing, since kindling a fire was impossible.

The rain lasted through the night and didn't let up until well into the afternoon of the next day. I forced myself to travel on, though all I wanted to do was find a farmstead and beg shelter. My feet hurt, my throat was raw, and I learned that wet cheese tastes bad but soggy bread tastes worse. I tried to make the best of things by imagining Morann and his party suffering from the weather as much as I was.

I wonder how much farther I have to go before I meet them, I thought as my shoes squished with rainwater. *I hope I hear them before I see them or they see me. I don't want to charge into their midst head-on. Better to step off the path, take to the woodland, and watch them from there for a while, just to make sure Morann's kept his word about bringing Devnet home.*

The rain ended and a chill night came on. When I went hunting for fuel to start a fire, I discovered that every stick in the forest was soaked through. I'd have to depend on my cloak again. I huddled like a caterpillar in its cocoon and buried my face in the fur collar. Even if the wolf's pelt did smell like wet dog now, it still brought me bittersweet memories of my lost friend, Kelan. I told myself that I would never part with it, not even if it turned to tatters.

And I'll never let this leave me either, I thought, reaching into my belt pouch and drawing out my special keepsake, the rusting shard of Kelan's shattered sword. My fingers closed around that precious talisman, and in spite of the cold I fell asleep.

There was no rain the next day, but a drizzle came and went, fraying my temper as thin as a strand of spiderweb and cheating me out of a fire yet again. *If this doesn't change, Morann will find me by the sound of sneezing long before I find him,* I thought with grim humor as I closed my eyes.

I was roused in the middle of the night by the voices and a glimpse of fire through the trees. *Morann,* I thought, and cursed him for everything he'd done *and* for owning the luck or skill to have a fire when I had none. Common sense told me to stay put until daybreak, but I was too eager to find out if Devnet was with him.

I'll just creep near enough to see, I told myself. Leaving my bag and staff behind so that I could move more nimbly, I edged closer to the beckoning fire.

As I approached, disappointment overtook me. The fire I'd spied was only one small blaze, nothing fit to warm a king, his hostage, and a dozen fighting men. There were only three voices. I contemplated whether it would be safe for me to step into the ring of firelight and ask these unknown travelers if I could warm myself in their company. I listened to their talk more attentively, hoping to find something in their conversation to tell me they were decent, honorable people.

What I heard made me catch my breath.

"What do you mean you saw a face up in that tree? Are you crazy?"

I knew that voice. It belonged to one of Father's men.

"I saw what I saw," came the stubborn reply.

The hairs on the back of my neck rose. There on the far side of the campfire sat Caílte, the warrior whose hand had ended Kelan's life. I saw his hated face clearly.

My lost friend's killer had come hunting me.

CHAPTER SEVENTEEN

The Price of a Life

"STOP TALKING LIKE a woman, Caílte," the first man said irritably. I recognized him as Daire, well known in Cruachan for having a bull's thick neck and often the beast's bad temper. "This stupid chatter about someone among the branches, spying on us? It was an owl, or a shadow, or nothing!"

"Not someone," Caílte replied. "Just a face."

The third warrior in their party made a disgusted sound. "He's like this whenever he has to leave Cruachan overnight." His face was in shadow, but I knew Ruadan by the way he drawled his words, as if he were forever half asleep. Such slow speech was misleading: he was one of the swiftest runners I'd ever seen. "I found that out the hard way when we last marched to Tara and I slept beside him. I mean I *didn't* sleep, for all his gabble about seeing things. Bad enough that he loses his wits when the sun goes down, but does he have to try and take ours too?"

"Don't talk about me like I'm not here or I'll find a way to remind you," Caílte growled, fingering the hilt of his knife. "I didn't mean to talk about the face, but he took me by surprise, grinning down from the tree that way."

"Too bad you can't ask your invisible friend to show us the trail that leads to our princess," Daire joked.

Ruadan sighed. "Remember Kelan? If he was still around, he could've found her in a heartbeat, even after a rainstorm like we had. That lad was a skilled tracker."

"That lad was a fool," Caílte muttered.

I thought I saw Daire frown, but it might've been a trick of the firelight. "Look, Caílte, you were within your rights to challenge him for . . . well, for whatever insult he gave you. It's been years and I don't recall it anymore. But the boy's dead. Why belittle him?"

"Daire's right," Ruadan chimed in. "Your quarrel was settled long ago, by his death. Let his good name alone."

"Tell him to stop haunting me!" Caílte shouted. He sprang to his feet, scooped up a rock, and flung it hard against the tree trunk shielding me.

"Calm down, calm down." Daire rose to pat Caílte on the back. "It's been a tiring day."

"Do you think we'll be the ones to find her?" Ruadan wondered aloud.

Daire shrugged. "Lord Eochu sent out six search parties. No one knows which way she went when she left home, but if she ran off for the reason *I* think, we're not likely to be the lucky ones."

"We'd better be," Caílte grumbled. His companions ignored him.

"What makes you say so, Daire?" Ruadan asked.

"This is the same road Lord Morann's got to take to reach Cruachan. What do you bet that our princess is smart enough to know that? And I say *he's* the reason she's fleeing home, so why would she run down the path that'll take her right into his arms?"

"What makes you think he's behind her going?"

"*Think* for a change! It's not too hard." Daire began counting off each point he made on his thick fingers. "Lady Maeve's happy in her home. There's never been serious talk of fostering her out *anywhere*. Lord Morann's messenger shows up. Next thing you know, Lord Eochu announces he's handing over his favorite girl, no warning, hardly any time before he takes her away to meet Lord Morann partway. But what happens right off?" He jabbed his thumb at the overhanging branches. "Lady Maeve's gone! You tell *me* there's some other reason for it."

"I guess you're right," Ruadan said. "We won't be the ones to find her. How much longer should we try before we go back?"

"And tell Lord Eochu what?" Caílte's voice rose. "That we couldn't find his favorite daughter? Do you know the fate he keeps for men who fail him where she's concerned?"

"Caílte, I pray that Lady Maeve is found safe, but we're only one of the search parties. At best, another one will bring her home, but if the worst happens—may the gods avert it—we can't be held responsible if—"

"We can! We will! Open your eyes and see the truth, Ruadan. Lord Eochu will destroy all of us if any harm touches his daughter." Wood on the fire cracked and sent a tower of sparks shooting into the sky, painting Caílte's contorted face the color of blood. *This is why Kelan died!"*

I couldn't breathe. I was earth. I was stone. I heard Daire shouting at Caílte, telling him he was insane and would end his days as a wandering lunatic, homeless on the roads of Èriu. I heard Ruadan trying to intervene and make peace. Their words seemed to come from a greater and greater distance.

I realized I had crept away from their camp, done it silently and without thinking. I was back at the spot where I'd left my staff and traveler's bag. I moved in a dream, finding my way to the road by the leaf-dappled light of the moon.

This is why Kelan died. . . . This is why Kelan died. . . .

Caílte's words echoed through my mind as I walked through the dark. I needed time and a safe place to think, away from Father's men. I'd been lucky, overhearing them without being discovered.

And what of Lord Morann's party? How close were they? I was too shaken to deal with them now. With my nerves this taut, I wasn't fit to spy on them. I'd make some clumsy move, reveal my presence, and then Lord Morann would have me and no need to set Devnet free.

I found the path and followed it, sweeping my eyes left and right with every step, seeking the telltale glow of campfires that might mean Lord Morann's people were here. I saw none. My road broke free of the trees and brought me to the woodland's edge. A moonlit meadow lay before me, embraced by a river whose rippling waters held the stars. A hill rose in the middle distance, its crest crowned with dark shapes that made it look like the lower jaw of some fantastic monster.

A gateway mound, I thought, remembering tales of how unnatural hills like this earned the Fair Folk another name: People of the Mounds. They sometimes adorned the tops of their underground retreats with giant standing stones. There was probably a portal to the Otherworld in the flank of the hill, the entry framed by weirdly carved blocks.

I should have been afraid.

I was, at first. I stood staring at it in wonder and terror, under a sky as black as the wings of the Morrígan's ravens, but splashed and spangled with silvery light. As I watched, a cloud raced across the moon, a phantom with wings of smoke and eyes of flame.

Ea! I called her name with my heart and started forward, across the open grassland. It didn't matter if I'd seen a wandering spirit or only a vision of my own creation. The memory of my brave, wondrous bird blew away my fear with the beating of her wings and drew my footsteps to the mound.

I circled it, seeking an opening, and found one on the side that faced away from the forest. A massive white stone lay across the entryway, a thick slab of rock whose face was completely covered with an intricate pattern of whorls and curves. The spirals were so artfully carved that it was like staring into an eddying stream. A dark passage lay beyond the barricade.

"People of the Mounds, I seek you," I said in a calm, reverent voice. "I am Maeve, princess of Connacht, daughter of Cloithfinn and Eochu Feidlech, who is High King of Èriu. Let me shelter here, and if the price of your protection is that I never see the sun again, I accept it." I straightened my shoulders, walked around the white slab, and crossed the boundary between worlds.

I didn't stop until I was entirely shrouded by shadows, with not even a strand of my hair or a thread of my hem touched by the moonlight falling across the threshold to the mound. I had entered a gateway to the Otherworld without any protective charm, such as a branch of the sacred rowan tree. There was no enchantment to shield me from the Fair Folk, if they decided they didn't want me in their realm uninvited. The few weapons that I had to defend myself were purely human—my walking staff and my knife. If the People of the Mounds sent monsters to destroy me for my brashness, I wouldn't survive, but I wouldn't die helpless or without teaching them that I was a hard mouthful to swallow.

I don't know how long I waited in the darkness. I didn't want to enter the Otherworld completely; I merely wanted to wrap its peace around me and muster my thoughts. I cocked my head toward the depths of the mound. The silence was a solid thing. Hearkening in the other direction, toward the mortal world beyond the white stone, I heard the faint rustle of a stray breeze over the grass, the song of night insects, and nothing more. I closed my eyes.

When I opened them, I saw the fires.

There were three, burning far away across the meadow, deep within the shelter of forest beyond. *Am I seeing this?* I wondered as I slowly emerged from the mound and laid one hand lightly on a carved slab before the entry. Yes, there they were, so small at that distance, but real. *Are they his? Morann's? Is Devnet with him?* I had to know.

Before I stepped away from my refuge, I thanked the People of the Mounds for their kindness. Even though I'd seen nothing within the gateway, I left feeling as though the powerful deities of the Otherworld had offered me the guest-bond. I was grateful.

Lord Morann's encampment boasted *five* fires, not just the three I'd seen from the shadows of the mound. All that light made it difficult for me to get close enough to take in everything that was going on without being detected, but I managed to see enough. Besides his twelve warriors he'd brought a pair of servants, his charioteer, and—

Yes, there was Devnet. Our bard sat flanked by two of Morann's fighting men, eating his dinner at the smallest fire, far from his captor. His ankles were bound. When he finished eating, one of the guards secured his wrists as well.

"Not too tight, friend." It sounded like he'd held on to his good humor despite everything. "I'd like to be able to play my harp again someday, even if it's just for the instant before your chief cuts off my head."

"There'll be none of that, don't worry," the guard tying Devnet's wrists said. "It won't be long until we meet up with Lord Eochu. Once his daughter comes to us, you'll be let go."

"And you think that will be the end of it?" Devnet chuckled drily. "How many kings do you know who'd simply let a bard go free after treating him like this?" He indicated his bonds. "Lord Morann knows the power of a song. He won't want that weapon turned against him, especially after he used it so skillfully to slander my sweet princess. There's only one way to be sure I keep silent, just as there's only one way for him to turn my lady Maeve back into the prize she was before her brothers were born."

The first guard's brow creased. "What are you saying?"

"What I heard Lord Morann himself say when I was still his guest and not his hostage. He asked if the three young princes were well when I left Cruachan. When I told him yes, he drank to their health but added, 'We must be glad for them while we can. Born so small, so soon, who knows what their future will be?'" Devnet made a face. "That was when I made the mistake of *hinting* that such talk might be called ill-wishing. He used my words as an excuse to justify *this*." He held up his bound hands.

"You're spinning tales," the second guard scoffed. "How could Lord Morann harm the princes of Connacht? It's impossible."

"You're young enough to believe that," Devnet replied. "But I've lived and traveled long enough to know that ambition has a way of trampling anything in its way, including what's 'impossible.' I'm glad I won't be there to see it happen. They're such sweet babies."

I slipped away while Devnet's guards barked at him to shut his mouth. If I hadn't been so horrified by all I'd heard, I would have laughed at this one *true* impossibility: compelling a bard to be silent.

I crossed the meadow of the gateway mound and paused for another look at the stone-crowned hill that hid a path to the Otherworld. What would I have found if I'd followed that dark passageway to its end? I knew I could be brave, but would I ever be brave enough to do such a thing? Would anyone— king, warrior, bard, or druid—have the courage to confront the Fair Folk face to face, in all their ageless power? There had been some, and the bards sang their praises, but much more often those who encountered the People of the Mounds feared and fled.

Feared and fled. The flash of an idea struck me. I knew what I must try in order to save Devnet. "Thank you," I whispered to the Fair Folk in their hidden realm, for my heart told me this inspiration was their parting gift to me.

I retraced my way to the campfire where Father's men were still talking. Their tongues froze when I stepped into the light.

"Lady Maeve?" Daire regarded me with clear mistrust. "It's you, isn't it?"

"Of course it's her, you idiot!" Ruadan recovered from his shock enough to punch Daire in the shoulder. "What do you think, we've captured a shape-shifting bean sidhe?"

"You *captured* nothing," I told him stiffly. "I've come to you of my own will."

Ruadan looked chastened. "I'm sorry, Princess. It's good to see you. Now we can head back to Cruachan in the morning."

"Yes," I said. "With your king's honor restored and our bard Devnet rescued. Let me sit by the fire—last night's rain ate my bones—and I'll tell you how you'll all earn my father's favor for life, more cattle than you have hairs on your head, and enough gold to bury each of them up to the tips of their horns."

Here's magic: if you give commands as if it's your right to do so, you will be obeyed, or at least be heeded. The three warriors listened as I told them my plan, their eyes growing wider at every word.

When I finished, Daire was the first to speak. "You say you saw twelve fighting men in Lord Morann's camp?"

I brushed his question aside. "Even if there were a hundred, it wouldn't matter. I'm not telling you to fight them."

"You're telling us to cut our own throats," Caílte growled. "The risk is too great. You could be killed."

"You mean *you* could be killed if anything happened to

me," I told him tartly. "Don't worry—I'm only valuable to Lord Morann alive."

He shook his head stubbornly and addressed his companions. "Too much could go wrong. We have to take her back to Cruachan. I'll carry her there myself if I must."

I lowered my voice so that all of them were forced to listen closely to every word. "Lord Morann's camp doesn't lie that far from here. Lay one finger on me and you'll see how well a scream carries on a still night. His men will be on us, take me, kill Devnet, and leave your king looking weak, gullible, and unfit to rule. Do you serve Lord Eochu or only your own fears? I am ready to risk this. Will you admit you have less courage than a girl?"

That did it. They were mine.

The moon was sinking as we crossed the meadow. I gestured to where Morann's campfires still burned. My men nodded and went ahead of me to scout the best positions for what they'd have to do. Alone, I took the bag of ashes I'd gathered from their fire and rubbed them through my hair to dim its telltale red. I spat into my hands, worked more of the ashes into a paste, and smeared it over my face. Next I snarled fistfuls of grass and wildflower stems through my curls.

I must look dreadful, I thought. *Like something not quite human.* A wicked grin curved my lips. *Perfect.*

My one regret was that I wasn't standing close enough to view Morann's campsite when I loosed the eerie, sobbing cry of the bean sidhe, the uncanny woman of the Fair Folk whose voice foretells death. I wish I could have seen his face when I howled his name and his doom.

At least I was able to hear how badly his voice shook as he commanded all his warriors to seek the source of that unearthly wailing. He was so ensnared by his own terror that he left them no chance to raise sensible objections—what good is it to pursue a creature of the Otherworld?—and as his loyal men they could not disobey.

I ran while they were still retrieving their weapons and lighting torches. I sent my voice trailing behind me, trying not to laugh while I continued howling portents of Morann's death. If any of them were sharp-eyed enough to catch sight of me before they gave chase, they'd see a wild phantom, not a girl.

When I broke from the forest, I sealed my lips and kept them sealed as I raced across the meadow. I'd fulfilled my part in the plot, rousing Morann's hounds and luring them away. Now I had to throw them off my scent or everything was lost. Labored breath and pulsing blood filled my ears. I never paused to listen for the sounds of pursuit. I had no time to ask myself if my pursuers were close enough behind me to guess my goal. With a few hasty words to beg the Fair Folk's pardon for this second invasion, I plunged into the mound.

I barely had time to enjoy the silence sheltering me when I heard the warriors' approach. They raced past the entrance to the mound, the flare of their torches such a brief wink of light that at first I thought my eyes had fooled me. I learned better soon, for they came back, this time pausing just on the other side of the gateway's guardian slab. One of them stared down the passageway so intently that I thought he'd spied me, even as deeply as I'd burrowed into the dark. My palms turned damp and I trembled in spite of myself. I leaned against the rough stone wall to stay upright under his penetrating gaze.

"Are you sure she went in there?" one of his comrades asked. "Because I could swear she blew away on the wind."

"I saw what I saw," the first man snapped, but he didn't sound certain.

"If she did, she's gone," a third warrior declared. "Gone back to her own people. We won't see her again. Not if we're lucky."

"*Was* that a bean sidhe?"

"What else could it be? Would any *human* girl go roaming the land at night or enter a fearsome place like that?" He gestured at the entrance to the mound with his spear.

"Maybe . . . if she was a wandering madwoman." The first man was the kind of hound who didn't let go easily once his jaws closed on his prey. "We should go in after her, to be sure."

"You first."

No one moved.

That was good, but I wanted something better: I wanted them gone. How to encourage that?

Guennola's angry hiss was easy to imitate. I cupped my hands to my mouth in order to amplify the sound and put a healthy breath behind it. The passageway into the mound added volume to the stoat's cry as well, making it echo loud enough to bring Morann's men to attention.

"Did you hear that?"

"What was it?"

"Something in there."

"Are you sure? Maybe it was a trick of the wind."

I took a fresh breath and gave one of Muirín's sharp yelps, then followed it with a rapid series of barks. It wouldn't have fooled another fox, but that wasn't my goal.

"Listen now! It *did* come from the mound." The men gaped at the passageway but not one of them dared to stir a step past the white stone barrier.

"What was it? It sounded like a dog."

"Not a dog . . . a fox, I think. But that hissing—"

I pitched my voice low and growled like a badger. The long, rough, rumbling call rolled out of the mound like thunder. Each new animal's cry that I added to my performance pulled the warriors' nerves tauter. It was unnatural to hear such a variety of beasts in one place, especially when that place was a route to the Otherworld. I paused only long enough to mutter a renewed petition to the Fair Folk, imploring their leniency for what I was doing on their threshold. I hoped that if they didn't find my presence insignificant enough to overlook, they'd find my ploy amusing enough to divert their retribution.

I dropped to my knees, scrabbling for stones on the passageway floor. I flung one, then another, then as many as I could throw in rapid succession. None of my missiles needed to hit a target. My aim was simply to make the men imagine that they'd stirred up the true inhabitants of the mound and now the warriors of the Fair Folk were massing to drive them away. As the last stone left my hand, I filled my lungs as deeply as I could and fairly screamed my Ea's familiar cry:

Kee-kee-kee! Kee-kee-kee! Kee-kee-kee!

Until that moment I had no idea that it's possible for a man to run away without actually *running*. No warrior worthy of the name would ever *flee* danger, especially when his fellow fighters were there to witness such a shame. Still, all of Morann's men managed to take themselves elsewhere, and quickly, before the last echo of my kestrel call died away. As their torches retreated across the meadow, back toward their camp, I rushed to the portal, rested my hands on the white stone, leaned forward, and craned my neck to watch them go.

I followed them at a safe distance, but it was hard to hold myself back and go slowly. I burned with eagerness to know if the rest of my plan had worked. I had the answer soon enough, when I heard their shouts of outrage and surprise up ahead.

A dozen fighting men are more than a match for three, but one man can single-handedly defeat all twelve just by holding his sword to the throat of their king. That was exactly what I saw Ruadan doing when I arrived.

He grinned when he saw me. "Well, my lady, it worked."

I lifted my chin. "Did you ever doubt me?" He had the wisdom and the courtesy not to answer that.

"Never, Princess." Devnet came forward to greet me, rubbing his wrists, now freed from their bonds. "I'm in your debt forever."

I hugged him close. "You owe me nothing. All this happened because you were trying to help me."

He shrugged. "If we keep pulling threads, trying to see which ones make the pattern, we unravel the cloth and are left with nothing but tangles. Let's have no more talk of debts." He cocked his head and studied my ash-smeared hair and face. "On second thought, you *do* owe me the tale of how you contrived my rescue. May Lugh give me the art to do it justice!"

The bard's words were poetry, but poetry could wait. I had practical matters to settle. I took Daire aside and gave him his instructions. I knew my orders for Morann's men would be followed more readily and with less balking if they came from his mouth, not mine. He sent the warriors on their way, letting them know that their king's continued health depended on their obedience. They took torches to light their road and left. A few cast speculative backward glances at me, in all my smudged splendor. At least two raised their eyebrows, realizing how they'd been deceived. One smiled.

Morann's servants were sent home with his men, but not the charioteer. Daire relayed the command that he take Ruadan back to Cruachan. "I don't care that it's still dark—you'll get started now," he told the driver. "As for you, Ruadan—"

"I know, I know," Ruadan drawled. "Tell Lord Eochu what's happened and have him and our warriors meet us on the way home. The Fir Domnann fighters are gone, but no sense trusting that they'll stay away." He nudged the charioteer. "Let's go."

Ruadan's departure left Daire and Caílte to share the duty of standing watch over Morann. "You should let Devnet and me help you, or you'll both be too tired when morning comes," I said.

"With respect, Lady Maeve, could you or our bard cut a man's throat if it came to that?" Daire asked.

I couldn't say yes and stay honest, but Devnet had a good answer: "If Lady Maeve and I stand watch together and Lord Morann's throat needs cutting, I think that we could find enough nerve *between* us for the job." Daire and Caílte exchanged doubtful looks, but conceded.

Lord Morann made himself a nest of curses and went to sleep. "Do you think we scared him?" Devnet whispered to me. I giggled.

As we sat together, keeping watch over our captive king, Devnet asked me to tell him how I'd come to spearhead his rescue. I did so, leaving nothing out, not even the strange attraction that had brought me over the threshold of the gateway mound.

"I was frightened at first," I said. "But when I saw my Ea's shape fly across the moon, I remembered her courage and went on."

"Ea?"

And all at once my heart opened and the sorrow and loss I'd carried there so long came pouring out. I told my friend about Ea and Odran, about the crannog and the joy I'd found there in healing helpless creatures, about the cold brutality with which Master Íobar had slain them, about how the slingstone that sent Ea to her death shattered me as well. Every word was a knife that opened an old wound. A few tears trickled down my cheeks, but I couldn't have the comfort of weeping out my grief for fear of waking Daire and Caílte.

"I wish you could have seen her, Devnet," I said. "When we go home, I'll show you the hood I made for her. It's my one remembrance."

"A hood?"

"We had to keep the smaller animals safe from her. A bird that can't see won't fly. It was my idea."

"Clever. In my travels, I saw some hawk trainers using the same thing to control their birds."

"Hawk trainers?" I wiped away my tears.

He nodded. "In the East, I met three people who'd taught raptors to hunt for them. They set them after small game birds. I hear that in some lands it's a common thing."

"I don't know if I'd ever have wanted Ea to chase game for me," I mused. "But I enjoyed watching her fend for herself. She was wonderful in flight."

"How do you know your Ea was a *she*?" Devnet asked.

"Male kestrels have blue-feathered caps. Odran told me so. Females have wide black stripes across their tails to set them apart."

"I thought you were going to say they wore more jewelry," Devnet teased. "When I was in the north, I met one pretty winged lady who owned a bracelet made of fire."

"What?"

"Oh, don't be alarmed, it didn't blaze too high—how could she fly, wrapped in flame? The fire was trapped in a braid of hair, made captive by its beauty. I asked her master what she'd done to earn her enchanted talisman and he said that he'd found her wearing it. Whenever he tried to remove it, she snapped at him, so he let it be."

Our bard went on to describe how the falcon's master discovered her while on a far-ranging hunt of his own. He took an immediate fancy to her, for even though she was badly wounded, she had a bold spirit that attracted him. At the price of some unavoidable damage to his fingers from the bird's beak and talons, he brought her back to the stronghold of Dún Beithe.

I recognized the name. "That's where Lady Íde's cousin rules."

"Lord Artegal, yes, and the young man I met is his son."

I begged Devnet to tell me more. He was glad to do so, for what bard ever turned down an invitation to talk? He spoke about how the fallen falcon's rescuer tended her, earned her trust, then taught her to hunt for him. I interrupted his account many times, posing question after question, but though I listened greedily to his responses, I was in a daze.

It's Ea, I thought. *How many kestrels wear a red braid? It must be her!* My heart longed to believe in the impossible: that she'd escaped death, that the druid's slingstone had only wounded her, that some merciful power had brought her into the care of a good person with the wit to heal her.

My spirit knew that somehow I had to find out if what I believed was true.

It was a good thing that Daire woke up and told us to get some sleep. I'd become too engrossed by the thought that Ea might still be alive, and distraction makes a bad sentry. I didn't think I'd be able to close my eyes, but I was exhausted and sleep claimed me.

We took the homeward road at sunrise. Morann walked with his head down and his shoulders hunched, saying nothing. Daire and Caílte alternated staying as close to him as his shadow. From time to time, Devnet would sing to entertain us.

"Before we reach Cruachan, I must finish creating the tale of how Lady Maeve saved me," he declared. "Every detail of her heroic exploits must be accurate." He turned to me with an innocent expression. "Now remind me, Princess. When I was attacked by that flying plague of fanged squirrels and you used a wild boar to bludgeon them all to death, did you pick the boar up by its front legs or its hindquarters?"

"By its tail," I tossed off in reply. "And shame on you for not remembering."

I spoke with a lightness I didn't feel. Now that Devnet was safe and there would be no further threat from Morann, my memory fell back to the moment I heard Caílte cry out the words that sent me wandering to the threshold of the Otherworld: *This is why Kelan died!*

What did he mean? I would not let the sun set until I had an answer.

The next time Daire took over as Morann's guard and Caílte dropped to the rear of our group, I fell into step beside him. "I want to talk to you."

"That's a change," he muttered, keeping his eyes straight ahead.

"I heard you last night, Caílte," I said. "Before I spied on Morann's encampment, I watched yours. I was behind a tree when you spoke of Kelan's death. You made it sound as if it didn't happen because of your stupid quarrel over the hero's portion."

"That was years ago. With respect, it doesn't concern you, Princess."

"I decide what concerns me."

He tightened his jaw and kept silent. A wall had dropped between us. I intended to tear it down.

"He haunts you, doesn't he?" I asked in a low voice. "You see his face when night finds you far from home. Aren't you afraid this will grow worse, with time? What will you do when the day comes that his face never leaves your sight, when you can't look anywhere, waking or sleeping, without seeing him, when—"

Caílte stopped dead and clutched my arm. "Have mercy, Princess." He spoke in a half-strangled whisper. Sweat beaded his brow. "Don't ill-wish me more than I already suffer. Do you think I *wanted* to kill him?"

"He said you didn't merit the hero's portion. You could have laughed it off. You could have made him pay for the insult with a beating."

"I wish I could have done that." Caílte's face fell. "I swear by my sword arm, I wish I'd had a choice. If I hadn't found cause to challenge him that night, it would have happened some other time. It had to be. If I'd refused, someone else would have done it, and badly. Kelan didn't deserve to die by butchery. I gave him a warrior's death, quick and clean. I don't regret that."

"Why did he deserve to die at all?"

Caílte spoke softly. "He failed the first duty of every man who serves the High King: He didn't protect Lord Eochu's greatest treasure. He taught a king's beloved daughter skills that put her in harm's way."

"I don't understand what—"

"The dog, Princess," Caílte replied. "That savage wolf-hound you fought off to save young Kelan's girl and the baby she carried. Your father called me to him after the lad admitted he'd been teaching you how to use weapons. The king had me meet him outside the ringfort, where no one could surprise us or overhear. I never saw him so enraged, not even when he dueled his enemies and the battle madness possessed him. His words are burned into me here"—he touched his brow—"and here." He touched his heart.

Don't tell me any more, Caílte! I thought, suddenly afraid of what I'd stirred up.

"What did he say?" I asked. Afraid or not, I had to know.

"He said that if Kelan hadn't meddled, hadn't taught a girl things no girl needed to know, you wouldn't have deceived yourself into thinking you could fight the beast. You'd have

run away, like a sensible girl, and gotten yourself out of danger. He said he was going to put an end to your ridiculous fancies of taking up a man's weapons by putting an end to the man who encouraged them."

"Why—" I could hardly find breath to speak. "Why did he need *you* to kill my friend? Why didn't he do it himself?"

Caílte smiled sadly. "You've answered that yourself, Princess. Kelan was your friend. You'd never forgive the man who killed him, and your father has always needed your love and goodwill. You're his daughter, but until your brothers were born, you were also his future, the lady of Connacht, the prize that all of us saw shining just beyond our reach—"

The hero's portion, I thought. *The bone to tempt the High King's hounds and keep them close and loyal. Is that what I was to Father? Is that who I am?*

"How do I know you're not lying, Caílte?" It had to be asked.

"What would I gain by deceiving you? I could give you my word of honor that everything I've told you is so, but would you accept it?" He laughed like the cawing of a crow. "Ask your father for the truth, Princess. Run and ask him why he let Kelan think he'd been pardoned when the lad's punishment waited for him in the shadows. And when you learn that I *have* told you the truth, ask him how he'll reward me for it." He shrugged. "Maybe it's time I took the payment I deserve for what I've done. Let it come. I'm tired of seeing that blameless boy's face everywhere I turn. I'm tired of fighting phantoms. I'm tired of living with evil dreams." He looked at me steadily. "Tell the king what I've told you, my lady, and let me sleep."

Chapter Eighteen

Road of Return

CAÍLTE GROANED IN his sleep all night long, struggling with Kelan's ghost. At least he could close his eyes. I lay wide awake, staring into the star-hung branches above me. My mind was filled with what that tormented man had told me before Daire called him away to take a turn herding Lord Morann.

How could my father, the man I'd loved and worshipped all my life, be so unjust? I was torn from throat to heart. It wasn't possible. It was wrong. I refused to believe it.

I did.

Caílte stirred well before dawn and sat up with his head in his hands. Daire was on sentry duty and glanced his way for an instant, then shrugged and ignored him. He'd grown accustomed to Caílte's midnight horrors.

I took the opportunity to creep closer and place a comforting hand on his arm. "Father won't know you told me about Kelan," I whispered.

Caílte's face remained impassive in the leaf-scattered

moonlight. "That's kind of you, Princess, but it's a secret you don't need to keep. The High King has never been a man to question the rightness of his actions. If you think less of him for this, he'll see it as a flaw in you, not himself."

I lowered my gaze. "Does my mother know?"

"That I killed the lad?" He sounded incredulous. As if anyone in Cruachan didn't know that!

"I mean does she know Father forced you to do something so unjust?" I looked up again to see him shake his head.

"Only a fool would say anything to Lady Cloithfinn that might turn her against her husband. He'd find out, and then it'd be just a matter of days before he repaid whoever did it." He gave me an uncertain look. "Of course he'd never touch *you* for carrying the tale to her, Lady Maeve, but . . . will you?"

I reassured him that I would tell Mother nothing. What good would it do? She'd hate Father for it, and that would poison her life as well as his. Worse, she might declare he'd done the right thing, and then I'd have to hate them both.

"Say, why are you two putting your heads together over there?" Daire called out cheerily. He was in a good mood, probably already feeling the weight of gold Father would put into his hands. "I thought we were all friends here."

"We are, which is why I wanted to speak with Caílte alone," I replied lightly. "I'm about to give him a gift and I didn't want you to feel neglected, seeing him receive it when I have nothing for you."

"Unfair! Our princess is playing favorites." Daire made a playfully exaggerated show of wounded pride. "Why does *he* deserve a gift?"

"Because he doesn't question his princess or keep a poor, weary bard from his dreams?" Devnet suggested sleepily.

My fingers dipped into the little pouch at my waist and plucked out the shard of Kelan's sword. Before Caílte knew what I was doing, I took his hand in one of mine, placed the sliver of iron on his palm, and curled his fingers around it. Leaning forward, I whispered in the warrior's ear, "This was Kelan's, and mine, and now it's yours, a token of peace, a charm to set you free. It carries his forgiveness. You won't see his face again."

Caílte opened his hand only enough to glimpse what I'd given him, then shoved the iron sliver deep into his own pouch, ignoring Daire's pestering him to reveal my gift. He lay down again, as did I. Now I could sleep.

The next morning, Caílte put an end to Daire's curiosity. "You want to see my princess's gift?" he asked, so pleasantly that his fellow warrior gave him a suspicious look. "Here it is." He displayed the iron shard.

"That's it?" Daire blinked. "*That's* your royal gift?"

"It is," Caílte said. "And it's wondrous."

"It's a rusty piece of nothing. Yet here you sit, grinning like a man who's been given gold, fast horses, and a beautiful, silent wife. Have you finally lost your mind?"

"No, nor will I. Lady Maeve's gift gave me the first peaceful night I've known in years. That's worth more to me than anything you've named." He fixed a grateful look on me. "Where did you learn to weave such magic, Princess?"

I could only smile back at him. There was no enchantment tied to the remnant of Kelan's shattered sword. I didn't

have a druid's power to bless or curse. All I'd done was offer a long-suffering spirit permission to accept my forgiveness and to forgive himself. If he chose to call it magic, I wouldn't tell him otherwise.

Father's party intercepted ours when the sun stood directly overhead, after we'd emerged from the forest. I braced myself for the moment when I'd have to face him. Would I be able to bear his touch or would I shrink back into myself when he embraced me? Would he question me for that or would he even notice? Try as I would, I couldn't summon up the ability to act as though nothing had changed between us. Every time I remembered what he'd done, the years that had passed between Kelan's death and now became no more than the blink of an eye.

Fechin was driving Father to meet us. They were accompanied by at least twenty armed men, some on foot, some on horseback. I could tell the exact moment he caught sight of us because that was when his chariot broke away from everyone else and spewed dust behind it. It took the mounted men a moment to gather their wits and urge their horses into a gallop, but soon they were pacing the High King, while the men on foot came pelting after.

"We're either about to get welcomed or trampled," Devnet murmured to me. "Maybe we should go back into the woods."

I was too tense to share his humor. As Fechin reined back the horses, Father leaped from his chariot and lifted me off my feet in an overpowering hug.

"Oh my Maeve, my spark, thank all the gods you're safe!" he cried.

Yes, thank them for that, I thought, feeling like no more than a bundle of cloth in his arms. *Or who would have to die this time for failing to protect the High King's prized possession?*

Father set me down and got a good look at me. I'd rinsed the ash paste from my face in a woodland stream but had done a slapdash job of it. I never had time to wash my gray-streaked hair at all. "What *happened* to you?" he exclaimed.

That question drew our bard like nectar draws bees. I had no hope of answering before Devnet came forward, the first words of our adventure already falling from his lips.

I never heard such an artful weaving of words. Devnet's clear, strong voice recounted my full participation in his rescue, everything from how I'd found a way for three men to overcome a dozen without shedding a single drop of blood to how I'd mustered the forces of the Otherworld to help me defeat Morann's men. He dwelled lovingly on the way I'd brought the fallen king to account for his sins, including the fact that he'd broken the guest-bond, had the effrontery to demand me for his fosterling, and worst of all . . .

"He broke my harp."

There was nothing maidenly about me in that telling. I wasn't the princess who depended on others for protection but the one who fought to defend what was precious to her. Devnet spoke only the truth—though of course he couldn't resist adding his own dramatic touches and tweaks. His skill took my exploits and served them up like salt seasoning a stew from tastelessness to savory perfection. He described me as the girl I was, the girl my father never wanted me to be.

I watched Father's face as Devnet spoke. He wasn't happy, but his warriors were. They kept up an ongoing chorus of

approval. The corners of Father's mouth were pulled down farther and farther with every shout of praise for what I'd accomplished.

Devnet lifted his hands, offering up the last of his tale. "I've often said that our princess has a warrior's spirit, which is a good thing in a woman. Our most formidable fighters have always inherited their daring, strength, and courage from *both* parents. Valiant mothers breed valiant sons. Your three boys will soon prove that, Lord Eochu, as your daughter will do once she finds her true mate. But where is the hero brave enough to hold her fire in his hands? Where is the man wise and bold enough to recognize her true worth without fearing it and to reward it fitly?"

The warriors roared agreement, beating their swords against their shields until it sounded like the thundering challenge that rose from both sides before a battle. Even Father seemed to accept what I'd done and gave me a look that was filled with pride.

But how long will this last? I thought. *How soon before he falls back into the old ways, trying to tether me? And how can I stand it, knowing what he's done and still might do to anyone who tries to help me cut that cord?* I absentmindedly twined a tress of hair around my finger. It was one of the few that had escaped being coated with ashes. As I looked at it, I imagined it braided and looped around a kestrel's foot, a bracelet made of flame, destined for flight. *Oh, Ea, if I stay here, I'm earthbound!*

"Maeve?" Father's voice roused me. "My little warrior, don't you know it's not polite to ignore your king when he's trying to reward your courage?"

"I'm sorry, Father. What were you saying?"

"Lord Eochu wants your aid, my lady," Devnet said. "He's smart enough to know that our heroism must bring you a much greater prize than cattle or gold, but he has no notion what that prize should be."

"That's true, my spark," Father said benevolently. "I leave it to you. Tell me what you'd like and it's yours." He winked. "Within reason. I can't give you Connacht and you'd have to fight me if you wanted to be High King."

I looked him in the eye. "Is that a promise? Do you give me your word as king?"

He drew back, put off balance by what I'd said. "If you wish." He sounded mystified, but took his oath before our bard and with his warriors at witnesses. "But I don't see why you need—"

"Send me away. I want to be like my sisters. I want to go into fosterage."

All Cruachan agreed that I'd asked for the most admirable reward in the world. It wasn't greedy or ambitious. It was a natural part of the lives of highborn children. It would benefit Connacht through the alliance it secured between us and the kingdom that accepted me.

And wasn't it touching that I'd requested to be placed with Lady Íde's beloved cousin, Lord Artegal of Dún Beithe? Father raised a brow to hear me take control of a choice that should have been his, but when I said, "I want to do this to honor Mother's loyal friend, the woman who devoted herself to the safe birth of my brothers," he had to hold his tongue.

As soon as we received Lord Artegal's enthusiastic consent to foster me, preparations began for sending me to my new life

in the north. Lady Íde was delighted that I'd be a part of her cousin's household. "Artegal is a wonderful man, though he and his wife can be a bit softheaded when it comes to that boy of theirs. I know they'll make you welcome." She and Mother worked furiously through their tears, driving the women of Cruachan in a dozen different directions in order to assemble all the things I'd need for my departure. Everything was ready in three days' time.

To my chagrin, I wasn't permitted to take part in any of the work. Mother insisted I use my remaining days for taking leave of the people and places I wouldn't see for years to come. Some I might never see again.

I was no longer kept at arm's length from my brothers. The triplets' nurses began presenting the *findemna* to me every chance they got, as if my brothers were three platters of choice food. The first time I took one of the babies into my arms, I was rewarded with a smile.

"Who are you, precious one?" I asked him tenderly.

"That's Lothar." His nurse spoke as proudly as if she'd given birth to the prince herself. "Do you feel how strong he is? He'll be walking before the next new moon!"

"Then he'll have to catch up with my Bres," a second woman declared. "He'll be walking *long* before that."

The two of them began to bicker over which of their infant charges was the cleverest, the better eater, the most advanced, until the third nursemaid quietly said, "Nár sleeps all through the night and never wakes me." This earned a pair of envious glares from her colleagues, but it also put an end to the argument.

The day before I left, I went to visit my cattle. It gave me a great sense of satisfaction and security to see how well they were doing. The cowherd took pride in showing me how they thrived and reassured me he'd continue to care for them well until my return.

On the way back, I met Devnet. "I've been looking for you, Princess," he said. "That is, your father asked me to find you and bring you to him for a private farewell. There are some things he'd like to tell you before you go that he can't say tomorrow in front of everyone."

"Thank you, Devnet," I said. "You won't have to escort me. I ought to be able to find him on my own."

"You *ought* to, but *will* you?" I couldn't deceive a man who lived by playing with all aspects of words, from their plainest meanings to their most secret subtleties. "I haven't seen you in Lord Eochu's company once since his return. Something's changed."

"Things do," I replied. I sped up my pace, but Devnet matched it.

"You're right, my lady," he said. "Things, people, hearts, truth, they all change. It's only our way of seeing them that's permanent."

A half-smile lifted one corner of my mouth. "That's not the way it is with truth and you know it."

"Well, I've lived long enough to know many things, especially about truth and change. As a bard, I've often braided both of them together." He smiled and kissed the top of my head. "Your leave-taking is a change I wish weren't true. How can Cruachan live without its princess? And such a princess! One who loves strongly and hates swiftly, who acts rashly and gives freely, who understands slowly but once she does, it's deeply and with a knowing heart. Above all, one who lives boldly." He lifted my chin with one fingertip. "Can my princess also learn to hide the truth just long enough to forgive her enemy graciously before she leaves his care?"

"Father's not my enemy." Rising tears choked my voice. "But what he did—"

"Hush. I knew there was a reason things had changed between him and you, but nothing about what caused it. I doubt I need to know. Keep this secret if revealing it will do more harm than good."

Is that enough reason to hide the truth? I wondered. But I said nothing. I'd been brought up to revere the bards and to accept their words as wisdom.

"I can't forgive him," I muttered. "Not yet."

"Then see him now and smile as though he's done nothing that needs forgiveness. It's only for a little while. You're going to a new life. For your own sake, take none of the old heartaches with you when you leave."

I did as Devnet asked, though not without a great burden of misgiving. I forced myself to see Father as I'd known him when he was still my champion, my hero, the shining warrior and king who could do no wrong and who always seemed to love me best. When the day of my departure came, he wept. So did I, but not because I was leaving him.

The journey to Lord Artegal's stronghold was long but made pleasant by good company. Devnet had declared he'd come with me, and no one wanted to tell a bard what he could and couldn't do.

I rode in the chariot we'd taken from Morann, the same one Father gave him when his stallions ran away with me. The former king of the Fir Domnann raised no objections. Two days after his arrival in Cruachan, our royal captive had made the serious mistake of insulting the High King grievously. That was what rumor claimed, for no one seemed to know any person who'd actually witnessed the affront. In any case, an armed challenge had been the only remedy.

Now Morann's head shared the lintel of our doorway with Fachtna Fáthach's. Devnet glanced up at it before we left. "What a price to pay for a broken harp," he said.

Father insisted that Fechin be my driver. The battle-hardened charioteer spent most of the trip recounting stories that all began with "I remember when you were just a baby" and all ended with "But now you're a young woman and you probably won't remember me when we meet again." It was very funny having to dry a grown man's sentimental tears and reassure him daily that he'd never be forgotten. Devnet's vehicle kept pace alongside and our bard was kindhearted enough to pretend he saw nothing of Fechin's distress.

When the heights of Dún Beithe came into sight, Devnet and I decided to walk the rest of the way, sending Fechin ahead to announce us. It was partly to stretch our legs and partly to escape from his ever-growing urge to sniffle his way through tales of my childhood. The driver of the cart carrying my possessions overtook us and we got some odd looks from him, but we waved him on and kept walking.

"You know, Fechin's not the only one who's afraid you'll forget him," Devnet remarked casually. He stopped and removed his gold earrings. "Take these to remember me by, Princess."

I held up my hands, fending off the gift. "They're too valuable. I'm afraid I'd lose them."

"So you've taken my advice to heart. You want nothing to remind you of your old life." He sounded disappointed.

"I *need* nothing for that," I corrected him gently. "I don't hold memories in my hand, but I'll never let them go."

He smiled. "It's too bad you were born a princess. You might have made a fine bard."

"*Might?*" I teased.

Suddenly a distant shape skimmed across the sky above Dún Beithe. I cried out joyfully, seeing the curve of wings, the grace that no bard's poetry could capture, the glorious spectacle of a falcon in flight.

"Is that your bird?" Devnet asked, shading his eyes.

"I don't know," I said in a hushed, awestruck voice. And then, "It doesn't matter."

That was no lie. In that moment, on that road to a fresh life, a new world, I knew the truth that touched my spirit: With or without wings, I, too, owned the power to fly. I owned myself. Nothing tied me to the past but what I chose to carry from it in my heart. I could be more than what other people named me, expected of me, decided for me. I would prove that I was something greater than the king of Connacht's daughter: I was no one's but my own. I was Maeve.

I was free.

AFTERWORD

Of Myths and Mash-Ups

As I continue adding new heroines to the Princesses of Myth series, even though they come from ancient cultures as distant and different from one another as Greece and Japan, Egypt and Ireland, there seems to be one thing that these young women have in common: Try as I may, I simply *cannot remember* where I first heard about them. Whether they are historical, mythical, or legendary ladies, I have no idea how we first "met" or how I became interested in their lives to the point where I wanted to *create* more about them.

It's the same with Maeve. I don't recall our initial meeting, but she must have made an absolutely smashing first impression. I'm a nearly lifelong reader, thanks to parents who always found the time to read to me and to tell me stories. I got started reading independently before I entered kindergarten, so over the years I've encountered countless tales of girls and goddesses. Only a few had the power to strike a spark in my imagination. A spark ignites and blooms into a flame. A flame lights the way into the shadows, where the untold portions of my heroines' stories stand waiting to be guessed at, built, embellished, and, ultimately, shared with you.

Maeve is not a historical person. She is a fictitious and fantastic part of Ireland's heroic past. If she had been real, she would have lived around the first century CE. Her chief claim to fame comes from the epic *The Cattle Raid of Cooley*. The earliest version of this story is found in a twelfth-century manuscript. There are several things mentioned in the epic that are anachronisms—that is, references to things that didn't exist in the first century. (If you watch a movie set in ancient Rome, you don't want to see Julius Caesar wearing a wristwatch.) The work itself was created earlier than that, but there's no way of knowing how old it really is.

A lot of things can happen to a story when there's a big gap between the time it's first told and the time it's first written down. A popular story that's been etched into a clay tablet, carved into the wall of a pyramid, inscribed on a scroll, printed in a book, or pixelated on your preferred e-reader is far more likely to remain unchanged than a story that's repeated from one person to another. If you don't believe this, watch a rumor morph into an urban myth or play a few games of "Telephone."

Here's something else you can believe about stories: When it's a traditional tale that's been spread by word of mouth alone—by bards and minstrels and marketplace storytellers and grandparents and kids at play—as soon as someone actually *writes it down*, the whole equation changes. Any variations are regarded as "wrong" because they don't jibe with the written version, which is considered "right" merely because it's not likely to change.

Permanence = Authenticity. The gates are locked; the playground is closed.

That's where I decide to climb over the fence, and Maeve is just the girl to give me a boost. It helps that she doesn't dwell in the realm of history and that the legends surrounding her leave out so much. Heroes of Ireland, like the great Cuchulain, have their childhood and youthful exploits detailed in song and story, but Maeve's girlhood remains an elusive phantom wandering through misty forests, haunted ringforts, and beautiful, treacherous bog land.

Maeve's closest cousin in the Princesses of Myth series is Helen. The places where their stories unfold are real enough—Sparta and Troy, Connacht and Ulster—but the women are not. There might have been any number of real young women who were very much like Helen and Maeve—spirited, independent, strong, and pretty—and their lives could have been the basis for the myths and legends that arose.

This is the same sort of thing that happened to King Arthur. Like Maeve and Helen, he didn't really exist, but someone like him *might* have existed. The "real" Arthur would have lived around the sixth century CE. We know this because some legend-spinners claim he defeated the invading Saxon army at the battle of Mount Badon, which actually happened around 500 CE. On the other hand, the *historical* records name a victorious British leader, Ambrosius Aurelianus.

When you hear the words *King Arthur and his knights of the Round Table,* what image comes to mind? I always picture them wearing the heavy plate armor and full-face visored helmets of the late Middle Ages, the type most people think of when they hear the word *knight.* I also imagine them riding armored horses, ready for a joust, and living in classic fairy-tale castles with drawbridges and stone towers.

None of these things existed in sixth-century Britain, but that didn't stop the centuries-long list of writers who composed their own variations on the theme of King Arthur. (For the best example of some very radical changes, read Mark Twain's *A Connecticut Yankee in King Arthur's Court*.) However, the writers did include some elements of the legends, the "flavor" of the old to enhance the new. The result? A blend of the traditional and the innovative.

A mash-up. (Yes, mash-ups *can* be zombie-, werewolf-, and vampire-free!)

That's pretty much what Maeve's story is, the way I've chosen to tell it. There's a taste of her personality from *The Cattle Raid of Cooley* (the formidable personality of a woman who knows what she wants and isn't about to quit until she gets it), a dollop of daily life in first-century Ireland, and the overall seasoning of legend, all properly combined and presented in the story of her girlhood as I've pictured it. As for matters geographic—the places and landscape where the action happens—you'll also encounter a mix of the real Ireland and the Èriu of both legend and my imagination.

Whatever the ingredients, I hope you find the finished dish to your liking. I'll be serving seconds in *Deception's Prize*. Enjoy!

A note about historical material: Iron Age Ireland was out of the mainstream culture, so the material available can be iffy. Some of the accounts of life there in Maeve's day are by writers who didn't hold other civilizations in high esteem. To be utterly flippant, it was often a case of Romans Rule, Celts Drool. Would you trust your enemy to write a fair newspaper story about *you*?

I didn't think so.

The first-century Irish people didn't leave any written versions of their own history. They did have a system of writing called *ogham,* but it didn't appear until the sixth century CE and was mostly used for gravestone inscriptions. The stories remained in the memories of the bards and in the hearts of the people.

May they remain with us as well.

Places and Faces, or "How Am I Supposed to Pronounce *That*?"

As a writer, I am sometimes called upon to read aloud from my books. I love seeing my readers' reaction face to face, without the smoke, veils, and anonymity of the Internet. I will know straightaway just by looking at them if they're not enjoying what I've written.

I will also know if they *do* like it.

It's one thing to write a book and another to read from it. I know how to spell words like *yolk* and *espresso* and *Givenchy*, but reading them aloud is something else. For example, the yellow part of an egg is the "yoke." I was pronouncing it "yolk" with an *l.* Sorry about that, folks.

So *now* what have I done? I've written a book filled with characters and places whose spelling often has little to do with how they should be pronounced. Welcome to the Romance of Romanization.

Not all languages use our alphabet. Some languages use a nonalphabetical system, such as the characters of written Chinese or the hieroglyphics of ancient Egypt. Romanization lets us take a word from Chinese, Arabic, Cherokee, Hawaiian, Nahuatl, or the Celtic tongue of Maeve's people and represent the sound of that word in a way that we can read.

I have no idea how the powers that be decide how to

represent the words of a particular language. Sometimes said powers even decide to change the previous Romanization. For example, the first dynasty of China—and the one that gave the country its name—was the 秦. This used to be Romanized as *Ch'in,* but now it's *Qin.* Another example is the capital of China, once written in English as *Peking* but now written as *Beijing.* The change in Romanization happened in China in 1949 and then was slowly adopted by Western countries.

I thought it would be handy to include a pronunciation guide for the Celtic names, places, and so on in *Deception's Princess.* In some cases, the pronunciation is so uncomplicated and obvious ("Tara") that you might wonder why I bothered. I say, better too much information than too little.

Remember, I'm doing this for myself as much as for you. I want to get it *right* when I read *Deception's Princess* before an audience.

By the way, there may be *alternate* pronunciations for many of the following names and terms, due to variables like dialect and locale. Example: My husband comes from Los Angeles and I come from Brooklyn. When the word in question is *horror,* he pronounces it "HOR-er" and I pronounce it "HAH-rer." Then we argue about who's right.

In other words, po-TAY-to, po-TAH-to.

Special thanks to Mary DeDanan, who helped me with this pronunciation guide.

1. Maeve and Her Family

MAEVE: MAYV
CLOITHFINN: KLETH-fin
CLOTHRU: KLAW-rah
DERBRIU: DJER (ah)-broo
ÈILE: AY-lah
EITHNE: EN-ah
EOCHU FEIDLECH (son of FINN): OH-ah FED-lekh
FINDEMNA: FINJ-djehm-nah
  The fair-haired triplets.
  BRES: BRESH
  LOTHAR: LAH-har
  NÁR: NAHR
MUGAIN: MUH-gan

2. Friends, Fosterlings, and Other Residents of the Ringfort

BLÁITHÍN: BLAW-heen
BRAN: BRAHN
CAÍLTE: KEEL-teh
CERA: KEHR-ah
COLLA: KAL-la
DAIRE: DAW-reh
DEALLA: DAW-lah
DEVNET: DJEV-nit
DONAL: DUN-al
FECHIN: FEH-heen
GUENNOLA: GWEN-no-la
ÍDE: EE-djah

ÍOBAR: EE-bvehr
KELAN: KIHL-lin
KINNAT: KIHN-nut
NIALL: NEE-ul
ODRAN: AH-drin
OWAIN: AH-win
RUADAN: ROO-ah-din
SABHA: SAW

3. MISCELLANEOUS PEOPLE AND DEITIES

ÁED: AYD
AENGUS: ENG-gus
ÁINE: AWN-ya
ARTEGAL: ar-teh-GIHL
BRIGID: BRI-ged
CAER IBORMEITH: KER eh-BROOM-mah
CINEÁD: kee-NOD
CONCHOBAR: koh-NA-ber
DANÚ: DAN-oo
DONN: DUN
FACHTNA FÁTHACH: FIR(tih)-na FWAH-ah
FLIDAIS: FLI-dish
GUAIRE OF THE GANGANI: GU(ah)-reh /
    GAN-ga-nee
LUGH:LEW
MORANN: MOH-rin
MORRÍGAN: MOHR-ee-gahn
ULAIDH: uh-LEE

4. Animals

DUBH: DOO
EA: AW
GUENNOLA: GWEN-no-la
MUIRÍN: mir-EEN
TREASA: TRA-sa

5. Places

AVALLACH: AH-va-loh
CONNACHT: kon-NAWKHT
CRUACHAN: KRUA-kihn
DÚN BEITHE: DOON BEH-heh
EMAIN MACHA: EM-en MA-ha
ÈRIU: AY-ru
TAILTEANN: TAL-ton
TARA: TAH-reh
TECH DUINN: tjekh DIN
TÍR NA NÓG: TEER na NOHG

6. Miscellaneous Terms

BEAN SIDHE: BAN SHEE
CRANNOG: KRAN-og
FIR DOMNANN: Fir DOM-nen
SLIOTAR: SHLIH-ter
TRIQUETRA: CHEH-kew-tra

7. Holidays/Holy Days

SAMHAIN: SOW-in
> November 1, festival honoring the dead, start of
> winter, and the Celtic new year

IMBOLC: IM-bolk

    February 1, festival of lambing and births

BELTAINE: BEL-ti-nuh

    May 1, festival of fertility, start of summer

LUGHNASADH: LEW-na-sa

    August 1, harvest festival, time for fairs

About the Author

Nebula Award winner ESTHER FRIESNER is the author of over 40 novels and 150 short stories. Educated at Vassar College and Yale University, she is also a poet, a playwright, and the editor of several anthologies. Her Princesses of Myth books include *Nobody's Princess, Nobody's Prize, Sphinx's Princess, Sphinx's Queen, Spirit's Princess, Spirit's Chosen,* and *Deception's Princess.*

Esther is married and a mother of two, harbors cats, and lives in Connecticut. Visit her at sff.net/people/e.friesner and learn more about her Princesses of Myth books at princessesofmyth.com.